The yellowbacks... classics of popular fiction

The yellowjackets or yellowbacks were a great series of bestselling adventure and crime thrillers that had its origins in the mid to late 19th century following on from the 'penny dreadfuls'. They virtually began the mass market revolution of the early 20th century with a clear standard format and imprint/series livery (what would today be called branding). Hodder & Stoughton published the yellowjackets in two main series with series run dates of: 1923-1939 and later 1949-1957.

As the tagline ('where thrillers really began') on the back cover implies, the imprint and series focused on thrillers that were the bestsellers of their time. This current reissue or retro revival if you will, brings back many of these masterpieces, now classics in their own way and extends it further by including key titles from that period that were either great crime or thriller or even general commercial fiction (including sub-genres of noir, horror, gothic, romance, westerns, etc.) influences of their time. There are some perennial favourites and many rarities either lost or not easily available being revived in the current series. Writers and characters ranged from adventure heroes like Bulldog Drummond, Allan Quatermain, Richard Hannay or the Saint through thriller grandmasters Edgar Wallace and E. Phillips Oppenheim, crime and mystery maestros like Patricia Wentworth, GK Chesterton, Agatha Christie and the Detection club, to western and swashbucklers like Zane Grey, Max Brand, Captain Blood and even romance or general fiction classics like Hermina Black, Denise Robins, Marie Corelli or Stella Morton. These were books that had storytelling at their heart and always entertained.

The yellowbacks had both hardback (with varying design elements) and paperback (which built the series look) versions with the latter still carrying the imprint 'yellowjacket'. The current reissues pay tribute to both and use an amalgam of elements from both editions while retaining the complete yellow (or 'mustard-plaster') livery with the author's name in blue beveled type with a 'simulated emboss' effect and a white outer 'outline', and the book title in black. These reissues retain the distinctive size of the original mass market paperback and follow the three main category variations—the thrillers (crime, westerns, mystery, adventure) had blue lettering for the author's name, while Romance and softer general fiction had red; and other categories like humour had green.

For more detail and a full list of titles visit https://www.hachetteindia.com/home/yellowbacks

THE RETURN OF SOLAR PONS

THE RETURN OF SOLAR PONS

August William Derleth (February 24, 1909 – July 4, 1971) was an American writer and anthologist. Though best remembered as the first book publisher of the writings of H. P. Lovecraft, and for his own contributions to the Cthulhu Mythos and the cosmic horror genre, as well as his founding of the publisher Arkham House (which did much to bring supernatural fiction into print in hardcover in the US that had only been readily available in the UK), Derleth was a leading American regional writer of his day, as well as prolific in several other genres, including historical fiction, poetry, detective fiction, science fiction, and biography. Derleth wrote more than 150 short stories and more than 100 books during his lifetime.

THE RETURN OF SOLAR PONS

August Derleth

Hodder and Stoughton Yellow Jacket

hachette INDIA

The Return of Solar Pons

First published in book form in 1958 by Mycroft & Moran

(Registered Name: Hachette Book Publishing India Pvt. Ltd.)
An Hachette UK Company www.hachetteindia.com

1

The texts in these editions in most cases have been reprinted as is, with minimal editorial changes and by and large no bowdlerizing for political correctness; though in some editions, a few words and phrases considered archaic, or those considered offensive now, along with archaic punctuation may have been modified in places to make the text more accessible to today's readers. The narratives, language, beliefs, social mores and/or cultural depictions, in these volumes are a reflection of their times and must be viewed as such. They may also contain certain cultural, racial and gender prejudices and stereotypes that may be outdated or clearly wrong then and wrong today; but their removal would be tantamount to claiming these prejudices never existed. The Publisher does not endorse or support those depictions or stereotypes; and these books have been made available for a discerning audience that will read it for entertainment value and a chronicle/record of popular fiction of past times.

Cover design by Priya Singh adapted from the original classic yellowjacket by Hodder & Stoughton.

Cover illustration by Ishan Trivedi.

Series note: Some of the books in the series (unless otherwise credited) may have cover or inside illustrations from the original yellowbacks or early editions, and while full restoration has been attempted, some images may be grainy or faded due to the condition of the original material. The end notes or bonus material or blurb details may have been sourced from the public domain or free use publications such as Wikipedia and attribution is hereby made also allowing similar free use reproduction from here. Sources requiring further specific attribution may write in and further detailing and/or corrections shall be made in subsequent printings/editions.

Reprint specifications may be subject to change including but not limited to finishes, paper, colour sections.

ISBN: 978-93-5731-185-4

Hachette Book Publishing India Pvt. Ltd.
4th & 5th Floors, Corporate Centre,
Plot No. 94, Sector 44, Gurugram - 122 003, India

Typeset in Electra LT STD 10/12.5 pt by Manipal Technologies Limited

Printed and bound in India by Manipal Technologies Limited

CONTENTS

AUGUST DERLETH
The RETURN of SOLAR PONS
INTRODUCTION BY
EDGAR W. SMITH

Foreword

CAPABLE HANDS
BY DAVID MARCUM

Following the publication of *The Memoirs of Solar Pons* in 1951, August Derleth, by then established as a very successful novelist of historical and mystery fiction, wrote three more new Pons stories that appeared the following year, in *Three Problems for Solar Pons* (1952). This little book is considered the rarest of the Solar Pons volumes. In it, Derleth wrote words which must have filled Pons enthusiasts with dread: "*These are quite possibly the last Solar Pons pastiches I shall write... I (am persuaded to) believe that filling the 'abhorrent vacuum'... is now in more capable hands than my own...*"

Edgar W. Smith, famed Sherlockian, references this quote in his introduction to *The Return*, believing that Derleth felt that way because of the forthcoming publication of *The Exploits of Sherlock Holmes* (1954), written by Adrian Conan Doyle, one of Sir Arthur's sons, and mystery legend John Dickson Carr. Whole volumes could be generated about the fractious story behind *The Exploits*, but this is not the place for that. Suffice it to say, at the time there was apparently quite a bit of backlash in the Sherlockian community against *The Exploits*, as Adrian Conan Doyle had gone out of his way for so many years to antagonize Sherlockians. From my position, having found and loved *The Exploits* while still in high school in the early 1980's, and going for years unaware of the darkness connected to it, I'm very glad that it exists, regardless of any of the drama that accompanied it when it first appeared.

I do find it interesting that Derleth felt that he could abandon Pons at this point, believing that the writing of new Holmes-like stories were now in "more capable hands" than his own – especially after the difficulties he'd had with the Conan Doyle Estate at the time his own first Pons collection, *In Re: Sherlock Holmes*, was published in 1945. The Estate had tried to suppress that book in the same way that they'd shut down *The Misadventures of Sherlock Holmes* (1944). At the time, Derleth had simply ignored them. Now, he seemed willing to walk away from his position as the Literary Agent for the adventures of Solar Pons.

Thankfully, he changed his mind, and continued to write new Pons adventures.

Following the pattern he established with *In Re: Sherlock Holmes* and *The Memoirs*, this book, *The Return*, has thirteen stories to match the thirteen in *The Return of Sherlock Holmes*. They are as strong as ever, and Derleth's writing only becomes more assured.

"The Devil's Footprints" examines an impossible crime in the snow-covered countryside. (The Sherlock Holmes novel, *The Case of the Devil's Hoofmarks* by Allen Sharp [1989], addresses the same question – both being based on a historical mystery. I'll leave it to you to decide who handles it better!)

"The Rydberg Numbers" is a treat, and confirms that 7B Praed Street, Pons and Parker's residence, has seventeen steps leading to the sitting room, just like another famous consulting room located not too far away. "The Dorrington Inheritance" features an introduction to someone – *Spoiler Alert!* – who will become quite important to Dr. Parker at a later date, although there is no indication here that this is anything more than another wonderful Pons investigation.

There are several stories here that reflect some of Sherlock Holmes's "Untold Cases" – "The Grice-Paterson Curse", "The Remarkable Worm", and "The Trained Cormorant". I have a special love for "The Grice-Paterson Curse" – see below – and never tire of re-reading it.

There is no doubt the Derleth's decision to continue writing Pons stories was the correct one. He had stated that "*filling the 'abhorrent vacuum'... is now in more capable hands than my own...*" How fortunate for us that his own hands proved to be so very capable after all.

For those meeting him for the first time, Pons is very much like Holmes. He solves crimes by using ratiocination and deduction. He plays the violin, smokes pipes, and lounges around his rooms in dressing gowns, as well as occasionally conducting chemical experiments there. His brother, Bancroft Pons, is an important fixture in the British Government, rather like Sherlock Holmes's brother, Mycroft. His landlady is Mrs. Johnson, and his closest contact at Scotland Yard is Inspector Jamison. And his friend and biographer, in the mold of Dr. John H. Watson, is Dr. Lyndon Parker.

While most of Holmes's Canonically-recorded adventures stretch from the 1870's until his retirement to Sussex in 1903, Pons operates in the post-World War I era, with his cases extending from when he and Dr. Parker meet in 1919, after Parker has returned to England following his war service, to 1939, just before the beginning of World War II. Pons had also served in the War, in cryptography, and when the two meet, Parker is disillusioned at the England to which he has returned. However, this is quickly subsumed as the doctor's interest in his new flat-mate and friend grows when he joins Pons on a series of cases that he later records.

For too long, the Solar Pons adventures have been too difficult to obtain. Fortunately, these new editions will change that. Here's how that came about.

In the late 1970's, I had been a Sherlockian for just a few years, having found Mr. Holmes in 1975. Those were the early days of the Sherlockian Golden Age that began with the publication of Nicholas Meyer's *The Seven-Per-Cent Solution* in 1974, and has continued to the present. Meyer reminded people that there were *other* manuscripts by Dr. Watson out there, still waiting to be found – hidden in attics, filed away in libraries, or suppressed by paranoid individuals for a plethora of reasons. These began to be discovered, one by one. Meyer himself subsequently published the amazing *The West End Horror* (1976), along with an explanation as to how the appearance of the first book had led to the second. Other Sherlockian adventures continued to surface – *Hellbirds* by Austin Mitchelson and Nicholas Utechin (1976), *Sherlock Holmes and the Golden Bird* by Frank Thomas (1979), and *Enter the Lion* by Sean Hodel and Michael Wright (1979), to name just a very few. The Great Sherlockian Tapestry, after consisting of mainly just sixty main fibers for so long, was about to get much heavier.

And around that time, someone with great wisdom realized that Solar Pons should be a part of that.

Pinnacle Books began reprinting the Pons adventures in late 1974, just months after the July publication date of *The Seven-Per-Cent Solution.* In the world of book publication, at least in those days when things took forever, Pinnacle certainly didn't jump on the bandwagon at the last minute to get the books immediately into print, after seeing how popular both *The Seven-Per-Cent Solution* and Sherlock Holmes were. Rather, the re-publication of the Pons books must have been planned for quite a while, and it was just their great good luck that their Pons editions appeared right around the same time as Meyer's *The Seven-Per-Cent Solution.* Planning and setup would have required a great deal of effort, as would designing the distinctive "Solar Pons" logo that they would use on both their Pons books, and later on Sherlock Holmes books by Frank Thomas. And most of all, they would have needed time to solicit the wonderful cover paintings of Solar Pons and Dr. Parker.

It was these paintings that drew me into the World of Solar Pons.

Living in a small town in eastern Tennessee, finding things related to Sherlock Holmes in the latter 1970's was difficult. My hometown had both a new and used bookstore, and I regularly scoured them looking for new titles. Strangely, several of my most treasured Sherlockian books from these years were found – not in the bookstores – but on rotating paperback racks at a local drugstore. However, it was at the new bookstore, a few weeks before my fourteenth birthday, that I happened to notice seven books lined up in a row, all featuring a man wearing an Inverness and a deerstalker.

I grabbed them, thinking I'd found a Holmesian motherlode. Instead, I saw that they were about... *Solar Pons?*

I had a limited amount of Sherlockian research material then, and I don't recall if I found anything about Mr. Pons to explain why he dressed like Sherlock Holmes. (I had quite forgotten then, although it came back to me later, that I'd first read a Pons story back in 1973 – before I'd ever truly encountered Sherlock Holmes. That story, "The Grice-Paterson Curse", was contained in an Alfred Hitchcock children's mystery anthology, and I credit how much I enjoyed it then with shaping my brain to be so appreciative when I first read about Holmes a couple of years later, in 1975. That one is still my favorite Pons story to this day.)

Those seven books haunted me, and I somehow managed to hint strongly enough to my parents about it that they ended up being birthday gifts a few weeks later – along with some other cool Holmes books. And so I started reading the Pontine Canon, as it's called – the first of countless times that I've been through it. (It's strange what the brain records. I vividly remember reading and re-reading those books frequently in an Algebra class throughout that year – particularly one story on one certain day, "The Man With the Broken Face". I was lost and behind for a lot of that year in that class, and instead of trying to catch up, I'd pull out a Pons book, which felt much more comfortable. The teacher, who later went on to be beloved and award-winning for some reason that escapes me, knew what I was doing and did nothing to pull me back. Pfui on her! But I did like reading about Pons.)

As time went on, I discovered additional Pinnacle paperbacks, featuring new Pons stories by British horror author Basil Copper. It was great to have more Pons adventures, but his weren't quite the same. Around the time I started college, I discovered that Copper had edited a complete *Omnibus* of the original Pons stories, and it was the first grown-up purchase that I made with my first real paycheck. (Many thanks to Otto Penzler and The Mysterious Bookshop!) I was thrilled to see that the stories had been arranged in chronological order, which appealed to me. (That kind of thing still does.) Little did I realize then that Copper's editing had been so controversial within the Pons community.

For it turned out that Copper had taken it upon himself to make a number of unjustified changes. For instance, he altered a lot of Derleth's spellings in the *Omnibus* edition from American to British, causing some people to become rather upset. I wasn't too vexed by that, however, as I was there for the stories.

Copper continued to write new Pons stories of his own, published in various editions. I snapped those up, too, very happy to have new visits to 7B Praed Street. Over the years, I noted with some curiosity that Copper's books came to take on a certain implied and vague aspect – just a whiff, just a tinge – that Pons was *his* and not Derleth's.

Meanwhile, the Battered Silicon Dispatch Box published several "lost" Pons items, and also a new and massive set of the complete stories, *The Original Text Solar Pons* (2000), restoring Derleth's original intentions. It was in this book that I read Peter Ruber's extensive essay explaining Copper's changes in greater depth, and the reaction to them within the Ponsian community. However, Ruber didn't mention what I found to be Copper's even more egregious sin. But first a little background...

Over the years, there have been various editions of the Pons books – the originals published by Derleth's Mycroft & Moran imprint, the Pinnacle paperbacks, the Copper *Omnibus*, and the Battered Silicon Dispatch Box *Original Text Omnibus*. (There has also been an incomplete set of a few titles from British publisher Robson Books, Ltd.) Only a few thousand of the original Mycroft & Moran books were ever printed, and for decades, Pons was only known to a loyal group of Sherlockian enthusiasts by way of these very limited volumes. The Pinnacle books made Pons available to a whole generation of 1970's Sherlockians – such as me – that would have never had a chance to meet him otherwise if he'd only remained in the hard-to-find original editions.

As time has passed, however, even these Pinnacle books have become rare and quite expensive. For modern readers who have heard of Pons and are interested in learning more about him, or for those of us who are Pons enthusiasts who wish to introduce him to the larger world, it's been quite difficult, as all editions of his adventures are now quite rare and expensive, unless one is stumbled upon by accident. The Mycroft & Moran books can be purchased online, usually for a substantial investment of money, and the Copper and Battered Silicon Dispatch Box *Omnibi* were always expensive and hard to come by, and now it's only worse. Finally, with these new publications, the Solar

Pons books will be available for everyone in easily found and affordable editions. With this, it's hoped that a new wave of Pons interest will spread, particularly within the Sherlockian community which will so appreciate him.

In 2014, my friend and Pons Scholar Bob Byrne floated the idea of having an issue of his online journal, *The Solar Pons Gazette*, contain new Pons stories. Having already written some Sherlock Holmes adventures, I was intrigued, and sat down and wrote a Pons tale – possibly almost as fast as Derleth had written his first Pons story in 1928. It was so much fun that I quickly wrote two more. After that, I pestered Bob for a while, saying that he should explore having the stories published in a real book. (I choose real books every time – none of those ephemeral e-blip books that can disappear in a blink for me!) When that didn't happen, I became more ambitious. Bob put me in touch with Tracy Heron of The August Derleth Society, and he in turn told me how to reach Danielle Hackett, August Derleth's granddaughter. I made my case to be allowed to write a new collection of Pons stories, as authorized by the Estate, and amazingly, I received permission. I introduced Danielle (in this modern email way of meeting people) to Derick Belanger of Belanger Books, and then set about writing some more stories, enough to make a whole book. Amazingly, the first new authorized Pons book in decades, *The Papers of Solar Pons*, was published in 2017.

But that started me thinking...

Realizing that this new book had the possibility to reawaken interest in Pons, or spread the word to those who didn't know about him, I wondered if the original volumes could be reprinted. After all, interest in Sherlock Holmes around the world is at an all-time high, getting the word out by way of the internet has never been easier, and shifts in the publishing paradigm mean that the old ways of grinding through the process for several years before a book appears no longer apply.

The Derleth Estate was very happy with the plan. Now came the hard part.

Being fully aware of the controversy surrounding Copper's *Omnibus* edition, it was evident that that new editions had to be from Derleth's original Mycroft & Moran volumes – for after all, he had edited and approved those himself. Thankfully, modern technology allows for these books to be converted to electronic files with only a moderate amount of pain and toil.

I had several friends, upon hearing of this project, who very graciously offered to help me to "re-type" the original books. I can assure you that, if these books had needed to be re-typed from scratch, there would have been no new editions – at least not as provided by me. Instead, I took a copy of each of the original Mycroft & Moran Pons books, of which I am a very happy and proud owner, and scanned them, converting them all into electronic files. So far so good – that only took several hours of standing at a copy machine, flipping the pages of the books one at a time, and hitting the green button. (And sometimes re-doing it if a scanned page had a gremlin or two.)

After that, I used a text conversion software to turn the scans into a Word document. That raw text then had to be converted into another, more easily fixed, Word document. Then came the actual fixing. Early on, it was decided to try and make the new editions look as much like the originals as possible. Therefore, many inconsistent things that niggled me as an editor-type remain in the finished product, because they were that way in the originals. For instance, Derleth's punctuation improved quite a bit from his early books to the latter – but it was very tempting to start fixing his punctuation in the earlier books. If you see something that looks not-quite-right, chances are it was that way in the original books.

There were times that a letter or a note, as quoted in a story, would be indented, while on other occasions it would simply be a part of the paragraph. I wanted to set up all of those letters and notes in a conistent way throughout the various books, but instead I kept them as they had appeared in the original editions, no matter how much the style varied from story to story. Finally, some of the racial stereotyping from those stories would not be written that way today. However, these are historical documents of sorts, and as such, they are presented as written, with the understanding that times have changed, and hopefully we have a greater awareness now than before.

Since the early 1980's, whenever I've re-read the Pons stories – and I've done so many times – it's been by way of the Copper *Omnibus* editions. I enjoyed having them all in one place in two matching handsome and heavy books, and I was very pleased that they were rearranged for reading in chronological order. The fixing of British-versus-American spelling didn't bother me a bit. This time, as part of the process to prepare the converted-to-text files, I was reading the stories as they had originally appeared, in the order that they had been published in the original volumes. I hadn't done it that way for years. The conversion process captures everything, and that means some items do have to be corrected. For instance, when setting up for printing, original books from the old days often *split* words at the end of a line with hyphens, whereas modern computer programs *wrap* the text, allowing for hyphens to be ignored. When converting the text of the original books, the program picked up every one of those end-of-line hyphens and split words, and they all had to be found and removed. Likewise, the text-conversion program ignores words that are italicized in the original, and these each have to be relocated and re-italicized. (However, in some cases, Derleth himself was inconsistent, italicizing a word, such as a book title or the name of a ship, at one point in a story, and not at a later point. That had to be verified too.)

I have long been a chronologicist, organizing all of the thousands of traditional Sherlock Holmes stories that I've collected and read into a massive Holmes Chronology, breaking various adventures (book, story, chapter, and paragraph) down into year, month, day, and even hour to form a *complete* life of Holmes, from birth to death, covering both the Holmes Canon and traditional pastiches. It was inevitable that I would do the same with Pons. For several decades, I've had a satisfying Pons Chronology as well, based on research by various individuals, and largely on Copper's arrangement of the stories within his *Omnibus* – with a few disagreements. By re-reading the original stories in their original form, for the first time in years, I realized that, in addition to changing spelling, Copper had committed – as referred to earlier – a far bigger sin.

I discovered as I re-read the original stories for this project that a number of them weren't matching up with my long-established Pons Chronology, based a great deal upon Copper's arrangement in his *Omnibus*. Some of the stories from the originals would give a specific date that would be a whole decade different from where I had placed the story in my own chronology. A quick check against Copper's *Omnibus* revealed that he had actually changed these dates in his revisions, sometimes shifting from the 1920's to the 1930's, a whole decade, in order to place the story where he thought that it ought to go. Worse, he sometimes eliminated a whole sentence from an original story if it contradicted his placement of that story within his *Omnibus*.

As a chronologist, I was horrified and sickened. This affront wasn't mentioned in Ruber's 2000 essay explaining why Ponsians were irritated with Copper. I can't believe that this wasn't noticed before.

There has always been ample material for the chronologist with the Pons books, even without these changes. Granted, the original versions, as written, open up a lot of problems and contradictions about when various stories occur that Copper smoothed out – apparently without anyone noticing. For this reason, and many others, I'm very glad and proud that the original Solar Pons adventures, as originally published by Derleth, are being presented here in these new volumes for a new generation.

David Marcum
"The Obrisset Snuffbox", PSI
(excerpted from the Belanger edition reissues)

A RETURN TO ADVENTURE

Solar Pons was created by August Derleth to provide the world with more Sherlock Holmes stories. From the beginning, though, Pons shifted away from the original Great Detective and began to become his own unique character. That shift became complete in *The Return of Solar Pons*, a collection sharing just the title concept with that of Sherlock Holmes.

In *The Return of Sherlock Holmes*, the Great Detective returned from the land of the dead after seemingly perishing over the Reichenbach Falls in the embrace of his foil, the fiendish Professor Moriarty. When Holmes appears in Watson's office and explains where he had been from 1891-1894, the time known as The Great Hiatus, it provides a triumphant return.

For Solar Pons, however, there was no tragic end. He did not fall to a fictional death over Niagara Falls at the hands of Baron Ennesfred Kroll. No, there was no such demise for the Sherlock Holmes of Praed Street. Rather, Derleth had the detective return to the great adventures he had been scribing all along.

Yet there is a bit of a shift in these adventures. We do get some straightforward adventures such as "The Adventure of the Lost Dutchman". We also get the telling of some untold tales from the Holmes Canon in "The Adventure of the Remarkable Worm" and "The Adventure of the Trained Cormorant".

But there is also an expansion of the Pontian world in "The Adventure of the Camberwell Beauty", where we meet The Doctor and Si-Fan, Derleth's take on the insidious Fu Manchu. This villain adds a master of an underground spy network as another foil to Pons, a foil unlike anyone Holmes ever faced in mental combat. There is also "The Adventure of the Grice-Paterson Curse", an unsettling gothic horror story with a conclusion worthy of Derleth's other muse, H. P. Lovecraft. The story is one of the best Solar Pons adventures, and yet I can't help but note that Doyle would never have penned such a tale in his Holmes Canon. That is fine with me, as it shows that Pons is very much his own man and a Great Detective in his own right.

Enjoy these excellent adventures of Solar Pons and discover why Pons is a worthy successor to Sherlock Holmes. Belanger Books and Arkham House are proud to make these adventures available once again.

Sincerely,
Derrick Belanger
May 2018

The Return of Solar Pons

INTRODUCTION
BY EDGAR W. SMITH
(From the 1958 Mycroft & Moran Edition)

There is no Sherlockian worthy of his salt who has not, at least once in his life, taken Dr. Watson's pen in hand and given himself to the production of a veritable Adventure. I wrote my own first pastiche at the age of fourteen, about a stolen gem that turned up, by some unaccountable coincidence, in the innards of a fish which Sherlock Holmes was serving to his client in the privacy of his rooms; and I wrote my second when I was fifty-odd, about the definitive and never-more-to-be-seen-in-this-world disappearance of Mr. James Phillimore in a matrix of newly-poured cement. It would be difficult to say which conception was the cornier of the two; but the point does not concern me too greatly, after all, because Mark Twain wrote a pastiche once, when he was somewhere between the ages of fourteen and fifty-odd, which was considerably cornier than either of them. The point that does concern me – and it is a point that all of us who are tempted to emulation should bear in mind – is that the writing of a pastiche is compulsive and inevitable: it is, the psychologists would say, a wholesome manifestation of the urge that is in us all to return again to the times and places we have loved and lost; an evidence, specifically, of our happily unrepressed desire to make ourselves at one with the Master of Baker Street and all his works – and to do this not only receptively, but creatively as well.

Besides Mark Twain and myself, the roster of those who have felt the impulse to produce a coin in counterfeit of the pure Watsonian gold includes such diverse seekers after the truth as Bret Harte, Agatha Christie, O. Henry, Anthony Berkeley, John Kendrick Bangs, Dr. A. Conan Doyle, Maurice Leblanc, J. M. Barrie, and practically every normal fourteen-year-old boy who has had the proper unbringing and an adequate supply of vitamins. Some of the product of this labor of love is good, and some of it is very bad indeed. It is the writers of high literary repute, by some quirk of fate, and those among them in particular who have turned to outright parody, whose product ranks in lowest esteem. Dr. Doyle, for example – one of the great historical novelists of his time, and a giant in many realms – did no more than scratch feebly at the surface with the two short passages in a lighter vein which he attempted (*The Field Bazaar* in *The Student*, of Edinburgh University, in 1896; and *How Watson Learned the Trick*, in *The Book of the Queen's Doll's House*, in 1924), and his shortcoming is all the more notable because of the opportunity he had, in his capacity as Dr. Watson's literary agent for more than forty years, to learn how Watson actually did the trick. Doyle's work falls below the standards attained by many who wrote from a longer perspective, and without their tongues too obtrusively in their cheeks; it is not to be compared – to cite one instance among few – with that of Vincent Starrett, whose *The Unique Hamlet* stands as a classic in the true genre of the pastiche.

The fact remains, in any event, that not many of the essays made at simulation of the Saga have brought satisfaction to any but the essayers themselves. The writing of pastiches is its own, and usually its only, reward; and this, for the true amateur and dilettante, is altogether as it should be. But there have been occasions when a more ambitious writer has taken it upon himself, in grim and feckless bravado, to launch a highly organized attack upon the whole front of the Sacred Writings, with the acknowledged intent of invading them, planting his banner in their very midst, and pushing his way to stand boldly at Watson's sainted side. This, I think, is carrying good, clean fun too far.

Just such an effort as this to enlarge the Saga was made, a few years ago, by Adrian Conan Doyle, the agent's son. What he did was to produce twelve stories, some of them deriving putatively from the manuscripts in the tin dispatch-box in the vaults of the bank of Cox & Co., at Charing Cross, which he proceeded then to offer to the public, straight-faced, as Canonical and heaven-sent. He worked at first with John Dickson Carr, that excellent exponent of the locked room and the unlocked solution, but disagreements arose between them, and the last six of the stories were by the Scion alone. The book containing the stories, when it was published, was called *The Exploits of Sherlock Holmes*, but to the cognoscenti it is known as *Sherlock Holmes Exploited*; the stories, in the vernacular of the Baker Street Irregulars, are not denominated as pastiches, but rather (shunning the crude term "forgeries") as simulacra. It is evidence of the appraisal given them, to put it in its mildest terms, that they have not been subsumed into the Canon.

That honor of subsumption came closest to being conferred in the instance of one pastiche which attained to such rarefied heights that it was published, in a national magazine, under the by-line of Sir Arthur Conan Doyle himself. The history of this episode – certainly one of the great biblio-bobbles of the century, if not of all time – is worth detailing.

The rumor had spread during the years of the Second World War that the manuscript of a new Sherlock Holmes story had been discovered among the papers left by Dr. Doyle at the time of his death in 1930. Hesketh Pearson quoted excerpts from it in his *Conan Doyle: His Life and Art*, in 1943, and the Irregulars clamored for its publication in full. The Doyle estate pleaded reluctance on the score of "unworthiness," but when the war was over, and the market for literary merchandise showed promise of a better financial return, the manuscript was sold to Hearst's *Cosmopolitan* magazine (although no British magazine would touch it) for what must have been a very tidy sum.

If you will open the issue of *Cosmopolitan* for August, 1948, and turn to page 48, you will see it there in all its textual glory, with beautiful illustrations by Robert Fawcett. THE CASE OF THE MAN WHO WAS WANTED, the headline screamed, BY SIR ARTHUR CONAN DOYLE, and, at the foot of the recto page, "Printed by Arrangement with the Estate of the late Sir Arthur Conan Doyle. Copyright, 1948, by Denis P. S. Conan Doyle, Executor of the Estate of the late Sir Arthur Conan Doyle." The blurb at the front of the issue said this: "We wish we could tell you a dramatic story about how the previously unpublished Sherlock Holmes story by Sir Arthur Conan Doyle on page 48 was discovered after all these years. But the facts of the matter are simply that Doyle stuck the manuscript into a hatbox which he put in a safe-deposit box back in 1922 without telling anybody about it. The bank finally decided to open the safe-deposit box last year and there it was."

That, in all conscience, is a dramatic enough story for anybody's wish – but the best is yet to come. The story, it turned out, was a fairly good one, but only fairly good: it contained anachronisms and un-Sherlockian doings and un-Watsonian sayings that led many a B. S. I. to question its authenticity, and disputation waxed on every hand. The circumstance seemed incredible that the one fixed point in a changing age had given way, and that the Canon now comprised not sixty tales, but sixty-one. But there the record stood: "*by* Sir Arthur Conan Doyle," which was to say, under the agential arrangements that had existed between them, by Dr. Watson.

And there, to all intents and purposes, the record stands today, despite the fact that neither Doyle nor Watson had anything whatsoever to do with the story's authorship. It was Vincent Starrett, praise be, who brought proof to confirm the suspicions still prevailing. Putting his sleuths in Britain on the trail, he uncovered the facts and published them in his column in the *Chicago Tribune*; and they were later reprinted and extended in the pages of *The Baker Street Journal*. And the facts were simply these: that an English gentleman by the name of Arthur Whittaker, now deceased, had written this pastiche, had sent it to Sir Arthur, and had received from him in return a small but generously-minded solatium; that Sir Arthur had tossed the manuscript on his shelf (there is no evidence that it ever got into a hat-box), and that it had lain there, forgotten, until his heirs and assigns discovered it several years after his death and ingenuously assumed it to be his. Fortunately, Mr. Whittaker had kept a carbon copy, and was able to prove his authorship beyond dispute. What settlement was ever made with him for the fee received from Mr. Hearst I do not know; but I do know that I have never seen any statement in print by either the Estate or *Cosmopolitan* retracting the egregious misrepresentations made and setting the record straight; nor have I seen mention of this horrendous example of mistaken identity in any publication other than the two mentioned above. It is terrifying to think that, in lack of more widespread testimony to the contrary, the world might come, in its innocence, to believe that this *Case of the Man Who Was Wanted* was a true Canonical Tale.

Here, typically, was a serious pastiche, calling Sherlock Holmes and Dr. Watson by their own names, bearing persuasively upon the Baker Street scene, and attributed, in the accustomed manner, to the man who was closer to the Master and his companion than any other ever was. And yet, as with so many similar efforts made by the hardest-boiled professional or the rankest amateur, the counterfeit clanked with a muffled sound when it was thrown upon the hard surface of the Irregular mind.

It has remained for one whose love of the Canon is as respectful as it is profound to abandon this pretense and to write a series of tales which are not, ostensibly, about Sherlock Holmes and Dr. Watson at all. The pastiches he has produced (for they are, to any but the utterly benighted, about Sherlock Holmes and Dr. Watson) come the closest of any that have been written, consistently, to capturing the true flavor of the Saga, and to making its people and its places and its happenings entirely credible. August Derleth, a prodigious man in many arenas, gave us, in 1945, after their publication in part in national magazines, his magnificent "*In Re: Sherlock Holmes: The Adventures of Solar Pons*". There were twelve stories in all, and they were followed by eleven more when *The Memoirs of Solar Pons* appeared in 1951, and by another trilogy in *Three Problems for Solar Pons*, published in a limited edition in 1952. Now, after too long a lapse, ten new stories – to which the trilogy of 1952 have been added – about this "tall, thin gentleman wearing an Inverness cape and a rakish cap with a visor on it," with "the thin, almost feral face; the sharp, keen dark eyes with their heavy, but not bushy brows; the thin lips and the leanness of the face in general," are brought together, happily in this present volume, *The Return of Solar Pons*.

The flavor is still there; Dr. Watson still walks and talks in the guise of Dr. Parker; the image of Sherlock Holmes is incarnate in the likeness of this man called Pons; and, though we are led by the hand to Mrs. Johnson's house on Praed Street, we know it is Mrs. Hudson who waits to receive us in hallowed Baker Street itself.

In his introduction to *Three Problems for Solar Pons*, Mr. Derleth wrote: "These are quite possibly the last Solar Pons pastiches I shall write... I (am persuaded to) believe that filling the 'abhorrent vacuum,' as Anthony Boucher put it...

is now in more capable hands than my own..." Mr. Derleth's mistaken deduction related to the forthcoming publication of the *Exploits*, to which I have made reference above. I am glad he has changed his mind since reading them, and that he has once again taken his own – or Dr. Watson's – pen in hand. We are left with the impression that, just as it was Dr. Doyle (in collaboration with ex-Professor Moriarty) who tried to kill Sherlock Holmes at the Reichenbach Falls, so it was the agent's son who almost brought about the death of Solar Pons. But both attempts resulted in failure, and we rejoice in the fact now as we rejoiced in it then. Sherlock Holmes returned; and here, for our delectation, is *The Return of Solar Pans*.

– Edgar W. Smith
221B Baker Street
Morristown, New Jersey
April 7, 1958

I

THE ADVENTURE OF THE LOST DUTCHMAN

When I look over my notes concerning the various adventures of my companion, Solar Pons, in the closing years of the 1920's, I am hard put to it to make a choice from a roster which includes the diabolical affair of the Devil's Footprints, the curious puzzle of the hats of M. Henri Dulac, the French consul, and the singular affair of the Little Hangman, but I doubt that there was another in those years which began as dramatically as the strange adventure of John Paul Renfield, clerk of Counsellors Extraordinary, Ltd.

The problem had its origin, as I recall, on a bright summer morning. The early sunlight still streamed into our quarters at 7B Praed Street, and Pons, having just finished putting into his files his own notes on the case of the Cloverdale Kennels, had come to the breakfast table, only a few moments ago laid by our estimable landlady, Mrs. Johnson. He carried the *Times*, and was just turning to the agony column, as was his custom, when there was a sound of running footsteps from the street below, followed by the flinging open of the outer door and a clatter on the stairs.

"A young man in distressing haste," observed Pons, his eyes twinkling. "He has forgotten to close the outer door."

His words were hardly spoken before there was an assault upon our door, and, before either of us could rise from the table, it, too, was flung open, and a hatless, disheveled young man bounded into the room, to close the door behind him and to stand there with his back against it, one hand still on the knob.

"Mr. Pons!" he gasped in great distress, "Save me! I've done nothing, but the police are bound to arrest me for the murder!"

"Pray compose yourself, young man," said Pons. "The police are occasionally guilty of gross stupidity, but they are as often capable of extremely able and level-headed work. I observe you have just come from your place of employment, which is not too far from these quarters, and which you yourself opened with your pass key not long ago – the hour lacks but a few minutes of being half after eight. You have been kneeling on a floor – not one which is your responsibility, for you yourself appear to be a singularly neat person, and would not willingly permit such dust to accumulate on any floor within your province to keep – and kneeling quite possibly beside the body, the discovery of which sent you in such headlong flight to us."

Our young client's jaw dropped, his mouth agape, and in his expression there was that amazement invariably aroused in the untutored at any exhibition of my companion's power of deduction, no matter how simple it was. He took a step or two into the room, and stood there, still trembling a little.

"Sit down, by all means," said Pons persuasively. "Perhaps you would care to join us in a bite of breakfast?"

The young man shook his head almost violently. "I couldn't eat – in truth, I couldn't! My God, sir! do you think you can do anything for me? They'll put it on me, as sure as I stand here!"

"Suppose you tell us your story from the beginning," urged Pons. "I daresay the body will not go off of its own accord."

Thus persuaded, our client dropped into the chair Pons pushed out for him, and sat for a few moments, his face lowered into his hands, until he could catch his breath and control himself. When at last he looked up, his features were more calm; indeed, he was not unhandsome; though his face was round and extremely guileless in its expression, his eyes were a strong blue, his nose and mouth soft, and a sand-colored moustache was faintly evident on his upper lip.

"Mr. Pons, my name is John Paul Renfield. I live in Highbury," he began. "About a month ago, I found myself unemployed. I had been a clerk in a small shop, which was bought up by a chain of shops, with the result that two of us were let out. I turned to the papers to find employment, and almost at once I saw a small notice from a firm called Counsellors Extraordinary, Ltd., on Edgware Road, not very far from here. The firm needed a clerk, and I went round at once to apply. The place had once been a shop, I guessed, but now it had been taken over by this new firm. The gentleman in charge was an elderly man who gave his name as Elwyn Pyncheon; he looked a scholarly sort of man, for he wore pince-nez with heavy brown rims, and he had a bushy brown beard, though I took notice that such hair as I could see coming out from under the skull cap he wore had a more reddish tinge.

"There was not much in the way of furnishings in the office. Just a worn old desk, a wastebasket, a hat-rack, and three chairs. Mr. Pyncheon was at the desk when I came in. I introduced myself and said I had come in reply to his advertisement. He looked me over carefully.

"'Married?' he asks me.

"I said I was not.

"'Family?' he asks me.

"I said as how I had a mother living in Northumberland, and a brother with her. One sister. My father died in the war.

"'You haven't got any close friends who'd be likely to drop in and take up your time?'

"'No, sir, I haven't,' I said.

"He wanted to know what experience I'd had, and I told him I had been clerk for Spotswood & Greenwell for almost seven years.

"'Ever kept books?'

"'Yes, sir. I have.'

"Well, Mr. Pons, the short of it was that he decided I was satisfactory, depending on what his partner said. For the time being, I was to consider myself engaged, and would be expected on the stroke of eight in the morning. If, however, I minded long hours, I needn't apply. He explained that the spareness of the rooms was due to the fact that his partner had ordered special equipment made, but the manufacturer had not yet completed the order, and for the time being we would be required to do our best with such equipment as we now had.

"I went around next morning and there he was, waiting for me.

"'My dear young man, my partner and I have decided that you are eminently fit for the position we want to fill,' said Mr. Pyncheon. 'You may, however, decide that our hours are too long, but we are prepared to pay you a fair salary to make it up to you. We'll expect you promptly at eight o'clock in the morning, and we won't expect you to leave the premises again until nine o'clock in the evening. Lunch and dinner will be sent in. The premises consist of this room, an adjoining bathroom, and one inner room, which is to be kept locked and which you are on no account to enter.

"'Whenever ladies or gents come in, take the name and address, such summary of their problem as they may wish to leave, and tell them that whenever an opening presents itself, we will write to them and make an appointment. However, there is one exception to this rule. You will notice as you sit at this desk, which will be yours, a small light bulb over the entranceway.' Here he turned me about so that I could see the bulb he meant. 'You'll keep your eye on that bulb, especially during the visit of any client. If at any time you see that it has been lit, you're to make whatever excuse you like to our client, withdraw at once, and leave the building for the remainder of that day, not to return again until the following day.

"'Now, then,' he finished, 'your first task for today will be to go through the city directory and make a list of all the stores which handle paper supplies.' And with that, Mr. Pons, Mr. Pyncheon put on his hat and left."

Our client would have gone on, had not Pons interrupted him. Pons had finished his breakfast and had left the table to take his favorite lounging chair next to the fireplace, where he sat deeply absorbed in Mr. Renfield's narrative. "I take it, Mr. Renfield," said Pons, "that you are repeating Mr. Pyncheon's words faithfully?"

"Yes, Mr. Pons, just as he spoke to me. When I was a lad, I used to like doing bits on the stage, and I was quite good at it, if I may say so, but of course, not good enough to earn my keep. I did learn to memorize and imitate quite well, but I am telling you what Mr. Pyncheon told me just as he himself spoke to me."

"Very well. Pray forgive my interruption."

"Mr. Pons, for day after day, I sat at that desk, making lists of one kind or another. Now and then clients came in, and I concluded that my employers were in the business of helping people in trouble – not the ordinary kind of trouble, by any means. I always took down names and addresses, and promised that they would hear from Mr. Pyncheon. Occasionally people came in in response to the unusual notices which Counsellors Extraordinary, Ltd., inserted in the papers. Here, I've brought some of them in for you."

So saying, our client took some crumpled clippings from one of his pockets and handed them to Pons.

"Hm!" murmured Pons, reading aloud from the clippings. "'Troubled by investments? See Counsellors Extraordinary.'

'We have acquired the lot of books and papers of the late Jarel Perkins, including maps, notes, documents. Anyone interested, please apply to Counsellors Extraordinary.' 'Genealogical reasearch? Family troubles? In-laws? Only the most difficult cases need apply to Counsellors Extraordinary.' Ah, here is Mr. Perkins again. 'We are experienced at all manner of intimate counsel.' private papers of Lord Recton. For sale or examination.' Mr. Perkins once more."

"Yes, Mr. Pons, some of the advertisements were repeated."

"Pray continue with your story, Mr. Renfield."

Our client went on. "I worked steadily there at the hours set, and I must say that, apart from the fact that I could not understand quite the reason for making the lists my employers required, I was not ill-used. I was paid weekly at the rate of three pounds a day, which is more wage than I was accustomed to at Spotswood & Greenwell. My meals were sent in from a nearby restaurant, and I must say that they were of good quality and quite sufficient for my needs. Once in a while my employer would pick up my accounts of names and addresses, and also the lists I made at his direction, but sometimes whole days would go by without a sign of Mr. Pyncheon. As for the names and addresses, I never heard another word of them from Mr. Pyncheon, though on four or five occasions visitors who had been in during my first week or two came back to complain that they had had no notification of an appointment as yet; I always took down their names and addresses again.

"However, to make this story appropriately shorter, last night, just as I was about to close up, a very rough-looking individual came in. He had one of our advertisements clutched in his hand. He came in somewhat furtively and suspiciously, but he seemed reassured when he saw me sitting in the middle of the well-lit room.

"'I'll take the lot of them papers,' he said.

"I was about to enquire which papers he had reference to, when I saw, much to my astonishment, that the light above the entranceway was lit. I suppose I had become so used to never seeing it after almost a month at work there, that I was the more astonished. Just the same, I remembered my instructions; I rose immediately, as I had been told to do, excused myself, and left the building, no doubt leaving our client to wonder what on earth I was about – unless he thought I had gone after the papers. I went directly home.

"This morning, when I was making ready to come down to work, I received a curt note informing me that my services with Counsellors Extraordinary, Ltd., were terminated. No reason was given, and I was upset by the ending of what I had come to regard as a soft berth. The matter would have ended there, perhaps, leaving me all in ignorance, if it had not been that I still had on my person the pass key to the premises of Counsellors Extraordinary, Ltd.; so I determined to go down as usual this morning and leave the key on the desk.

"As I came into the building, I was immediately aware of two things. The first was the fact that someone had disturbed the desk, which was much pushed about. A chair had also been turned over. The second was a peculiarly acrid smell, which I took for the smell of gunsmoke. Even so, Mr. Pons, I would have left my key and taken myself off, had I not chanced to see, leading out into the office from under the door of the room I had been forbidden to enter, a dark, glistening stain, which, on walking over to look at it, I saw was blood. Mr. Pons, I then tried the door. It was not locked. And just beyond it, in an almost empty room, lay the body of our client of last night, sprawled on his face. He had been shot, Mr. Pons. Before he died, he had tried to write something in the dust on the floor with his finger – a word which was meaningless to me, but unfortunately, he could not finish it, because he died before he could do so. There was no sign of my employers.

"Mr. Pons, I knew my duty. The police must be informed. But even as I decided that I must telephone them, I realized I had absolutely no corroboration for what I had to tell them. The note I received this morning was typed on the same machine I had used for the past month. The signature was also in typescript. So far as I could prove, I had been alone in the building when I left the victim; there would be only my word for it that I had left him alive. However much I could say about my employers, I realized that I actually knew nothing of their whereabouts. Mr. Pyncheon had never mentioned his home address, and there was no hint of it among the papers I had handled.

"Mr. Pons, I fear I lost my head. I closed and locked the door once more and came over here as fast as my legs would carry me."

By this time, Pons' eyes were fairly dancing. "Singular, most singular," he muttered. "Counselors Extraordinary, indeed! What diligence! What unusual tenacity! We shall just look in at their address. Once we have examined the premises, we shall get our old friend, Inspector Jamison, on the wire. I fancy there is no time to be lost. Our quarry already has a night's lead. Come, Parker, bestir yourself. I am at your service, Mr. Renfield."

"Thank heaven! I did not come in vain," cried our client.

"I have yet to turn away anyone who brightens my day with the promise of an adventure," replied Pons as he clapped his deerstalker on to his head.

The premises occupied by Counsellors Extraordinary, Ltd., seemed indeed to have been converted from a small shop. While the place was outwardly neat, it was not prepossessing. No name had been painted on the door or otherwise emblazoned on the building except for a very small business card attached to the outer door; this alone identified the tenant. Our client produced his pass-key and threw open the door.

The office was indeed uncommonly barren, and clearly gave evidence of a struggle. Mr. Renfield had described it accurately – the desk had been pushed to one side, a chair had been turned over, and another chair stood well offside, as if it had been kicked there without having fallen. The door to the lavatory stood ajar. However, it was the inner room in which Pons was primarily interested, and he walked across to it to open the door, revealing the body of the last client of Counsellors Extraordinary, Ltd.

It was that of a man past middle-age, clad in rough but not cheap clothing. He was grizzled and burly in appearance, thick of body but not fat, a large-boned, well-muscled man who might have given anyone a bad time in an encounter. He lay on his face, his arms sprawled out, and there was sufficient evidence in the dust to indicate that he had been wounded in the center of the room, but had subsequently crawled toward the door, and, weakened by loss of blood, had attempted to leave a message on the dusty floor. He had been shot twice, once in the right lung, once in the abdomen, and he had been dead, I ventured, almost twelve hours.

The message itself showed in the dust just away from the index finger of the right hand. Pons' eyes fixed upon it at once. "Is that not most curious, Parker!" he exclaimed.

"Poor fellow! If only he could have finished it!"

"Can you read it?"

I peered at the letters in the dust. "It begins with an 'l', I think, and goes on with 'a – s – ' Is that another letter after, or does he go on to the next? And that is a 'd', surely, followed by 'u - t' – what follows may be a 'c' or not; at any rate, at that point he lost consciousness."

"Capital!" exclaimed Pons, and went on to examine the room.

The death room was as comparatively barren as the front office. It consisted only of a cot, on the floor beside which lay a host of cigarette stubs. Pons was already at the bed, examining cot and floor alike, his magnifying glass in his hand. He moved from this corner of the room to another, examining footprints in the dust, picking up a pair of pince-nez with a torn cord, which lay on the floor, and came at last to the dead man, whom he examined as closely as he dared without disturbing the body. He not only went through the empty pockets in vain, but we went so far as to scrape grains of earth and particles of dust out of the dead man's trousers' cuffs, and to cut away a portion of the cuff itself and put both into the little envelopes he was accustomed to carrying in the hope of finding some object to analyze in that corner of our quarters given over to his chemical laboratory.

Having finished this, he returned to the outer office, and subjected that room to the same intense scrutiny, often on his hands and knees. It was only when he had finished examining the desk so recently our client's that he came back at last to the pathetic message which the dying man had attempted to leave in the heavy dust of the inner room. He brought with him a sheet of onion skin paper from the desk in the outer office, and proceeded to trace the letters carefully without disturbing the dust itself.

This done, Pons was ready to leave.

"Now, then, Mr. Renfield. If you will telephone Inspector Jamison at New Scotland Yard, I fancy the police will soon be here to take your statement and assume control. I daresay your Mr. Pyncheon will not be coming in today."

"I'll just stop in next door and call the Yard, Mr. Pons."

"If you'll give me your address, Mr. Renfield, I will keep you informed of developments."

"Number 31, Moundgrove Road, N. 5, Mr. Pons."

"And you might ask Inspector Jamison to step around to our quarters for a word with me when he finishes here."

Once back at 7B, Pons busied himself at his chemistry. He said nothing of his work while he was absorbed in it. Only when he had completed it did he come over to the mantel, dip into the toe of the slipper affixed to it for a pipeful of shag, and sit down to look at the tracing he had made.

"I daresay you've arrived at some conclusions, Parker," he said finally.

"None but that this is a most unusual affair."

"With a distinct odor of the fraudulent."

"I would not have thought our client was deceiving us."

"No, no, not he," replied Pons impatiently. "Dear me, you have a reprehensible habit of thinking the worst of people, Parker. The circumstances, the circumstances."

"Ah, you mean the spare furnishings of the headquarters of this so-called Counsellors Extraordinary, Ltd."

"Capital, Parker! You make progress. Yes, indeed, the furnishings literally scream aloud of the temporary. But is not the business of this unusual firm in itself totally out of the ordinary?"

"Indeed it is."

"So much so that it is difficult to believe in it?"

"Well nigh impossible," I agreed.

"Yet these enterprising employers of our Mr. Renfield seem to have advertised in rather costly space in every paper in London. The clippings I examined came from no one of them alone. Let me see – did not one of them offer the papers of Lord Recton?"

"I believe so."

"Let us just look into Burke's. I cannot recall such a title; I am inclined to think it is as false as the business advertising the mythical lord's papers."

For a few moments Pons pored over Burke's *Peerage*. Then he looked up with twinkling eyes. "No one of that title is listed here – nor, I daresay, anywhere else."

"Surely that is an idiotic procedure!"

"I submit there is method in it. Consider Mr. Renfield's story. Every client who came was turned away – put off with the promise of being called in for an appointment. He made no mention of any one having ever been called subsequently. But one client alone excited the curious Mr. Pyncheon's interest – and this one he knew by sight, for, as you will recall, Renfield had not yet discovered the nature of the client's business before he was aware of the light burning above the entranceway. Does not this suggest something to you?"

"Elementary! The room was being watched."

"Scored again! It was being watched by the occupant of the inner room. For someone kept a constant vigil from that room. The cigarette stubs indicate a period of long tenancy by a man of substantial flesh and medium height, whose footprints indicate that he has rather a small foot – he wears a size eight shoe and has sustained an injury to his right leg, either as the result of an accident or an early sickness, which causes him to walk with his right foot slightly at an angle, perhaps not with a noticeable limp."

"Ah! Mr. Pyncheon's partner," I venture.

"I fear Mr. Pyncheon's partner does not exist," retorted Pons. "There is every indication that Mr. Pyncheon was alone in the matter. His talk of a partner was only to allay Mr. Renfield's doubts, just as his explanation of the bareness of his 'office' was. There is but one murdered man. I submit that the whole extraordinary stage was set up for the sole purpose of finding someone whom our Mr. Pyncheon wanted very badly to find, and who might be drawn by the nature of the advertising sponsored by Counsellors Extraordinary."

"You are setting yourself an almost impossible task, Pons."

"It is not as difficult as you think. For one thing, our client's elusive employer is most certainly of comparatively recent American origin. You will have Renfield repeated his words. No Englishman, for example, would say 'stores' when he meant to say 'shops.' That peculiarly offensive diminutive, 'gents,' is another word of which no British professional man is likely to be guilty. Nor is the Englishman accustomed to speak of shops keeping supplies as those which 'handle' them. I have no doubt you observed even more such peculiarities of speech.

"I have also made some little examination of the particles I removed from the dead man's cuff, and find it possible to come to certain conclusions regarding him. I subjected the cloth of the cuff to close scrutiny and chemical analysis. I found in cuff and cloth both, apart from the customary specimens of London grime, tiny fragments of quartzite, stone dust, and – perhaps most suggestive of all – gold dust. Add to that discovery the fact that the murdered man's hands were well calloused, and I fancy we are not very wide of the mark if we conclude that the victim was an American miner by calling."

"Why American?" I objected.

"Ah, well, even if the cut of his clothes did not suggest as much to you, it is surely entirely credible that Mr. Pyncheon, an American, sought a fellow American – or was himself the object of such search on the part of his victim."

"I fear I cannot follow you, Pons."

"It is not the first time. Yet the reconstruction of events leaves precious little else in explication. I submit that Mr. Pyncheon and his victim each possessed something the other was most anxious to obtain. Mr. Pyncheon fled to London and set a trap for his victim, who, deceived by the guilelessness of our client, whom we may be sure he observed from outside before he entered the premises of Counsellors Extraordinary, fell into it, lost his life, and perhaps also that possession of his so much desired by Mr. Pyncheon."

"That is all highly speculative, Pons."

"I don't think so. I suggest you look at all the facts. Here is an American setting up a business which is surely fraudulent in that, according to such evidence as we have, no counsel is actually given to anyone. Unknown to his employee, our client, he conceals himself in the back room of the shop and keeps a vigilant watch on every client who enters. When at last he catches sight of his victim, he rids himself of his employee by a prearranged signal, and takes his victim by surprise."

"Now that is as far-fetched as anything I have yet heard from you," I cried. "How would one American find another, hiding from him, somewhere in all London?"

"Why, by dint of advertising. Our American brethren are profound believers in the power of the printed word. Counsellors Extraordinary, Ltd., ran daily advertisements of a size all out of proportion to the services offered. If his victim were indeed in London, as Mr. Pyncheon had reason to suspect – there is some reason to believe each knew the other would be here – then it was surely within the laws of average that sooner or later his eye would fall upon an advertisement which was directly pertinent to his reason for being here."

"And that reason?" I countered.

"All in good time, Parker. Let us turn now to that enigmatic dying message."

So saying, he placed the tracing he had made on the arm of his chair. I came over and bent above it, looking at it closely.

"There can be no doubt of the first three letters," I said.

"They are 'l', 'a', and 's'. Then he straggled off to what appears to be a 'd', followed by a 'u' and a 't'. There was some attempt to write further, but death prevented it."

"Surely that fourth discernible letter is a capital 'D'," said Pons.

"It might be."

"I submit further that the second letter is an 'o', not an 'a', and that there was an attempt to write a fourth letter to precede the capital," continued Pons. "Let us set down the first word as lost'."

"No, it is surely 'last'," I protested. "The victim was trying to tell us that it was the last survivor of a group of criminals who did him in."

"Ah, Parker, you're wasting your talents writing up these tame little adventures of mine. You should be in the department of sinister Orientals and the cosh-and-bag'em school. What would it be? Last Dutberry – Last Dutwinkle?"

"That next unfinished letter is not 'b'," I cried in hot protest. "It looks more like a 'c'."

"So it does. But let us leave this for the nonce. Just hand me that *American Almanac*, Parker."

I gave him the book and sat mutely watching as he turned its pages.

"I fancy the section on mines and mining might prove instructive," he murmured as his eyes traveled rapidly over the pages. "Ah, here we are. Los Amarillas – Goacher's – Bowie Mine – Jose Vaca's Cave – the Lost Nigger." He lingered to read a page. "Now here is a curious tale, Parker. Let me read it to you. 'In 1865, a band of Apache Indians, wishing to do a service to a military post doctor named Thorne, who had been kind to them, led him blindfolded on a horse into a range of mountains, known by the Spanish as the Sierra de la Espuma – the Mountains of the Foam – which rise in Arizona just east of what is now the city of Phoenix. When the blindfold was removed, Dr. Thorne found himself at the site of a gold mine so rich that all he had to do was pick gold up from the surface of the earth. He filled two saddle bags with almost six thousand dollars worth of gold ore, and then, blindfolded again, was led out of the mountains, pledged to silence. Six years later, two prospectors named Jacob Waltz and Jacob Weiser, having heard rumors of this mine, went into the mountains in search of it. They had to guide them only a tale the doctor had told of seeing a tall, needle-like crag. This they assumed to be a rock called Weaver's Needle, after a pioneer woman of the Southwest. Some time later, Weiser staggered out of the mountains to die in a Pima Indian village, and bequeathed to the village doctor a rawhide map showing the location of the fabulous mine. The doctor retained it for many years, and at least one copy, subsequently destroyed, was made of it.'"

I conceded that the legend was interesting.

"It is not a legend," said Pons. "It suggests nothing to you?"

"I suppose it is similar to scores of other such tales."

"Jacob Waltz is hardly an English name. Though nothing was ever heard of him again, it was he who gave the name, indirectly, to the mine. Waltz was a Dutchman."

"The Lost Dutchman!" I cried.

"Precisely. I submit it was this that Mr. Pyncheon's victim was trying to write in the dust in the room where he was so foully murdered." He paused and cocked his head a little to one side. "I thought it was surely time for Jamison to come."

The sober tread which had reached Pons' keen ears now fell upon my own, and in a few moments Inspector Jamison opened the door and stepped into the room. The customarily cheerful Inspector looked both wrathful and troubled. He greeted us perfunctorily and immediately voiced his grievance.

"The duty of every Englishman is to report to the police any crime on the instant of its discovery," he said sententiously. "The Yard does not look kindly on the efforts of amateurs to take the place of the police."

"Ah, that is well spoken, Jamison. Doubtless, however, my little interference has not prevented you from solving the case."

"No, it hasn't. We've detained Mr. Renfield, though I don't see why he should have done it. And come back to it, too! No evidence of robbery, and the motive is anything but clear."

"Mr. Renfield is merely the unfortunate dupe of the man, Pyncheon."

"Pyncheon, Pyncheon! That's all I've been hearing. Can Renfield bring forward one other person who has seen him? No, he can't."

"Tut, tut, my dear fellow. You can always find trace of Pyncheon by the regular police methods. Someone must have engaged the shop for conversion to the offices of Counsellors Extraordinary, Ltd. Someone must have posted the advertisements and paid for them. I have no doubt that the usual efficiency of the Yard will in due time discover the murder weapon. I fear, however, we shall not have time now to pursue this model routine. We must act more quickly. Just hand me today's *Times*, will you, Jamison?" asked Pons, his eyes twinkling.

Jamison did so, however grudgingly, and sat down, disgruntled and still reproachful. He pushed his bowler back on his head and watched Pons look into the paper.

"Ah, here we are!" cried Pons. "The S. S. *Sheffield* sails from Liverpool for New York in just one hour. There has been no prior sailing for America since the murder, and I should think it highly probable that our Mr. Pyncheon is aboard her. Let us lose no further time. We can fly from Croydon, and, to play it safe, you can wire ahead for the ship to be held until we reach there!"

"Pons, you cannot mean it!" protested Jamison, a wild gleam of hope in his eyes.

"I was never more serious. Come, time does not wait on us."

I pass over that mad, airborne dash to Liverpool.

We reached the port city just at the hour S. S. *Sheffield* was scheduled to sail. We raced in a cab from the landing field to the docks, and were soon mounting the gangplank to the *Sheffield*, the captain and purser of which, duly impressed by the majesty of New Scotland Yard, waited for us. The captain identified us at once and stepped forward to greet us.

"Captain Lacey, at your service, Inspector. What can we do for you?"

Jamison gestured toward Pons.

"Captain, you are likely to have aboard a gentleman of middle age or over, with red or chestnut-red hair," said Pons. "He is clean-shaven and walks in a slightly crab-like fashion due to an impediment in his right leg. He is somewhat above middle height, and the index and second fingers of his right hand are quite probably stained with nicotine since he is an inveterate cigarette smoker. The bridge of his nose may bear the marks of pince-nez, of which he has no need, but which were part of his disguise and were torn from him in a struggle last night. He has rather small feet, and wears a size eight shoe. The gentleman in question is American, very probably from the Southwestern part of that country."

Captain Lacey turned inquiringly toward his purser.

"We do have a man who answers that description, sir," said the purser.

"Can you make it possible for us to see him?" asked Pons.

"Certainly, sir. Follow me."

We made our way through the throngs of people milling about the deck, following the purser toward the cabins. We had not quite reached his destination, however, when the purser slowed up and paused.

"Here he is now, sir, coming toward us."

A red-haired man, carrying a large Ingersoll watch open in his hand, came walking toward us. The pedal impediment on which Pons had insisted was scarcely noticeable. He was clearly perturbed.

"See here, purser," he said, as he approached. "It's past sailing time. What the devil's the delay?"

"I'm sorry, sir. We're hoisting anchor in five minutes."

The red-haired man snapped his watch shut and turned on his heel. He would have gone back the way he had come, had not Pons spoken.

"If you please, Mr. Perkins."

Perkins whirled about.

"Otherwise known as Pyncheon," continued Pons.

A wild look came into Perkins' eyes.

"Late of Counsellors Extraordinary, Ltd."

A scream of rage and defiance broke from Perkins, and, just as Jamison pushed forward, saying, "I hold a warrant for your arrest..." he broke from us and ran to the rail.

Jamison was too quick for him. Surprisingly agile for his bulk, he flung himself on Perkins before he could throw himself over the rail. But he was not quick enough to prevent Perkins from throwing into the sea something that fell like a heavy cloth.

"The map, Jamison! The map!" cried Pons.

But his warning came too late.

Defiant in Jamison's stout grasp, Perkins shouted savagely, "If I can't have it, no one else will either!" He flung a similar piece to the deck. "And the one's no good without the other!" He struggled wildly for a moment, to no avail, for the purser and several passengers drawn by the disturbance had gone to Jamison's assistance. "Curse him!" he cried in a voice that rang with despair. "I should have finished Stark when I had the chance."

"You did," said Jamison. "The charge is murder."

Pons bent and retrieved a piece of rawhide on which was drawn half a map of a secret, almost inaccessible spot in the mountains of western Arizona.

"How you could have known it was a map – or half a map – Perkins was after is beyond me," I said when once we were settled in the compartment of the train taking us back to Euston. "And what a lucky shot at his real name!"

"Elementary, Parker, true – but not luck. It could have been none other," said Pons. "It was perfectly clear from the circumstances narrated by our client that the late Mr. Stark possessed something Perkins wanted very much. By the same token, Perkins had something Stark wished to own. Since Stark was obviously connected with gold mining in some capacity, and since he had attempted to write down in the dust in his dying extremity the name of a fabulous lost mine, what more probable but that the object each so ardently desired was half of a map showing the location of the Lost Dutchman?

"How then to attract Stark's attention, once Perkins had reached London and permitted Stark to know where he had gone with his half of the map? He hit upon a most ingenious device, and then, to make sure that Stark would take the bait, he made it doubly attractive by advertising repeatedly the 'lot of books and papers of the *late* Jarel Perkins, including maps, notes, documents'. Poor Stark was thrown off his guard, and still more so when he came around for a look at the place, only to see our guileless client in charge before he came face to face with the very man he had thought dead.

"A fetching little problem, Parker," concluded Pons, settling himself for the ride to London. "And its final act was fitting in that the map was rendered useless. Enough blood has already been shed over the Lost Dutchman in the past half century. The lust for gold curses its possessors."

II

THE ADVENTURE OF THE DEVIL'S FOOTPRINTS

As I came into our cozy quarters at 7B Praed Street at midnight one cold January night late in the 1920's, I found Solar Pons just putting on his deerstalker. His Inverness was already on his shoulders. He did not turn at my entrance, quiet as it had been, but spoke at once.

"Ah, Parker," he said with satisfaction, "you are in time to come along on a little excursion into the country past the Chiltern Hills – if you're not too tired."

"I'm never too tired for an adventure – but at this hour!" I protested.

From the mantel to which he had stepped for shag with which to fill his pipe, Pons replied, "I had a wire but two hours past from Detective-Sergeant Athelny Moore of Aylesbury – you may remember him from that little matter of the Sulgrave Squire two years ago – about the disappearance of the vicar who has the living of Tetfield parish. Moore is on his way here to take us to Tetfield, a hamlet not far from Aylesbury. The matter would seem to be urgent, and, since I have the highest regard for Sergeant Moore's judgment, I fancy the problem will be interesting."

There was no need for me to remove my coat, for, within a few moments the sound of a car at the kerb outside was followed by the appearance of Detective-Sergeant Moore himself. He was a young man of medium height, thin of body and of face, with strong blue eyes, an aquiline nose of more than usual length, and a closely cropped moustache over a full mouth.

"I hope you will forgive this late hour, Mr. Pons, but I am utterly at sea," he said. "The Reverend Mr. Ambrose Diall is a man of the most exact habits, well-liked by everyone, and just the opposite of the reforming clergyman, with which too many parishes are unhappily afflicted. Besides, he's well along in years, very frail, and not given to any diversion, unless his dislike of owls may be so accounted. Yet he walked out of his house sometime during the night, and the marks in the snow indicate that he has vanished without so much as leaving the confines of the rectory and church grounds."

"Let us be on our way, Sergeant," suggested Pons. "If there are marks to be seen in the snow, we shall not want to risk rising temperature tomorrow before we have had opportunity to examine them."

"Now, then," said Pons, when we were ensconced in the car, with Sergeant Moore at the wheel, driving northeast toward Willesden on the way to Aylesbury, "suppose you tell us what has taken place."

"Ah, if only I could, Mr. Pons," cried the sergeant. "But the fact is I cannot begin to do so. Mr. Diall walked out of his house late last night, carrying his gun. His housekeeper, an old woman named Jennie Kerruish, said that since he took his gun, he would have been going after owls. There had been a snowfall late that afternoon and early in the evening, and this has not thawed appreciably since then. Thus it is possible to trace the vicar's movements. He went out of a side door of the rectory, which is an old, rambling building, and moved toward the church, keeping pretty well to the shadows. He had arrived at an old beech tree and came to a pause at that place. But there his footprints end; they neither turn back nor go off to the side. And yet – and here I come to the most perplexing aspect of the matter – leading away from the vicar's footprints toward the road is a strange pair of hoofprints – that is what they are, Mr. Pons – hoofprints! 'Devil's footprints,' Mrs. Kerruish calls them, and says that for some time past the vicar had seemed to be afraid of the Devil! There has been no trace of Mr. Diall since then."

"No one else occupies the rectory?"

"No one, Mr. Pons."

"So that Mrs. Kerruish's story is without other than circumstantial corroboration?"

"Except for the fact that the vicar's habits were quite well kown. The sexton, Silas Elton, says that to his knowledge what Mrs. Kerruish says of the vicar is correct. Mr. Diall was a reclusive man, given to seeing no one except those members of the parish who sought him out or called on him to do the duties of his office. Tetfield is one of those small parishes which are usually without vicars, other than one attached to a larger parish of the neighborhood. Tetfield was for some time attached to Aylesbury, and the vicarage and church had fallen into disuse when the bishop was persuaded to send the present vicar to the living seven years ago."

"Is there any reason to suspect foul play?" I put in.

Sergeant Moore hesitated a moment before replying. "None."

"I fancy your brief hesitation was not without cause, Sergeant," said Pons.

"Well, Mr. Pons, I don't know that it's worth mentioning. Mrs. Kerruish did think the vicar had been acting troubled for the past week. She gave me a curious kind of letter he had received. But you'll hear as much from her, and you'll see the letter all in good time. I'm sure it's only the imagination of an old woman no longer as sharp as once she might have been."

"How old is Mr. Diall?'

"Sixty-seven."

"I take it there is no evidence of senility."

"None, Mr. Pans."

With this Pons was content to relapse into silence. He rode the rest of the way without speaking again.

The rectory and church grounds at Tetfield, which, together with a small cemetery, were all in one parcel of land, were on the Aylesbury side of the village, and we came to the site of the vicar's disappearance almost upon our entrance into the village. Dawn had not yet arrived, and Sergeant Moore's car, coming to a stop before a low hedge broken by a path, revealed a constable on guard in the glow of its headlamps.

"We've managed to keep most suspicion quiet about the vicar," explained Moore. "So we've not had to deal with the curious." He spoke as he led the way by the light of an old-fashioned dark lantern, which seemed oddly appropriate in this ancient setting of great old yews and gnarled beeches.

"Nothing has been disturbed, except for the footprints we've made in the snow alongside the vicar's. Now, here, Mr. Pons, is the side door, and there are the vicar's footprints."

Pons took the dark lantern from Sergeant Moore and walked along beside the vicar's tracks. The way led across the lawn in the direction of the church, and, ultimately, into the cemetery, where the footprints made a circuitous route among the stones. It was apparent even to me that the vicar seemed to be searching for something, and the housekeeper's theory that he had gone out to shoot an owl took on substance, for the footprints suggested as much. They moved this way and that, toward the darker trees, and the stance the vicar took beneath the trees indicated that he had stopped to peer about.

But there, beneath an old beech tree, the vicar's footprints came to an end. It was plain to be seen that he had walked to this point and paused; thereafter he had not taken a further step, yet there was an unmistakable line of hoofprints leading on from that point, quite as if an eldritch metamorphosis had taken place, and the man who had paused there had become a hoofed creature.

"Those are surely the prints of a two-legged creature with hoofs!" I cried.

"Elementary," said Pons dryly. "Perhaps it was Pan. I have always suspected the concealed compulsions of the clergy."

"Mrs. Kerruish fell to praying at sight of them," said the sergeant.

"I commend her reaction to you, Parker," said Pons. "At the moment, however, I am somewhat more interested in these other marks. It seems quite clear that the vicar dropped his gun; the print in the snow is adequate proof. You have not mentioned retrieving the gun, Sergeant; I take it therefore that someone else did so, either the vicar himself or that enterprising agency which spirited him away."

He shot the rays of the dark lantern to the tracks leading away from those of the vicar. "What do you make of that slight mark which occurs at intervals alongside the hoofprints, Sergeant?"

I looked to where Pons had directed the light and saw at intervals a light brushing in the snow – scarcely enough to more than disturb the evenness of the snow cover – almost as if a lopsided tail had dragged there!

"I've been unable to come to any tenable conclusion about it, Mr. Pons."

"Let me commend it to your attention, Sergeant. Now, then, let us just see what happens to these curious prints. Devil's footprints they are indeed, Sergeant; Mrs. Kerruish may be more right than she knows, even if her acquaintance with devils is limited to that traditional hoofed figure of our Christian belief."

He walked on.

The hoofprints led outward from the cemetery in a straight line toward the road. But they did not reach there, for just as abruptly as the vicar's footprints had come to a stop, so did these. The road was still twenty rods away. Pons dropped to his knees and scrutinized the last of the prints with the greatest care. Then he got up, brushing the snow from his knees, and looked around, flashing the dark-lantern on all sides and up into the trees. From this cursory examination, he went on to another; bidding us stay where we were, he began to walk in ever widening arcs from one side to another of the line of prints, until he arrived at the road; there he went up and down, looking vainly for any sign that either the vicar's footprints or the hoofprints had been renewed.

Coming back, he retreated along the line of hoofprints to the last prints of the vicar; there he dropped to his knees once more and subjected both sets of prints to the most intense examination before he stood up again.

"I daresay you have already determined that the hoofed being of this little drama was not carrying anything of any great weight from this spot, Sergeant," he said.

"Yes, Mr. Pons."

"And that the weight of the two – the vicar and the other – was not equal?"

"I felt we had reason to believe so."

"Capital, Sergeant! Granted, then, that two people walked here, both seemingly inexplicably with incompleted trace. Now, I think you will have noticed that the author of the hoofprints could have made his way to the road with ease by swinging from one branch to another of the low-limbed trees between the places where the hoofprints end and the road begins. That is almost certainly the method of egress from the grounds; a close scrutiny of the final set of hoofprints indicates that the creature went up. The vicar's footprints, however, do not give such a clear indication. Here he stood – his prints are not clear; he shifted from one foot to the other; he moved in his tracks. Yet, there is but one direction in which he could have gone."

So saying, Pons flashed the light of the dark lantern up into the ancient beech tree which loomed overhead.

"Mr. Pons, there's nothing in those branches," said the Sergeant.

The light traveled through the tree to the roof of the church.

"I submit that anyone in the tree might have ready access to the church," said Pons.

"It could be done, Mr. Pons," said Sergeant Moore cautiously.

"Come along and give me a hand, Sergeant. I'm going up into the beech."

Pons climbed up into the dark tree. He had returned the Sergeant's dark lantern in favor of a smaller pocket-flash of his own, and from time to time the light of the flash was visible to us below. He climbed well up into the tree, examining bole and limbs, and even ventured out along one sturdy old limb toward the church roof on the far side before he came back down.

"The weather, I think you said, was cold yesterday, Sergeant?" he asked.

"Yes, sir. There was no thaw."

"And the prediction for yesterday's weather?"

"That was a mistake, Mr. Pons. Warmer weather was predicted; it didn't come."

Pons chuckled. "If I am not mistaken, this little scene was played to the weather."

"I'm afraid I don't follow you, Mr. Pons."

"No matter. I submit that if the vicar's footprints had not been eliminated by the expected thaw, the hoofprints leading outward would prove equally mystifying, even as they have done. As it is, we are entertained by both sets of prints – the one scarcely meant to be seen, the other otherwise designed. Now, then, it lacks but an hour of dawn. If I may, I should like to take a look into the church. Is the key available?"

"I have all Mr. Diall's keys, Mr. Pons," said Sergeant Moore. "Mrs. Kerruish lives apart from the vicarage, just across the way, and recognized that we should have access to the vicarage. But the church is usually kept unlocked."

Pons led the way, carefully skirting the line of mysterious footprints. He went through the cemetery to the church, which immediately adjoined the cemetery. It was an attractive building of stone, several centuries old. Pons opened the door upon the dark interior. In the light of the dark lantern, the church proved to be singularly barren of any but the traditional Anglican trappings; here there was no touch of the High Church, but only an austerity that harked back to the Reformation.

Without thought of us, Pons moved rapidly about the church, paying particular attention to the south wall and the altar. But he evidently did not find what he sought, if indeed he sought anything, for he roved restlessly about until the light of the dark lantern fixed upon a long trap-door just before the vestry. He went directly to this and tugged at it. As it came up, it revealed well-worn steps leading down into the church crypt. Without hesitation, Pons pushed forward.

The crypt was almost as devoid of ornament and fixture as the church. The wall directly under the altar was a catacomb; it consisted of three rows of burial niches. Along the north wall stood the paraphernalia of church bazaars and picnics – wooden tables, benches, and the like – together with certain tools, which were certainly those most often used by the sexton in his role as gravedigger. The west and south walls were clear of impedimenta.

Pons' primary attention was for the burial niches. He passed rapidly from one to another, subjecting each to the most intense scrutiny. Suddenly a muffled exclamation escaped him, as he paused before one of them. He held the light of the dark lantern on it, and with his free hand touched its surface, where minute scratches were visible; these were of comparatively recent origin, though the date on the receptacle was 1780.

"Does this not bear marks of having been tampered with, as if it had been recently opened, Sergeant?"

"Indeed it does, Mr. Pons. Though I couldn't imagine who might have opened it. These niches hold the mortal remains of former vicars who have had the living and had no other place of burial. This crypt has not been used for burials for decades, however."

"Hold the lantern, Parker."

While I held the light steady, Pons worked at the niche. In but a few moments he had it open, disclosing a stone coffin beyond. This in turn he pulled out. Its cover had fallen inward. Pons took the light and shone it into the coffin. There lay exposed not the burial remains one might have expected, but a black attaché case of appreciable size.

"Let us just look inside that case, Sergeant."

Sergeant Moore took the case from its hiding place. "It's locked, sir."

"Break the lock."

Sergeant Moore did so. As the case fell open, a sharp gasp escaped him. In the light of the dark lantern lay a small fortune in gold and bank notes!

"The Reverend Mr. Diall's offertories seem to have been extraordinarily good," observed Pons dryly.

"Mr. Pons – you expected this?" asked Sergeant Moore.

"I fear I cannot say so. I am looking for something more sinister. What better place than these burial niches? This diversion, however, throws a little different light on the matter.

Let us impound the contents of the case, and return the case itself to its place of concealment. You and Parker should be able to pocket this little cache."

Pons waited until we had emptied the attaché case. Then he swung away from the burial niches to pass slowly along the south wall of the crypt, flashing the light on wall and floor until he came to a place approximately half way along the wall. There he stopped.

"Ah, here we are!" he cried. "Fresh earth, missed by the broom where the wall joins the floor, And here – as you can see – the stones have recently been moved. Lend a hand, Sergeant. Let us see what lies behind them."

I helped the Sergeant work out the stones. Slowly, a kind of tunnel came into sight. It was half filled with earth, some of which slid forward into the crypt when the stones were being taken away.

"There's a shovel over along that wall," said Sergeant Moore, inclining his head toward the north. "I saw it when we came down."

"We'll not need it at the moment," said Pons, who was showing the light into the opening we had disclosed. "You can see a pair of shoes, soles facing us. Clerical shoes, unless I am in error. The late Mr. Diall is still in them. It was manifest that he must be here somewhere, for there was only one direction he could go from the place where he vanished. That was up. He had not been carried away. He was not in the tree. Therefore he went up through the tree, caught by a noosed rope swung over a limb so that he could easily be drawn up out of his tracks. And from the tree he went over to the church roof, down the wall of the building, and in, through a door or a window, and was carried to his grave here, after which his murderer went back the way he had come and, once ready to leave the beech tree, donned those fanciful hoofs and carried on from the vicar's tracks, trailing his rope sufficiently to leave but a brushing in the snow at intervals – like a Satanic tail."

"What a cunning scheme!" exclaimed the Sergeant. "Who could have wanted to harm so inoffensive a man as Mr. Diall?"

"That remains to be discovered. Now, then, it lacks but little time before dawn. How long do you suppose we shall have to wait on Mrs. Kerruish?"

"Not at all, Mr. Pons. The good woman proposes to present herself at any hour for your inquiry."

"Very well. For the moment, we can do nothing for Mr. Diall. Let us just close up that opening once more and repair to the vicarage."

Contrary to my expectations, the vicarage was furnished almost to the point of opulence. Somehow, I had conceived of the vicar as a dry-as-dust sort of man, content to vegetate in so quiet a spot, where his living could hardly have been enough to keep him in more than the most niggardly circumstances, as so many vicars of the Church of England are unhappily kept. The study gave evidence of a very large library, the most recent model of the wireless, and well-stocked liquor cabinet.

"This room is just as the vicar left it," said the Sergeant. "Mrs. Kerruish has not disturbed anything."

"And Mrs. Kerruish?"

"She lives nearby. But here she is now."

The sound of footsteps at the back of the house was followed by the opening and closing of a door. A short, heavy, white-haired woman, who was not without a certain kinship to a Belcher portrait, came to the threshold of the room. She had mild blue eyes, a much lined face, and an uncertain mouth; her hair straggled down the sides of her face, giving evidence of her haste.

"I see the lights go up, and I guessed the gentlemen from London had come, Sergeant Moore," she said. "So I got up and dressed and came over."

"And just in good time too, Mrs. Kerruish," said the Sergeant. "This is Mr. Solar Pons. I wish you'd tell him just what you told me."

"That I will," she replied as she came in to the study and sat down.

"It all started about a week before the good man walked out of this house and never came back, God save him," she began. "Up to that time he'd been his same old self, jolly as a parson ought to be. 'Good morning, Mrs. Kerruish,' he'd say to me every morning he came down. 'And how's my Cornish lass this morning?' A good man, through and through, and I'm an old woman who's seen a parcel of men in my time. After breakfast he'd go into this room and do his work – writing letters and such, though, truth to tell, it was precious few letters he ever wrote – once in a while his report to the bishop, and a subscription to a magazine – scarcely any more.

"You can see by looking about he got a good many papers. *The Times*, the *Observer*, and the *News of the World*, and he liked to read 'em. Well, sir, that morning he'd just settled down to read the paper, when he got up quick-like, muttering to himself, and he came back to the kitchen where I was at work, and wanted to know had I seen the sexton about? I said no, I hadn't; so he went and got his hat and set out to walk over to where Silas lives – that's just on the other side of the church. After a while he came back, and he was mighty quiet, didn't have hardly a word for me, but acted like he was bothered about something. He went to the papers again and he looked 'em all through from first sheet to last, and then he turned on the wireless and listened to the news. All the rest of that day he did scarcely anything else; there was a report due the bishop, too, but it wasn't for two days after that he got around to making that out.

"Next day it was he began to watch the post most anxiously. Before that time the post never mattered very much to him;

sometimes he never even looked at it for a day or two. But this past week, he could hardly wait to get it. Then one day, just three days ago it was, he got a letter from London. I heard him give a sort of groan, and I hurried to the study just as he crumpled up a letter and threw it into his wastebasket. 'Is there anything wrong?' I asked him, but he says only, 'I'm perfectly all right, Mrs. Kerruish,' like I was somebody he met casual on the street. But I begun to notice his color was off, and he didn't hardly eat anything, and he seemed to be watching and listening and waiting for something, and every time he heard an owl, he'd take his gun and go out after it. Many an owl he's shot here, Mr. Pons; he couldn't abide 'em, nor can I – nasty, creepy things, and they do say as when they call near a sick person that one will die. I've known it to happen.

"Well, sir, last night I was working late, ironing his things, when I heard that owl call – a brown owl, I think it was, that sad, wailing kind of call. And he heard it, too. He came out to the kitchen for his gun, looking sort of wild, and went by me without a word, out by the side door. I was just about done, I had about quarter of an hour to do, and I did it and went home. He wasn't back when I left, but there was nothing strange to that. But this past morning, when I came in I see he hadn't come home, and when I went out lookin' for him, I see those devil's footprints, and I went right over and reported, quiet-like, that the vicar hadn't come home."

For a few moments after she had finished her story, Pons sat in thoughtful silence, his eyes closed, his lean, ascetic face in repose, the index finger and thumb of his right hand stroking the lobe of his ear, in that gesture so typical of him. Presently his eyes flashed open; he looked intently at Mrs. Kerruish.

"You saw the vicar throw a letter into the wastebasket, Mrs. Kerruish. Did you save the letter?"

"No, Mr. Pons. But I hadn't burned it when the Sergeant asked. I empty the wastebasket into a larger basket and burn it when that's full. I got the letter out for Sergeant Moore." Here she looked inquiringly at the Sergeant, who nodded at her and came forward with the letter in question, smoothed out and unfolded so that Pons might read the curious message at a glance.

I will come for you soon. Otus.

There was no superscription, nor was there any date. The envelope, which Sergeant Moore now put down beside it, bore a date four days before; it had been posted in Notting Hill. Pons glanced at it and turned for the time being from both letter and envelope.

"The vicar had never before shown any sign of being troubled, Mrs. Kerruish?"

"None, sir. He was as cheerful as a lark."

"And would you say, now, if it devolved upon you to say so, was he ill or otherwise troubled?"

"Oh, he wasn't ill, Mr. Pons. He had something on his mind, and it troubled him, deep."

"Since you did not burn the wastepaper, perhaps you have not disposed of Mr. Diall's daily papers, either, Mrs. Kerruish?"

"No, sir, I have not. All the papers for the last week or so are stacked right up alongside the study table."

Pons' glance flickered to the papers she pointed out, and returned to her. "I daresay the sexton ought to have risen by this time. It is dawn."

"He said to fetch him, Mr. Pons."

"Very well. That is all, Mrs. Kerruish, thank you."

"Oh, I do hope you'll be able to find him, Mr. Pons. That poor man! Him being so frail and all, and the nights so chill!"

The moment we were left alone – Sergeant Moore having gone off to fetch Silas Elton, and Mrs. Kerruish having returned to her cottage – Pons turned to the newspapers neatly stacked beside the study table.

"Let us see – a week ago. That would be last Tuesday week. It is now Wednesday morning, Ah, here we are. All three are together. If you'll run through the columns of the *Times* and the *Observer* for some possibly relevant item, I shall do the same with the *News of the World*. Some item must have given Mr. Diall quite a turn."

"I hardly know what to look for," I protested.

"Nor I, at the moment. However, since the subject is to all appearances a retiring country clergyman, it ought not to be too difficult to discover what might have affected him. It might be notice of a financial loss..."

"It is elementary that that is not likely," I interrupted.

"Ah, why do you say so, Parker?"

"Because in that case you would have taken the *Times* to look through the financial column yourself."

"Capital, Parker!" exclaimed Pons with a deep chuckle. "Something of the ratiocinative process seems to be rubbing off on you."

We had hardly commenced our labors when Sergeant Moore came with the sexton.

Silas Elton was a tall, gangling fellow of about sixty years. He had the appearance of a rough countryman, and his clothes spoke for his menial occupation. He had huge, rough hands, which now held his cap. That he had not long since risen from sleep was evident in his red eyes and in his touseled hair, which had not been combed.

"You wanted to see me, Mr. Pons?" he said.

"Yes, Mr. Elton. You had opportunity to observe Mr. Diall during the past week?"

"Yes, sir."

"Did he seem out of sorts to you?"

"Mr. Pons, he was deadly scared of something."

"Ah, we make progress. Did he let drop any hint of what he feared?"

"No, sir."

"Now, Mr. Elton, we understand that approximately a week ago, when the change in the vicar came about, he left the house suddenly and went over to see you. What about?"

"He wanted new and stronger locks put on the vicarage."

"Did you put them on?"

"Not yet, sir. The locks are all good ones, but I could see 'twas no use arguing with him. He'd made up his mind, and he was mortal scared."

"Mr. Elton, how long have you known Mr. Diall?"

The sexton was taken aback by the question, but he rallied quickly. "Why, almost as long as he's been here, sir. Ever since I came to the village."

"On the night of the vicar's disappearance, did you hear anything out of the ordinary?"

"No, sir."

"The cry of an owl, for instance?"

The sexton smiled apologetically. "Wouldn't think to mention that, Mr. Pons. There's always plenty of brown owls about."

"Then you did hear the cry of an owl?" pressed Pons.

"I did, yes. And I knew he'd be setting out after it. He was death on owls, sir, 'struth. And he did go. Cook showed me his tracks next morning – and them others." He shuddered, and his face blanched a little. "Like as if the devil took him." He shook his head wonderingly.

"Could you say, was it an owl that called – or a man imitating an owl?"

The sexton looked startled, as if this idea had never occurred to him. "Why, sir, I thought... But it might have been a man. It's not hard to mock the brown owl."

"So that, if someone had taken it into his head to draw the vicar out, such an imitation would have achieved that end?"

"Yes, sir, I expect it would."

"Thank you, Mr. Elton. We may wish to speak to you again."

"Whenever you need me, sir."

When the three of us were alone again, Pons turned to the letter Sergeant Moore had passed to him.

"You had some opportunity to study this, Sergeant. Did anything about it strike you?"

"Yes, Mr. Pons. The writing seemed to be disguised. It seemed labored – as if whoever had written it had had a hard time getting his letters right."

"Yet Mr. Diall, to judge from his reaction, had not the slightest doubt as to the sender's identity. I commend that fact to your attention, Sergeant. Now, then, just have a look at this paragraph in the *News of the World*."

He laid it on the table before us as he spoke.

It was a curiously inappropriate bit of news.

MUNSON ROBBER RELEASED

> Leonard Wimberly, 67, was released from Dartmoor today, after serving fifteen years for the robbery of Munson's, Ltd., a Midlands bank. He was the leader of the Owl Gang, which was responsible for many crimes of robbery and burglary fifteen to twenty years ago. Two confederates, Alfred Storer and Willie Compton, who gave evidence for the Crown, served reduced sentences of five years each. The stolen money from Munson's was never recovered, Storer swearing that Wimberly alone knew where it was cached, and Wimberly stating on oath that Storer had concealed the money.

Sergeant Moore shook his head in perplexity.

"You cannot mean that this is the paragraph which so agitated the vicar?" I cried.

"I submit it is," said Pons, with maddening superiority. "Let us look again at the letter. 'I will come for you soon.' It is signed 'Otus.' Is that not a most curiously suggestive name, Parker?"

"Very probably a variation of Otis or Oates, neither of which is uncommon."

"But Otus, I submit, is uncommon. Surely it is more than a coincidence that it is part of the name given to the closest American counterpart of our common tawny or brown owl – the screech owl, the Latin name of which is *Otus asio* – the same name applied in part to our own somewhat rarer Scops owl – *Otus scops*."

"That is as far-fetched a connection as I've ever heard you make," I retorted.

"An appropriate pen-name for the leader of the Owl Gang, is it not? They took their name, incidentally, from the habitual use of owl calls as signals."

"Oh, come, Pons," I cried, "You are having us!"

"On the contrary, I was never more serious. I submit that it is more than coincidence that we should come upon owls so frequently in this little matter without a manifest connection among them. Mr. Diall was well known to his housekeeper and his sexton for his aversion to owls, so much of an aversion, indeed, that the mere cry of one sent him for his gun and compelled him to kill the inoffensive bird. Yet he is otherwise pictured as a gentle, retiring, jolly fellow. Is this picture not somewhat inconsistent?"

"It is entirely within the limits of possibility," I protested.

"Oh, entirely," agreed Pons amiably. "But when it is coupled with the attendant factors, its probability grows increasingly remoter."

Sergeant Moore moved uneasily, cleared his throat, and said cautiously, "As I understand you, Mr. Pons, you are suggesting that Wimberly, as the head of the Owl Gang, wrote to Mr. Diall immediately on his release and sent him what could be construed as a threat. Can you possibly mean that the money we found in the crypt is the swag from Munson's?"

"My confidence in you is not misplaced, Sergeant," said Pons, smiling. "Appearances are often deceptive. Mr. Diall has lived such an exemplary life in Tetfield that no one tends to think of what his life might have been like before his tenure here. He came to Tetfield seven years ago. He was released from prison ten years ago. He had three years to alter his identity and to prepare for the ministry, after which he had to find some remote parish where he could settle down to enjoy the harvest of the Munson robbery. I submit that our Mr. Diall was formerly better known as Alfred Storer. Since Alfred turned King's evidence at the trial, it was far more probable that the authorities would believe him against Wimberly when each claimed the other had hidden the swag, though it was Wimberly who told the truth. Small wonder that Mr. Diall could hardly bear the sound of an owl's cry – the gang's onetime signal; he was haunted by his betrayal of Wimberly and the fear of what he might expect if ever Wimberly discovered his whereabouts. Now, then, has any stranger come to Tetfield within the past few days?"

"Mr. Pons, I don't know. I can have enquiry made."

"You may be sure that once Wimberly has set out to find the swag, he will not be far away from it. For the moment, however, let us not forget that we have a body to dispose of. Would it not be best to let the sexton know that we have found the vicar?"

"He will take it hard."

"Fetch him, Sergeant. I have one or two questions to ask him before he learns of our discovery."

"All crime is little short of idiotic," observed Pons, after Sergeant Moore had gone for Silas Elton, "and this one is particularly so. Storer would very probably have surrendered his swag without protest in exchange for his life; he had had ten good years of it."

"Wimberly must be an exceptionally strong man to have hoisted Storer aloft," I said.

"The vicar was a small, frail man, remember. But here is the Sergeant with Mr. Elton. Come in, come in, Mr. Elton. I fear we have bad news for you."

The sexton came in before Sergeant Moore. He had combed his hair and looked considerably more presentable.

"You've had trace of the vicar, sir?"

"Indeed we have, Mr. Elton. We found him in the wall of the church crypt – half dead, but fortunately he'll be able to tell us soon who tried to do him in. We have him upstairs in bed."

Hardly had Pons spoken, when the most extraordinary change came over the sexton. His jaw dropped, his eyes widened, he began to tremble. Then, with a sound that was half cry, half sob, he turned. Had it not been for Pons, he would have leaped from the kitchen. With a bound, Pons was out of his chair and on top of him, his long powerful arms around Silas Elton's neck, bearing him to the floor. For a moment Sergeant Moore was too stunned to act; then he, too, flung himself upon the sexton to secure him. Once the handcuffs were on Elton, Pons stood up.

"Willie Compton, alias Silas Elton – at your service. I congratulate you, Sergeant Moore. Do not hesitate to charge him with the murder of Mr. Diall, once Alfred Storer."

"A pathetic example of thieves falling out," said Pons, as he sat looking from the window of our compartment to the lovely landscape flashing past on our way to London later that day. "A crime that was as unnecessary as it was impulsive. It had probably not occurred to Compton until the day Storer came over to announce his discovery in the *News of the World*. That put the wind up Compton, as well, and, as most guilty men do, he wanted to take flight. Storer did not; he was satisfied with his lot, and not as frightened as Compton – had he been, he would hardly have gone out to challenge what might have been a signal to him on that fatal night. Besides, Storer was very probably certain that Wimberly would have a difficult time to find him. Compton was not content to wait and find out.

"The writing on the warning note was disguised because Storer might very well have recognized Compton's hand, but might be too frightened, as it turned out, to recognize that the script was in a disguised hand. To have the letter sent from London and afford the police a perfect clue pointing straight to Wimberly cost Compton little effort, far less than those ridiculous hoofprints in the snow. On the chosen night, he need only climb into the beech tree – from the church – cry out like an owl, and be confident that Storer would come out for him. You may be sure he had rehearsed his little plan, but the snow added a complication which he contrived to lend an aspect which might appear highly sinister to the superstitious. Devil's footprints, indeed! He might more easily have simply disappeared with Storer's cache, since he had undoubtedly learned where the swag was hidden in the vicarage, and took the first opportunity – before or after the murder – to remove it to the crypt, from which he could take it in his own good time, whenever he was ready to leave Tetfield, once the investigation had died down.

"His guilt was obvious from the moment I learned that he had come to the village at about the same time as the vicar. There had clearly been an understanding between Compton and Storer. Fundamentally, however, Compton's crime violated the law of probability. It was hardly probable that Wimberly would either have warned of his coming or announced his arrival. It was improbable that he could so quickly learn the whereabouts of the other members of the Owl Gang, or, having known, would have discovered so rapidly the details of the setting insofar as they were necessary to exacting that vengeance Compton sought to persuade us to believe had been accomplished. Only

Compton was equipped with this knowledge. Finally, it was highly unlikely that Wimberly would be released from prison, with the Munson swag still unfound, without being followed and watched.

"Compton and Storer were living in a quiet paradise all their own. Poor Compton! The guilty flee when no man pursueth. The real devil's footprints were invisible!"

III

THE ADVENTURE OF THE DORRINGTON INHERITANCE

It was on a wild winter night of the seventh year I shared with my companion, Solar Pons, at his quarters, 7B Praed Street, that there came to his attention a singular matter which was to have a more profound and lasting effect on me than on him. For to Pons the affair of the Dorrington inheritance was but another in a long sequence of challenging problems, while to me – ah, but that is a different matter, extraneous to this account, which is primarily concerned with the unique talents of the private enquiry agent who did me the honor of suggesting that I share his rooms.

Pons had been more than usually restless that night. Nights of storm and weather tended to stir him, as if the wind's rune along Praed Street, and the occasional patter of rain or whisper of snow at the panes were a path to the memory of more exciting times. He was pacing to and fro, filling the room with the fumes of the strong shag he smoked, when there was a pull at the bell below. Pons paused and turned toward the door. In a few moments the outer door could be heard opening and closing, and a step fell upon the stair.

"Our good landlady is coming up with a message," said Pons.

A tap on the door was followed by Mrs. Johnson's troubled face looking in at us. She held an envelope in her hand.

"I do hope this won't take you out on such a night as this, Mr. Pons," she said.

"Thank you, Mrs. Johnson. I am always at the service of those who call upon me. We shall see."

As she withdrew, he tore open the envelope and took a short letter from it. He read it with sparkling eyes and tossed it to me.

"We are about to have a visitor," he said cheerily, rubbing his hands together in anticipation.

The letter was straightforward and direct, simplicity itself.

"Dear Mr. Pons,

"I beg you to see me at half after eight tonight. My father refuses to take steps for his own protection, as if he feared some scandal. I am convinced that unless such steps are taken, his life will be forfeit to the scoundrels who are hounding him, but, fortunately, have so far failed of accomplishing this goal. I am, sir, yours sincerely,

"Constance Dorrington."

"What do you make of it, Parker?" asked Pons, as I lowered the letter.

"Well, it is certainly admirably clear," I ventured. "Written by a lady of purpose."

"And quality, for the stationery is expensive."

"Determined."

"Not to be crossed without intelligence."

"Refined."

"Of such sensibilities as one would like to see in all women, true – and which one finds, alas! too seldom. She writes a fine, flowing hand, but with a certain restraint; she has an eye to the proper balance – note how well she has arranged her letter on the paper! – and she promises us an intriguing little puzzle on which to sharpen our wits."

"Her father's life threatened," I murmured.

"Ah, more than that, I fancy. There is more here than Miss Dorrington intended to meet the eye. 'As if he feared some scandal.' *Dorrington*. Does not that name ring a familiar chord?"

"None whatsoever."

Pons turned to his voluminous notebooks and paged rapidly through them, pausing now and then with the ghost of a smile at his thin lips, or the faintest twinkle in his keen grey eyes as memory of some success was jogged by the passing pages. Finally he paused.

"Ah, here we are," he cried. "Dorrington, Alexander – Discovered and long part owner of the Premier Diamond Mine, Kimberly. Owner of the Maracot Diamond.' And so on. He had one son, Amos T., presumably our client's father. He belonged to a great many clubs and societies, and died only three years ago. Evidently Amos T. was his only heir." He closed the book and looked calculatingly at me. "I thought I knew that name. The Maracot takes rank with the Kohinoor and the Hope diamonds for size and value. Where there is treasure, Parker, there is also likely to be tribulation." He cocked his head alertly toward the windows. "Was not that the sound of a cab? I daresay our client is at the door."

The ringing of our bell came hard upon his words. "Rung with decision and determination," murmured Pons. "There is no hesitation there."

Within a few moments, Mrs. Johnson showed into the room a surprisingly beautiful young woman in her mid-twenties. Though she wore a long cape which came almost to her trim ankles and accentuated her height, she had no covering on her head, despite the raw weather, and her thick, lustrous, chestnut brown hair, snow-flecked and touched with raindrops, gleamed and shone in the light of the room. Her eyes seemed both green and blue; her mouth was small in appearance, but full; her cheekbones were high; and her eyebrows had the look of being brushed up, untouched by any shaping instrument, which lent her face the challenging and breathtaking beauty of an aroused madonna's.

She came straight toward Pons and extended one long slender arm.

"Mr. Pons, it's good of you to see me. I am Constance Dorrington. I hope you'll forgive my precipitate coming, but I would withstand my impulse no longer."

"I trust I shall always be at home to a beautiful lady," said Pons, with unaccustomed gallantry. Then, turning to me, he added, "This is my companion and friend, Dr. Lyndon Parker, who – I see by that look of soft and yielding awe – would like even more to be at your service."

She flashed him a charming glance of gentle reproach for thus having brought a touch of color to my own cheeks as well as to hers.

"Pray sit down, Miss Dorrington," Pons went on. "Dr. Parker, I see, is already waiting on your cape."

The removal of our client's cape disclosed a figure which in every way complemented the beauty of her features. Moreover, she was modestly and inexpensively dressed. Apart from a diamond on her engagement finger, she wore little jewelry – though, truthfully, no gems could have enhanced her appearance.

She sat down in Pons' favorite chair, and, while he stood with one elbow on the crowded mantel, listening, she began with unusual directness to tell her story.

"My father, as you may know, is the only son of the late Alexander Dorrington, who was in the diamond mines of South Africa. He left my father a considerable inheritance, but I've begun to believe that father's inheritance includes something more sinister than the pecuniary rewards of diamond mining. My father has admitted that there was some question about the fairness of the arrangement by which grandfather bought out his partners. To put it as plainly as possible, Mr. Pons, I'm afraid grandfather cheated his partners badly. These gentlemen, who were named Bartholdi and Conyers, did make some ineffective protest at that time, but grandfather appears to have had the law – such as it was – on his side. If this is indeed the case, I suggested to my father that he make restitution to the families of his father's partners – Mr. Conyers is dead, but Mr. Bartholdi still lives in Kensington – but he will not hear of it."

"You made the suggestion because his life had been threatened?" asked Pons.

"Not alone that, Mr. Pons. Because it seemed to me only honest. I hadn't learned of the matter before."

She opened a small bag she carried and removed three envelopes from it. These she gave to Pons, explaining that they were the warnings her father had received. I stepped to Pons' side and peered over his shoulder.

All had been posted in Kensington. Each was addressed to our client's father by means of a sequence of letters cut from newspapers, crudely pasted together. The letters enclosed were similarly made. The first of them had been sent seven weeks previously. It read simply:

"Your days are numbered."

The second, posted three weeks later, read:

"Grown fat on stolen diamonds! How fat was B. when he died – a pauper? Put your affairs in order."

The third, posted but a week ago, was in similar vein:

"Count your days. The Old Man failed honour and justice. We will not fail again."

Pons read these with tight lips and narrowed eyes. He made no comment, however, other than to signal our client to continue her story.

"When father received the first of these warnings, he was with us."

Pons interrupted her. "You speak of 'us,' Miss Dorrington. You have neither brother nor sister, and your mother is dead."

"Forgive me. My fiancé, Count Carlo di Sepulveda, was with us at the time. Being Spanish, he is excitable, and he wanted my father to summon the police at once. Father was so reluctant to even consider doing so, that my fiancé was astonished. Then father admitted that grandfather's enemies might still hope to gain a part of his inheritance, and told us about the advantage grandfather had taken of his less educated partners. I suggested at that time that restitution might be made, but both my father and my fiancé agreed that the method of approach selected by these people merited no such consideration, and I suppose, in a way, they were right, for I'm sure father would have listened to any straightforward plea. Besides, we had no way of knowing whether the warnings came from Conyers' heirs or from Bartholdi – or from someone close to them who might have learned about the affair.

"When the second letter came, father guessed that Bartholdi or some close associate of Bartholdi, was behind it. He believes that the reference to 'B.' as being dead was meant to misguide him, for it's Mr. Conyers who is dead, and it's true that Mr. Conyers died in unhappy circumstances. Exactly ten days after this note was received, the first attempt was made on my father's life. He narrowly escaped being shot or bludgeoned to death that evening when he was accosted and held up by two masked men carrying weapons. Only the fortunate arrival of a policeman prevented the success of the ruffians, who had begun to beat father, though he had offered them his wallet and watch. He didn't connect them with the warnings at that time, even though it appeared to be deliberate. It wasn't until he received the third warning, with its reference to not failing 'again,' that he realized an attempt had been made. Even then he wouldn't call the police. Now that the third letter has come,

I've grown increasingly fearful for his life, and I cannot simply sit idly by waiting and wondering how they will strike next time.

"I've come here in a compromise between my wish and my father's. You are not the police, Mr. Pons, and I would like you to prevent anything happening to my father. I've thought that if some intermediary could approach Mr. Bartholdi – or the heirs of Mr. Conyers – and suggest that restitution for any wrong might be made without the necessity of resorting to violence, father could be persuaded to agree. I have Mr. Bartholdi's address here, but I don't know Mr. Conyers' heirs."

Pons hesitated a moment before replying. "I do not usually act as such an intermediary, Miss Dorrington," he said presently, "but there are points about your problem that interest me."

"You'll act for us, then, Mr. Pons?"

"Say rather, I will act for you, Miss Dorrington. I have no commission from your father. I shall, however, have to meet him. Perhaps tomorrow evening might be convenient?"

"Certainly, Mr. Pons. Perhaps you and Dr. Parker could come to dinner?"

Pons glanced at me, his eyes twinkling. "Dr. Parker would be delighted. As for me – we shall see."

"Seven o'clock then, Mr. Pons," she said, rising.

"Dr. Parker will see you to your cab."

I escorted Miss Dorrington to her cab with pleasure, and returned to find Pons seated in the chair she had just vacated. His long legs were stretched out before him, his chin was sunk to his chest, his lips were pursed, his eyes closed, and the fingers of one hand played with the lobe of an ear. He did not make any sign at my return, and did not, in fact, speak until some time had elapsed.

"If you had a moment, Parker," he said then, "to stray from your admiration for the form and features of our client, did you observe anything of unusual moment about her story?"

I admitted I did not.

"It does not strike you as highly ingenuous?"

I laughed, I fear, somewhat brittlely. "Not half so much as many of the problems you have taken in hand."

"She is a courageous young lady. Engaged to a foreigner, too, by the sound of it. We would be happier with more of her kind at home."

"Married to a fishmonger, no doubt, so long as he is an Englishman."

Pons glanced at me with a droll raising of his eyebrows. "Or a doctor – who knows?" he said. "Let us just have a look at the *Peerage*."

I gave him the book and waited.

"'Sepulveda,'" he murmured presently. "Certainly an old Spanish family, with or without the 'di.' But somewhat more at home in the New World than in the old during the last century or two. The Sepulvedas were among the founding families of Spanish California, and there are still streets, settlements, and byways in California cities named in their honor. The Spanish line appears to have all but vanished."

"An American then."

"I know of no such anomaly as a titled American. He is not that. Either he belongs to the last remnants of the Spanish line or he is an American who affects the title to which he has a right when abroad. But his name is less familiar than that other – Bartholdi."

"Was there not a German government officer of that name?"

"Indeed there was, Parker. The name, however, is Swiss."

"Will you call on him with our client's offer?"

"I should be inclined to delay that a little. I submit that would put myself in an incongruous position indeed were I to make an offer I could not subsequently support. I shall have to talk with Amos Dorrington first." He shook his head. "Just the same, I may stroll about the vicinity of the address Miss

Dorrington left with me. In the meantime, let us look once more at those little missives sent to Mr. Dorrington."

I handed these to him and replaced the *Peerage*.

"What do you make of these, Parker?"

"Is there anything to be made of them but what is so clearly set forth?"

"There are certain points of interest," Pons answered. "Do they not seem curiously vague to you?"

"No more so than many of which I have read."

"Ah, in the fiction of detection, no doubt. But this, I remind you, is life."

"Oh, come, Pons, they are simple enough in their meaning."

"I regret to say I do not find them so. The first one, for example, makes no mention whatsoever of the reason why Mr. Dorrington's days should be numbered. If he were willing to make restitution for his father's sins, there is not even a hint that the business of the sale of the diamond mine is the *raison d'être* for the warning. I submit this is a strange approach indeed."

"It was meant to frighten Dorrington into a receptive state of mind."

"One would have thought his father's old associates could have guessed that something of the old man's ruggedness might come down to his son."

"The second warning is indicative enough," I said. "'*Stolen diamonds*.' Could you ask for more?"

"Indeed I could. Is it not singularly odd that Mr. Dorrington should be given time to put his affairs in order?"

"Clearly that is an invitation to make restitution."

"You think so?"

"I am positive of it."

"Pray remember that the late Ambrose Bierce held that to be positive meant to be a fool at the top of one's voice." He shook his head. "To whom, then, ought he to make restitution? No name is signed. There is nothing to show whether it is Bartholdi or Conyers' heirs who pursue him. I submit that the invitation is not nearly as simple as you make it out to be."

"And the third?" I asked.

"In this matter the third is somewhat more explicit. The mention of '*B.*' in the second note might well have been intentionally misleading..."

"It could not have been anything else."

"On the contrary," retorted Pons, "it could have been a simple error. The mention of the 'Old Man,' the name by which the senior Dorrington was known among his crews in Kimberly, suggests a wider knowledge of the possible motive for this persecution of our client's father. Does it not strike you as curious that 'honour and justice' can be served only by Dorrington's death?"

"However strange it may seem, that is precisely what the warning does suggest."

"Gently, Parker, gently," said Pons. "I agree. You need not raise your voice to make your point. However, there are other points. The grammar is flawless – yet Dorrington's partners were referred to as 'less educated.' This suggests nothing to you?"

"Nothing but the elementary – that it is not Bartholdi who is behind this, but one of Conyers' heirs."

"That is surely the most obvious conclusion," agreed Pons soberly. "I am not quite happy with it at this stage, however. Let us sleep on it. Perhaps tomorrow will bring us new insight."

I did not see Pons again until noon of the next day, for he was up and about long before I rose. He came in to find me at a frugal lunch. His eyes were dancing, and he had about him an air that suggested an ill-kept secret. He wore ordinary street-clothes, and was obviously going out again for he did not remove his hat.

"I stopped by to discover whether you were free to come along," he explained.

"By all means," I replied.

"I've been making a few inquiries in Kensington and have managed to turn up Conyers' son, Adrian. He has a small business where he sells tobacco, newspapers, and magazines."

"Ah, you've talked with him?"

Pons shook his head. "I reserved that pleasure for this afternoon. I wanted your help, since I hope to be able to look around a little free of his surveillance."

Since he could scarcely conceal his impatience to be away, I rose from table.

We set out immediately by cab, and in good time found ourselves in Kensington. There Pons walked through the warm winter sunshine toward a little park. He walked with purpose, but presently slowed and drew my attention with an inclination of his head to an old man sitting on a park bench not far ahead of us.

"He has a wide circle of friends among the pigeons of Kensington," murmured Pons.

The old man was even now feeding pigeons. He appeared to be the epitome of amiability. His lined and bearded countenance was benign, and his uncovered white hair caught the sunlight and seemed to make a kind of halo about his head. He was well dressed, almost expensively so; it was evident at a glance that he was not a poor man, and sat there not by necessity but by choice. A silver-headed cane lay against the bench at his side.

We drew abreast of him and stopped short of disturbing the pigeons.

Slowly the old man grew aware of us. He raised his leonine head and regarded us out of pale hazel eyes.

"Forgive us if we disturb you," said Pons. "The picture you make among the pigeons is one of such serenity it catches the eye."

The old man smiled, but a certain sharpness seemed to come into his glance. "At my age, young man, nothing disturbs me," he said in a confident voice, "and everything is a part of my world – of which so little is left to me."

"These birds would seem to know you, sir," said Pons.

The old man chuckled. "They should! I've been feeding them ten years or more."

"Ah, retired," said Pons.

"Long ago," said the old fellow.

Though the food had now been exhausted and devoured, the pigeons showed no inclination to leave the old man. They perched on his shoulders and knees, sat on his shoes, and walked all about before him as if expecting more largesse from his hand.

"I fancy," said Pons, "these birds would willingly go into your pot if you were of a mind to take them."

The old man's eyes turned suddenly cold. "Sir, the things of this earth were put here for man to enjoy – not to destroy."

Pons apologized handsomely, after which we took our departure.

"Bartholdi," said Pons, once we were out of earshot.

"I thought as much," I answered.

"An amiable fellow, well over eighty years old."

"Such a harmless guise may well conceal a black heart."

"I have known it to do so," said Pons thoughtfully. "However, Mr. Conyers is a man of quite another stamp. His shop is only two streets away. We will not go in together, however, Parker. I will go first. You will follow within a few minutes, in just long enough time to enable me to examine what is obvious. I intend to look about a little, and I want him out of the place for a short time, if you can manage it. When you come in, ignore me. Look around for a magazine to buy. When you find it, edge toward the door without paying for it and walk off down the street. Make sure Conyers sees you. I want him to pursue you. Delay him as much as you can."

"What if he gives me in charge?" I protested.

"Not Conyers. He'll want only his money."

After a short walk, we came within sight of Conyers' little shop. Pons bade me wait and went on ahead. The shop was hardly more than a hole in the wall, one of no great depth, with outside racks. I observed that though people stopped at the racks to read the leads of newspaper stories, comparatively few went in to buy.

Presently I followed Pons into the shop. Conyers was alone behind the small counter which separated his customers from the shelves of tobacco. He sat on a stool, a short, powerfully-built man, roughly clad. He chewed at a match held between his thick lips, and his small, dark eyes, which had been following Pons around, turned frankly to me as I entered. His glance was suspicious, and his face wore a look that indicated a profound distrust of the world.

I thought it best to buy a cigar, before looking over the rack of magazines. Finally I selected the most recent issue of *The Strand*, and, carrying it in plain sight, walked casually over to the door and out.

"Guv'nor!" I heard Conyers cry.

I pretended I had not heard and walked rapidly away from the shop down the street.

"You – Guv'nor!" I heard him call out angrily.

Then there was the sound of the stool being kicked over.

Three doors past Conyers' shop, I paused to look into a display window, keenly aware of Conyers' running footsteps.

He came up and took me roughly by one shoulder.

"Guv'nor!"

I turned, feigning surprise. "Eh? What is it?" I asked.

"You didn't pay me for the magazine," Conyers said belligerently.

"Magazine?"

He pulled *The Strand* almost savagely from my grasp and waved it before my face. "This one! This one! See?" he shouted.

"Upon my soul!" I said. "So I did."

I reached into my pocket.

"You must forgive me," I said apologetically. "I'm a little absent-minded."

He was somewhat mollified. "I could see you wasn't too sharp," he said grudgingly.

I took as much time as I could fumbling about among the coins I had pulled from my pocket before I managed to find the proper amount. He took the money, favored me with a darkly suspicious glance from narrowed eyes, and turned back toward his shop.

I walked on slowly, until Pons once again fell into step at my side, carrying a pound of shag he had bought.

"That fellow's a bad man to cross," I said.

"I believe he would be difficult," agreed Pons. "He is not yet sixty, very vigorous, and dourly suspicious."

"You'll remember that little deduction of my own," I said. "I find it extremely gratifying to learn that Mr. Adrian Conyers maintains a newspaper shop. How simple it is for him to have access to the printed letters he would need for the warnings posted to Mr. Dorrington! Or have you overlooked that significant point?"

"Not at all. Indeed, you will be happy to learn that your drawing him out of the shop gave me the opportunity to rummage through a stack of papers beneath his counter. I found these."

He drew from inside his coat three newspaper pages and held them up before me. I saw at a glance that letters and words had been carefully cut out of them.

"Aha!" I cried, with a glance, I fear, of undoubted triumph.

"It would indeed seem to be suggestive," admitted Pons.

"'Suggestive'!" I cried, not without a touch of scorn. "I should say it is the strongest possible circumstantial evidence – particularly as the dates seem to correspond on these papers with the approximate time of the mailing of at least one of the letters to Mr. Dorrington."

"I have given the matter some thought," replied Pons. "Yet I remain troubled about one or two little details, and I am loath to charge Conyers with authorship of this singular persecution until I am settled in mind about him. For one thing, Bartholdi and Conyers are in touch with each other, and Bartholdi has access to Conyers' counter and newspapers. Access, in fact, is rather public. For another thing, the attack on our client's father bespeaks the hiring of toffs."

"Then it could be either Conyers or Batholdi – or both!"

"I fear it could. Yet the studied crudeness of the method does not ring true."

"You have not said they were literate men."

"They are not. But neither are they illiterate. I submit that the method stands in odd contrast to the letters themselves."

"They may have employed someone to prepare the letters."

"Quite true," agreed Pons. "It is also eminently possible that there is a group of them working toward a common end. There are other Conyers heirs."

"Have you tracked any of them down?"

Pons shook his head. "I understand they are as much in need of money as Mr. Adrian Conyers."

"A clear motive, then."

"For money, Parker, yes. Not for Dorrington's death." He hailed a cab and we stood waiting for it to swing to the kerb. "I think it is time to have a talk with Mr. Dorrington. We shall look forward to dinner."

We were not destined to share dinner with our client and her father that evening, however. In late afternoon Miss Dorrington sent frantic word that her father had been run down and gravely injured; moreover, her fiancé had just barely escaped a similar fate. Both men had been pushed into the path of a speeding car, and Count di Sepulveda had also been bludgeoned. Miss Dorrington was close to hysteria, and Pons lost no time setting out for the Park Lane home of our client.

Miss Dorrington herself met us at the door. Though she had been weeping, she was now composed.

"Both father and Carlo are in bed. Carlo is not too badly injured – he was struck on the head by what must have been a sandbag, but he managed to avoid the car which ran down my father. Both were knocked down, and they failed to take the number of the car. Carlo remembers only that it was a large black Daimler, and that two swarthy men drove it."

"Where did the attack take place, Miss Dorrington?"

"At the Embankment Gardens, near the Charing Cross tube station. My father had made a visit to his solicitor, who is ill at his home. Carlo was with him. As the two of them crossed the street, someone who must have been following them pushed them into the path of a car that came around the corner and raced down the street. Carlo was agile enough to twist away from the car before he fell, but my father fell in its path. But you will want to talk to Carlo."

"If he can talk comfortably."

Count Carlo di Sepulveda lay in a double bed at the head of the stairs. He was a pleasant, open-faced young man, not without trace of a certain elegance in his manner, even in his prone position. His head was bandaged over packing behind his right ear. At our entrance, his brown eyes widened in surprise.

"You didn't tell me you had visitors, Constance," he said in mild reproof.

"This is Mr. Solar Pons, Carlo – Dr. Parker is with him. Mr. Pons has come at my request to look into the persecution to which father has been subjected."

"I'm glad to hear it," he said heartily. "We urged him to go to the police weeks ago, Mr. Pons."

"Miss Dorrington has given me most of the facts," said Pons. "Can you tell us more? Where, for instance, could your assailant have been concealed?"

"I didn't see him – or them, Mr. Pons. But an appreciable amount of shrubbery grows at the Embankment Gardens, and I suppose, having followed us, he had hidden himself there and run out upon us as soon as he saw his confederates' car approaching. There were two men in the car; both seemed to me quite dark, almost foreign-looking. I had the impression, from the brief glimpse of them Mr. Dorrington had, that he recognized them."

"Ah," murmured Pons. "Yet they seemed to you foreigners?"

"Either that, or men long exposed to sun."

"You yourself were struck with a sandbag?"

"I took it to be that."

"Yet you managed to prevent being flung after Mr. Dorrington?"

"Yes, Mr. Pons. I twisted to one side, since I was aware of the car's approach. I don't think Mr. Dorrington saw it coming until he was pushed. I lost consciousness as I fell."

Pons' keen gaze drifted from the bed and its occupant to look at the appointments of the room. He bent casually and picked up a pair of highly polished shoes, now slightly scuffed. "Your shoes, Count Sepulveda?"

"Yes, Mr. Pons."

"They certainly retain a high degree of polish."

"I stop at Claridge's, Mr. Pons," answered Miss Dorrington's fiancé, with a mild trace of hauteur.

Pons replaced the shoes and went on. "Was there no other traffic at the hour of the accident? Half after three, I believe, was the time."

"That's correct, Mr. Pons. As bad luck would have it, there was very little traffic at that time. Just the same, the car evidently didn't dare to return so that the driver could make sure of our condition. Pedestrians had seen the accident, though no one has come forward to offer information."

"Did you happen to see any pedestrians other than yourselves as you started to cross the street?"

"No, sir, I can't say that I did. One doesn't think of those things – one tends to one's own affairs, not so?"

Pons turned to our client. "Perhaps Dr. Parker might have a glimpse of Mr. Dorrington?"

"By all means," agreed Miss Dorrington. "Dr. Duell has left strict instructions that he is not to be disturbed, but we can go quietly and need not wake him."

Mr. Dorrington lay in the room across the hall, also in a large double bed. There was a nurse in attendance. At a sign from Pons, I stepped up and made a cursory examination of the old man who lay there. He was a stocky, muscular man, just short of being corpulent. Our client watched with some apprehension, and the nurse favored us with a coldly disapproving stare. The patient was still unconscious, but his breathing was regular, and his pulse only a trifle fast.

In the hall, afterwards, I said, "His condition is grave, but he has a good chance."

"That is just what Dr. Duell said," replied Miss Dorrington.

We descended the stairs. All the way down, Pons was extremely thoughtful and very silent. At the foot of the steps he took hold of Miss Dorrington's arm firmly but persuasively and drew her close to him.

"I'm sure you are very fond of both your father and your fiancé , Miss Dorrington," he said in a low voice.

"Of course," she replied, mystified.

"I fear I must tell you I expect a final attempt to be made on your father's life tonight."

"Here! In his own house!" She was incredulous.

"In his own room," said Pons. "I took the opportunity to look out the window. The room is relatively easy of access from outside."

"Mr. Pons, you must be joking."

"I assure you, I have never been more serious. Count Sepulveda himself suggested as much when he said he thought your father had recognized the men in the car which ran him down. If they, too, felt that he did, they have no alternative but to silence him before he can speak."

"Then I'll notify the police at once."

"Stay, not so fast," cautioned Pons. "The police have been known to bungle. Let me suggest that, unknown to anyone, Dr. Parker and I conceal ourselves in the room where your father lies, to spend the night on guard beside him."

"Mr. Pons, I could not ask you..."

"Miss Dorrington, you have retained me to save your father's life. I mean to do so by every avenue at my disposal. I fancy we will not only be able to save his life, but also to net the author of this scheme."

"The night nurse must know."

Pons looked at his watch. "When is she due?"

"At eight."

"Adjure her silence, Miss Dorrington."

"Certainly, Mr. Pons."

"Very well. We shall return here at eight – unknown to anyone, mind! Even your father, should he return to consciousness, is not to be told. As long as no announcement of his death has been made, he is in grave danger."

Our client was still hesitant and troubled, but finally she acquiesced. "Very well, Mr. Pons, if that is your wish."

As we left the house, I turned on Pons. "Aren't you subjecting Miss Dorrington to unnecessary worry?" I demanded indignantly.

"I think not."

"How do you deduce that a final attempt will be made on Dorrington?"

"Any other attempt will be too late," said Pons. "You heard Sepulveda say that Dorrington appeared to have recognized the men in the car. Now then – exercise your ingenuity – is it Bartholdi or the Conyers' heirs behind this persecution?"

I ignored his challenge. "And what, pray tell," I went on, still indignant, "was the point of inquiring about Count Sepulveda's shoes?"

"Ah, forgive me, Parker – I fear I try you. I was interested only in the excellence of their polish, which did not extend to beneath the instep."

"I myself have never worn a pair better polished," I said.

"Ah, you have never stayed at Claridge's, Parker," answered Pons, with a little smile.

"And now?" I asked.

"We shall take the precaution of taking weapons tonight. You may have the revolver, Parker. I will content myself with my leaded stick. Unless I am much mistaken, we shall have the opportunity of bringing this matter to a successful conclusion before the night is done."

Shortly after eight o'clock, Pons and I were concealed in Amos Dorrington's room. The patient was still unconscious, and the night nurse was rather relieved than not at the presence of a doctor in the room, since it lightened her task, however mystified she was that we were there. The room was quiet, but for some time there was considerable movement in the room across the hall; servants and – I had no doubt – our client herself, came and went at the wish of the patient, who would be up in a day of two, since the nature of his wound did not necessitate our client's fiancé's staying abed.

The night wore on. Pons had set me to watch the windows, but to stay out of line with them, so that I might not be seen against the faint frame of light. He himself had taken his stand behind the door. The room was lit only by a small bedside lamp, which threw a glow over the patient where he lay, but cast a very faint illumination about the rest of the room. Sounds from outside diminished, and gradually the house itself quieted down in sleep.

As the night deepened, Pons sent the nurse on one aimless errand after another – quite as if he actually wished her out of the room – until I became so indignant that I restrained my protests only with the greatest difficulty. Half an hour past midnight, Pons urged the nurse to go below stairs to brew us some hot tea, promising that I would watch over the patient.

She had hardly gone, when there was a quick rustling sound outside the door. I turned expectantly. The door opened, slowly at first, then swiftly, and closed again as someone slipped into the room. Almost at once I was aware of the odor of chloroform as a dark figure moved quickly toward the bed, his intention patent.

Before I could cry out a warning, Pons had crept up behind him. Just as the intruder bent above the patient, Pons raised his leaded stick and struck him down. He crumpled to the floor without a murmur.

"Arouse Miss Dorrington, Parker," said Pons. "I'll stop up that chloroform."

I hastened out.

When I returned with our client, even more attractive in her negligee and gown than in street apparel, Pons stood before the door of the room. He caught hold of Miss Dorrington's hands and looked earnestly into her startled face.

"My dear lady, if you could free your father from the danger which hangs over him with but one diamond," he said, "would you do so?"

"Indeed I would!" she cried passionately.

Pons turned his hand so that Miss Dorrington's left hand rested lightly on his. He touched the diamond on her finger. "This is the stone, Miss Dorrington. Return it."

So saying, he threw open the door of Amos Dorrington's room, and turned up the light. There, still where he had fallen, lay Count Carlo di Sepulveda. "I fear I have had to add to the blow he so calculatingly bestowed upon himself," said Pons.

Our client cried out and ran over to him. She came to her knees beside his still form.

"Mr. Pons, you've killed him!"

"I think not."

Then she grew aware of the odor. "Chloroform!" she exclaimed. She shot a glance at Pons, her eyes wide with revulsion and apprehension. "Oh, Mr. Pons – you can't mean... ?"

Pons nodded gravely. "I do, Miss Dorrington. The author of all your troubles and your father's persecution is none other than your fiancé – who is as bogus a count as I have ever had the misfortune to encounter. No one staying at the best hotels could fail to have his footwear as highly polished below the instep as his shoetops.

"There would seem to have been some slight misunderstanding in this little problem, Miss Dorrington. It was by design, but no one coming to your difficulty with an open mind could fail to be aware of it. There was only one diamond that was important – that is the stone you are at this moment removing from your finger – since it provided the motive for your fiancé's deeds. The motive was not in seeking to gain part of your father's inheritance, but all your own."

Later, as we stood in the street waiting for a cab, Pons could not forego the chance of scoring over me.

"My dear fellow, the entire matter was as plain as a pikestaff. The crudely done but grammatical warnings were a lesson in developing the power of observation. The first of them was nothing less than a feint; it dredged up more than the rumor which had inspired it. But Sepulveda did not listen closely; in his second note he made the error of referring to Bartholdi as the other deceased member of the trio who once owned the Dorrington mines. His attempt to implicate Mr. Adrian Conyers by 'planting' the cut-out papers under his counter was merely fatuous, for neither the Conyers heirs nor Bartholdi had any valid reason for waiting so long after Alexander Dorrington's death to press any claim they felt they had.

"In the third warning, Sepulveda gave the show away by referring to the elder Dorrington as the 'Old Man,' which could have been known only to Dorrington's associates or to someone who had sat at the family councils. If we eliminate the former associates and their heirs, only Sepulveda is left with motive and opportunity, however improbable he might seem as the likeliest suspect. Who else but he sat at those councils?

"And who else but he knew of Dorrington's plan to visit his solicitor at his home? Only Sepulveda could have arranged for his accomplices to be ready for Sepulveda's pushing Dorrington ahead of the car, after which he sandbagged himself and roughed himself up. Doubtless his accomplices returned quickly enough to mix with the gathering crowd and make off with the telltale weapon. Undoubtedly Dorrington was aware of the identity of his attacker – but Sepulveda had not counted on the car's failing to kill him; so he had no choice but to attempt to silence Dorrington before the old man could name him.

"A plan bounded by folly. Had he succeeded, Sepulveda would have been at the mercy of the toffs he had hired for years to come."

He paused just as a cab came toward the kerb.

"By the way, Parker, I submit that even though the bogus Count di Sepulveda has been collared by the police, our client might very well be in need of just that kind of comfort only a solid man of your stamp could offer her."

"At this hour?" I cried.

"The hour is never too late for gallantry, Parker."

"Do you think so?" I asked, I fear, much too eagerly.

"I do indeed," he said gravely, getting into the cab and giving the driver the address of our quarters. He leaned out in the face of my hesitation and added, "Pray give her my compliments on her dispatch in acting against her father's persecutor. I have a feeling we shall see more of the lady."

Once again time proved my astute companion only too correct in his deduction.

IV

THE ADVENTURE OF THE "TRIPLE KENT"

If Solar Pons had not visited Sussex that summer of 193–, it is very probable that the singularly sanguine affair of the triple murder in Kent – filed among my notes under the unimaginative heading of the "Triple Kent" – might not have come his way, and I would have been deprived of a notable example of that fascinating power of ratiocination which was indisputably his.

We were on the way back from the South Downs, where Pons had paid an almost reverential visit to an old bee-keeper whose retirement concealed the identity of a brilliant genius to whom Pons habitually referred as "the Master," when the train drew to a stop at Tunbridge Wells. Pons had been slumped in his seat in our compartment, his head on his chest, his arms folded, and his lean, ascetic face in repose, when suddenly his eyes flashed open, he raised his head, and became instantly alert.

"There is some disturbance ahead, Parker," he said. "What can it be?"

At the same moment, I was aware of the commotion.

"Ah, someone is going from compartment to compartment, opening and shutting the doors," said Pons.

"Looking for someone?"

"That is all too likely," agreed Pons.

So saying, he lowered the window and stuck his head out. Almost immediately, he drew back again, his eyes twinkling. "I know you're in haste for London, Parker, but I fear we shall not be on this train. Did not Mrs. Johnson know our destination?"

"Indeed, she did. I never leave without telling her where you can be reached."

"I fancy I am about to be reached."

As he spoke, the door of our compartment was opened. An apple-cheeked young police sergeant stood there. At sight of Pons, he gave a glad cry of relief.

"Mr. Pons! At last! Thank heaven you weren't on the earlier train, or I'd have missed you."

"Pray compose yourself, Sergeant Lester. Will you come in?"

"Mr. Pons, I cannot. I implore you instead to step out. There has been a terrible crime in the vicinity and I am at my wits' end for some clue by means of which to fathom it. I telephoned you earlier. Your landlady was kind enough to tell me you had gone on a holiday in Sussex, and to give me an address where you might be reached. I telephoned there only to learn that you had gone. I hoped you might be on this train, and I have not been disappointed."

My companion looked to me. "What do you say, Parker? Can your practise spare you for another day?"

"My *locum tenens* will manage very well without me," I said.

"Capital!" exclaimed Pons.

Forthwith he came to his feet, snatched his small bag, and stepped from the train. I followed.

"I have a car waiting, Mr. Pons," said Sergeant Lester. "I have only just now left the scene of the crime, and we're waiting on my finding you to move the bodies."

"Bodies?" repeated Pons.

"Bodies, Mr. Pons," said the Sergeant again, with the utmost gravity. "Three of them. Three harmless ladies murdered. They are at their cottage, which is not far from Tunbridge Wells. But here is our car. After you, Mr. Pons."

"Now, then," said Pons, when we were riding off, "let us have a brief résumé of the affair. There is no doubt it is murder, I take it?"

"None whatever, Mr. Pons. The three ladies were found shot to death. We haven't discovered either the weapon or the shells. A shotgun was used."

Pons listened without interruption, sitting with his eyes closed, one arm folded across his chest, the other resting on it and held aloft, with his fingers gently stroking one ear-lobe.

"The victims are Mrs. Edith Norwood, who was forty-five; her daughter, Louise, who was twenty-three; and her housekeeper, Miss Elizabeth Sothern, who was fifty-two. Mrs. Norwood owned the house. She and her daughter were found in their sitting-room; Miss Sothern was some distance from the house, in a little coppice. All three ladies had been shot in the back at quite close range.

"The most curious part of the problem," concluded Sergeant Lester, "is the complete absence of motive."

"Say, rather, obvious motive," said Pons. "What is obscure today may not be so tomorrow."

"As far as can be determined," said Sergeant Lester then, "nothing has been removed from the cottage. There is, in fact, not the slightest sign of any disturbance, apart, of course, from the havoc caused when one of the poor ladies fell against a tea-table and knocked it over; as a result, there is an upset table, and broken crockery is scattered on the floor. The ladies were evidently at tea."

"And Mr. Norwood?" asked Pons.

"Mr. John Norwood was in London. He has been notified and is on his way here. The bodies were discovered by a postman three hours ago. I should tell you, however, that these three ladies were the sole occupants of the cottage. Mr. and Mrs. Norwood had been divorced five years ago. Since then, Mr. Norwood has remarried, and he and his second wife live in a house in Crowborough. He was a frequent visitor at the home of his first wife, and so on occasion was his second wife. They were all on the friendliest of terms, and apparently had been old friends before the divorce and remarriage of Mr. Norwood. He seemed very much distressed at hearing this sad and shocking news and volunteered to come immediately.

"The late Mrs. Norwood and her daughter lived on a competence afforded them by her ex-husband. Another daughter of the couple, who will inherit the cottage and all else left by her mother and sister, is married and lives in the United States. Her inheritance now also includes the competence from her father, and she remains his only child, since no children were born to him by his second wife. No one within reach thus stands to gain by the death of Mrs. Edith Norwood and her daughter."

"You have eliminated robbery and gain," mused Pons. "What remains?"

"Mr. Pons, I do not know. The ladies lived very quietly. Except for Miss Norwood, who went to London occasionally, they went nowhere save very rarely to Crowborough to take an afternoon or an evening with Mr. and Mrs. Norwood there. Apart from the reciprocation of these visits, there was little social life at the cottage. The ladies were much given to reading, listening to the wireless, and playing cards. They were highly respected, regularly attended church services, and contributed to every charity. They had no known enemies."

"But one unknown," murmured Pons.

"The house is just ahead here," continued the Sergeant. "As you see, it lies over a knoll in a little valley, which explains the fact that no one heard the shots."

"The police have examined the bodies to determine the time of death?"

"Yes, Mr. Pons. The ladies were shot some time yesterday afternoon."

He finished speaking as the car drove up to a gate which opened on to a well-kept lawn. A constable stood on guard there. Another was stationed at the door of the house. A few people had collected curiously in the road outside, but, since nothing of the crime was visible from that point, they shifted uneasily and moved restlessly to and fro, unable to get past the constable.

"No one has been in but the doctor and myself," explained Sergeant Lester. "In the circumstances, it was thought best to disturb absolutely nothing so that any assistance you might be able to extend to us would not be hampered by the destructive curiosity of the people."

"Commendable," said Pons, but already his keen eyes were darting here and there, looking past a trio of fruit trees to the only visible coppice nearby, doubtless the scene of Miss Sothern's death.

The path leading to the house was of crushed gravel, and carried no footprints. The house itself was a modest cottage, snug behind laburnum bushes, and naved by yew and box-elder trees. Some roses blossomed beside the door, of a color which was no less bright than that which had burst forth inside, and was now darkened by the intervening hours.

For the scene inside was shocking, indeed. Two comely women – one in her prime, the other at the height of her beauty and youth – lay done to death. One was almost at the threshold, with the appearance of having crumpled against the doorframe before striking the floor; this was the younger. The other had knocked over the tea-table and lay in the midst of crockery, spilled tea, and scones. Both lay in dark pools of blood, which had flowed from gaping wounds in their backs.

Pons picked his way delicately to stand beside the body of the older woman. He crouched over her for a few moments, his sharp eyes scanning the floor, flickering from object to object.

Then he walked over to the body of Miss Norwood, stepped around her, and vanished into the adjoining room.

He reappeared in a short time.

"I take it the coppice and Miss Sothern's body are ready of access from the outer door leading off the kitchen?" he asked the Sergeant.

"Yes, Mr. Pons."

"Let us leave Miss Sothern for the moment," said Pons, returning to Mrs. Norwood's body. "Is there not something singularly suggestive about this scene?"

Sergeant Lester looked his perplexity at Pons.

"Let us ask rather," said Pons, "what the scene suggests to you?"

"Obviously, the ladies were having tea," answered Lester.

"Say, rather, about to have tea. If you will look closely at the broken cups, you will find that none had as yet held tea. But there is even more to be seen in these shards? Are there not four cups? I fancy if you piece them together, you will discover four, not two or three. Two would account for Mrs. Norwood and her daughter. A third possibly for Miss Sothern."

"They were very informal people," put in Sergeant Lester. "They would certainly not exclude the housekeeper for tea."

"Very well, then. I submit they were expecting a visitor to tea."

"Would not their visitor have found them thus and reported their murder to us?" asked Sergeant Lester.

"I should be inclined to doubt it very much, in these circumstances," said Pons dryly, "because it is fairly certain that their visitor was their murderer. Moreover, I submit that the murderer's primary objective was the death of Mrs. Norwood;

Miss Louise and Miss Sothern were slain because they could reveal the identity of their visitor."

Sergeant Lester stood for a moment in deep thought. "I fail to follow you in that, Mr. Pons," he said presently.

"It is elementary, my dear fellow. Consider – the presence of four cups on the table indicates that a visitor was expected. The presence of the tea itself suggests that the approach of their expected visitor had been observed, and tea had been brought in. The fact that it had not been poured is sufficient to enable us to postulate that their visitor had only just arrived. Mrs. Norwood was surely on a basis of casual and friendly relations with her murderer. She was almost certainly about to pour tea when she was shot from behind. Miss Norwood was very probably a witness to her mother's death; as she turned to flee, she, too, was shot. The housekeeper, perhaps having come far enough to discover what had taken place, turned and ran, pursued by the murderer, who shot her in the coppice. The primary object of the murderer's attention was, then, Mrs. Norwood. The other ladies were shot only because they witnessed the first murder. A singularly callous and brutal crime. But, tell me, Lester – it suggests nothing to you that in these circumstances a place had been laid for Miss Sothern?"

"No, sir, except that the Norwood ladies were not departing from their custom of having their housekeeper to take tea with them."

Pons smiled enigmatically. "Pray consider it, while I look about outside."

So saying, he was off, pushing through the kitchen. Sergeant Lester turned and went out the way he had come in. I followed. From the front of the house we could see Pons moving toward the body which lay as it had fallen among the trees of the coppice. Once there, however, he dropped to his knees and proceeded to make the closest possible scrutiny of the grassy ground, crawling back part of the way he had come.

When he had finished, he rose and went around the house, vanishing from sight. He next appeared around the corner of the cottage nearest us. There once again he dropped to his knees beneath a window which opened from the room in which the dead ladies lay. Sergeant Lester watched him in absorbed silence, until at last Pons rose, brushed grass blades from his knees, and came toward us.

"Miss Sothern's footprints are quite clear," he said. "She ran from the cottage. Her flight was erratic. She was evidently so shocked and frightened that she ran without direction and only turned toward the coppice when she saw that she was being pursued. Her pursurer, however, caught and killed her."

"We found no trace of his footprints, Mr. Pons," said Sergeant Lester.

"There is indisputable evidence of the pursuit of Miss Sothern," said Pons. "I commend a closer examination of the turf to you. Manifestly, Miss Sothern was not shot at as close range as her employer and the young lady; but her wound was no less mortal. The murderer then apparently gathered up such shells as were ejected and quietly made off."

As Pons spoke, the constable at the gate came up the walk and bent to whisper to Sergeant Lester.

"Let him come in," said the Sergeant. Turning to Pons, he explained, "Mr. Norwood has arrived."

A patently agitated man of approximately fifty years of age came hurriedly up the walk at the constable's direction. He was broad-shouldered. His eyes were a light blue, his mouth was sensuous, and his pale cheeks were very full. He was well dressed, wore a dark moustache, and carried gloves with a walking stick.

"My God! My God! Sergeant Lester, where are they? Who has done this dreadful thing?" he cried, as he came up.

"Pull yourself together, Mr. Norwood. Your daughter and Mrs. Norwood are just inside. Miss Sothern is in the wood. Perhaps you had better not go in, sir."

But Norwood had already pushed past and into the cottage, from which presently came a heartrending cry of anguish. In a few moments Norwood came unsteadily out, visibly shaken. His face was ghastly. He sat down heavily on the stoop before the door, dropping gloves and stick, and covered his face with his hands, fighting for control.

Sergeant Lester, however, gave him but a few moments of respite. Then he moved grimly closer.

"I'm sorry, Mr. Norwood, but we must ask you a few questions."

Norwood looked up haggardly. "I understand," he said quietly.

"Do you know of any enemy of Mrs. Norwood's who might have done this thing?" asked the Sergeant.

"No, sir. None of them had an enemy in the world. They were gentle and kind. You know that, Sergeant."

"Yes, Mr. Norwood," replied Lester. He would have gone on, had not Pons indicated that he wished to question Norwood. The Sergeant stepped back.

"Tell me, Mr. Norwood," said Pons, "was your ex-wife in the habit of allowing Miss Sothern to set a place for herself at tea?"

"At all meals, sir," said Norwood. "Except, of course, in case of special guests. At such times, Miss Sothern served. Otherwise everything was always very informal. It was a family tradition."

"You have another daughter."

"I spoke with her by transatlantic telephone before I came down," answered Norwood. "She and her husband live in Baltimore."

"Does Mrs. Norwood have any other surviving relatives?"

"A sister, Mrs. Sybel West, lives in Brisbane – Australia."

"Your ex-wife's sole heir is your other daughter?"

"Yes, sir."

"We understand that you and the present Mrs. Norwood occasionally visited here?"

"Yes, sir. Sometimes I stopped myself on my way up to or down from London, where I have my office. Sometimes, of a Sunday, Iris and I came together to spend the afternoon here. You should understand, sir, that my present wife and my first wife were neighbors and friends before my estrangement and divorce. We lived on adjoining places near Twickenham. After my divorce, I married Iris, who was the widow of a Colonial officer."

"When did you last visit here, Mr. Norwood?"

"I spent a day here within the week – just five days ago, sir."

"Alone?"

"My wife was indisposed. She knew I had been invited to visit Louise and Edith, of course."

"Who else commonly visited here, to your knowledge?"

"I know of no one." At this point a note of caution entered his voice. "Of course, you must realize that Edith and my daughter lived their own lives. Who came here between my own visits I have no way of knowing. But I should be inclined to think that they entertained no one regularly, or I should very probably have heard."

"Mrs. Norwood would have told you?"

"Yes, Edith would have mentioned it, I feel sure."

"Your first wife lived on a competence you paid her. How is this now affected by her death?"

"Not appreciably, sir. It continues, though in reduced form, and goes to our American daughter."

Pons appeared to be briefly lost in thought, noticing which, Sergeant Lester excused himself and went back around the cottage toward the coppice, signalling to one of the constables on guard.

"The present Mrs. Norwood," resumed Pons, "is a small, light woman?"

"Yes, Mr. Pons. She was a dancer and actress before her first marriage."

"In England?"

"In the provinces particularly. She was first married in Calcutta. Though how you could know of her is beyond me."

"The first Mrs. Norwood suggests the contrast. Second marriages are often made to very different types," said Pons with unusual glibness.

Norwood, however, was quite satisfied. He came to his feet just as Sergeant Lester returned.

"I'm afraid, Pons, your vision is better than mine," said Sergeant Lester. "There are none but the woman's prints in the turf between the house and the wood."

"I hardly think your vision is at fault, Sergeant," said Pons. He took out his watch. "Mr. Norwood appears quite shaken, and, since Crowborough is not very far away, do you think it possible for us just to drive him home?"

The Sergeant was somewhat taken aback, but, despite Norwood's immediate protestations, he rallied to Pons' suggestion.

"I must give instructions to Mr. Denton for the removal of the bodies," he said. "Then we will set right off."

In a short time we were on the way, passing along the lime-trees of the Pantiles in Tunbridge Wells and then by the gorse- and bracken-grown Common and the curious sandstone High Rocks on the way to Groombridge. The day was ideal; the summer sun shone upon a landscape which soon changed from the Tunbridge Wells Common to the Weald with its forests of oak. A light wind blew from the Channel coast, and the freshness of the sea reached even so far inland as the road along which we travelled. Now and then, out of the forest areas that remained of the Weald, rose picturesque rocks, and at last the towers of Eridge Castle. Crowborough was indeed not far away.

"This was Jefferies country, if I'm not mistaken," I said.

"Yes, Richard Jefferies had the Downs Cottage," answered Norwood.

"There is also a certain literary doctor living near Crowborough," said Pons, with a twinkle in his eye. "In more than one way a colleague of yours, eh, Parker?"

I did not reply, for at that moment Norwood leaned forward to direct our driver, and in but a very little while we drew up before a pleasantly-situated cottage on the outskirts of Crowborough.

"This is the Brown House," said Norwood. "I thank you for bringing me home."

He got out and would have shut the car door, had not Pons intervened. "I have a fancy to look about, if you do not mind, Mr. Norwood."

"But of course not, Mr. Pons. Do come in. Perhaps Mrs. Norwood could brew a cup of tea for us?"

"There will hardly be time, Mr. Norwood," said Pons, getting out of the car. "Do Mrs. Norwood and you live here alone?"

"No, sir. We have a housekeeper, Mrs. Mayfield, and her son, Fred. My wife retained them when we took the house."

Pons turned to Sergeant Lester. "Perhaps we had better let Mr. Norwood go in before us. His news will grievously upset his wife, and these little scenes are scarcely to my liking. Come, let us walk about a bit."

"Just as you like, Gentlemen," said Norwood.

Pons' consideration was futile, as it happened, for even as we were turning away, a slender woman came running from the house toward Norwood. She was a pretty, sweet-faced woman in her forties, and she had obviously been weeping. Oblivious of us, she threw herself into her husband's arms.

"Oh, John, John – I heard it on the wireless. How terrible!"

"Yes, my dear. But, please – we have visitors."

We were formally introduced. Mrs. Norwood held back her emotions with effort, and clung rather pathetically to her husband. He was plainly needed at home, for the triple murder had shocked her profoundly.

Pons, however, was not to be diverted from his purpose. He had meant to walk around the property and now, excusing himself, he set out. Sergeant Lester elected to remain with Mr. and Mrs. Norwood as they walked toward the house, from one window of which a short, slender, thin-faced elderly woman stood watching us.

There was a row of sheds along one line of Norwood's property, and it was toward them that Pons bent his steps. The door to one of them stood open, and the figure of a man could be seen moving about inside. It was to this shed that Pons went.

The man inside observed our approach and came to the door. He was a dark-faced fellow, with high cheekbones and a small mouth, and his brown eyes watched us suspiciously.

"I take it you're Mayfield," said Pons, coming up.

"That's right," he answered, crisply.

"Mr. Norwood has given us permission to look around a bit," Pons went on. "I see you've a fine array of tools here."

"Mr. Norwood's."

"Is all this then Mr. Norwood's? I should think he scarcely had time to work at the bench here, or to fish, or hunt."

"Oh, the fishing gear and the guns are mine," said Mayfield. "He don't have time, no, that he don't. He do sometimes get down here by noon or thereabouts from the city. But he don't often take out a gun and never a fishing pole."

"And Mrs. Norwood?"

Mayfield grinned. "She's afraid of fish. Can't look a fish in the eye, or a worm, either. And as for hunting – hoh! Why, the other day, she says, 'Teach me how to shoot that gun there, Fred' – that's the shotgun," he explained, obviously with a poor opinion of our knowledge of weapons – "and she took it out and practised, but she couldn't hit much with it, not as I'm saying she couldn't if she tried a lot – and yesterday she went out with twelve shells and came back with the gun unused. Got so scared, she did, she just threw the shells away and brought the gun back."

"It looks a fine gun."

"That it is, sir. Just feel how light it is."

He lifted the gun out of the rack and tossed it to Pons, who caught it deftly. Pons held it close to his face.

"But this gun has been fired recently, and not cleaned," said Pons. "The smell of the powder is still strong."

"Could be Ma had it. She's a crack shot, she is."

Pons handed the gun back to him and stood looking idly around. Then he asked, "Does not Mr. Norwood own a car?"

"Yes, sir, that he does. Mrs. Norwood took it in to Crowborough yesterday at noon for repairs. It's still there." He probed in the pocket of his vest. "I expect I ought to go in after it; they've had it long enough." He drew a receipt from his pocket. "Ah, yes, here 'tis. They received it at twelve-thirty-five. Should have had plenty of time, I expect. Mrs. Norwood waited for it, but it took longer than they thought, and she came back on foot just before he came down from London."

"Thank you, Mayfield. If you'll excuse us, we'll join Mr. and Mrs. Norwood."

Pons walked toward the house in deep and troubled silence.

"You suspect someone, Pons," I said.

He shook his head. "No, Parker, I have long passed beyond suspicion. I know who killed those unfortunate ladies."

"Indeed! I suppose you've seen something Sergeant Lester couldn't see."

"No, no, the very nature of the crime was enough. Thereafter every little shred of evidence which presented itself fit the suggested pattern. I have had to do many disagreeable things in my life, Parker, but this I am about to do is bound to be one of the most unpleasant. There is no need to prolong it. Did you not observe anything interesting about Mayfield's features?"

"I can't say I did."

"He has the same high cheek-bones, the same dark complexion, the same kind of hair as Mrs. Norwood. He is certainly her brother. Very probably the housekeeper is their mother, all unknown to Norwood himself. His wife, you will recall his saying, retained the staff."

We had reached the house, the door to which stood open.

Pons tapped lightly and walked in. Mr. and Mrs. Norwood were sitting together on a couch, and Sergeant Lester sat facing them. They ceased to speak as we came in, but only for a moment; then Mrs. Norwood spoke.

"Will you have some tea, Gentlemen?"

"Thank you, no," said Pons with unaccustomed brevity. "I am sorry, Sergeant Lester, but it is your duty to place Mrs. Norwood under arrest for the murder of Mrs. Edith Norwood, Miss Louise Norwood, and Miss Elizabeth Sothern yesterday afternoon."

For a moment there was not a sound. Then Norwood, his face blanched, rose with a growl of rage in his throat. His fists were clenched. Sergeant Lester was too surprised to make a move. Pons stood his ground grimly, unalterably, while across from him the pretty, sweet face of Mrs. Iris Norwood underwent a horrible transformation – the sweetness washed from her features, her eyes took fire, her mouth was contorted. Then, even before her husband could reach Pons, she sprang at Pons like a tiger.

Pons caught her by the hair, twisted it, and brought her to her knees, clawing at his hands.

"Sergeant Lester," commanded Pons curtly. "Mr. Norwood, control yourself."

There is no need to dwell upon that painful scene – the subduing of Mrs. Iris Norwood, the collapse of John Norwood, and the ultimate taking away of Mrs. Norwood by officials from Crowborough, acting at Sergeant Lester's direction. Afterward, riding back toward Tunbridge Wells, Sergeant Lester spoke anxiously.

"I suppose, Mr. Pons, that the evidence is all there – but for the life of me, I haven't seen it."

"Perhaps it is all too elementary, Sergeant," said Pons. "Some of us have an unhappy tendency to make a problem far more complex than it is. The evidence is not quite all there – some of it you must turn up for yourself. For instance, guards on the train will need to be found who remember Mrs. Iris Norwood's having traveled to Tunbridge Wells yesterday; I daresay you'll find them. Mrs. Norwood certainly left her car to be repaired when the receipt indicates, and entrained immediately afterward for Tunbridge Wells, after telephoning to say she was coming for tea at the Norwood cottage.

"But, of course, the facts which present themselves at the scene of the murder are circumstantially quite conclusive. Was not the crime essentially that of a woman? Indeed it was. The table had been set for four, including Miss Sothern. Yet we were given reason to believe that Miss Sothern would not have been seated with Mrs. Norwood and her daughter if their guest had been any but a familiar one. The very incidence of tea at a cottage occupied by three women suggests another woman; if a strange man had come for tea, Miss Sothern would have been serving, not joining them.

"An examination of the turf beneath the window of the sitting-room indicates that Mrs. Iris Norwood stood there for a moment to look in. The circumstances suggest that she may even have shot Mrs. Edith Norwood from that window. She may also have stepped quietly into the house and shot her from the threshold of the room. Certainly Mrs. Edith Norwood was shot in the back. Her daughter fled, and was shot down. Then Miss Sothern in turn took flight, with Mrs. Iris Norwood in pursuit. You said, you will remember, 'There are none but the woman's prints in the turf between the house and the wood.' Not the 'woman's', Sergeant – but the 'women's' – a close scrutiny will show you that one of the women was somewhat heavier than the other – that was Miss Sothern. Hers was a size six shoe, but there are also prints, however similar to the untutored eye, not as heavily indented, made by a slight woman who wears a four and a half shoe, Mrs. Iris Norwood's size.

"The very reclusive nature of life at the Norwood cottage left one with but little alternative in the identity of the murderer. Did not every testimony we had, including that of Norwood himself, indicate that the ladies entertained very few people? Indeed, the only names which were ever brought forward as familiar visitors, were those of John and Iris Norwood. An intimate serving of tea to a solitary woman guest in midafternoon suggests only Iris Norwood.

"She used her brother's gun, certainly. I fancy she convinced him she could not shoot, so that he was ready to believe her story that she had thrown away the shells rather than shoot. She threw them away, beyond question – both the unused and the used shells she calmly gathered up after her brutal crime."

"But her motive, Mr. Pons?" protested Lester.

"There is surely but one possible motive, Sergeant. The woman was jealous of the first Mrs. Norwood, nor was her jealousy of any recent origin. It must have existed a long time ago, even before she managed to break up the Norwood home. Norwood himself never suspected it. He mentioned that she had been an actress. She was never anything else. She fiercely resented every visit he paid to that house, and his spending a day there within the past week was finally the goad to activate her jealousy toward so cruel a crime, the effect of which now falls equally upon her murdered victims and the man she strove to possess so completely. There is no hatred so great as that of one woman for another.

"An ugly, stupid crime, peculiarly feminine in its essential nature. Do you wonder that I subscribe so firmly to single blessedness?"

V

THE ADVENTURE OF THE RYDBERG NUMBERS

I have hesitated many years before setting forth the curious events concerning the disappearance of the left-handed physicist which occupied the attention of my friend, Solar Pons, in the same year in the 1920's which saw us through the incredible case of the fantastic horror at Burlstone and the baffling problem of the Swedenborg Signatures. But the march of scientific progress has voided the qualms which prevented me from yielding heretofore to the inclination to chronicle this unique adventure.

It began, as I recall, one October morning. I had risen early, only to find Pons already at crumpets and tea, and bearing every evidence of having been up for at least an hour. My companion looked at me with dancing eyes.

"You are just in time, Parker. We are about to have a most distinguished visitor."

"At this hour?" I protested.

"His step is on the stair."

There was indeed a heavy tread on the stairs leading to our quarters.

"Who is it?" I asked. "The Prime Minister?"

Pons shook his head. "One who is far more seldom seen in these rooms."

"Not His Majesty!"

Pons chuckled. "I am always at His Majesty's command without requiring his presence here."

The door to our quarters was unceremoniously flung open to reveal the portly, almost massive figure of my companion's brother, Bancroft. His eyes were even sleepier than on the one previous occasion I had seen him some years before, regarding the curious behavior of the reclusive cryptographer, Ricoletti. He came but slightly forward into the room, pushed his cane firmly to the floor, and looked from one to the other of us.

"I detest above all things being awakened at such a barbaric hour," he said peevishly.

"For my part, I welcome any hour of the day or night which may offer me some little problem in human travail," replied my companion. "It takes none of my powers to conclude that only such a problem would have brought you to our humble quarters. I am surprised that the Foreign Office permitted your sleep to be disturbed."

"It has nothing to do with the Foreign Office," retorted Bancroft. "You are not at your best at this hour, Solar. Since it is too early for any activity at the Foreign Office, it is patent that no event or circumstance arising from my modest position there brings me here. No, sir, confound it, I have been aroused from my bed by an hysterical young woman, and I am persuaded it is you she wishes to see, not me."

"How did she come to you?"

"I have some acquaintance with her brother. It is he who seems to have disappeared."

"Ah, at last we are coming to the matter in hand."

"I have the young lady below in a cab. I should tell you she has defective eyesight; she is partially blind, in fact. Her name is Lillian Pargeter. She is under considerable strain."

"By all means, let her come up!" cried Pons.

"Before I fetch her, does the name *Rydberg* convey anything to you, Solar?"

Pons tugged at his left ear and sat for a moment with closed eyes. "I believe that Per Axel Rydberg is or has been until recently the curator of the New York Botanical Garden..."

"I doubt that he would be the one."

"Then there was Abraham Viktor Rydberg, who died in 1895, a Swedish novelist and writer on various subjects. Swedish Academy in 1877, I believe, and professor of ecclesiastical history at Stockholm from 1884 onward. He was for many years on the staff of the Göteborg *Handels-och sjöfartstidning*, where such novels as his *The Freebooter on the Baltic* and *The Last of the Athenians* appeared. He wrote poems, ecclesiastical studies, and various other tomes, among them *Magic in the Middle Ages*."

"Surely it is not he!" exclaimed Bancroft testily. "And *Mendelyeev*?"

"Dmitri Ivanovich Mendelyeev, author of the Periodic Law, the standard table."

"Quite probably that is the man. The missing man seems to have been at work on some problem involving physics or physical chemistry. Physics and chemistry are not my forte, as you know, Solar. Pargeter was employed by the government in research. To the best of my knowledge, he was not involved in any major research. He is considered by the department a minor if persevering physicist and has a record of competence, but not brilliance. He is a man of thirty-five; his sister is somewhat younger."

"He is, in short, a person of little consequence in the eyes of the government," said Pons. "Let us just have a talk with the young lady."

"I'll get her," I offered.

"Pray do," replied Bancroft, obviously relieved. "Seventeen steps to these rooms! I am not given to running needlessly up and down them."

I descended to the street and opened the door of the cab on a not unattractive young woman, with dark hair and pale blue eyes. She was one of those fine-featured young women so typical of certain areas of England, though the thick-lensed glasses she was required to wear lent her fragile face an oddly owl-like appearance. I introduced myself and took her slender hand in mine to help her from the cab and up the stairs into our quarters.

"Ah, Miss Pargeter," said Pons, coming to meet her and conduct her to a seat near the fireplace. "Sit here and tell us what has alarmed you."

"It is about my brother, Stanley," she began. "He said to me not long ago, if anything was to happen to him. I should see Mr. Pons. I understood him to mean Mr. Bancroft Pons, but I may be in error. Oh, dear! I am so upset!"

"Pray take your time, Miss Pargeter," said Pons persuasively. Bancroft Pons snorted impatiently.

"I have no doubt my brother has not been at his best," Pons continued. "I beg you to overlook his idiosyncrasies. You must understand my brother has a position of some importance in the government."

"The object of this gathering is to inquire into the circumstances concerning the disappearance of Stanley Pargeter," observed Bancroft with icy detachment. "I suggest you get on with it, Solar."

"How long has your brother been gone, Miss Pargeter?" asked Pons.

"Oh, that is the trouble, Mr. Pons. I don't know. I think it has been all of two days now, perhaps three, but I cannot be sure."

Pons glanced quizzically at his brother, but Bancroft flickered not an eyelash.

"I know you'll think me hysterical or mad. I assure you I am not. As you have surely seen, I cannot see very well. My brother and I have lived together at Number 27 Conant Place for the past four years, and I believe I know him very well. I am accustomed to his step, his manner, his actions. It would be difficult to deceive me. Yet just such an attempt has been made. I could not be positive until last night, but then I grew certain, and I could not wait to see you. I know something dreadful has happened to Stanley, and I beg you to find him."

"Something took place last night to increase your certainty?" prompted Pons.

"Forgive me, I am distraught. Yes, a little thing. He took hold of my hands. Then I knew this man who had lived in our house for at least two days and perhaps three was not Stanley. You see, Mr. Pons, Stanley is left-handed. This man, too, appeared to be left-handed. But when he took hold of my hands last night, I felt there were more callouses on his right hand than on his left. That isn't true of Stanley. Yet in every other respect, I had thought him to be Stanley – perhaps with a slight change here or there, true, but nothing of great consequence. His voice, for instance, suggested that he was coming down with a cold; I have heard Stanley sound just so. His manner was identical, he was as considerate as Stanley has always been, and even the sound of his walk rang true most of the time. In appearance, he certainly resembled Stanley. But I know now it is not he. And I know that something has happened to Stanley, something he may have expected.

"I cannot imagine what it can be. I have wracked my poor brain in an effort to discover anything he might have said to me. But it is only his request about you that comes to mind. And his work."

"What work, Miss Pargeter?"

"Mr. Pons, Stanley's work was not really important. It was what he did at home that seemed to matter to him."

"Did he speak of it?"

"No, Mr. Pons. He would have thought I could not understand, and I am sure he was right. But one evening I came silently into his rooms, and I heard him say to himself, 'Ten to one the old man didn't know what he had!' I thought this of no consequence, for Stanley is by nature solitary, and I interrupted him on the matter about which I had sought his advice, and went out again. But recently he spoke quite often of people named Rydberg, Balmer, Mendelyeev, Bohr, and others with whom I am not familiar, I am sorry to say. He has spoken so much, too, with some excitement of something he called quanta and the Rydberg numbers and constants, but it is all beyond me."

Pons sat for a long minute with his head sunk on his chest in an attitude of deep concentration.

"Who were your brother's associates, Miss Pargeter?"

"He had none, Mr. Pons."

"He did not go out of an evening?"

"On occasion, yes." She spoke doubtfully. "Our father left us a competence. There was no need for Stanley to work, but he has always been keenly interested in chemistry and physics, and he wished to do so for his own gratification. We have few friends, but we do occasionally go out to parties, usually among friends on Park Lane. Seldom anywhere else. They are always rather private parties, though not limited in size as much as I would like. But perhaps I am too sensitive about my affliction."

"Yet your brother himself had no particular friend, no confidante?"

"If he had, I know of none. I should be inclined to doubt that people would take kindly to Stanley. Please do not misunderstand me; I don't mean to disparage him. I mean only he is so engrossed in his work that he had no interest in talking of anything else, and he is therefore a very poor listener."

Again Pons appeared to muse for a few moments in silence.

Presently he asked, "It was two or three days ago when you first became suspicious, Miss Pargeter. Why?"

"Yes, sir." She clenched one hand and made a futile gesture. "Oh, it's difficult to explain, Mr. Pons. Perhaps it was nothing more than intuition. People who are afflicted in one of the senses are often compensated by a sharpening of those which remain unimpaired. Perhaps it is so with me. I *felt* that something was wrong with Stanley; I didn't dream at first it was not Stanley who was with me, for he seemed no different from his usual self. Until last night. Then, of course, I knew."

She spoke with such assurance that it was not easy to doubt her. Glancing at my companion, I saw his keen eyes alight with interest. Bancroft Pons, for all the sleepiness of his expression, was no less alert. Both men appeared to be waiting upon Miss Pargeter's words with more than ordinary attention.

"Mr. Pons, what am I to do?" she cried.

"I fear yours is a most difficult task, my dear young lady," replied Pons immediately. "You must return home as if nothing had taken place, and you must conduct yourself without a single betrayal of your doubts."

"Oh, I cannot!"

"I am sorely afraid you have no alternative. I may say that your brother's fate rests on your doing so."

"Mr. Pons, it will be beyond me."

Pons was inexorable. "For his sake, perhaps for your own, there is no other way. Your substitute brother is employed as usual?"

"Yes. He goes and comes just as Stanley did."

"Very well then. I will call on you in the course of the day. Let us now waste not a further moment."

Bancroft came to his feet with catlike grace. "I will see you to the cab, Miss Pargeter," he announced.

Thus impelled, our client had no other course but to take her leave.

"Is that not a singular occurrence, Parker?" asked Pons, while yet their steps sounded on the stairs. "It would seem to be an hallucination. I believe they are not uncommon in cases where there is a clear diminution of one of the senses."

Pons clucked in disapproval. "Dear me, you medical gentlemen find it difficult to credit the unusual. Why are the scientific gentry always so ready to dismiss the admittedly inexplicable and substitute a rationalization which negates the evidence? I submit that our client is a young lady of more than ordinary intelligence, of some considerable perception, refreshingly free of unnecessary emotionalism, and not at all given to hallucinations."

"Hallucinations!" echoed Bancroft Pons, who had come silently back up to the threshold. "Bosh and twaddle! That young lady suffered none. But whoever made off with her brother must indeed have been laboring under illusions."

"Why do you say so?" asked Pons.

"Come, come," said Bancroft impatiently. "Had he gone of his own free will, there would have been no need of a substitute. His sister is not a child; she could have been told if he wished to go away. Since there was a substitute, Pargeter was abducted. If so, the abduction must be concerned with his work. He could hardly have been mistaken for anyone else – but stay! there is young Samuel Pargitton, who is at work on bacteriological warfare."

Pons smiled. "You have eliminated him, surely. I submit that such an elaborate attempt at deception could not have been made in error, and could have been done only to prevent anyone from taking note of Pargeter's absence. Have you enough personal acquaintance with Pargeter's work to be assured that it could not be of interest to any foreign power?"

"Certainly. I have all our men at my fingertips."

Pons smiled again. "But how many chemists, foreign agents, intriguers, physicists, and experts in the various fields of interest to our Foreign Office can occupy your fingertips? That must surely be a question as academic and incapable of solution as the number of angels believed to be able to occupy the point of a pin. Ninety, was it not? There are more chemists than that, to say nothing of the others. The experts always abound."

"The hour is too early for this kind of sport, Solar," said Bancroft testily. "Let us have done with it. The man did routine work. Consider, if he had not done so, a substitute might not have been so readily put forward. A consummate actor, after studying Pargeter for weeks, perhaps months, might readily deceive all who knew him; but if precise and specialized knowledge were required of him in so restricted a field as that in which Pargeter worked, he could hardly hope to excel in this, also. No, in this I brook no question; Pargeter's work was routine, no more. But the matter in hand would seem to be one of importance."

"Of the utmost importance," added Pons. "No pains have been spared to deceive Miss Pargeter and prevent knowledge of her brother's disappearance. It is evident that Stanley was thoroughly and comprehensively studied over a considerable period of time. We are faced with the obligation of inquiring whether the missing man has access to any vital information."

"None."

"Then if his vocation offers nothing, perhaps his avocation?"

"Were they not the same? I believe Miss Pargeter said as much."

"The field is not so restricted as you suppose," said Pons, waving toward his corner table filled with retorts and chemicals.

"Our German friends have an expressive word for this: *Kinderspiel*," interrupted Bancroft. "I shall expect to hear from you in good time, Solar. In deference to you, I shall have Pargeter's work reexamined; if I have not sent word to you by noon, you may consider that his position offers us nothing of possible interest pointing toward a solution of the riddle. Let us hope that the game will not be too long afoot."

With that, Pons' distinguished brother took his leave. Pons turned merry eyes on me. "I fear Bancroft is nettled. Something has escaped him. We shall have no word from him."

"You are certainly confident," I said.

"I submit that our client's brother's status is not one which enlists the profound interest of the Foreign Office. The question which instantly occurs is – why not? I daresay it is for the very reason my brother has set forth – his work is not important. Of the nature of his work we have had some hint – radiation of heat and light. Now this strikes me as a field with most interesting possibilities, though it is admittedly difficult to grasp at the moment just how Stanley Pargeter may have come into information which might conceivably be of concern to someone other than an academician. I fancy our next move is an examination of Pargeter's home."

So saying, Pons retreated into meditative silence. From time to time, he looked into certain of his reference books; now and then he sawed away at his violin, which was a great trial to anyone within earshot, for whatever his talents, Pons was not a violinist; on occasion he dipped into his files. He was roused by nothing of the immediate mundane world, neither the familiar street sounds nor the ringing of our own telephone when a patient called me.

He proved correct in his assumption that there would be no further word from his brother, though he did him the courtesy of waiting upon him until noon, when, after a light repast set before us by Mrs. Johnson, he announced his intention of calling upon our client without further delay.

Our goal proved to be a rather old-fashioned house of two storeys, well-appointed, but clearly a dwelling which belonged to another era. Obviously it had been the home of our client's parents, and had at one time been an imposing residence. Miss Pargeter had been expecting us. She seemed now somewhat more composed than she had been in the morning, but she was still plainly under strain.

"Oh, I am so glad you've come, Mr. Pons," she cried. "I've been wracking my poor brain to find some explanation, but I'm more puzzled than ever. My poor brother can assuredly not be of interest to anyone. Why, he has been going on to his friends for months, for trying years, about the numbers..."

"What numbers?" asked Pons sharply.

"The Rydberg numbers, as I'm sure I told you," she replied.

"Tell me, Miss Pargeter, has your brother's substitute in any considerable way altered his books and papers?"

"I fear I would not be able to say. Would you like to see his room?"

"By all means."

Our client took us upstairs and ushered us into a spacious room, which bore an appearance of some disorder.

"My brother is not a good housekeeper," explained Miss Pargeter.

Pons went immediately to a large and handsome, but obviously home-made desk which was littered with papers in every conceivable disarray. Some of them had overflowed into a capacious wastebasket at one side of the desk; others were piled with comparative neatness at the far side. There was every evidence to show that many of the papers had been removed from the desk drawers, some of which stood open. Half-open books lay carelessly face up or down among the papers, so that, at cursory inspection, the desk bore the look of utter confusion.

Pons, however, showed none of the bewilderment I felt. He seated himself at the desk and attacked the papers with the utmost caution, careful to disturb none of them. His keen eyes flickered rapidly from one to another, as he turned each over following his scrutiny. Some failed to hold him; indeed, most of them were apparently trivial by nature. But there were few papers which he put aside.

Miss Pargeter watched him in perplexity. She looked to me from time to time for some explanation of his conduct, but there was nothing I could reply save to reassure her silently as best I could.

Pons was at Pargeter's desk for a most wearing hour. Miss Pargeter finally took her leave of us, descending to the floor below, and when Pons completed his perusal of Stanley Pargeter's papers, he bestowed upon the rest of the room only the most superficial of examinations before following our client.

"Miss Pargeter," he began without preamble, "I have appropriated several of your brother's papers. Since these were in the stack on the left end of the desk, I am quite certain they will not be missed by your brother's substitute, who must be kept free of your suspicion at all costs until we have come upon the track of your brother. Now, you have mentioned Stanley's attendance at social events and especially his propensity for talking of his work. Did you have reference to his employment or his studies at home?"

"Oh, what he did at home, Mr. Pons. He talked of this interminably."

"So that anyone attending a party also attended by your brother might have heard him when he spoke of his work?"

"Mr. Pons, my brother spoke to everyone. I'm afraid he was most trying. He seemed to be unable to gain an ear in quarters associated with his work, since his theories were – I am sure, quite properly – dismissed as untenable, and therefore he felt impelled to speak of them to anyone who would listen, and, I fear, many who would rather not have listened."

"Could you possibly recall the names of people to whom your brother broached his beliefs?" asked Pons. "I suggest, of course, only those who appeared to be willing listeners, and who gave him time enough in which to understand him."

Miss Pargeter looked dubious. "I'm afraid it would be very difficult."

"Pray do your best. I shall need also a photograph of your brother. I will expect you to communicate with me in the morning."

On this note we took our departure.

Once back at 7B, Pons went straight to his small library of books pertinent to physics and chemistry. He was soon lost in Sir Richard Glazebrook's *Dictionary of Applied Physics*, so lost, indeed, that he refused dinner, much to Mrs. Johnson's indignation. His table rapidly came to bear an aspect similar to the desk in the room of the missing man, for Pons was studying the papers he had taken from that room in relation to data he assimilated from the books at his command.

All evening he sat in uncommunicative silence, as if the very walls of the room had ceased to exist for him, together with all else within them save the papers and books at his fingertips. His meditation was profound, and by the hour of my retirement, he had begun to cover sheets of paper with his jottings.

It was so I found him still at dawn. He had gone without sleep, but he now sat before a table in less disorder than it had been on the previous evening. He had arranged some of his papers and had brewed a pot of tea for himself. His eyes, when he met my reproving glance, were bright.

"Pray spare me the medical point-of-view on loss of sleep, Parker," he said crisply. "I have had before me a singular and most tantalizing task, and one, I regret to say, without positive solution. I have been trying to arrive at some conclusion about the subject which occupied Pargeter."

"I'm afraid you're off on a wild goose chase, Pons," I said. "Everyone – including his sister and your brother – is convinced that Pargeter is at best an enthusiast without much to lend credence to his views – at worst, a profound bore."

"I submit that not quite everyone is so convinced, Parker," replied Pons. "Myself, for one. For another, that gentleman who had sufficient foresight to bring about Pargeter's abduction. I fancy we are all too prone to accept the opinion of the majority; it may be in error. It frequently is. Let us suppose, on the contrary, that Pargeter has hit upon something."

"The majority," I said with asperity, "are entirely likely to be right."

Pons smiled tolerantly. "Ah, I should hesitate to commit myself to the mercy of the majority," he answered. "In this case everyone seems to take it for granted that Pargeter's theories, whatever they are, are untenable. You know my methods, Parker. Let us assume that the contrary is true."

"The experts..."

"With all due respect for science – and none is more fulsome in his praise of the scientific method than I, you must agree – I confess to a profound distrust of 'experts'."

At this juncture, Mrs. Johnson knocked and came in with our breakfast on a tray. The good woman had doubled Pons' portions, explaining with an injured air that inasmuch as Pons had not eaten his dinner the previous night, he would need "the extra." Pons hailed her appearance volubly, and gently praised her generous breakfast, so that she went out beaming with pleasure.

"Now, then," said Pons, brusquely pushing his breakfast to one side, "take a look at this. What do you make of it?"

He pushed toward me one of the papers I recognized as among those he had found on Pargeter's desk. On it was written a curious series of figures and letters.

"N/c (equal to 109,677.76 cm. –i.)
"$N - 3.28888 X 10^{15}$
"$n = \frac{n_o - N}{(m + u)^2}$"

"These would seem to be formulae," I ventured.

"Capital, capital!" exclaimed Pons. "These are Rydberg numbers. N over c is the Rydberg constant, with the numerical value of N as stated. The reference is to the theory of radiation of heat or light. I fear the matter is too complicated to permit of precise explication, regrettably. Its beginning lies in the measurement of the distinct lines or bands occupying definite positions, which is to say, showing definite wave lengths, given off by gases and vapors heated to incandescence, and visible under spectroscopic examination. J. J. Balmer, as early as 1885, set down the atomic spectrum of hydrogen. The Rydberg constant was pronounced subsequently, following upon which came Planck's quantum theory, and Ritz's principle of combination, which gave us the Rydberg-Ritz Formula. The experiments of Niels Bohr, Paschen, Rutherford and, not long ago, Brackett, have added to our store of information about radiation.

"Some of the theories which have been advanced are considered revolutionary and radical by scientists the world over. Rutherford's postulate that electrons rotate rapidly about a nucleus, so that outward centrifugal force balances the inward attractive force, for instance – Niels Bohr's suggestion that an electron always moves in a closed orbit, without absorption or emission of radiation, a theory enunciated only a little over a decade ago, were not set forth without encountering very strong opposition."

"Surely this is all in textbooks," I interrupted. "I acknowledge it is out of my depth."

"Yes, it can be found in Glazebrook."

"In that case, what would Pargeter have to offer which could not be more readily ascertained than by abducting him?"

Pons smiled enigmatically. "It does not occur to you that Pargeter may just possibly have gone beyond the lines of thought suggested by the developments outlined by Messrs. Balmer, Rydberg, Bohr, et al.?"

"Pray inform me where such developments could lead?"

"Ah, Parker, I fear I am incapable of doing so. At best I have certain tenuous suspicions, little more. But is it not tantalizing to consider that scientific thought in regard to certain fundamentals may be in error and these radical gentlemen may be right?"

"Oh, that's the dream of every dabbler in physics and chemistry," I retorted. "And Pargeter is surely no more than that."

"Is he? I wonder."

"You have certain tenuous suspicions. What are they?"

"Well, suppose that further experiments lend support to the radical theories thus far outlined and lead some scientists to conclude that certain of our fundamental scientific laws are not, after all, unalterable."

"For example?"

"The law regarding the fissionability of the atom."

"My dear Pons!" I protested. "Here we are a quarter of the way into the twentieth century. For decades, our greatest authorities, living as well as dead, have held to the unshakable belief in the indivisibility of the atom. This is not my field; neither is it yours."

"No, it is Pargeter's," said Pons dryly.

At this moment the outer bell rang, and in a few moments Mrs. Johnson trudged into the room with a letter for Pons, which had just arrived by special messenger.

Pons tore open the envelope and glanced at the single sheet of paper it contained, ignoring for the moment the photograph of our quarry which fell to the table. "Ah!" he cried, "Here is a list of names from Miss Pargeter." His eye went down the paper. "Sir Hilary Saunders – no, of course not. Nelson Warrender – no, it cannot be he." He read for a few moments in silence. "Aha! Crandall Barrington. I fancy that is our man."

"Why do you say so? Is he not the actor?"

Pons nodded, as he drew his breakfast toward him at last.

"What would a minor actor know of such abstruse scientific matters?"

"One of Barrington's closest friends during the past twelvemonth has been Karl Heinrichs, who is on the staff at the German embassy," answered Pons.

"You are surely not suggesting that the German ambassador is implicated in Pargeter's disappearance!" I protested.

"There is only one man in London who conceivably has the imagination to suspect that Pargeter may have got on to the track of something, and at the same time the determination to find out what it is and the skill and ingenuity necessary to have accomplished his abduction in the manner in which it was done. He is not in any obvious way connected with the German embassy. Yet he is an espionage agent employed by the German government. He moves freely in social circles and lives near Park Lane, in a somewhat secluded house where he entertains lavishly now and then. I refer to Baron Manfred von Grafenstein."

"A notoriously fanciful dilettante who poses as a patron of the arts," I said, unable to conceal my dubiety.

"And a consummate actor. Heinrichs is his friend. I do not doubt that Barrington spoke of Pargeter and his theories to Heinrichs, and Heinrichs in turn carried information to von Grafenstein, whose imagination is not bound by the traditional acceptance of scientific fundamentals."

"But what could be gained from Pargeter?"

"The direction of Pargeter's theories and/or experiments, if any have been made, which I am inclined to doubt, knowing the stuffiness of departmental heads. These can be transmitted to scientists in Germany, who may be more open to suggestion than our own men."

"He could hardly hope to get Pargeter out of the country."

"Not without exposing his hand. No." Pons shook his head, "If indeed he has taken Pargeter, he will have him imprisoned at his home. Consider the advantages of von Grafenstein's gambit. Not only would Pargeter be unable to say just where he had been kept, but he would not even be able to prove he had been abducted, since a dozen people could testify that he had been at home and at work with unfailing regularity. Pargeter can be kept away from work indefinitely; von Grafenstein has no reason to suspect that Pargeter's absence has been noticed. If Miss Lillian Pargeter were to betray alarm, her brother's double could immediately notify his employer, and Pargeter could be returned. If, that is, there is any thought of returning him," Pons added darkly.

"What is your next step, then?"

"I fear it is one I cannot take. It is one the government will not take. Moreover, the tribulations and ramifications of going to Scotland Yard are insufferably delaying. No, I fancy this is a matter for the boys. It is Guy Fawkes' day; the night could not be more ideal. I shall send for Alfred Peake."

By Pons' reference to "the boys" I understood that he meant the group of gamins he called his Praed Street Irregulars. They were a little army of street urchins, ranging in age from eight or nine years into their teens, alert and venturesome lads who would do anything within reason for a guinea. Alfred Peake was their acknowledged leader; it was through him that Pons was accustomed to dispatching his assignments.

Promptly within an hour, Alfred presented himself. Pons' message had found him in school, he had obtained an excuse, and here he was. He was a bright-eyed boy in his early teens, though small for his age, and he stood before Pons now with his arms akimbo and his eyes alight with anticipation.

"Alfred, my lad, I have a little task for you," said Pons. "I shall need a dozen to a score of dependable boys. Can you find them?"

"I think so, Mr. Pons."

"Capital! Today is Guy Fawkes'. How many of the boys, do you think, will have costumes appropriate for the occasion?"

Alfred looked dubious. "I don't think many will, sir."

"Very well, then. I shall entrust you with five pounds with which to outfit yourselves. Now, then, take a look at this photograph."

Alfred obediently bent over the photograph of Stanley Pargeter which his sister had sent to Pons. He studied it carefully.

"Do you think you could recognize this man if you saw him?"

"Yes, sir."

"Let us suppose, as is not unlikely, that you encounter him in bed, with his face bandaged."

Alfred looked dismayed.

"If I told you it was necessary to do so, could you bring yourself to tear off the bandages to see whether it was he?"

Alfred grinned and nodded.

"Ah, willing lad! Now, then, look here."

Pons spread before him a map of London folded to the region just west of Hyde Park. "Can you find Waverton Street?"

"Yes, sir," said Alfred, after but a few moments, and put his finger on it.

"Good! Now there is a certain house on that street, Number Twelve. I believe the man we want is in that house. He is being held a prisoner there against his will. He may be locked in a room. He may be abed under guard. He may be under a sedative."

"Doped, sir?"

Pons smiled. "Doped, Alfred. We want this man. I may say, Alfred, our government wants him."

"What do you want us to do, Mr. Pons?"

"At mid-evening, which is to say between nine and ten o'clock, I suggest that you boys venture upon Waverton Street in Guy Fawkes costume and make a nuisance of yourselves. You know 'trick or treat'?"

"We always do it, sir."

"Good. I shall expect you to do it. At Number Twelve, however, I shall expect you to invade the house. I'm afraid you may have to be quite rough. Can you find yourselves some sandbags?"

"I think so, sir."

"Capital! Don't hesitate to use them. I'm afraid they must be used on all the occupants of the house. I cannot say how many men may be there. Perhaps as many as five, perhaps but two. Our quarry is in all likelihood among them. I need hardly say you are not to use the bags on him. Proceed with discretion, my lad, and caution. I shouldn't like any one of you to be shot."

Alfred's eyes widened, but not with apprehension.

"This man is to be found. The house must be searched from top to bottom. They will not suspect an army of roistering children until it is too late. Once you find him, bring him with you. We will be waiting in a Daimler limousine just around the corner from Waverton on Hill Street looking toward Berkeley Square. As soon as you've delivered him, abandon your costumes and scatter. Are you willing to undertake the assignment, Alfred?"

"Yes, sir," responded the lad eagerly.

"Very well. You may promise the boys a guinea each. Whether you succeed or fail, you may present yourself here tomorrow for your reward. Take the photograph with you, so there may be no mistake. Now be off with you."

"Pons, this is madness," I protested, once Alfred Peake had gone clattering down the stairs.

"Ah, I thought it rather ingenious myself," answered Pons. "Now I shall require only Bancroft's assistance. I shall want a government car which is not likely to be stopped between Waverton Street and Praed, in case of a flaw in the arrangement."

A few minutes after nine o'clock that night, Pons, his brother Bancroft, and I, were sitting in a darkened Daimler limousine which bore certain official insignia which would guarantee us uninterrupted passage through London. Waverton Street crossed behind us. Pons' brother had complained bitterly at Pons' tactics, but had interposed no obstruction. Within ten minutes of the time of our arrival at our post, a small army of boys in costumes typical of Guy Fawkes' day materialized and swept down the street.

Soon there was a veritable bedlam of noise. Doorbells were rung, the boys banged away on various unmusical instruments, and ran shouting and crying from house to house. There must have been easily twenty of them or more. Pons sat unresponsive to Bancroft's muttering plaint about the discomfort he suffered; once, in the glow of my cigarette, I saw Pons' face masked with a Sphinx-like grin.

The bedlam receded down the street and diminished.

"Ah, they have got in," murmured Pons. "There was always the off chance that no one would answer the assault on the door."

Five minutes passed with interminable slowness. Ten.

Then the bedlam resumed, sweeping back toward the corner where we waited. The noise increased, exactly as before it had diminished, and abruptly the horde of boys swept around the corner and bore straight down upon the car. In their midst stumbled one who was taller, clad in white, and apparently similarly crowned.

Pons was out of the car in a flash.

The boys gave way to him. Within a moment Pons was pushing his quarry into the Daimler. After them came one of the boys, who, when his mask was doffed, was revealed as Alfred Peake.

"Mr. Stanley Pargeter, I presume," said Pons. "Allow me. Solar Pons, at your service. We are accompanied by my brother, Bancroft, whom you may know, and my companion, Dr. Lyndon Parker. Pray wrap yourself in this blanket."

The car was already drawing away toward Berkeley Square. Of the Praed Street Irregulars there was no sign; they had melted away into the night.

"They must have torn my skin, taking off those bandages," Pargeter said ruefully.

"Sorry, sir," said Alfred. "We were in a hurry, and couldn't tell how many more men might be in the house."

"How many were there, Alfred?" asked Pons.

"Three, sir – not counting this one."

"They gave you trouble?"

"Yes, sir. The last one had a gun. The tall guy opened the door. A butler, he was. Whitey hit him and he went down. We met the next one on the stairs. He was fooled, too. But the last one – he was in the hall upstairs – he had the gun. He almost stopped us, but Mick Green – he's the one always reading cowboy stories from the States – he lassoed the gun. We tied him up. Then we found him here, in bed, like you guessed he might be."

"We will hear more of this from von Grafenstein," murmured Bancroft Pons.

"I doubt it," answered Pons. "Instruct the driver to go round and drop Alfred at his home."

Back at 7B, Stanley Pargeter revealed himself as a thin, pale-faced young man who clearly took himself with challenging seriousness. I was able to outfit him with some clothing, and helped clear his head of the bandages which remained, for Alfred had torn away only enough of them to assure himself that he had found his quarry. Bancroft waited with mounting impatience until Pargeter could tell his story.

He had been abducted in the simplest way imaginable. Hailing a cab, he had got in to find it already occupied. He knew nothing more until he awoke in a strange bed. Since then he had been questioned daily. At first he had been told he had had an accident; he had talked freely. But then, as the tenor of the questions became apparent to him, he had said nothing more. He had not as yet been mistreated, but there had been certain disquieting signs. Nor had he been allowed to see anyone, or even to view those who questioned him, for his eyes had been kept bandaged.

"Now, Mr. Pargeter," said Pons, when the young man had finished his recital, "let me ask about the direction of your theories. My brother, as you know, is connected with the Foreign Office."

Pargeter looked somewhat dubious. His pale eyes glanced from one to the other of them. "I've been ridiculed so often, Mr. Pons," he said at last, "I hardly know what to say. I'm convinced that not even this attempt to extract information from me about my line of thought will convince my superiors that it's worth following. I am exploring radical ground."

"So much seemed apparent," said Pons. "Let me guess. I have examined some of your papers. As perhaps you know, I am not bound by the beliefs of your departmental heads. I do not recognize the impossible until all other avenues have been closed. Judging by the papers left in your home, you are working toward research tending to show that the nucleus of the atom is not necessarily always profoundly stable."

Pargeter grinned. "Somewhere, Mr. Pons, there must be an atom with a nucleus sufficiently unstable to be fissionable." Pons looked toward his brother with dancing eyes.

"I am afraid the government's position holds your views untenable, Mr. Pargeter," said Bancroft.

"I know it, sir. But I'm far from convinced they are untenable. I'm certain they'll give my views no more hearing now than before."

"I am convinced they will not," assented Bancroft.

Pons interrupted. "You gave some of these theories to your captors, Mr. Pargeter?"

"None of any importance, I am sure."

"Nevertheless, would that not be a treasonable act, Bancroft?" asked Pons.

"I believe it would," agreed Bancroft, a cunning smile beginning to show at his lips.

"So that it might be the wisest course to charge Stanley Pargeter with giving information to foreign agents and put him under immediate detention to be held incommunicado and tried under the Official Secrets Act."

Pargeter looked at him, startled.

"I will have it done," said Bancroft.

"Pray do not be alarmed, Mr. Pargeter," said Pons. "I refer to the man who has been occupying your home and your position as your double since your abduction. As for yourself, I fancy there is a gentleman in America who may appreciate your talents. If you have no objection, I will give you his name and address. Our American cousins may be less traditional in these matters than our own scientists."

Pargeter left for the United States within a fortnight, and, as events in the years that followed amply proved, Pons was correct in his estimate of our American cousins' appreciation of Stanley Pargeter and his radical theories.

VI

THE ADVENTURE OF THE GRICE-PATERSON CURSE

"No, Parker," said my friend Solar Pons suddenly, "you need have no fear that the ants, for all their social organization, are close to taking over mankind."

"The prospect is horrible," I cried – and stopped short. I turned. "But how did you know what I was thinking? Pons, this is uncanny."

"Tut, tut – you are too much given to overstatement. It is only the simplest deduction. You have been reading Mr. H. G. Wells' admirable fantasies. When I observed you just now staring at an ant on the pane with an expression that can only be described as one of horror, it was not too much to conclude that you have at last read *The Empire of the Ants*."

"How simple it is, after all!"

"As most seemingly complex matters are simple." He gestured toward the windows. "Draw the curtains, will you, Parker?"

I stepped across the room to shut the weather from sight.

Rain whispered steadily at the panes, and from the street came now and then the sound of vehicles splashing through the water, for the warm, late summer rain had been falling the better part of the day, bringing a misty fog to shroud London. It was now twilight, and the yellow glow of lights in windows and along the street could be seen dimly.

"Tell me, Parker, does the name of Colonel Sir Ronald Grice-Paterson recall anything to your mind?" asked Pons, as I walked back toward him.

"Nothing but that I seem to remember him as Governor-General of some part of the British Empire. Was it not Malaya?"

"It was indeed."

Pons stretched forth a lean arm, took an envelope off the mantel, and held it out to me. I took it, unfolded the paper inside, and glanced at it.

"From a woman, I see," I said. "She uses a highly individual perfume."

"A musk."

"'Dear Mr. Pons,'" I read. "'Against the wishes of my family, I am writing to ask that you receive me tomorrow night at eight on a most urgent matter pertaining to the curse of our unhappy family.'" It was signed, "Edith Grice-Paterson." I looked up. "His daughter?"

"I believe the Colonel's daughter pre-deceased him. His granddaughter, perhaps. What do you make of the postmark?"

I looked at the envelope. Though the stamps were British, the postmark was not; it read "Isle of Uffa," and in its geometrical center were stamped the initials "G. P."

"Where in the world is Uffa?" I asked.

"Ah, Parker, I fear my geography is lacking in the information you ask. But I seem to remember that on his retirement from Malaya, Grice-Paterson went to live out his life on an island estate which exists in a state of quasi-independence from Great Britain. If memory serves me rightly, it lies off the coast of Cornwall, east of the Scilly Isles. It has a status similar, I believe, to the almost incredible Isle of Redonda, which has been a separate little kingdom, though allied to Great Britain, for decades. Uffa, however, is close to England, whereas Redonda is in the Leeward Islands, in the British West Indies."

"I'm afraid both are beyond my knowledge."

"You have never chanced to encounter them."

I turned again to the letter. "She writes in an agitated hand."

"That is hardly surprising. The papers carried a brief notice within the week of the finding of the body of Lt. Austen Hanwell, described as her fiancé. Certain mysterious circumstances attended his death. Let me see, I believe I clipped the account."

Pons opened one of his huge scrapbooks, which was lying among newspapers on the table. From a group of loose clippings waiting to be added to the storehouse of criminous occurrences between those covers, he selected one.

"Yes, here we are."

I walked to where he bent and looked past him. The story was indeed brief. "Tragic Death," read the short heading. "The body of Lt. Austen Hanwell, 27, was discovered early yesterday in a study at The Creepers, the home of his fiancée, Miss Edith Grice-Paterson, on the Island of Uffa. He appeared to have been asphyxiated or choked to death, though routine inquiries failed to turn up any evidence of foul play. Lt. Hanwell was a native of Brighton. His death is the third in a series of tragedies which have beset the family of the late Col. Sir Ronald Grice-Paterson."

"It is careful to charge no one with murder," I pointed out.

"Is it not, indeed!" agreed Pons. "There is more here than the press is willing to print. Perhaps our client can enlighten us further. I hear a car driving to a stop below, and, since it is just past the hour set in her letter, I daresay it is she."

In a few moments our client stood before us. She was a tall, willowy young lady, a pronounced blonde, with strong blue eyes. Though she gave evidence of some trepidation, there was an air of grim determination about her also. She was dressed entirely in black, and was enveloped in a full cape, which served both to keep her dry and to protect her from the wind. Once she had thrown back her cape, she had the bearing of a young woman well on her way to spinsterhood, so somber was her manner.

She ignored the chair Pons stood out for her and burst at once into speech. "Mr. Pons, I have no one else to turn to. The police of Helston have declined jurisdiction, on the ground that Uffa has a separate government and that its status in relation to Great Britain has never been clearly defined. That is all nonsense – we are part of England – but they do have certain valid reasons for their reluctance to act. Nevertheless, I am determined to bring to an end the curse which has hung over our house ever since I can remember." Though she spoke with suppressed feeling, there was no mistaking the firmness of her resolve. She paused dramatically before she added, "Mr. Pons, in the past eleven years, three persons have died very strangely under our roof, in circumstances which strongly suggest murder – but, if so, it is murder without meaning and motive, murder which the authorities are reluctant to accept as that."

She strode up and down before the fireplace, clasping and unclasping her fingers in agitation she fought to control.

"Pray compose yourself, my dear lady," said Pons quietly. "You are the granddaughter of the late Colonel Sir Ronald Grice-Paterson?"

"I am. I am the mistress of The Creepers."

"The late Colonel had two sons and a daughter?"

Our client drew in her breath for a moment and clenched her hands. "His two sons were the first and second victims of the curse which has fallen on our family, Mr. Pons. My aunt, my father's sister, died when she was quite young. My mother died in an accident at sea. There are left of our entire family now only my two brothers and myself. Both are younger than I, and for the time being, they live with me at The Creepers.

"My grandfather died eleven years ago, and the estate – that is, the Island of Uffa – fell to his three children. My only aunt and one uncle died without heirs; so the estate fell to my father. He in turn died as mysteriously as his brother, and my poor Austen, within a year after he came down from London to assume possession of Uffa. All the children had been living away from the house when my grandfather died; he was a solitary man, very introspective by nature, and with a strong streak of misanthrophy. He lived alone but for one servant, and discouraged even his children's visits. His sole occupations were the writing of his memoirs, which were never published, and his devotion to horticultural pursuits. While he made or seemed to make an exception in my case, in that he showed a fondness for me on such occasions as we visited Uffa while my father was employed in London, he was rebelliously rude and cantankerous with everyone else."

Pons sat for a moment in silence, his fingers tented before him, an enigmatic smile on his thin lips. "Will you tell us something of the – 'the curse,' I believe you called it?" he asked presently.

"Very well, Mr. Pons, I'll do the best I can," said our visitor. "It began – no, let me say rather that the first time I was aware of it was about a year after grandfather died. I was then seventeen. My grandfather's house had always seemed a very gloomy place to me – for he had surrounded it with all manner of plants and trees, and it was overgrown with creepers, which give the house its name – and we did not visit there often. However, on that occasion – my seventeenth birthday – we journeyed down from London to spend a week with my Uncle Sydney.

"It was at about this time of the year. My uncle was in the best of spirits, though there had never been much love lost among the members of my father's generation, or, for that matter, between my grandfather and his children. On the morning of the second day of our visit with him, my uncle failed to come down to breakfast. When my father and one of the servants went to see what detained him, they found him stretched out on the floor, dead. Mr. Pons, he had been strangled in some remarkable fashion. There were curious bruises around his neck, as well as on his face, his arms, back, and chest. There was the appearance of a violent struggle, but the room was locked, the key was in the lock on the inside, and, while the window was open, there was no mark to show that anyone had climbed into the second storey window either by ladder or by means of the thick creepers along that wall.

"The medical evidence seemed inconclusive; it was not called death by strangulation, but death by misadventure; his doctor believed he had had some kind of seizure, and, while a cursory investigation was made by the only police sergeant on the island, there was nothing at all that might be called evidence turned up. No strange craft had landed on Uffa; no one had any reason to want Uncle Sydney dead; and my father, who inherited my uncle's share of Uffa, had far more wealth of his own through his business interests and his investments in the City."

Our client struggled visibly to control herself. She was clearly still under great strain, and had undoubtedly forced herself to make the journey to consult my companion. "Mr. Pons, I didn't see my uncle lying there – but I did see my father in exactly similar circumstances just seven years later, almost to the day – and now, God help us all! – I've seen my fiancé similarly slain – all without motive, as if it were an act of a vengeful God! Mr. Pons, our family – our house – our Uffa is cursed! Now my brothers are urging me to sell, to give up Uffa, and move to England. I have no wish to do so, for I am sentimentally attached to our island, but certainly I cannot sell until I can be sure that only the Grice-Patersons and those who are close to us are victims of this dread curse which seems to know no limitation of time."

"Do I understand you to say that all these deaths have taken place in the same room, Miss Grice-Paterson?" asked Pons.

"No, Mr. Pons. Two of them occurred in the same room on the second floor – my uncle's and my father's. My fiancé was found on the ground floor, in the study directly below that room. He had been reading late, and had apparently fallen asleep. The circumstances of my father's and uncle's deaths were very much the same – that is, the door was locked, the open windows showed no sign of disturbance. In the case of my fiancé, the door was ajar, but nothing had been disturbed. There were the same strangling lines about his neck..."

"Pons!" I cried out suddenly, memory flooding me – "A dacoit!"

Our client flashed a startled glance in my direction, and then gazed wonderingly back toward Pons.

"Pray forgive Dr. Parker, Miss Grice-Paterson. He is addicted to the reading of the exploits of Dr. Fu Manchu, who employs thugs and dacoits to accomplish his lethal work for him."

"You may well make sport of me," I answered hotly, "but it's certainly not beyond the bounds of possibility that the one-time Governor-General of Malaya may have brought back with him some sacred symbol, the recovery of which has brought about these strange deaths."

"Perhaps not beyond the bounds of possibility, but certainly of probability," countered Pons.

Our client fingered a curiously-wrought golden brooch at her throat, a thoughtful expression on her attractive features. "It is true I've heard my grandfather speak often of the mysteries of Malaya – of the strange customs and the unbelievable things one might learn from the ancient native culture – but I'm quite certain he was not the kind of man who would have made off with anything which did not belong to him. He was no doubt a martinet in many ways, and in most ways a typical British colonial administrator, I am convinced – but, Mr. Pons, he was not a thief."

"I should be inclined to agree with you, since I know something of your grandfather's record," said Pons soothingly, his eyes warning me to be silent. "Now tell me, would it be possible for Dr. Parker and myself to examine the body of Lt. Hanwell?"

Our client bit her lip, and an expression of anguish washed into her face. "Mr. Pons, he has been put into his coffin, and we're shipping his body home to Brighton tomorrow. Do you think it necessary?"

"It may be helpful," replied Pons.

"Very well, then, if we were to leave immediately – my car is below, and there will be a boat waiting to take us to Uffa at Penzance – we might be able to accomplish what you ask before the body is sent away."

"Capital! We shall leave at once."

Pons leapt to his feet, threw aside his purple dressing-gown, kicked off his slippers, and in a thrice was ready, deerstalker, Inverness and all, having moved with an agility only too typical of him, and managing to chivvy me for my slowness at the same time. He did not speak to our client again until we were comfortably ensconced in her car, a handsome Rolls-Royce, driven by a chauffeur.

"Tell me, Miss Grice-Paterson, has there ever occurred any other untoward incident at The Creepers?"

In the darkness of the car, our client's sensitive face was visible only in the light of passing street-lamps. She appeared to ponder Pons' question before she answered.

"Mr. Pons, I cannot say. Perhaps in the light of life in an ordinary suburban villa or semi-detached house, there have been strange events at The Creepers. Our inability to keep dogs, for instance."

"Ah, what of that?"

"They die, Mr. Pons. Despite the fact that our winter temperatures rarely fall below forty-five degrees, and our summer temperatures do not often rise above eighty degrees, our dogs have been unable to weather a year at The Creepers. We have lost no less than seven of them in the course of the past decade. Of all kinds, too. And two cats, I might mention, shared the dogs' inability to live on Uffa."

"Is this a general condition on the island?"

"Well, now that I think of it – it isn't. There is a dog in a tenant house at the other end of the island. An old sheep dog. He doesn't seem to have been troubled by the atmosphere of Uffa. He may be an exception. Then again, it may be the atmosphere of The Creepers, which brings me to another of the incidents you asked about – the night of the perfume – when the entire island seemed to be pervaded with a most bewitching and demoralizing perfume, as cloying as that of heliotrope, and giddying. It came, of course, from one of my late grandfather's rare plants, which had come into blossom after many years of sterility.

"Then there are, I suppose one might add, the strange, whispering sounds of the leaves, which seem to caress one another even on the most windless nights. Oh, Mr. Pons – how can I speak of these things which are so much a part of the house and of life on Uffa, when I am still bowed by the curse of the Grice-Patersons! How shall I ever again survive the month of August! I shall never spend another summer on Uffa."

She spoke with passion and determination.

"You do not live alone at The Creepers?"

"No, Mr. Pons. My brothers Avery and Richard live there with me. Mrs. Flora Brinton is our cook. Aram Malvaides is an old servant who was my grandfather's orderly for many years. He is the gardener, and he has an assistant who comes some days from the mainland. There are certain other minor servants, responsible to Mrs. Brinton or to Aram."

"You've not mentioned hearing any outcry in the case of any one of the three unfortunate deaths, Miss Grice-Paterson."

"None was heard. The crimes took place late at night, evidently after the victims were asleep."

"Yet there was evidence of struggle in each case?"

"Yes, Mr. Pons."

"Does it not seem strange to you that none cried out, that no struggle was overheard?"

"No, Mr. Pons. The Creepers is built in the shape of a T with a short stem. The family usually sleep in the west wing, or the left arm of the T, whereas our guest rooms and winter quarters are in the east wing. There is the entire length of the house to separate the one from the other. Even if there had been an outcry, there's no certainty that it would have been heard by any of us. But there was none, for the servants would surely have heard a cry if one had sounded."

Pons flashed a baffling smile at me and lapsed into silence. Once or twice I caught sight of his hawk-like face in semi-repose, but soon we were out of London, away from the occasional gleams of light, riding through the dark countryside into the southeast.

At dawn we rode out of Dartmoor into Cornwall, and soon we were catching glimpses of what is surely one of the most beautiful faces of England – the Cornish coast near Truro, and then Camborne, and then at last, Penzance, where there was indeed a boat awaiting us – it was no less than a small yacht. But of Uffa there was no sign from land; our client explained that it lay over the horizon. Her car was quartered in Penzance, since there was little use for it on Uffa, which consisted of but a small settlement in addition to The Creepers and the immediate grounds of the estate, though the entire island was the domain of the Grice-Paterson family, and had been for two centuries.

The morning was free of fog, and presently Uffa rose out of the sea like the embodiment of a dream, like fabled Lyonesse, all green, save for a few rocks along one coast, and for a cluster of white which was the little fishing village on the opposite shore. It was there that we landed. A carriage waited for us there, driven by a dour, dark-skinned old man.

"This is Aram, Mr. Pons," said Miss Grice-Paterson.

Aram gazed at us with the darkest suspicion manifest on his features. His attitude was aloof and unfriendly.

"I don't know what my brothers will say," our client went on, as we got into the carriage. "They may be rude; if so, I hope you will forgive them. It is I who am mistress here, and the decision is mine to make. They've opposed your coming – they fear 'any further scandal' – as they put it."

"We shall see," said Pons imperturbably.

The Grice-Paterson brothers were indeed displeased to the point of rudeness at sight of us. Avery, the older, was but a year younger than his sister; he was a dark-haired brute of a man, as massive as our client was well-proportioned, with the shoulders of a professional athlete. Richard was as fair as his brother was dark, and slight of build against Avery's thickness. Neither was entirely civil at our introduction, and neither was co-operative, being disinclined to answer the few questions Pons put.

We did not linger in their company, however, for Pons was anxious to view the body of Lt. Austen Hanwell before its removal. We therefore followed our client from the house through the heavily overgrown lawns and gardens east of the widespread dwelling, past the abandoned dog kennels, to the old stone family vault, where the coffin containing the body lay waiting to be sealed by the authorities before being taken on shipboard.

"Forgive me," said Miss Grice-Paterson at the great iron door. "I cannot bear to see him again. I'll wait here beside the path."

The coffin stood just inside. Pons left the door ajar, and so we had ample light at the entranceway to the vault, though Pons had brought his pocket flash. He lost no time in raising the coffin lid, exposing to view a handsome, moustached face, that of a man who looked even younger than his years. But face and neck – when his clothing was withdrawn – still showed the livid marks our client had described to us.

"Your department, I think, Parker," said Pons, holding his light close to the dead man's skin.

I examined the marks with the greatest care, though I was at a distinct disadvantage in doing so two days past the event. But there was no mistaking what I saw, and, when I had completed my examination, I said so.

"These are the marks of thin but powerful cords, applied with great pressure."

"Enough to cause death?"

"Enough, in my opinion."

"There are no wounds except the marks of the cords?"

"Only on the marks themselves. Here and there small openings in the flesh, which might have been made by rough spots on the cords. You may laugh at me all you like, Pons, but if this is not the work of dacoits, I shall be very greatly surprised."

For a few moments Pons said nothing. He bent to examine the marks himself. When he straightened up, his aspect was grave as he replied, "I fear it is something far more sinister, my dear fellow, than dacoits. Look again. Are those tears in the flesh not regular punctures?"

I threw up my hands. "It's one and the same thing." Pons closed the coffin and stood aside for me to pass.

We found our client standing at some little distance from the vault. Beyond her, approaching the place, was a complement of four men from the ship in the harbor, preceded by an official who was clearly a member of the police. Miss Grice-Paterson, however, avoided meeting them by stepping down a side path.

"I will take you around to the room where my fiancé was found," she said. And in a moment she indicated the east wall of the building, a towering mass of creepers. "See, those are the windows – those two there. And directly above them are the windows of the other room in which my uncle and my father died."

The windows were framed in singularly beautiful crimson flowers, which adorned the creepers massed upon the stone wall of the house. In the bright morning sunlight, their appearance was remote indeed from the nameless horror which had taken place just beyond them.

Pons paused a moment, crossed over, and smelled a blossom.

From the proximity of the windows, where he stood intently examining the earth below, he asked, "Should something happen to you, Miss Grice-Paterson, who will inherit the property?"

"My brother Avery."

"And after him?"

"My brother Richard."

"And then?"

Miss Grice-Paterson looked at Pons, puzzled. "How curious you should ask that, Mr. Pons! Or perhaps you knew of my grandfather's strange will. If some catastrophe were to wipe out our family, the entire estate is to go to old Aram. We have no other close relatives. My grandfather had a brother with him in Malaya, but he was killed in an accident there. His only son succumbed to one of those mysterious East Indian diseases, while he, too, worked as a commissioner on my grandfather's staff. I told you," she concluded grimly, "that there is a horrible curse on our family – I assure you most earnestly I was not exaggerating."

"I believe you," answered Pons. "Tell me, if you know – what were your grandfather's relations with his brother and his nephew?"

She shrugged. "I cannot say, except by what I've heard. Grandfather was a hard man. I understand the change came on him after grandmother's death."

"Was she, too, a victim of the curse?"

"Oh, it is all of a piece, Mr. Pons," she cried. "Grandmother was accidentally killed at a family birthday party. Grandfather went to pieces. He brooded for days, and never afterward seemed to come out of his shell except as an irascible old man, filled with hatred of mankind."

"I see. Now let us have a look at the room in which Lt. Hanwell met his death."

Once more we braved the scowls of Avery and Richard Grice-Paterson, as we passed through the front part of the house on our way to the east wing. The room in which Lt. Hanwell had been found was a spacious one, lined with shelves of books on all but one wall, and handsomely apportioned to be as pleasant as possible for anyone who chose to spend his time in it. Our client indicated a comfortable old leather-covered chair between a table lamp and the near window.

"Austen had apparently been reading there and had fallen asleep. He was found between the chair and the window. The chair had been kicked out of place, and the table moved somewhat out of its usual position. The lamp had fallen over; it was still alight when we found him."

"The window was open?"

"Yes, Mr. Pons. Our windows are unscreened because we are never troubled with insects of any kind."

"So that anyone might have entered that way?"

"There was no sign of such entry."

"Nevertheless, it was open."

"But who would have motive for such an act, Mr. Pons?"

"Ah, Miss Grice-Paterson, I am not so bold as to say. But let us suppose it was to someone's interest to prevent your marriage."

"Why?"

"To prevent any change in the line of succession. Or am I mistaken in that your marriage would alter the provisions of your grandfather's will?"

She colored briefly and looked down. "No, Mr. Pons," she said in a scarcely audible voice. "The property would go to my oldest child."

"As for the absence of signs of entry by way of the windows..." began Pons.

"A dacoit could manage it without leaving a trace," I said with asperity.

Pons did not so much as blink an eye in acknowledgment. "Lt. Hanwell slept in the room above?" he asked.

"Oh, no, Mr. Pons. Austen slept in the west wing, where we all sleep. We seldom use the east wing, except in winter, when we move out of the west wing for this."

Pons examined the window and its frame. Then he looked over the chair, studying what appeared to be lines of wear, after which he got down on his hands and knees to look about on the rug, having been assured by our client that it had not been cleaned. He seemed to find nothing there but fragments of drying leaves, which he discarded. Then he went back to the window, opening it and leaning out. By bending down, he could almost have touched the ground, which he had scrutinized outside. The sphinx-like expression on his face told me nothing as he drew back into the room and closed the window.

"And now the room upstairs, if you please," he said.

In a few minutes we stood in a gracious, sunlit bedroom which was the very antithesis of a murder chamber. The room contained a large double bed immediately adjacent to the window; if this were the position of the bed at the time of the death of the two Grice-Patersons, I could not help thinking how immoderately convenient it was for any murderous dacoit.

Pons must have been thinking along similar lines, for he crossed at once to the window and leaned out to test the strength of the creepers, the heady perfume of the flowers of which wafted into the room as soon as he opened the window.

"They look as if they would bear the weight of a small man," I could not help saying.

"They would bear a two hundred pound man," replied Pons.

"My grandfather planted them when he came into the estate, just after grandmother's death in Malaya. He was on his first visit home," explained our client. "We naturally thought of someone's climbing them to come in through the window, but there was no mark on them, and the creepers would surely carry some sign of having been climbed, Mr. Pons."

"It is reasonable to assume so – in all but an exceptional case. These windows, too, were open on those lethal dates?"

"I believe so, Mr. Pons. I remember the questions that were asked when my uncle was found. I was seventeen then, as I told you."

"And your brothers?"

"They were sixteen and fourteen."

Pons stood looking about, but there was nothing to be seen, for the room was spotlessly clean. Then he appeared to come to a sudden decision. "Can it be arranged for us to spend the night in this room, Miss Grice-Paterson?"

"Why, yes, Mr. Pons. I had expected to put you into the west wing – but perhaps you would have greater privacy here."

"Thank you. We'll try this room for a night or two."

For the next few hours, Pons wandered through The Creepers, questioning the servants and making a vain attempt to inquire about certain events of the Grice-Paterson brothers, who remained patently unwilling to be of any assistance, a circumstance I regarded with the gravest suspicion, though Pons shrugged it off. He walked about the gardens and lawns, marveling at the variety of exotic plants, shrubs and trees which abounded there – the fruit of the late Colonel Sir Ronald Grice-Paterson's industry. Indeed, so overgrown was the estate that it seemed almost as if the one-time Governor-General of Malaya had sought to create here on this island off the coast of Cornwall a home reproducing, as far as the climate permitted, his residence in the Malay States. Nor was Pons content with the environs of the house; he wandered all over the island, pausing in the little harbor village, quite as if he were on holiday instead of busy at an inquiry into as dreadful a crime as either of us had encountered for a long time.

Our lunch we had taken alone. Our dinner was taken with the family. This proved to be an extremely uncomfortable meal for all but Pons, for the Grice-Paterson brothers took no pains to conceal their animosity to us. Pons, however, he affected not to notice. Now and then he turned to one or other of them with a question.

"Tell me," he said to Avery on one occasion, "were you aware of the terms of your late grandfather's will?"

"You're fishing for motive, aren't you, Mr. Pons?" answered Avery hostilely. "You should realize, sir, we've had enough scandal without your meddling."

"The question, Mr. Grice-Paterson," insisted Pons, his enthusiasm for the leg of lamb on his plate not at all diminished by Avery's manner.

"Answer him," said our client angrily.

"I was," said Avery sullenly.

And to Richard, later, Pons said, "I cannot escape the impression that neither of you cared very much for Lt. Hanwell."

"Oh, we didn't," answered Richard. "We're solitaries, my brother and I. And you'll find, if you dig deep enough, Mr. Pons, that when I was a boy I could get up and down those creepers like a monkey. Without trace," he added with heavy sarcasm.

Pons thanked him gravely, and continued to show no annoyance when all his other questions were similarly treated by the brothers.

Not until we were once more in the room in the east wing, following that stiff, uncomfortable meal, did Pons relax his insistent casualness.

"Now, then, Parker, have you given up that fancy of yours about the stolen idol and the dacoit?"

"No, Pons, I haven't," I answered firmly. "I can think of no other theory which fits the facts so well. Yet I concede that there is the little matter of the succession – I've failed no more than you to notice that, except for Miss Grice-Paterson's fiancé – and perhaps he, too, indirectly – each of these deaths has furthered the succession of the estate."

"Ah, death always furthers something of the kind," said Pons. "Would that not make the ultimate author of these murders, to your mind, then Aram Malvaides?"

"Who else? Mark this – he alone of all the parties who have an interest in the Grice-Paterson estate was present on the occasion of each murder. The boys were not."

"Ah, that is well reasoned, Parker," admitted Pons.

Thus encouraged, I went on. "If Miss Grice-Paterson had married, there might be still more heirs to dispose of."

"You conceive of his wanting to eliminate everyone who stood between him and the inheritance?"

"Would it not have to be all or none?"

"Indeed it would, if your theory were tenable. But why wait so long between crimes, when he is not growing younger?"

"No one knows the dark mind of the murderer."

"And just how did he manage to gain entry without leaving a clue?" pressed Pons. "Pray spare me that dacoit, Parker. I find it inconceivable that a convenient dacoit would be standing by on call to suit the whims of so reluctant a murderer."

"I have not yet come to any conclusion about his clueless entrance," I was forced to admit.

"I fear that is the flaw in most armchair rationalization – particularly when it is based so largely on romance."

Once again I knew Pons was laughing at me; I was nettled.

"No doubt you already know the identity of the murderer?"

"I suspected it before we left London."

"Oh, come, Pons. I am a patient man, but..."

"I never knew a more patient one, to tolerate my idiosyncrasies for so many years," replied Pons handsomely. "But there are several salient factors which, I submit, may have some bearing on the matter. I am no lover of coincidence, though I am willing to concede that it takes place far more often in life than could be justified in fiction. It has not occurred to you that it may be significant that all these deaths should have taken place at approximately the same time of the year?"

"Coincidence."

"I feared you would say as much. The family occupies the east wing only in winter. Why? I have made certain enquiries, and understand that this practise was inaugurated by Sir Ronald; the family only followed his custom. This does not seem meaningful to you?"

I confessed that it did not.

"Very well. I may be in error. Yet I suggest that there may be a connection to certain other curious factors. I fancy we are in agreement that ingress was accomplished through the open window in each case?"

With this I agreed unreservedly.

"It does not seem to you curious, if that is so, that there was no mark to be found on any occasion? – no footprint below the ground floor window, though there is a respectable area where one might be impressed on the ground there; – no abrasion of the creepers to indicate the presence of a climber to this room – nothing?"

"Someone sufficiently light – and trained – could accomplish all that was done without leaving a trace."

"Surely that would be almost insurmountably difficult," protested Pons.

"Richard has admitted that as a boy he did it."

Pons smiled. "Richard was having us."

"You may think so, if you like," I retorted hotly. "But hasn't it occurred to you that these murders may have been started by someone else, and only carried on in this generation by another hand?"

"It has indeed," answered Pons. "Let us for the moment concede that it may be possible for undetected entry to have been made by way of the creepers. Let us look at another aspect of this strange little horror. Why should there be so long an interval from one crime to the next?"

"Obviously to diminish attention."

"If diminishing attention were of importance, surely some less dramatic manner of commiting the crime might have been found?"

"Except to one specially trained in the chosen method."

"Ah, we are back once more to the dacoit. I had no conception of the depth of your devotion to the sinister Doctor."

"You're making sport of me, yet I'm in deadly earnest," I said. "Is there any other solution which so admirably fits all the facts?"

"Manifestly."

"What is it?"

"That which was in fact the method and motive for the crimes."

"That is a riddle unworthy of you, Pons."

"Surpassed only by the true solution of the curse of the Grice-Patersons."

"If you're so sure of the solution," I cried, "why are we dawdling here? Why haven't you arrested the murderer?"

"Though I am sure, I want a little more verification than my deduction alone. I am entitled to wait upon events for that verification, just as you are for the dacoit to make a return engagement, for our presence in this room this hot summer night will duplicate the superficial aspects of the situation prior to each of the three crimes which have been committed."

"Except for one," I hastened to point out. "We are not heirs to the estate."

"You have your revolver with you, I notice," Pons went on. "That should be adequate defense against your dacoit. I have asked that the Colonel's old sword be sent up; that, in turn, should serve me long enough to sever any cord which may loop about us."

"Surely you're not expecting another attack!"

"Say, rather, I am hoping for one. We shall hope to catch the murderer in the act."

"Pons, this is absurd. An attack on us would be completely without motive; it would be a basic flaw in our concept of the motive for this sequence of events."

"Pray permit me to correct you – your concept of the motive, not ours."

"If I were to act, I would have Malvaides under arrest without delay."

Pons smiled grimly. "Yet it is no less logical to suppose that somehow our client's late father slew his brother; that she herself slew her father; that her brother, Avery, likewise developed enough agility to make away with Lt. Hanwell – they, too, were directly or indirectly in line to inherit.

"And now, Parker, it's past the dinner hour; night will soon be upon us. In hot latitudes, people take siestas after lunch; we did not. It is almost hot enough here for the torrid zone, and I for one am going to take a little rest before what I hope will be a strenuous night."

A strenuous night, indeed!

How often since that time have I recalled the singular events of that night spent in the twice fatal room of The Creepers on the Island of Uffa! We retired together at a late hour, despite our tiredness, but I was soon drowsily aware that Pons had left our bed and had gone to sit instead in a large, old-fashioned rocking-chair which stood opposite the open window, so that he could face them and still keep an eye on the bed.

Behind him, the door to the room was locked. We had prepared, as he put it, the identical situation which had maintained on the occasions of the two previous murders which had taken place in this room. Had I not been so exhausted after our long night ride and the difficulty of following Pons about during the day, I would not have slept, for the room and the night were cloyingly hot and humid; but the distant roar of the surf was lulling, and I was soon asleep. My last memory was of Pons sitting grimly on guard, the late Sir Ronald's sword ready to hand, even as my revolver lay beneath my pillow, ready for instant firing.

I do not know how many hours I slept before I was awakened, gasping for air, trying to call out, in the grip of a deadly menace. Before I could reach for my revolver – before I was sufficiently awake to grasp what was taking place – I felt myself being drawn bodily from my bed.

I had a horrified glimpse of Pons whipping away with the sword, even as the life was being squeezed out of me, and I felt a dozen pinpoints of pain upon my throat, my wrists, my face. Briefly, I was aware of a distorted picture, inexplicably terrible, filled with the imminence of death, of Pons' desperation against an enemy I could not see but only feel, of the tightening cords wound so insidiously about me...

Then I swooned.

When I came to, Pons was bending above me, chafing my brow.

"Thank God, Parker!" he cried. "I would never have forgiven myself if anything had happened to you in my anxiety to satisfy my suspicions!"

I struggled dazedly to a sitting position. "The murderer?" I gasped, looking vainly for him.

"The murderer – if murderer there was – has been dead these twelve years," answered Pons. "Colonel Sir Ronald Grice-Paterson. Only his unique weapon remains."

Then I saw all around me on the floor the severed, fleshy creepers from the plant with the crimson flowers that covered the east wall of the house, and knew what it was that had sought to clasp me in its lethal embrace, even as it had taken the Grice-Patersons and Lt. Austen Hanwell in their sleep.

"I believe it to be an experience without par," said Pons, helping me to my feet. "I had slipped into a doze and woke to a sound from the bed. The creepers had come through the window seeking the prey they sensed lay there – indeed, the entire opening was filled with the waving tendrils and limbs. I shall never forget the sight!"

In the morning, in our compartment of the train making its way from Penzance to London – for Pons would not permit our client to have us driven home, remaining only long enough to assist in the destruction of Sir Ronald's deadly creeper – Pons spoke reflectively of our strange adventure.

"The limiting circumstances of the deaths suggested a limited agent from the beginning," he said. "Each death had taken place in a room on the east side of the house – the same side on which the dogs and cats were found dead at various times of summer mornings – and each at the height of summer. 'How shall I ever again survive the month of August!' cried Miss Grice-Paterson. Furthermore, each had taken place at night, while the victims slept, thus enabling an insidious and silent slayer to transfix its victims in a fatal embrace which a waking man would readily have escaped.

"The creeper was unquestionably a mutation developed by Sir Ronald himself, a relative of the upas tree, and, like certain other plants, was carnivorous, becoming especially active at the height of its growth, which was its time of flowering – mid-summer. An importation from Malaya, beyond question. Curiously, no one seems to have thought of examining the dead men or animals for loss of blood, for the creeper was, quite literally, vampiric.

"Sir Ronald knew its properties, there can be no doubt. He knew very well why he avoided the east wing in summer, and only the family's habit of following his custom explains their survival. Otherwise they might all have died long before this.

"Sir Ronald's motive in planting and cultivating the creeper on Uffa is obscured by time. Did his misanthropy indeed compel him to lay so effective and mortal a trap for those who succeeded him in the ironic intention that his one-time orderly should come into the estate? Or did his hatred of mankind unbalance him? We have had repeated reference to the old man's dislike of the human race, which included his own family. Perhaps in that lay the root of the evil that was the curse of the Grice-Patersons. It makes an interesting speculation, though we shall never know."

VII

THE ADVENTURE OF THE STONE OF SCONE

That memorable Christmas morning, my friend Solar Pons woke me with a firm hand on my shoulder well before dawn. Our quarters were still dark, save for the glow of a light Pons had lit in the sitting-room. Bending above me, he waited until he was sure I was awake before he spoke.

"A merry Chirstmas to you, Parker," he said in an infectiously gay voice. "We are about to have the best Christmas gift of all – a client is on his way here."

"At this hour!" I cried. "It can't be more than four o'clock."

"A quarter of the hour. Ah, but it is even more extraordinary than you think. It is my brother Bancroft who is coming. You may judge for yourself the gravity of a situation which dislodges that lover of his comfort from his bed at this incredible hour."

I got out of bed with alacrity.

"You may as well dress, Parker, if you mean to accompany me. My brother needs no assistance at armchair theorizing; so I fancy we shall be required to do some leg work, at which Bancroft does not shine."

I had hardly joined Pons in the sitting-room, when I caught the sound of a car drawing up to the kerb outside, and, glancing at Pons, I saw by the anticipatory gleam in his eyes that he had no doubt his brother was below. Nor was he mistaken, for within a few moments Bancroft Pons had made his usually silent ascent to our quarters and stood on the threshold. I marveled anew at the ease with which so massive a man moved so soundlessly. As usual, he stood for a moment surveying us, taking in our dress, at which he nodded his impressive, almost leonine head, in approval. His customarily sleepy eyes were alight, his proud, sensuous mouth was almost a-tremble, and as he came into the room I observed that he was agitated.

"I need hardly say I know you have come on a matter of the utmost gravity," said Pons. "One not connected with the Foreign Office – at this hour. Extraordinary! You have been somewhere on your hands and knees. In dust, too. One of the government buildings?"

"Spare me these exercises," said Bancroft testily. "It is an extraordinary matter indeed!"

"I meant," interposed my companion gently, "it was extraordinary to discover you had been on your hands and knees."

Bancroft Pons made an impatient gesture and grimaced. "Let us have done with this *Kinderspiel* and come to the matter in hand. It is this – the Stone of Scone has been stolen from Westminster Abbey."

"This bids fair to be the merriest of Christmases!" cried Pons, smiling his delight.

"If chasing about the countryside is accounted a pleasure, it may well be," agreed Bancroft in distaste. "The theft was discovered over an hour ago. The night watchman making his round at eleven found all in order. There was a change of watchmen at that hour and the next watch passed through Edward the Confessor's Chapel shortly after two o'clock. He saw marks on the carpet that suggested a heavy object had been dragged down the altar steps. At the altar, he discovered that the Stone had been pried loose from under the Coronation Chair.

"The trail led away through the transept, past the Dryden memorial and the graves of Browning and Tennyson, and out of the building at a side door near the Poets' Corner. Presumably a car waited near there. You may well imagine into what consternation this singular event has thrown the government, since it is known that there are certain strong anti-monarchists who might wish to embarrass His Majesty and strike a blow for republicanism."

"I can, indeed," murmured Pons. "The government have always been more fearful of losing face than an Oriental. I daresay the Prime Minister's assassination could not have disturbed them more."

"Any matter which has brought me to my hands and knees is not a subject for drollery," said Bancroft. "The matter has thrown the Metropolitan Police and Scotland Yard into the most unimaginable uproar. The borders have been closed and all cars traveling into Scotland, Wales, and Ireland are being stopped and searched. The Police are preparing to drag the Thames and the Serpentine. But I need not set forth for you the various steps so inevitably taken by the gentlemen of the Yard."

"No one witnessed the theft of a stone weighing almost five hundred pounds?" asked Pons.

"No one," said Bancroft. "Pray refresh your memory. Last night was Christmas Eve, one of revelry. One might expect that the wits of the constabulary would be less sharp and they themselves less suspicious than usual."

"The Stone's value?"

"Only symbolic. Hardly four shillings. An idiotic crime!"

Pons smiled. "How like the government to concern itself far more over a symbol than something of true value!"

Bancroft refused to rise to Pons' needling. "My car is waiting," he said. "Everything has been left undisturbed at the Abbey, though photographers are there and it is abominably cluttered by the police and government officials."

Pons had already donned his Inverness and deerstalker.

In the car, Pons turned to his brother. "That was surely sandstone on your trousers, Bancroft. The Stone was damaged?"

"It would appear to have been," replied Bancroft cautiously. "Not at the Chair, where it was pried loose, but just a bit from it, before it was taken through the transept. You may not have known, Solar, but there has been a fissure in the Stone; the treatment accorded it tonight may well have widened and broken it."

Pons said no more for the remainder of the journey.

Curious celebrants of the Christmas Eve had gathered outside Westminster Abbey, and stood in wondering groups staring at the official cars before the building. Inside, there seemed at first to be even more people, but most of them were being kept in the vicinity of the hut-like tomb of St. Edward, which rose in a railed enclosure before the Coronation Chair.

The scene of the desecration now lay before us. The Stone of Scone had been enclosed beneath the Coronation Chair. It had been held in place by a small bar of wood, not of itself a part of the Chair. This had been splintered and broken, so that the Stone could be pried from beneath the Chair and slid out. The marks of the heavy Stone, which weighed four hundredweight, were plainly to be seen; it had been dragged down from the Coronation Chair and off toward the transept to the right. Not far from the Chair lay a marked deposit of sandstone dust and particles where the damage Pons had deduced had taken place.

The photographers had finished their work, and our old friend Jamison, now a Commissioner of Scotland Yard, who appeared to be in charge, beckoned us forward and greeted us with manifest pleasure.

"I'm afraid they'll be wasting your time, Pons," he said. "I told them these fellows have left a trail wide enough for an amateur to follow."

"In that case," observed Bancroft Pons dryly, "I should have thought you would be following it. Admittedly, anyone can follow it out of the Abbey; beyond that, the problem is a little more complicated."

Pons had not troubled to do more than smile at Jamison. Already he was on his hands and knees before the Coronation Chair, beckoning for the clearer light of one of the electric torches carried by the police. Two or three torches were immediately directed at the Chair; one of them Pons appropriated when he finished there. With it, he began to follow the trail of the Stone through the transept toward the Poets' Corner door out of which the Stone had gone from the Abbey.

Just beyond the Poets' Corner door in a direct line with it was a wrought iron gate. Pons went straight to it.

"No, no Pons, the Stone went around here and to a gate in the fence off to the left, at the Masons' Yard," protested Jamison.

"All in good time, Jamison," answered Pons, who now busied himself with a close scrutiny of the gate. "You've observed these marks and scratches, I take it?"

"The gate around the corner has been jimmied open," said Jamison flatly.

"Just so," said Pons. "Let us have a look at it."

So saying, he again took up the trail of the Stone, following it to the left of the Poets' Corner door, and down along a solid wooden fence separating the lane outside from the Masons' Yard between fence and Abbey. He turned the light of his torch on this door, which stood slightly ajar, and then, finished with his examination of it, he opened it and stepped into the lane outside. We were now not many yards from the gate before the Poets' Corner door, which rose up spectrally on the right.

Without turning, Pons said, "You will have observed that this lock was opened from inside, while the Poets' Corner door was forced from outside. This was then only a place of exit; the Poets' Corner was used for both entrance and exit."

"We noticed that," said Jamison curtly.

"Was there a policeman on duty in the vicinity?" asked Pons then.

"Yes, we have him inside," answered Jamison. "We've thought of all that, Pons. He saw a car here."

"At this gate?"

"No, nearer that iron gate up there."

"Let us just speak to him again."

Jamison led the way back into Westminster Abbey.

Police Sergeant Trowbridge was a pale-faced young man, now plainly nervous in the presence of so many of his superiors. He listened quietly to Jamison's instructions to answer Pons' questions.

"What kind of car did you see outside the Abbey?" asked Pons.

"A Ford Anglia, Mr. Pons."

"At what time?"

"It was near to three o'clock. There was a young couple in it, sir. Kissing and such-like. Nothing unusual, especially for Christmas morning. There were a lot of people moving about: there always are Christmas morning. Almost like the New Year's, Mr. Pons. Some of them a little the worse for drink."

"That was the only car?"

"No, sir. The only car at that hour. There was another about four, and there was one earlier. But in the same time, there were people moving up the lane. A quartet of drinking companions about quarter to three. Two couples at ten minutes past. And so on. In all, I should think there were perhaps fifty people seen between midnight and four o'clock, and seven cars. But the one at Poets' Corner gate was there at the right time."

"You spoke to them?"

"Yes, Mr. Pons. I went up and flashed my torch at them. I said, 'Here, here, what a ruddy time and place for the likes of this!' And the young fellow turned to me with the marks of her all over his face, and said, 'It's Christmas Eve, officer.' And I said, 'Christmas Eve, is it! It's three o'clock Christmas morning!' And he said, 'Ochone! Ochone! Is it that late it is already?' 'Private property you're on,' I said to him. And he said, 'I know we shouldn't be here.' And then she opened up, a pretty, dark-haired girl right enough, and said to me, 'But where can we go? The other streets are so crowded.' And so they were, and she gave me such a look, I felt sorry for them, and I said, 'There's a dark car park not far along.' And she said they were just in from the country, too late for rooms, and with the look of being too much in love – holding hands all the time they talked to me – and all, and maybe I could run them in and give them a bed in the cells. So I said, 'There's not a policeman in London apt to arrest you tonight,' which was the fact, since none would take kindly to having to appear against anyone in court on Boxing Day. I walked off then and left them there, and when I came back quarter of an hour later, they were gone."

"They were young people?"

"Maybe twenty-four or -five, Mr. Pons."

"Thank you, Sergeant Trowbridge." Pons turned to Jamison. "Now, Jamison, what has been done apart from the closing of the border?"

"We are preparing to drag the Serpentine and the Thames. We intend to question all known anti-monarchists and Scottish Covenanters."

"It can do no harm," said Pons with a quixotic smile. "Though I believe almost two million Scots signed the Covenant. I don't envy you your task."

"Pons, the Stone of Scone must be recovered as rapidly as possible. His Majesty must not be embarrassed by any republican coup," said Jamison.

"If His Majesty and the government are so easily embarrassed, then they have already been embarrassed," answered Pons. "However, I doubt very much that there will be any immediate further developments. I am confident the investigation is in capable hands, Jamison." He turned to me. "Come, Parker, I fancy we have finished here."

In the car once more, Bancroft Pons observed caustically, "I have seldom known you to be more ambiguous, Solar."

"Ambiguity has its uses, my dear Bancroft. Consider, for instance, how much more felicitous it will be to have that good bumbler, Jamison, off on a hue and cry dragging the waters of London for an object which is most certainly not in that quarter. The police sometimes have a bedeviling habit of getting in the way."

"Ah, you are prepared to lay hands on the Stone?"

"Nothing of the sort. I haven't the slightest idea where it is at the moment, save in the hands of four young Scottish Nationalists, three men and a woman, somewhere in the vicinity of London, certainly not across any border. Its ultimate destination is undoubtedly Scotland. But it will not be transported until the hue and cry has died down. We shall just wait for the abductors of the Stone to tip their hands. It seems to me the most sensible course. I submit that the whole plot has not long ago appeared in print."

"It has a familiar ring," conceded Bancroft Pons.

"I believe we share admiration for the many-faceted writings of Compton Mackenzie, particularly his brilliant comedies."

"Ah, *The North Wind of Love*."

"Precisely. In that novel the author describes a conspiracy to return the Stone of Scone to Scotland. It fails in his book. This time it appears to have succeeded, initially, at least. Perhaps that ardent Scottish Nationalist is unconsciously the author of this crime."

"Three men and a woman," mused Bancroft. "It would need not more than two men to drag the Stone. Why a third?"

"The marks on the Poets' Corner gate indicate that three men climbed over it. The door there was jimmied from the outside, but the gate in the wooden enclosure was pried open from within. At least two men went into the Abbey for the Stone, quite possibly all three went in. One returned in advance of the Stone. What more logical than to assume he came back to the car where the young lady waited, bearing the broken portion of the Stone, which, I should judge by the line of sandstone dust and particles marking the break, could we hardly have a been less than a quarter of the Stone, or a weight close to hundred pounds? His arrival must have taken place fortuitously just prior to Sergeant Trowbridge's appearance, at which he and the young lady posed as lovers. The other two subsequently brought out the Stone and, once the Sergeant had gone on, loaded it at the opened gate, to which point the car was doubtless driven on their signal.

"The whole plot was evidently the result of long and careful planning. The habits of the night watchmen of the Abbey were certainly known. The night selected for the deed was one on which pedestrians and cars which ordinarily would seem suspicious would pass almost unnoticed. The proximity to Boxing Day was surely also by design. The Stone of Scone has meaning for no one else but Scottish Nationalists. It has no monetary value. The abductors mean to return it to Scotland, where, they hold, it belongs. The Scots refer to it, by the way, as the *Lia Fail* – the Stone of Destiny, and some ascribe supernatural powers to it. Our Nationalists, however, are no super-naturalists, let it be known. I daresay they intend to make as much capital of this event as possible; we shall hear more of the Stone at their discretion."

"Scotland is an appreciable area to hunt," said Bancroft Pons dryly.

"For a man readily dismayed by even a tramp in the heather, I have no doubt," agreed Pons. "But I fancy all Scotland is not necessarily subject to search. The Stone of Scone is associated with but a few places – the Abbey of Scone in Perthshire, where it was the base of the Coronation Chair of the Kings of Scotland; Dunstaffnage in Argyllshire, which was the headquarters of the Scots Chieftains before the line of succession was begun. I should hardly expect to find it very far from Glasgow."

"Why Glasgow?"

"Is that not the seat of the Scottish Covenant movement, from which stem all the Nationalists? I believe it is. I daresay a little journey to Glasgow is not ill-advised, and, if Parker is free to go, I think we will just run up to Glasgow in a few days. There is no haste, as long as the border is closed; wherever the Stone now is, it is likely to remain for the time being."

Bancroft Pons bade us farewell at the kerb before 7B Praed Street. The grey day had now dawned, and neither of us was in the mood for more sleep. Pons was as keen as always when the game was afoot, eager to be up and about on the track of the desecrators of Westminster Abbey; but he was so obviously limited by the circumstances of the problem that he was forced to wait upon events.

Our entrance to our rooms coincided with Mrs. Johnson's arrival with breakfast and some little gifts to mark the holiday. We, too, had gifts for our patient landlady and took the opportunity to bestow them upon her, amid her protestations. This over, we settled to our breakfast, which, in keeping with the season of festivity, was a hearty one.

"You are not averse to a journey into Scotland, Parker?" Pons asked across the table.

"Not at all. Though how you hope to catch the vandals is beyond me."

"All in good time. 'Vandals', however, is a hard word. I fancy they look upon themselves as patriots."

"Yes," I retorted, "as Robin Hood looked on himself as a patron of the poor rather than as a robber."

Pons chuckled. "Dear me, I fear you grow more conservative every year. I noticed in my examination of the Coronation Chair that singular care had been taken to do it no damage. In one place, true, three letters had been crudely drawn – 'J F S' – surely 'Justice for Scotland' – but the Chair, which might easily have been badly broken in the haste that was necessary, was otherwise untouched. And the Stone itself was at least partially wrapped, as the trail with sandstone particles along two sides and not in the middle clearly suggests. No, I venture to say that the perpetrators of what tomorrow's wireless and newspapers will call 'this desecrating outrage' are young people of remarkable fire and imagination, and with a certain respect for such relics, determined to strike a blow for Scottish Nationalism in a fashion dramatic enough to stir a similar fire in the imagination of all England. The *Lia Fail* is the symbol of Scottish independence and surely the logical object of the Covenanters' attention."

"It will certainly arouse England," I agreed.

"And the Scottish Nationalists," said Pons. "Tomorrow's papers will carry apt quotations from the leaders of the movement. The Duke of Montrose will 'not regret the fact that the Stone is on its way back to Scotland'; the Scottish Patriots' Association will say the Stone has been 'retrieved, not stolen'; Mr. Compton MacKenzie will issue a round of hearty applause, and, as a patriotic Scot, will express his 'elation'; and the *Times* will most certainly stigmatize the act as 'a coarse and vulgar crime'."

"I must confess," I admitted guardedly, "I'm not sure just what the Stone of Scone is, except that it is the ancient Coronation Stone of the Scots."

"Actually, it is probably a piece of the red sandstone to be found near Dunstaffnage Castle, though some believers hold that it is the very stone on which Jacob rested his head in Biblical times. It is about twenty-six inches long, and sixteen wide, and weighs considerably over four hundred pounds, almost five. Some centuries ago, two iron rings were attached to it to aid in its transportation. It first came into Scottish history when King Kenneth II of Scotland set it up to mark his conquest of the country in 840 A.D. Thereafter, the Scottish kings were crowned on a throne which rose above the Stone. When Edward I of England turned from ravaging Wales to subdue Scotland in 1296, he seized the Stone and brought it to England. During the years that followed, Edward II, in the Treaty of Northampton, promised to return the Stone to Scotland; but that article of the treaty was never honored, and the Stone remained in Westminster Abbey until its disappearance this morning."

"Then the Scots have a right to it!" I cried.

"I have no doubt of it."

For the remainder of that day, Pons busied himself with his scrapbooks. He apparently gave no further thought to the problem in hand, and I forebore to question him about it, though more than once the impulse was strong to do so, for it was not his custom to sit idly by and wait upon events. The next morning, when I came into our sitting-room, I found him at the wireless, chuckling, as he listened to the venerable Dean of Westminster making an impassioned appeal for the return of the Stone of Scone.

"He will 'go to the ends of the earth' to recover it," said Pons dryly. "Can he have imagined that some supernatural agency has transported it there?" He turned on me, shutting off the wireless. "The BBC has just announced that no less than eight thousand policemen are searching for the Stone, a venture that will cost His Majesty's subjects a tidy sum every hour."

"At least you're not one of them," I said, not without irony.

"Happily no," Pons agreed. "I submit that the Stone is very probably hidden in the environs of London. I venture to say that not a tenth of the searching policemen would recognize it if they saw the Stone. Despite its size, it ought to lend itself easily to concealment. Quite openly among other stones, for instance. Pushed under a ledge of rock. Buried. In any case, the next move is up to the Stone's abductors. If no word has been received from them in ten days, I shall call in the Praed Street Irregulars and see what we can do. But I fancy we shall have word of them in good time."

As usual, Pons was correct in his surmise. Within the week, the Glasgow *Daily Record* – significantly – published a petition, addressed to His Majesty, which the newspaper had received by mail. It was unsigned, but its terms left no doubt that the Stone of Scone had indeed been taken by ardent Scottish Nationalists, for it begged His Majesty to accept the return of the Stone on condition that it would remain in Scotland "in such of His Majesty's properties or otherwise as shall be deemed fitting by him." The same issue of the *Record* announced the rumor that the Stone of Destiny was in Scotland at last.

Pons read both the petition and the article with dancing eyes. "Now they are preparing to move the Stone into Scotland," he said.

"The paper clearly indicates it is already there," I pointed out.

"A ruse to draw off the border police. No, the Stone is still in England, to be moved across, once the border has been re-opened. Let us lose no time getting off to Glasgow."

Accordingly, we took a train at Euston next mid-morning, and arrived in Glasgow early that ahead for accommodations at the Beresford on Sauchiell Street. Despite the tiring, daylong journey, Pons showed no inclination to resume his leisurely habits of the past week. Here he was all bustle. He hardly stopped for supper before he took himself off.

I did not see Pons again for twenty-four hours, for I was asleep when he returned that night, and he was gone next morning before I woke. But at the supper hour of the following day, he walked into the dining-room of the Beresford. I saw by the look of satisfaction on his lean, hawk-like face, that he had made some discoveries.

"I hope you haven't noticed my absence over-much, Parker," he said, sitting down at the table. "I have spent much of the last evening and today at the Mitchell Library looking into the literature of the Stone."

"I thought you remarkably well informed about it," I said.

"Ah, my interest was not in reading about the Stone, but in discovering who might have been reading about it within the past months. Would you not say it was more than a coincidence that every scrap of information about the Stone of Scone lodged in the Mitchell Library has been scrutinized within the six weeks prior to the theft of the relic by a young student known for his Scottish Nationalist sympathies?"

"Indeed I would. Who is he?"

"His name is Ian MacCormick. He is twenty-five and a student in law. He has today set out with two companions in a Ford Anglia on what appears to be a journey of some distance. I submit he is on his way to England for the Stone."

"Have you arranged to have him followed?"

"I fancy there is no need. If he is not caught at the border, he will return here with the Stone, prepared to take it to its ultimate destination."

"And that?"

"He is an impulsive, imaginative young man. In one of the books dealing with the subject, there were certain notes I took to be in his hand. He had set down three names. They were the Abbey of Scone, Dunstaffnage Castle, and Arbroath Abbey. Of these, he had crossed out the first two, manifestly because they were too obvious in their historical connection to the Stone."

"I don't recall your mention of Arbroath Abbey before. Where is it?"

"Some eighty miles to the north, above Dundee, on the east coast. It has a notable association with the Scottish Nationalists, for it was at Arbroath Abbey that the Estates of Scotland met in 1320 to reaffirm their freedom. I rather think he and his companions mean the Stone to make its reappearance at one of these three places, since there is nothing to be gained for their cause, and indeed, all to be lost, by their retention of the Stone. It will do them no good laid away somewhere in a cellar. To properly dramatize their daring theft, the Stone must make as dramatic a reappearance as it did a disappearance. But the Abbey of Scone and Dunstaffnage Castle are too close in their association with the *Lia Fail* to venture there; Arbroath Abbey is not, and yet bears an equal significance to the cause of the Scottish Nationalists."

"And you propose to wait for MacCormick and the Stone here?"

"Not here, but at Arbroath. Pray do not stir yourself, Parker; there is no hurry. The young men left only today. The journey to London will take them many hours, since London is some four hundred miles from here. Then they must recover the Stone, conceal it in their car, and make their way back here – an overall journey of close to nine hundred miles, added to which is the distance to Arbroath Abbey in winter weather. We are in no haste for Arbroath."

The third day after found us at the ruins of Arbroath Abbey, to which we came by hired car, which the custodian of the Abbey concealed at our request. We spent all that day in vigil there, and waited well into the night.

No one came.

Next day we were back, and at midday Pons' patience was rewarded.

At high noon a Ford Anglia appeared on the road to the Abbey and came directly to the ruins. Three young men got out and, opening the back of the car, took from it a heavy object wrapped in the Scottish flag of St. Andrew. Among them, they carried the Stone into the ruins and directly to the high altar, behind which Pons and I stood with the custodian.

They deposited the Stone on the altar, and their leader, a handsome, fair-haired young man, spoke out in a ringing voice the words of the Estates of Scotland, words first affirmed in this place centuries before – "For so long as a hundred of us are left alive, we will yield in no least way to English domination. We fight not for glory nor for wealth nor for honor, but only and alone for freedom, which no good man surrenders but with his life."

At the conclusion of his speech, Pons stepped out from behind the high altar and advanced on the speaker. "Mr. Ian MacCormick, I believe. Those are well spoken words. My name is Solar Pons. We have an engagement for dinner."

"A 'tec, by St. Andrew!" cried one of MacCormick's companions in astonishment.

MacCormick only smiled.

There is little more to be told. At dinner young McCormick and his fellow conspirators, together with the young woman who had aided them in London – all likable young people – told their story of the theft of the Stone of Scone. There was yet one more drama in which they hoped to take part – their prosecution.

"Then we shall be able to tell the world," said MacCormick, his eyes shining. "The entire world will know of the Nationalist cause!"

Pons smiled and shook his head. "I'm afraid you will be disappointed," he said. "I fancy England will be satisfied with the return of the Stone and will refuse to make martyrs of you."

Nor was Pons in error. Scotland Yard duly announced the recovery of the Stone of Scone – quite as if it had been an achievement of the police – and thereafter no one said one word of the identity of the abductors or of prosecution for the theft.

VIII

THE ADVENTURE OF THE REMARKABLE WORM

"Ah, Parker!" exclaimed Solar Pons, as I walked into our quarters at 7B Praed Street late one mid-summer afternoon in the early years of the century's third decade, "you may be just in time for another of those little forays into the criminological life of London in which you take such incomprehensible delight."

"You have taken a case," I said.

"Say, rather, I have consented to an appeal."

As he spoke, Pons laid aside the pistol with which he had been practising, an abominable exercise which understandably disturbed our long-suffering landlady, Mrs. Johnson. He reached among the papers on the table and flipped a card so that it fell before me on the table's edge, the message up.

> "Dear Mr. Pons,
>
> "Mr. Humphreys always said you were better than the police, so if it is all right I will come there late this afternoon when Julia comes and tell you about it. The doctor says it is all right with Mr. P., but I wonder.
>
> "Yours resp., Mrs. Flora White."

Pons regarded me with a glint in his eye as I read it.

"A cryptogram?" I ventured.

Pons chuckled. "Oh, come, Parker, it is not as difficult as all that. She is only agitated and perhaps indignant."

"I confess this is anything but clear to me."

"I do not doubt it," said Pons dryly. "But it is really quite simple on reflection. She makes reference to a Mr. Humphreys; I submit it is that fellow Athos Humphreys for whom we did a bit of investigation in connection with that little matter of the Penny Magenta. She wishes to consult us about a matter in which a doctor has already been consulted. The doctor has not succeeded in reassuring her or allaying her alarm. She cannot come at once because she cannot leave her patient alone. The patient, therefore, is at least not dead. She must wait until Julia comes, which will be late this afternoon; it is not amiss, therefore, to venture that Julia is her daughter or at least a schoolgirl, who must wait upon dismissal of classes before she can take Mrs. White's place and thus free our prospective client to see us.

"Since it is now high time for her to make an appearance, she has probably arrived in that cab which has just come to a stop outside."

I stepped to the window and looked down. A cab was indeed standing before our lodgings, and a heavy woman of middle age was ascending the steps of Number 7. She was dressed in very plain housewear, which suggested that she had come directly away from her work. Her only covering, apart from an absurdly small feathered hat, was a thin shawl, for the day was cool for August.

In a few moments Mrs. Johnson had shown her in, and she stood looking from one to the other of us, her florid face showing but a moment's indecision before she smiled uncertainly at my companion.

"You're Mr. Pons, ain't yer?"

"At your service, Mrs. White," replied Pons with unaccustomed graciousness, as his alert eyes took in every detail of her appearance. "Pray sit down and tell us about the little problem which vexes you."

She sat down with growing confidence, drew her shawl a little away from her neck, and began to recount the circumstances which had brought her to our quarters. She spoke in an animated voice, in a dialect which suggested not so much Cockney as transplanted provincial.

She explained how she "says to Mr. 'Umphreys," and he "says to me to ask his friend, Solar Pons; so I done like he said," as soon as her niece came from school. Pons sat patiently through her introduction until his patience was rewarded. He did not interrupt her story, once she began it.

She was employed as a cleaning woman at several houses. This was her day at the home of Idomeno Persano, a solitary resident of Hampstead Heath, an expatriate American of Spanish parentage. He had bought a house on the edge of the heath eleven years before, and since that time had led a most sedentary life. He was known to frequent the heath in the pursuit of certain entomological interests. As a collector of insects and information pertinent thereto, he was attentive to the children of the neighborhood; they knew him as a benign old fellow, who was ever ready to give them sixpence or a shilling for some insect to add to his collection.

Persano's life appeared to be in all respects retiring. Judging by what Mrs. White told in her rambling manner, he corresponded with fellow entomologists and was in the habit of sending and receiving specimens. He had always seemed to be a very easygoing man, but one day a month ago, he had received a postcard from America which had upset him very much. It had no writing on it but his name and address, and it was nothing but a comic picture card. Yet he had been very agitated at receipt of it, and since that time he had not ventured out of the house.

Mrs. White had been delayed in coming to her employer's home on this day; so it was not until afternoon that she reached the house. She was horrified to find her employer seated at his desk in an amazing condition. She thought he had gone stark mad. She had striven to arouse him, but all she could draw from him was a muttered few words which sounded like "the worm – unknown to science". And something about "the dog" – but there had never been a dog in the house, and there was not now. Nothing more. He was staring at a specimen he had apparently just received in the post. It was a worm in a common matchbox.

"Och, an 'orrible worm, Mr. Pons. Fair give me the creeps, it did!" she said firmly.

She had summoned a physician at once. He was a young *Locum tenens*, and confessed himself completely at sea when confronted with the ailing Persano. He had never encountered an illness of quite such a nature before, but he discovered a certain paralysis of the muscles and came to the conclusion that Persano had had a severe heart attack. From Mrs. White's description, the diagnosis suggested coronary trouble. He had administered a sedative and had recommended that the patient be not moved.

Mrs. White, however, was not satisfied. As soon as the doctor had gone, she had consulted "Mr. 'Umphreys", with the result that she had sent the note I had seen by messenger. Now she was here. Would Mr. Pons come around and look at her employer?

I could not refrain from asking, "Why did you think the doctor was wrong, Mrs. White?"

"I feels it," she answered earnestly. "It's intuition, that's what, sir. A woman's intuition."

"Quite right, Mrs. White," said Pons in a tolerant voice which nettled me the more. "My good friend Parker is of that opinion so commonly held by medical men, that his fellow practitioners are somehow above criticism or question by lay persons. I will look at Mr. Persano, though my knowledge of medicine is sadly limited."

"And 'ere," said our client, "is the card 'e got."

So saying, she handed Pons a colored postcard of a type very common in America, a type evidently designed for people on holiday wishing to torment their friends who are unable to take vacations. It depicted in cartoon form a very fat man running from a little dog which had broken his leash. The drawing was bad, and the lettered legend was typical: "Having a fast time at Fox Lake. Wish you were here." The obverse bore nothing but Persano's address and a Chicago postmark. "That is surely as innocuous a communication as I have ever seen," I said.

"Is it not, indeed?" said Pons, one eyebrow lifted.

"I could well imagine that it would irritate Persano."

"'Upset' was the word, I believe, Mrs. White?"

"That he was, Mr. Pons. Fearful upset. I seen 'im, seein' as how 't was me 'anded it to 'im. I says to 'im, 'Yer friends is havin' a time on their 'oliday,' I says. When 'e seen it, 'e went all white, and was took with a coughin' spell. 'E threw it from him without a word. I picked it up and kept it; so 'ere 'tis."

Pons caressed the lobe of his right ear while he contemplated our client. "Mr. Persano is a fat man, Mrs. White?"

Her simple face lit up with pleasure. "That 'e is, Mr. Pons, though 'ow yer could know it, I don't see. Mr. 'Umphreys was right. A marvel 'e said yer was."

"And how old would you say he is?"

"Oh, in 'is sixties."

"When you speak of your employer as having been 'upset', do you suggest that he was frightened?"

Our client furrowed her brows. "'E was upset," she repeated doggedly.

"Not angry?"

"No, sir. Upset. Troubled, like. 'Is face changed color; 'e said something under 'is breath I didn't 'ear; 'e threw the card away, like as if 'e didn't want ter see it again. I picked it up and kep' it."

Pons sat for a moment with his eyes closed. Then he took out his watch and consulted it. "It is now almost six o'clock. The matter would seem to me of some urgence. You've kept your cab waiting?"

Mrs. White nodded. "Julia will be that anxious."

"Good!" cried Pons, springing to his feet. "We will go straight back with you. There is not a moment to be lost. We may already be too late."

He doffed his worn purple dressing-gown, flung it carelessly aside, and took up his Inverness and deerstalker.

Throughout the ride to the scene of our client's experience, Pons maintained a meditative silence, his head sunk on his chest, his lean fingers tented where his hands rested below his chin.

The house on the edge of Hampstead Heath was well isolated from its neighbors. A substantial hedge, alternating with a stone wall, ran all around the building, which was of one storey, and not large. Our client bustled from the cab, Pons at her heels, leaving me to pay the fare. She led the way into the house, where we were met by a pale-faced girl who was obviously relieved to see someone.

"Been any change, Julia?" asked Mrs. White.

"No, 'm. He's sleeping."

"Anybody call?"

"No 'm. No one."

"That's good. Yer can go 'ome now, that's a good girl," Turning to us; our client pointed to a door to her left, "In there, Mr. Pons."

The light of two old-fashioned lamps revealed the scene in all its starkness. Mrs. White's employer sat in an old Chippendale wing chair before a broad table, no less old-style than the lamps which shed an eerie illumination in the room. He was a corpulent man, but it was evident at a glance that he was not sleeping, for his eyes were open and staring toward the curious object which lay before him – an opened matchbox with its contents, which looked to my untutored eye very much like a rather fatter-than-usual caterpillar. A horrible smile – the *risus sardonicus* – twisted Persano's lips.

"I fancy Mr. Persano is in your department, Parker," said Pons quietly.

It took but a moment to assure me of what Pons suspected. "Pons, this man is dead!" I cried.

"It was only an off-chance that we might find him alive," observed Pons. He turned to our client and added, "I'm afraid you must now notify the police, Mrs. White. Ask for Inspector Taylor at Scotland Yard. Say to him that I am here."

Mrs. White, who had given forth but one wail of distress at learning of her employer's death, rallied sufficiently to say that there was no telephone in the house. She would have to go to a neighbor's.

The moment our client had gone, Pons threw himself into a fever of activity. He took up one of the lamps and began to examine the room, dropping to his knees now and then, scrutinizing the walls, the bookshelves, the secretary against one wall, and finally the dead man himself, examining Persano's hands and face with what I thought to be absured care.

"Is there not a peculiar color to the skin, Parker?" he asked at last.

I admitted that there was.

"Is it consistent with coronary thrombosis?"

"It isn't usual."

"You saw that faint discoloration of one finger," continued Pons. "There is some swelling, is there not?"

"And a slight flesh wound. Yes, I saw it."

"There is some swelling and discoloration of exposed portions of the body surely," he went on.

"Let me anticipate you, Pons," I put in. "If the man has been poisoned, I can think of no ordinary poison which would be consistent with the symptoms. Arsenic, antimony, strychnine, prussic acid, cyanide, atropine – all are ruled out. I am not prepared to say that this man died of unnatural causes."

"Spoken with commendable caution," observed Pons dryly. "I submit, however, that the evident symptoms are inconsistent with coronary thrombosis."

"They would seem so."

With this Pons appeared to be satisfied. He gave his attention next to the table before which Persano's body sat. The surface of the table was covered with various objects which suggested that Persano had been in the process of trying to identify the remarkable worm when he was stricken. Books on entomology and guides to insect-life lay open in a semi-circle around the opened matchbox with its strange occupant; beyond, in the shadow away from the pool of light from the lamp on the table, lay a case of mounted insects in various stages of their evolution from the larval through the pupal. This, too, suggested that Persano was searching for some points of similarity between them and the specimen unknown to science.

I reached out to take up the matchbox, but Pons caught my arm.

"No, Parker. Let us not disturb the scene. Pray observe the discarded cover of the box. Are there not pin-pricks in it?"

"The creature would need air."

Pons chuckled. "Thank heaven for the little rays of humor which your good nature affords us!" he exclaimed. "The worm is dead; I doubt that it ever was alive. Besides, the parcel was wrapped. Let us just turn the cover over."

He suited his actions to his words. It was at once evident that the pin-pricks spelled out a sentence. Together with Pons, I leaned over to decipher it.

"Little dog catches big cat."

I flashed a glance at Pons. "If that's a message, certainly it is in code."

"Surely a limited message, if so," demurred Pons.

"But it's nothing more than child's play," I protested. "It can have no meaning."

"Little, indeed," agreed Pons. "Yet I fancy it may help to establish the identity of the gentleman who brought about Idomeno Persano's death."

"Oh, come, Pons, you are having me!"

"No, no, the matter is almost disappointingly elementary," retorted Pons. "You know my methods, Parker; you have all the facts. You need only apply them."

With this he came to his knees at the wastebasket, where he sought diligently until he found a box six inches square, together with cord and wrapping paper.

"This would appear to be the container in which the worm arrived," he said, examining the box. "Well filled with packing, so that the specimen should not be jolted, I see. Does that convey nothing to you, Parker?"

"It is the customary way of sending such specimens."

"Indeed." He looked to the wrapping. "The return address is plainly given. 'Fowler. 29 Upper Brook Street.' Yet is was posted in Wapping, a little detail I daresay Persano overlooked. Some care for details is indicated. Fowler will doubtless turn out to be a known correspondent in matters entomological, but most definitely not the source of this remarkable worm."

At this moment Mrs. White returned, somewhat out of breath. At her heels followed the young *locum tenens* she had evidently gone to fetch after telephoning Scotland Yard; and, bringing up the rear, came Inspector Walter Taylor, a feral-faced young man in his thirties who had more than once shown an unusual aptitude for the solution of crime within his jurisdiction.

With his arrival, the Inspector immediately took charge, and soon Pons and I were on our way back to 7B Praed Street, Pons bearing with almost gingerly care, with Inspector Taylor's permission, a little parcel containing the extraordinary worm which had sent Idomeno Persano to madness and death.

In our quarters once more, Pons carefully uncovered the remarkable worm and placed it, still in its matchbox, under the light on his desk. Thus seen, it was truly an imposing sight. It was furred, like a caterpillar, but also horned, like some pupal stages, with not one horn, but four, one pair rising from the back but close to its head, the other facing the first pair, but rising from the other end of the worm. Its head was bare of fur and was featured by a long proboscis, from which uncoiled a slender, thread-like tongue. It appeared to have no less than four rows of feet, double rows extending all the way along its length, as multitudinous as those of a centipede, and very similar in construction. Double antennae rose from back of its head, reaching to the height of the horns, while its tail was thick and blunt. It was perhaps four inches in length, and at least two inches in diameter.

"Have you ever seen its like before?" asked Pons delightedly, his eyes twinkling.

"Never. How could I, if even science does not know it?"

"Ah, Parker, do not be so ready to take someone's word for such a judgment. There is no such thing, technically, as a worm unknown to science. Any worm discovered by a scientist can be readily enough classified, even if not immediately identified with precision."

"On the contrary," I retorted with some spirit. "It lies before us."

"Let me put it this way, Parker – if the worm is unknown to science, there is no such worm."

"I'm afraid we are reversing roles, Pons," I said with asperity. "Is it not you who scores me constantly for my didacticism?"

"I am guilty of the charge," he admitted. "But in this case, I must give you no quarter. This worm is unknown to science for precisely the reason I have stated – there is no such worm."

"But it lies here, refuting you!"

"Pray look again, my dear fellow. I submit that the head of this interesting creature is nothing less than the head of a sphinx moth – commonly known also as a hawk moth or hummingbird moth – quite possibly the common striped sphinx, *Deilephila Lineata*. The elaborate legs are nothing more than complete centipedes cunningly fitted in – six of them, I should say; these appear to be a centipede commonly found in the northern part of North America, *Scutigera forceps*. The antennae apparently derive from two sources – the furred pair suggest the *Actias Luna*, or common Luna moth; the long, thin green pair are surely those of *Pterophylla camellifolia*, the true katydid. The fur is as equally a fabrication, and the horns – ah, Parker, the horns are little masterpieces of deception! This is a remarkable worm indeed. How closely did you examine the wound in Persano's finger?"

"I examined it with my customary care," I answered somewhat stiffly.

"What would you say had caused it?"

"It appeared to be a gash, as if he had run his finger into a nail or a splinter, though the gash was clean."

"So that you could, if pressed, suggest that Persano had come to his death by venom administered through a snake's fang?"

"Since my imagination is somewhat more restricted, of scientific necessity, than yours, Pons..." I began, but he interrupted me.

"Like this," said Pons.

He seized hold of a tweezers and caught the remarkable worm of Idomeno Persano between them. Instantly the four horns on the creature's thick body shot forth fangs; from two of them a thin brown fluid still trickled.

"Only one of these found its mark," said Pons dryly. "It seems to have been enough." He gazed at me with twinkling eyes and added, "I believe you had the commendable foresight not to include snake venom in that list of poisons you were confident had not brought about Persano's death."

For a moment I was too nonplussed to reply. "But this is the merest guesswork," I protested finally.

"You yourself eliminated virtually all other possibilities," countered Pons. "You have left me scarcely any other choice."

"But what of the dog?" I cried.

"What dog?" asked Pons with amazement he did not conceal.

"If I recall rightly, Mrs. White said that Persano spoke of a dog. A dog's tooth might well have made that gash."

"Ah, Parker, you are straying afield," said Pons with that air of patient tolerance I always found so trying. "There was no such dog. Mrs. White herself said so."

"You suggest, then, that Mrs. White misunderstood her employer's dying words?"

"Not at all. I daresay she understood him correctly."

"I see. Persano spoke of a dog, but there was no dog," I said with a bitterness which did not escape Pons.

"Come, come, Parker!" replied Pons, smiling. "One would not expect you to be a master of my profession any more than one could look to me as a master of yours. Let us just see how skillfully this is made."

As he spoke, he proceeded with the utmost care to cut away the fur and the material beneath. He was cautious not to release the spring again, and presently revealed a most intricate and wonderfully-wrought mechanism, which sprang the trap and forced the venom from small rubber sacks attached to the fangs by tubes.

"Are those not unusually small fangs?" I asked.

"If I were to venture a guess, I should say they belonged to the coral or harlequin snake, *Micrurus fulvius*, common to the southern United States and the Mississippi Valley. Its poison is a neurotoxin; it may have been utilized, but certainly not in its pure state. It was most probably adulterated with some form of alkaloid poison to prolong Persano's death and complicate any medication Persano may have sought. The snake belongs to the Proteroglyphs, or front-fanged type of which cobras and mambas are most common in their latitudes. The 'worm' was designed to spring the fangs when touched; it was accordingly well packed so that its venom would not be discharged by rough handling in transit." He cocked an eye at me. "Does this deduction meet with your approval, Parker?"

"It is very largely hypothetical."

"Let us grant that it is improbable, if no more so than the worm itself. Is it within the bounds of possibility?"

"I would not say it was not."

"Capital! We make progress."

"But I should regard it as a highly dubious method of committing murder."

"Beyond doubt. Had it failed, its author would have tried again. He meant to kill Persano. He succeeded. If he tried previously to do so, we have no record of it. Persano was a secretive man, but he had anticipated that an attempt would be made. He had had what was certainly a warning."

"The postcard?"

Pons nodded. "Let us compare the writing on the card with that on the wrapping of the package."

It required little more than a glance to reveal that the script on the wrapping of the package which had contained the lethal worm was entirely different from that on the postcard. But if Pons was disappointed, he did not show it; his eyes were fairly dancing with delight, and the hint of a smile touched his thin lips.

"We shall just leave this for Inspector Taylor to see. Meanwhile, the hour is not yet nine; I shall be able to reach certain sources of information without delay. If Taylor should precede my return, pray detain him until I come."

With an annoyingly enigmatic smile, Pons took his leave.

It was close to midnight when my companion returned to our quarters. A fog pressed whitely against the windows of 7B, and the familiar sounds from outside – the chimes of the clock a few streets away, the rattle of passing traffic, the occasional clip-clop of a hansom cab – had all but died away.

Inspector Taylor had been waiting for an hour. I had already shown him the remarkably ingenious instrument of death designed by the murderer of Idomeno Persano, and he had scrutinized the postcard, only to confess himself as baffled as I by any meaning it might have. Yet he had an unshakable faith in my companion's striking faculties of deduction and logical synthesis and made no complaint at Pons' delay.

Pons slipped so silently into the room as to startle us.

"Ah, Taylor, I trust you have not been kept waiting long," he said.

"Only an hour," answered the Inspector.

"Pray forgive me. I thought, insofar as I had succeeded in identifying the murderer of Idomeno Persano, I might trouble also to look him up for you."

"Mr. Pons, you're joking!"

"On the contrary. You will find him at the 'Sailor's Rest' in Wapping. He is a short, dark-skinned man of Italian or Spanish parentage. His hair is dark and curly, but showing grey at the temples. He carries a bad scar on his temple above and a little retracted from his right eye. There is a lesser scar on his throat. His name in Angelo Perro. His motive was vengeance. Persano had appeared against him in the United States a dozen years ago. Lose no time in taking him; once he learns Persano is dead, he will leave London at the earliest moment. Come around tomorrow, and you shall have all the facts."

Inspector Taylor was off with scarcely more than a mutter of thanks. It did not occur to him to question Pons' dictum.

"Surely this is somewhat extraordinary even for you, Pons," I said, before the echo of Taylor's footsteps had died down the stairs.

"You exaggerate my poor powers, Parker," answered Pons. "The matter was most elementary, I assure you."

"I'm afraid it's quite beyond me. Consider – you knew nothing of this man, Persano. You made no enquiries...."

"On the contrary, I knew a good deal about him," interrupted Pons. "He was an expatriate American of independent means. He dabbled in entomology. He lived alone. He had no telephone. He was manifestly content to live in seclusion. Why? – if not because he feared someone? If he feared someone, I submit it is logical to assume that the source of his fear lay in the United States."

"But what manner of thing did he fear that he could be upset by this card?" I asked.

Pons tossed the card over to me "Though it may tell you nothing, Parker, manifestly it conveyed something to Persano."

"It could surely not have been in the address. It must be in the picture."

"Capital! Capital!" cried Pons, rubbing his hands together. "You show marked improvement, Parker. Pray proceed."

"Well, then," I went on, emboldened by his enthusiasm, "the picture can hardly convey more than that a big fat man is running away from a little dog who has broken his leash."

"My dear fellow, I congratulate you!"

I gazed at him, I fear, in utter astonishment. "But, Pons, what other meaning has it?"

"None but that. Coupled with the suggestion of the holiday which appears in the commercial lettering, the card could readily be interpreted to say: 'Your holiday is over. The dog is loose.' A fat man running to escape a dog. Persano was corpulent."

"Indeed he was!"

"Very well, then. The postcard is the first incidence of a 'dog' in the little drama which is drawing to a close at Inspector Taylor's capable hands in Wapping. Mrs. White, you recalled to my attention only a few hours ago, told us that her late employer muttered 'the dog' several times before he lapsed into silence. That was the second occurrence. And then, finally, this matchbox cover announces 'Little dog catches big cat.' My dear fellow, could anything be plainer?"

"I hardly know what to say. I have still ringing in my ears your emphatic pronouncement that there was no dog in the matter," I said coldly.

"I believe my words were 'no such dog'. Your reference was clearly to a quadruped, a member of the Canis group of Carnivora. There is no such dog."

"You speak increasingly in riddles."

"Perhaps one of these clippings may help."

As he spoke, Pons took from his pocket a trio of clippings cut from *The Chicago Tribune* of seven weeks before. He selected one and handed it to me.

"That should elucidate the matter for you, Parker."

The clipping was a short news-article. I read it with care.

"Chicago, June 29: Prisoners paroled from Ft. Leavenworth yesterday included four Chicagoans. They were Mao Hsuieh-Chang, Angelo Perro, Robert Salliker, and Franz Witkenstein. They were convicted in 1914 on a charge of transporting and distributing narcotics. They had served eleven years. Evidence against them was furnished by a fifth member of the gang known as 'Big Id' Persano, who was given a suspended sentence for his part in their conviction. 'Big Id' dropped out of sight immediately after the trial. The four ex-convicts plan to return to Chicago."

Two of the convicts were pictured in the article; one of them was Perro. Pons must have made the rounds of hotels and inns in Wapping, showing Perro's photograph, in order to find him at the "Sailor's Rest".

"I take it 'Big Id' was our client's employer," I said, handing the clipping back to him.

"Precisely."

"But pray tell me, how did you arrive at Perro as the murderer?"

"Dear me, Parker, surely that is plain as a pikestaff?"

I shook my head. "I should have looked to the Chinaman. The device of the worm is Oriental in concept."

"An admirable deduction. Quite probably they were all in it together and the worm was the work of the Chinaman. But the murderer was Perro. I fear your education in the Humanities has been sadly neglected.

"The card, which was postmarked but two days after this item appeared in the papers, was an announcement from a friend of Persano's to tell him that the 'little dog' was free. The 'little dog' undoubtedly had information about Persano's whereabouts, and knew how to find him, even if Persano perhaps did not realize how much of his life in London was known in America. Persano understood the card at once.

"Had Perro not wished Persano to know who meant to kill him, I might have had a far more difficult time of it. 'Little dog catches big cat.' Perro is a little man. Persano was big. Perro is the Spanish for 'dog'. It should not be necessary to add that Persano is the Spanish for 'Persian'. And a Persian is a variety of cat.

"An ingenious little puzzle, Parker, however elementary in final analysis."

IX

THE ADVENTURE OF THE PENNY MAGENTA

From his place at the window one summer morning, Solar Pons said, "Ah, we are about to have a visitor and, I trust, a client. London has been oppressively dull this week, and some diversion is long past due."

I stepped over to his side and looked down.

Our prospective visitor was just in the act of stepping out of his cab. He was a man somewhat past middle-age, of medium height, and spare almost to thinness. He affected a greying Van Dyke and eyeglasses in old-fashioned square frames. He wore a greening black bowler and a scuffed smoking jacket, beneath which showed a waistcoat of some flowered material, and he carried a cane, though he did not walk with any pronounced impediment.

"A tradesman," I ventured.

"The keeper of a small shop," said Pons.

"Dry-goods?"

"You observed his clothing, Parker. His square spectacles and his walking stick are both old-fashioned. I submit he is in antiques or something of that sort. The nature of his business is such as to permit the casual, since he evidently wears his smoking jacket at his work."

"Perhaps he came from his home?"

"On the contrary. It is now ten o'clock. Some time after he arrived at his shop this morning something occurred that has brought him to us."

But our caller was now at the threshold, and in a moment our good landlady, Mrs. Johnson, had ushered him into our quarters. He bowed to her, and, his glance passing over me, he bowed to Pons.

"Mr. Solar Pons?"

"I am at your service. Pray sit down."

Our visitor sat down to face Pons, who was now leaning against the mantel, his eyes twinkling with anticipation.

"My name is Athos Humphreys," said our client. "I have a small shop for antiques, old books and stamps near Hampstead Heath. Other than that I doubt your need to know."

"Save that you are a member of the Masonic order, a bachelor or widower accustomed to living alone, without an assistant at your shop and with insufficient business to demand your unremitting attendance there," said Pons. "Pray continue, Mr. Humphreys."

Our client betrayed neither astonishment nor displeasure at Pons' little deductions. His glance fell to his Masonic ring, then to the torn and worn cuffs of his smoking jacket, which no self-respecting woman would have permitted to go unmended and finally to the lone key depending over the pocket into which he had hastily trust his chain of keys after locking his shop.

"I'm glad to see I've made no mistake in coming to you, Mr. Pons," he continued. "The problem doesn't concern me personally, however, as far as I can determine, but my shop. I must tell you that for the past three mornings I have had indisputable evidence that my shop has been entered. Yet nothing has been taken."

A small sound of satisfaction escaped Pons. "And what was the nature of your evidence that the shop had been entered, if nothing was taken, Mr. Humphreys?" he asked.

"Well, sir, I am a most methodical man. I maintain a certain order in my shop, no matter how careless it looks – that is by design, of course, for an antique shop ought to have an appearance of careful disorder. For the past three mornings I have noticed – sometimes not at once on my arrival – that some object has been moved and put back not quite where it stood before. I have never discovered any way of entry; all else, save for one or two objects, remains as I left it; so I can only suppose that whoever entered my shop did so by means of the door, to which, I ought to say, I have the only key."

"You are fully aware of your inventory, Mr. Humphreys?"

"Positively, sir. I know every item in my shop, and there is nothing there of sufficient value to tempt anyone but a sneak thief content with small reward for his pains."

"Yet it is patent that someone is going to considerable pains to search your shop night after night," said Pons. "A man in your business must lead a relatively sedentary life, Mr. Humphreys. Did you, immediately prior to this sequence of events, do anything at all to attract attention to yourself?"

"No, sir."

"Or your business?"

"No, sir." But here our client hesitated, as if he were about it speak otherwise, yet thought better of it.

"Something caused you to hesitate, Mr. Humphreys. What was it?"

"Nothing of any consequence. It is true that a week ago I was forced to post a small personal asking that relatives of the late Arthur Benefield come forward and call on me at the shop."

"Who was Arthur Benefield?"

"A patron of mine."

"Surely an unusual patron if you knew neither his address nor his heirs," said Pons. "For if you did, you would hardly have had to extend an invitation to his heirs through the columns of the papers."

"That is correct, Mr. Pons. He left no address. He appeared at my shop for the first time about a month ago, and brought with him a manila envelope filled with loose stamps. He had posted the envelope to me – apparently at a branch post office – but had then immediately retrieved it from the clerk, evidently someone whose acquaintance he had made – and brought it in person. He appeared to be an American gentleman, and asked me to keep the stamps for him. He paid a 'rental' fee of five pounds for that service during the month following his visit. He also bought several stamps from my collection and added them to his own.

"Mr. Benefield was run down and killed in an automobile accident ten days ago. I saw his picture in one of the papers, together with a request for relatives to come forward. Let me hasten to assure you, Mr. Pons, if you are thinking that the entry to my shop has anything to do with Mr. Benefield, I'm afraid you're very much mistaken. I took the liberty of examining the contents of Mr. Benefield's envelope as soon as I learned of his death. It contains no stamp worth more than a few shillings. Indeed, I doubt very much if the entire lot of mixed stamps would command more than ten pounds."

Pons stood for a moment in an attitude of deep thought. Then he said, "I fancy a look at the premises would not be amiss. Are you prepared to take us to your shop, Mr. Humphreys?"

"I would be honored to do so, Mr. Pons. I have a cab waiting below, if you care to return with me."

Our client's was indeed a little shop. It was one of those charming, old-fashioned places not uncommon in London and its environs, standing as if untouched by time from 1780 onward. A pleasant, tinkling bell announced our entrance, Mr. Humphreys having thrown the door wide and stood aside to permit us to pass. Then he in turn passed us, hanging his bowler on a little rack not far from the door, and throwing his keys carelessly to his counter. His shop was crowded, and wore just that air of planned carelessness which would intrigue the searcher after curios or unusual pieces for the household. Shelves, floors, tables – all were filled with bric-a-brac, knick-knacks, and period pieces. One wall was given over to books of all kinds, neatly arranged on shelves which reached from floor to ceiling. At the far end of the shop – next to a curtained-off alcove which was evidently a small place in which our client could brew himself tea, if he liked, for the sound of boiling water came from it – stood Mr. Humphreys' desk, a secretary of Chippendale design.

Our client was eager to show us how he had discovered that his shop had been entered in the night. He went directly to a Chinese vase which stood on top of a lacquered box on a table not far from the counter.

"If you will look carefully, Mr. Pons, you will see that the position of this vase varies by a quarter of an inch from the faint circle of lint and dust which indicates where it stood before it was moved. I have not had occasion to move this piece for at least a week. Of itself, it has no value, being an imitation Han Dynasty piece. Nor has the lacquer box on which it stands. The box, I have reason to believe, has been opened. Of course, it is empty."

Pons, however, was not particularly interested in our client's demonstration. "And where do you keep Mr. Benefield's stamps?" he asked.

Our client went around his counter and placed his right hand on a letter rack which stood on his desk. "Right here, Mr. Pons."

"Dear me!" exclaimed Pons, with an ill-concealed smile twitching his lips, "Is that not an unorthodox place for it?"

"It was where Mr. Benefield asked me to keep it. Indeed, he enjoined me to keep it here, in this envelope, in this place."

"So that anyone whose eye chanced to fall upon it would think it part of your correspondence, Mr. Humphreys?"

"I had not thought of it so, but I suppose it would be true," said Humphreys thoughtfully.

"Let us just have a look at Mr. Benefield's collection of stamps."

"Very well, Mr. Pons. It can do no harm, now the poor fellow is dead."

He handed the manila envelope to Pons. It was not a large envelope – perhaps four and a half inches by six and a half or thereabouts, but it bulged with its contents, and it had been stamped heavily with British commemorative issues of larger than common size. It had been addressed to Mr. Humphreys, and the stamps on its face had been duly cancelled; manifestly, if Mr. Humphreys' story were true, Mr. Benefield had had to apply to someone in the Post Office for its return to his hand, so that he could bring it in person to our client's shop. Pons studied the envelope thoughtfully.

"It did not seem to you strange that Mr. Benefield should make such a request of you, Mr. Humphreys?"

"Mr. Pons, I am accustomed to dealing with all manner of strange people. I suppose the collector is always rather more extraordinary in his habits and conduct than ordinary people."

"Perhaps that is true," pursued Pons. "Still, the circumstances of your possession of this envelope suggest that it contains something of value – of such value, indeed, that its owner was extremely reluctant to let it out of his sight long enough for the postman to deliver it, and left it here only because of dire necessity."

"But if that were true," objected our client reasonably, "what had he to gain by leaving it here?"

"In such plain sight, too, Mr. Humphreys," said Pons, chuckling. "I submit he had to gain what he most wanted – effective concealment. There is a story by the American, Poe, which suggests the gambit – a letter hidden in a torn envelope on a rack in sight of anyone who might walk into the room. What better place of concealment for an object – let us say, a stamp – than in the letter rack of a man who does a small philatelic business?"

"Mr. Pons, your theory is sound, but in fact it doesn't apply. I have gone over the stamps in that envelope with the greatest care. I assure you, on my word as a modest authority in philately, that there is not a stamp in that collection worth a second glance from a serious collector of any standing. There is most certainly nothing there to tempt a thief to make such elaborate forays into my humble establishment."

"I believe you, Mr. Humphreys," said Pons, still smiling. "Yet I put it to you that this is the object of your malefactor's search."

"Mr. Pons, I would willingly surrender it to him – if he could prove he had a right to it, of course."

"Let us not be hasty," said Pons dryly.

So saying, he calmly opened the envelope and unceremoniously emptied its contents to the counter before us. Then, much to our client's amazement, he bestowed not a glance at the stamps but gave his attention again to the envelope, which he now took over to the window and held up against the sunlight. The manila, however, was too thick to permit him any vision through it.

"It would seem to be an ordinary envelope," he said. "And these stamps which were to have paid its way here?"

"They are only British Empire Exhibition adhesives, issue of 1924, not very old, and not worth much more than their face value."

Pons lowered the envelope and turned to look toward the curtained alcove. "Is that not a tea-kettle, Mr. Humphreys?"

"Yes, sir. I keep hot water always ready for tea."

"Let us just repair to that room, if you please."

"It is hardly large enough for us all."

"Very well, then. I will take the liberty of using it, and you and Parker may guard the door."

Our client flashed a puzzled glance at me, but I could not relieve his dubiety nor inform him of Pons' purpose. That, however, was soon clear, for Pons went directly to the teapot on Mr. Humphreys' electric plate, and proceeded without a qualm to hold the stamped corner of the envelope over the steam.

"What are you doing, Mr. Pons?" cried our client in alarm.

"I trust I am about to find the solution to the initial part of our little problem, Mr. Humphreys," said Pons.

Our client suppressed the indignation he must have felt, and watched in fascinated interest as Pons finally peeled back the stamps.

"Aha!" exclaimed Pons, "What have we here?"

Beneath the stamps lay revealed, carefully protected by a thin square of cellophane, a shabby-looking stamp of a faded magenta color. Indeed, it was such a stamp that, were I a philatelist, I would have cast aside, for not only was it crudely printed but it had also been clipped at the corners. Pons, however, handled it with the greatest care.

"I daresay this is the object of the search which has been conducted of your premises, Mr. Humphreys," said Pons. "Unless I am very much mistaken, this is the famous one-penny magenta rarity, printed in British Guiana in 1856, discovered by a boy of fifteen here in our country, and originally sold for six shillings. After being in the collection of Philippe Ferrari for many years, it was sold to a rich American at auction for the fabulous price of seventy-five hundred pounds. Correct me if I am wrong, Mr. Humphreys."

Our client, who had been staring at the stamp in awe and fascination, found his voice. "You have made no error of fact, Mr. Pons, but one of assumption. There is only one penny magenta known to exist, despite the most intensive search for others. That stamp is still in the collection of the widow of the American millionaire who bought it at the Ferrari auction in 1925. This one can be only a forgery – a very clever, most deceptive counterfeit – but still, Mr. Pons, a forgery, with only the value of a curiosity. The original would now be worth close to ten thousand pounds; but this copy is scarcely worth the labor and care it took to make it."

Pons carefully replaced the stamps on the envelope, keeping the penny magenta to one side. Then he returned to the counter and put the loose stamps back into the envelope.

"If you have another, larger envelope, Mr. Humphreys, put this into it, and label it 'Property of Arthur Benefield'," instructed Pons. "I am somewhat curious now to know more of your late customer. Was he a young man?"

"Mr. Pons, I can only show you the clipping from the *News of the World*. It conveys all I can tell you," replied Humphreys.

He went back to his desk, opened a drawer, and took out the clipping.

Pons bent to it, and I looked over his shoulder.

The photograph was that of a young man, certainly not over thirty-five. He was not ill-favored in looks, and wore a short moustache. He appeared to be of medium weight. The story beneath it indicated that the photograph had been found in his billfold, but that no address had been discovered. From the presence of American currency in the billfold, the authorities had concluded that Benefield was an American tourist in London. They had had no response to official inquiries at the usual sources, however.

Benefield had been found in the street one night. Evidence indicated that he had been struck and killed by a fast-traveling car; police were looking for one which must have been severely damaged by the force of the impact. Car and driver had vanished, as was to be expected.

Pons read this in silence and handed it back to our client.

"Our next step," he said, "will be to catch the intruder. I have no question but that he will return tonight."

Athos Humphreys paled a little. "I should say, Mr. Pons, I am not a wealthy man. I had not inquired about your fee..."

"Say no more, Mr. Humphreys," replied Pons with animation. "If you will permit me to retain this little stamp for its curiosity value, I shall feel amply repaid."

"By all means, Mr. Pons."

"Very well, then. Parker and I will return here late this afternoon prepared to spend the night in your shop, if that is agreeable to you."

"It is indeed, sir."

We bade our client farewell and repaired to our lodgings.

We returned to Athos Humphreys' antique shop just before his closing hour that evening. It was not without some patent misgivings that our client locked us into his shop and departed. Clearly he was doubtful of our success and perhaps concerned lest our venture result in a scuffle in the narrow confines of his premises, and concomitant damage to his stock.

Pons had insisted that both of us be armed. In addition, he carried a powerful electric torch. So protected, we took up a cramped position concealed behind the curtain in the little alcove leading off the shop. Once we were alone, Pons warned again that our quarry was likely to be more desperate than I had imagined, and adjured me to keep my eyes on the door of the shop.

"You are so positive he'll come by the door," I said. "Suppose he opens a window and drops in from behind?"

"No, Parker, he will not. He has a key," replied Pons. "Surely you observed how careless Humphreys was with his keys when he came in with us this morning! He simply threw them to the counter and left them in plain sight. Anyone prepared to do so could have made wax impressions of the lot. I have no doubt that is what took place, as soon as our client's advertisement appeared and apprized our quarry that Humphreys undoubtedly possessed something belonging to Benefield, and what, more likely, than the very object of his search? I see him as a patient and dangerous man, unwilling to be caught, but determined to have what he is after."

"The penny magenta? But why would anyone take the trouble to conceal a forgery so carefully?"

"Why, indeed!" answered Pons enigmatically. "It suggests nothing to you?"

"Only that the man who wants it is deceived as to its actual value."

"Nothing other?"

"I can think of nothing."

"Very well, then. Let us just look at the problem anew. Mr. Athos Humphreys, a comparatively obscure dealer in antiques, is sought out by an American as a repository for a packet of stamps, all of no great value. Mr. Benefield has gone to the trouble of achieving a cancellation of his stamps, and then to the even greater trouble of recovering the packet to bring it in person – a considerable achievement, considering the rigidity of our Post Office. He pays at least half what his packet of stamps is manifestly worth to make sure that Humphreys keeps it where he directs. And where does he direct that it be kept? In plain sight in Humphreys' own letter-rack, after Benefield has made certain that it bears every appearance of having been posted to Humphreys. Does all this still suggest nothing further to you, Parker?"

"Only that Benefield seemed certain someone wanted the packet."

"Capital! You are making progress."

"So he made sure it wouldn't attract attention, and, if seen, would be mistaken for other than what it was. The envelope bore no return address, and the name of Humphreys was hurriedly printed in blocks. That, I presume, was so the man who wanted it wouldn't recognize Benefield's handwriting, which very probably he knew."

"It gives me pleasure to discover how handsomely your capacity for observation has grown, Parker. But – no more?"

"I fear I have shot my bolt, Pons."

"Well, then, let us just say a few words about Mr. Benefield. It does not seem to you strange that he should have so conveniently met with a fatal accident after reaching London?"

"Accidents happen every day. It is a well-known fact that the accident toll exceeds the mortality rate in wartime."

"I submit that the late Benefield and his pursuer were in this matter together. I put it to you further that Benefield slipped away from his partner in the venture and came to London by himself to offer the penny magenta for sale without the necessity of dividing the spoils with his partner, who followed and found him but has not yet found the stamp. It is not too much to conclude that it was his hand at the wheel of the car that caused Benefield's death."

"Ingenious," I said dubiously.

"Elementary, my dear Parker," said Pons.

"Except for the fact that the penny magenta is a forgery," I finished.

"Ah, Parker, you put my poor powers to shame," he answered with a dry chuckle. "But now I think we had better keep quiet. I should tell you I have notified Inspector Taylor, who will be within earshot waiting upon our signal."

I had begun to drowse, when Pons' light touch on my arm woke me. The hour was close to midnight, and the sound of a key in the lock came distinctly to ear. In a moment the outer door opened, and, from my position behind the curtain, I saw a dark figure slip into the shop. In but a moment more, the shade of a dark-lantern was drawn cautiously a little to one side. Its light fell squarely upon the counter and there, framed in it, was the envelope on which our client had written Arthur Benefield's name.

The light held to the counter.

Then, in four rapid and silent strides, the intruder was at the counter. I saw his hand reach down and take up the envelope.

At that moment Pons turned on his electric torch and silhouetted a well-dressed, thin-faced young man whose startled glance gave him a distinctly fox-like look. He stood for but a split second in the light; then he dropped, spun around, and leaped for the door.

Pons was too quick for him. He caught up a heavy iron and threw it with all his force. It struck our quarry cruelly on the side of one knee; he went down and stayed down.

"Keep your hands out of your pockets; we are armed," said Pons, advancing toward him. "Parker, just open the door and fire a shot into the air. That will bring Taylor."

Our quarry sat up, one hand gripping his knee painfully, the other still clinging to the envelope of stamps. "The most you can charge me with," he said in a cultured voice, "is breaking and entering. Perhaps theft. This is as much my property as it was Arthur's."

"I fancy the charge will be murder," said Pons, as Inspector Taylor's pounding footsteps waxed in the night.

Back in our quarters at 7B Praed Street, Pons lingered over a pipe of shag. I, too, hesitated to go to bed.

"You do not seem one whit puzzled over this matter, Pons," I said at last. "Yet I confess that its entire motivation seems far too slight to justify its events."

"You are certainly right, Parker," he answered with maddening gravity. "It does not then suggest anything further to you?"

"No, I am clear as to the picture."

"But not as to its interpretation, eh?"

"No."

"I submit there is a basic error in your reasoning, Parker. It has occurred to you to realize that one would hardly go to such lengths, even to commit murder, for a counterfeit stamp worth five pounds at best. Yet it does not seem to have occurred to you that the penny magenta I have here as a gift from our client may indeed be worth, as he estimated, ten thousand pounds?"

"We know that the single copy of that stamp exists in an American collection."

"Say, rather, we believe it does. I submit that *this* is the only genuine British Guiana penny magenta rarity, and that the copy in the America collection is a counterfeit. I took the liberty of sending a cable this afternoon, and I fancy we shall have a visitor from America just as fast as an aeroplane will make it possible from New York to Croydon."

Pons was not in error.

Three days later, a representative of the American collector presented himself at our quarters and paid Pons a handsome reward for the recovery of the penny magenta. Both Benefield and his partner, who had been identified as a man named Watt Clark, had been in the collector's service. They had manufactured the false penny magenta and exchanged it for the genuine stamp, after which they had left their positions. The substitution had not been noticed until Pons' cable sent the collector to the experts, whose verification of Pons' suspicion had resulted in the dispatching of the collector's representative to bear the fabulously valuable penny magenta home in person.

X

THE ADVENTURE OF THE TRAINED CORMORANT

"It has been a full six months since I have seen a dog-cart in the streets of London," said Solar Pons, as we rounded a corner into Praed Street and bore down upon 7B, "and that one, if I mistake not, is the work of an unreconstructed individualist. I permit myself to hope it may be a harbinger of some little problem to break the monotony of our summer days."

The object of Pons' interest stood before the steps to our own quarters, and, as we drew near, I could appreciate more fully Pons' comment. The dog-cart was in itself a little master-piece of brown, tan and grey-white wood of all kinds.

"Wrought by hand in its entirety," murmured Pons, his eyes gleaming. "And come from some distance, would you not say, Parker?"

"Mud on the wheels – chalk and dust – elementary," I said. "Folkestone – Dover?"

"Say, rather, further round the coast. The mud is a clay found in South Kent, the chalk dust lies over it, and what surmounts both is the dust of London." Pons was bending over the dog-cart in close scrutiny as he spoke. "Moreover, it has been driven here by a man with a wooden leg, who carried a parcel of some kind strapped to the cart."

"His portmanteau," I suggested. "He is a sycophant come to London to take lodgings with us and study your methods."

"Ah, you are waggish this evening, Parker," said Pons, smiling. "No, it was not a portmanteau. I should venture to guess a crate, containing, if the evidence before my eyes is not deceptive, a bird." He caught up a downy feather between thumb and forefinger and released it into the gentle breeze which made its way down Praed Street.

"I'm willing to concede the bird," I said. "But surely you can say more of our visitor than that he has a wooden leg. I can see those markings very well for myself in the bottom of the cart."

"Ah, how familiarity does breed contempt!" exclaimed Pons with a droll expression on his usually saturnine features. "I can say but little more, my dear fellow – save that our caller is a man past middle age, of some little weight, obviously a man of the sea, for his cart is the result of his own craftsmanship wrought upon what must have been for the most part driftwood, one might add, on venture, a stubborn, determined man who drives himself as hard as he did in his youth. He is given to smoking a homely mixture of shag which would put even my own to shame in its potency, and he wears, at the moment, orange corduroy trousers, as the threads on the rough edge of his seat suggest. But enough of this; let us just see what he has to say."

So saying, Pons turned to mount to our lodgings on the second floor of Number 7.

Our visitor was sprawled comfortably in Pons' own chair beside the fireplace. At our entrance, he came to his feet with a grizzled smile, and doffed his cap. He was a man of some sixty-odd years, more grey than dark of hair, with a rough, weather-beaten face. He stood on a wooden leg, visible from knee to floor, and did indeed wear orange corduroy trousers, with a dark blue jacket of like material. He was not corpulent, but he was heavy and solidly built. Moreover, he had been waiting for some time, as the dottle in the fireplace and the strong pungent odor of tobacco suggested.

"Beggin' your pardon, Mr. Pons," he said, inclining his head to my companion. "Captain Andrew Walton."

"Once in the China trade. Late of the *Welkin*, I see," said Pons, eyeing a scarf knotted about his neck.

"Aye, and the *Barbados* before her, and many a ship before that."

"Not long retired."

"Two years, sir."

"Living on the south coast."

"Aye, sir. Not far from New Romney, above the Dungeness Lighthouse."

Pons had removed his Inverness and deerstalker as he spoke. He slipped into his worn purple dressing-gown, exchanged his shoes for his slippers, and settled himself with a pipeful of shag, while our visitor waited politely for Pons' signal to continue.

"Me and Adelaide," he went on then, "have come all the way to London from our little house..."

"Surely you didn't bring Mrs. Walton with you on such a long journey by dog-cart!" I put in.

Our visitor favored me with an astonished stare.

Pons laughed heartily. "Forgive me, Parker. Your little deductions never fail to touch me," he said. Coming to his feet, he strode across to the chair in which our visitor had been sitting, caught hold of it, and turned it to one side, revealing a large crate in which sat a solitary black bird. "This is Captain Walton's 'Adelaide'."

"A raven!" I cried.

"A cormorant," retorted Pons. "A fishing bird well known to England's waters, and in various parts of the world, but most especially Japan and the China coast, where the bird is gainfully employed and highly prized by coast fishermen."

"Aye, and a better fisher than Adelaide hasn't been born, and you may lay to that, Mr. Pons. I've had her nigh on to seven years, and I wouldn't have brought her along on such a trip, only that I'd no way of knowing what might go on while I was away from the house..."

Pons' eyes twinkled. "I take it, Captain Walton, something has disturbed the even tenor of your days."

"Aye, sir, that it has."

So saying, our visitor leaned forward and phlegmatically unstrapped his wooden leg, from the cushion of which he extracted a compact case of what appeared to be black leather. It was somewhat rectangular in shape, very much like a gentleman's large flat pocket wallet, except that it was not folded and was rather more bulky. This he handed to me for Pons. I was surprised at its lightness.

"Cork lined," observed Pons, the moment he touched it. "Meant to float." His eyes danced. "I trust I am not amiss in guessing that the faithful Adelaide brought it to you?"

"Aye, sir. Now have a look at it. It's just as I found it, with one exception. It had a little waterproof wrapping around it; that I took off."

"Why haven't you brought it?"

"I'll be coming to that in my time."

Pons opened the cork-lined case and disclosed two small pockets, from one of which projected a letter evidently intended to be posted. Pons removed it without comment. From the other pocket he removed two objects – a thin-paper copy of a letter, and a postcard, unstamped, evidently not meant to be posted, for it bore no address. On one side of the card typescript stood out. The thin-paper letter was folded and had evidently not long reposed in the package, for it was still relatively clean and bore only the wrinkling impress of Captain Walton's knee-stub. The thin-paper letter was clearly a copy of a letter written to the intended recipient of the other letter, which was stamped and enclosed in an envelope, bearing a typescript address – "The Rt. Hon. Geoffrey Crayle, M. P., 15 Bourget Street, London S. E." – and appeared to come from "John T. Evans, Dungeness Lthouse., nr. Lydd, Kent."

The envelope contained little more than one page of letter, to judge by its weight. It was slightly longer than the customary envelope, but not of legal size, and its flap was straight, rather than wedge-shaped. Pons examined the envelope perfunctorily, then dropped it to the table before him. He unfolded the thin-paper letter and read it with somewhat more care; it was an ordinary letter of commendation from a constituent to his representative in Parliament, approving the Member's recent stand on a public matter affecting the constituency. He favored the card with but little more attention. It was a perfectly plain post card, bearing neither superscription nor address, and carrying but four lines of typescript, which read:

> Fifth without fail.
> Do not come to us.
> We will come to you.
> Sailing 10th *Normandie*.

Having finished his cursory examination, Pons looked up.

"Let us just have some hot water ready, Parker," he said to me, and, to our visitor, "Pray continue, Captain Walton."

"Well, sir," began the Captain with deliberation, "as you've heard, I'm a coast dweller, I make a little money beside my pension by carving out driftwood and the like, and I've got Adelaide trained to pick up whatever she can carry and bring it in – that is, beside the fish. A week ago yesterday, that would be the third, she came in with this. I don't get out much, but it was my intention to post the letter just as soon as I got into Lydd, but one thing and another came between, and it was three days before I found time to do it.

"By that time, there had been some queer goings-on. I don't mean to say I was suspicious right off, but someone was about making inquiries concerning me and Adelaide – round-about, you understand, not so much from me as from my neighbors. Once or twice I caught a glimpse of sunlight flashing off a spyglass – it's a sight I'm familiar with. So I knew somebody was watching the house."

"This unwelcome attention began when, Captain?" Pons put in. "Before or after the sixth?"

"Four days ago, sir."

"Ah, the seventh. Two days after the 'Fifth without fail'."

"On the evening of the eighth, I was that suspicious. I put the packet where you saw it, and went off along the coast after driftwood. While I was gone, someone got into my house and searched it, top to bottom. The only thing missing was the waterproof wrapper in which this packet had been kept dry."

"There was nothing, then, to show that you had not sent off the letter by post?"

"Nothing. But there was more to come. Little things – you might say, innocent things, except that they'd never happened before. Next day somebody came down from Folkestone and made enquiries about Adelaide. Did I have a fishing license for her? And the like. A strange, dark man, square of face – looked like a police officer. Did I want to sell my house, with all in it? On the eighth, someone shot at her – tipped her wing, he did. That was enough for me, Mr. Pons. I came to the conclusion that this packet is the cause of it all, and I asked myself why they couldn't have come direct and said to me they'd lost it and could they have it back? There's something mighty queer about it. If it belonged to Mr. Evans, why was it floating off the lighthouse unless he lost it by accident? If so, he had the right to come after it, if he thought I had it."

"Quite so," agreed Pons.

"I was in two minds about it at first – whether to go to the lighthouse or to the police. But the police are suspicious and apt to be troublesome, and Mr. Evans has been unfriendly – to say the least – keeping to himself. So I recollected you'd done a bit of work for Miss Norton and she'd spoken highly of you; so here I am. Now, sir, if I can just leave this with you, I'll be on my way back."

"Let us not be hasty, Captain Walton," cautioned Pons.

Our visitor looked inquiringly at Pons, as my companion got to his feet and took a turn or two about the room, his face a study. He walked over to the windows and back, paused a few moments at the mantel, where he flipped through two or three letters transfixed to it by his knife, and stood for a time before the fire, his keen eyes thoughtful, his brow furrowed, his lips pushing out and in, his hands clasped behind his back. He turned finally to Captain Walton.

"There is nothing demanding your presence at home?" he asked.

"Well, nought – save that I'm not over-fond of the city."

"I suggest then that you spend a few days in London."

"Eh? And what for, Mr. Pons?"

"It doesn't occur to you that it may be dangerous to return home just now?"

"I'm not strange to danger, Mr. Pons," said our visitor stoutly.

"Quite so. Let us say until you hear from me, then. I'll just give you a letter to the keeper of a lodging house not far from here. We may find it necessary to run down to Dungeness ourselves; if so, we can all go together."

Pons himself saw our visitor and his cormorant down the stairs. He came bounding back into the room, rubbing his hands together in a highly pleased manner.

"Now, then, Parker," said he as he seated himself before the objects our visitor had left behind, "what do you make of it?"

"I have never known your hunger for new adventure to overcome your judgment," I answered. "There's hardly any mystery here. Evans simply dropped his wallet overboard on his way to mail his letter..."

"Conveniently wrapped in a cork-lined container, to make sure it floated," interposed Pons.

"And the bird recovered it before he could do so," I finished doggedly. "I must say, Pons, you have a distressing tendency to make mystery where none exists, but I suppose that is only to be expected."

"Let me see," mused Pons, "you have been with me over a decade, almost twelve years, and in all that time it is only one of my cases which turned up something more – more, mind you, not less – than a mystery. And that, let me prod your memory, was the matter of Mr. Amos Dorrington's inheritance – you've been dancing attendance on his lovely daughter, Miss Constance, ever since."

"Nevertheless," I persisted, "I maintain if we ask Evans at the lighthouse, he will confirm my theory."

"Would it not be to his interest to do so? I should assume so." Pons shook his head. "But this discussion is purely academic, for I am very much afraid Mr. Evans is in no position to be asked any questions whatsoever."

"Why do you say so?"

"Unless I am very badly mistaken, Mr. Evans is dead," said Pons, with the same imperturbability he might have assumed were he ordering an egg for breakfast from our landlady.

"Pons, you are mad!" I exclaimed indignantly.

Pons clucked with growing impatience. "You have a disconcerting tendency to turn yourself into an alienist the moment your pet theory is challenged," he said. "I submit to some unwillingness always to abandon the obvious conclusion, but in this case yours is far from obvious. Let us just look into the matter a little more closely, setting aside the peculiar harassment to which Captain Walton and his cormorant have been subjected. I submit that it would hardly be logical of Mr. Evans to carry about with him at the same time both a letter to be posted and the duplicate copy of that letter."

"Of course not. He would file the duplicate."

"Precisely."

"But, hold on, Pons!" I protested. "Aren't you jumping to conclusions? We have no evidence to show that the thin-paper copy is a duplicate of the letter enclosed in the envelope."

"Except the fact that it is there in the same packet – as were it to make sure Mr. Evans knew what he had written his M. P."

"You suggest that Mr. Evans is not the author of the letter purporting to come from him?"

"I do, indeed. I submit he never saw it, and thus needed to have the duplicate so that he might know what he had supposedly written."

"My dear fellow," I said, not without scorn, "if ever I have read an innocuous letter, it is that duplicate copy. It isn't even such a letter of which a copy is necessary!"

"Except, of course, for the most cursory preference as to what it contained." He glanced over toward the burner. "But let us just settle the point without further delay. We have ample steam up."

So saying, Pons rose and carried the letter to the steaming kettle, where he held its sealed flap over the steam. He hummed a little tune as he stood there, a particularly obnoxious practise I inevitably found all the more so when he was at his most recalcitrant in the face of my opposing views.

In a few moments he returned with the open envelope in one hand and the unfolded letter in the other. He put the letter down before me without comment. It was indeed the same in content as the thin-paper duplicate. Pons' interest, however, was not in the letter, but in the envelope.

"I fancy this is the reason for Captain Walton's harassment," said Pons, indicating the back of the open envelope.

He placed it face downward on the table. At first I could see nothing, but presently I realized that the line of sealing gum on the envelope was slightly raised. Even as I noticed it, Pons had unclasped his pocket knife, prepared to operate on the envelope. In a trice, he was furling back a very thin strip of cellophane and disclosing an even thinner dark line beneath. It was this Pons drew forth with an exclamation of triumph.

"But what is it?" I cried.

"Microfilm," answered Pons, holding it up to the light.

I looked through the film but saw little save what appeared to be concrete structures in various stages of completion. They were interior photographs.

"Fortifications," said Pons.

"But where?"

"That, I daresay, is somewhat more in my brother's department than in my own. At this hour he should still be on his private wire at the Foreign Office."

When he returned from the telephone, it was with word that Bancroft Pons, a most enigmatic individual whose connection with the Foreign Office was of such a pervasive and inclusive nature that one could never guess at the importance of his post, save to conclude that it was of the greatest significance, was soon to join us.

"Now, then," continued Pons imperturbably, turning once more to the contents of our recent visitor's curious packet, "doubtless you have already arrived at the conclusion that this packet – like others of a similar nature – was dropped into the sea, very possibly from passing aircraft or a ship, for Mr. Evans to find, save that in this case Adelaide's vigilance was greater than Evans' own."

"But is not that an absurdly roundabout procedure?" I protested.

"In espionage nothing is too roundabout, my dear Parker, especially if it comes from abroad – from France, perhaps?"

"But France is an ally!"

"Exactly."

"Even if our country needed information it could not obtain by regular channels, there would be other alternatives open to it."

Pons smiled patiently. "It suggests nothing to you that Mr. Evans transmits such letters as these to a country politician in London, and receives duplicate copies of his letters with the originals?"

"Perhaps the letter is in cipher?"

Pons shook his head. "I thought of that at once. There is a poorly concealed message contained on the card, in addition to what the card conveys – that this letter must be delivered by the fifth and that by the tenth emissaries will act on its behalf. The so-called sailing date is nothing more or less than a time-limit, surely, since no such boat as the *Normandie* is scheduled to sail from any known port, as you will find if you take the trouble to scan the ships' registries. And, since today is the eleventh, the time limit has expired, and the warning must be put into effect."

"What warning?"

Pons tossed the card over to me. "That contained in the line-end syllables of this apparently innocent message."

I looked at the card again and read the four line-end syllables:

fail us you die

"I submit," said Pons, "it is not too much to assume that the threat so plainly set forth may already have been executed."

"Great Heavens, man! Why are you sitting there idly then?" I cried out.

"Because Mr. Evans is the merest cog in the machine. No, our quarry is somewhere in London. All we can do in that matter of Mr. Evans is to run down to Dungeness in the morning and make such enquiry as is possible, and perhaps at the same time notify the local police. If by some chance Evans is still alive, he can be taken readily enough when he is wanted."

"You are taking a singularly cold-blooded view of the matter. It is unlike you, Pons."

"Say not so," replied Pons, unmoved. "I fear any concern over Mr. Evans at this late date is ill-ventured. Let us rather attend to those more immediate aspects of the matter which may affect the welfare of our country. We must now wait upon Bancroft's coming."

My companion's elder brother made his appearance within an hour, coming soundlessly up the stairs and into the room almost before Pons seemed aware of his approach.

"How now, Solar?" he asked quietly from the threshold, his broad shoulders and massive, leonine head filling the doorway. "What troubles you to the extent of sending for me?"

"This," said Pons, tapping the strip of microfilm.

Bancroft came forward with his catlike tread, took up the film, and held it to the light. His face paled.

"If you had known what these were, you would not have sent for me," said Bancroft Pons.

"Elementary, my dear brother," answered Pons. "Fortifications of some kind. In France, I should assume. Extensive, since these would appear to be pictures of focal points of the substructure."

"These are interiors – and important secret interiors – of the Maginot Line fortifications," said Bancroft. "How came they here?"

Without a word, Pons indicated the hiding place of the microfilm. Keeping to his feet, Bancroft slipped his walking stick under one arm, took up the letter and the envelope, and subjected both to rapid, intense scrutiny.

"The Honorable Geoffrey Crayle would seem to be of primary interest," said Pons, "since the microfilm was addressed to him."

"Tut, tut, let us not jump to unwarranted conclusions, Solar," reprimanded Bancroft. "Say rather the letter and the envelope were addressed to him."

"Ah, then he is a man of impeccable character."

"Unimpeachable."

"Married?"

"A bachelor."

"No longer young?"

"Sixty-seven."

"He lives alone?"

"With a housekeeper."

"Dear me, how well informed you are about our country politicians!" said Pons.

"It is only a trifling part of my obligations to His Majesty's Government. Now, then, what of this fellow Evans?"

"I will make some inquiry in the morning. Otherwise, I leave him to you."

"He could not have been the writer, obviously. Merely an agent, then. The letter – and perhaps others before it – must have come from France, and it must be intended for German agents – possibly Russian – in London. How did it come to hand?"

My companion narrated rapidly and succinctly the circumstances of Captain Andrew Walton's visit.

"A cormorant," mused Bancroft. "By what humble phenomena of nature are the best-laid plans of men betrayed! I apologize to Mr. Burns. Adelaide, indeed! Where are they now?"

"In London, pending disposal of the matter."

Bancroft appeared to muse for a moment. Then he touched the letter with one finger. "This letter?"

"I may have use for it. Take the microfilm; I shall not need that."

"What do you expect to do?"

"First, to ascertain how these messages, addressed to an elected servant of His Majesty, a servant who is above reproach, could fall into the hands of a potential enemy of France and therefore, also, England. Secondly, to rid the country of him, since I am not sanguine enough to believe that our own government in its merciful tenderness would move so boldly as to strike down the whole body of them – for it is manifestly only a small segment of an espionage ring upon which we have unwittingly stumbled here. Our French allies are less circumspect in these matters, and not so prone to respect the claims of diplomatic immunity."

Bancroft Pons wrinkled his nose in almost haughty distaste. He carefully pocketed the microfilm, and stepped soundlessly to the threshold once more. "You have my number. Call on me if you need our help."

After his brother had gone, Pons sat for some time with his head sunk upon his breast, his eyes closed, his fingers tented before him. He offered nothing more by way of explanation, nor did I venture to ask, for fear that his replies would confuse me the more.

Early next morning found us on our way to New Romney, bound for the Dungeness lighthouse, a journey of a little over an hour by rail from Charing Cross, leading through the beautiful Sevenoaks and Tunbridge Wells country to the region of the Cinque Ports. But throughout our journey, Pons was too preoccupied to look beyond the floor and walls of our compartment. Convinced as he was that our journey would gain him nothing but the verification of his deductions of the evening before, he sat in deep thought, with his eyes half closed and his head lowered.

Once at New Romney, we changed to the cars of the quaint miniature railway which runs to Dungeness from that ancient port, a short journey to the tip of the spit of land which points to the lighthouse, a desolate area, with the wide Denge Marsh reaching inland to Lydd and back toward New Romney. Dungeness itself presented its customary isolation – one of pubs and fishermen and their little houses, dominated by the lighthouse in the sea. We had no trouble engaging a boat to take us to the lighthouse, and there we found the keeper, a bush-bearded old fellow named Elijah Moorehead.

"Evans!" he exclaimed in response to Pons' query. "So you came to ask me about Evans! A strange thing he should be missing."

"Ah," murmured Pons. "How long has he been gone?"

"Two days, Mr. Pons."

Pons glanced significantly at me, while Moorehead continued.

"He set out in his boat – he was as much at home in it as he was here – and he has not returned. The boat has shown up, capsized. I've reported him missing to the authorities."

"Quite right, Moorehead. You say he was much in his boat. Was he not bound to his duties here?"

"Oh, yes, sir. But he had more freedom than I liked. We were much troubled with aeroplanes flying too close, and he had devised some sort of chain of red flares on buoys to be made visible even in the dense fogs which plague us here. So he was much about looking after them. Still, he was an able hand in his boat."

"What was his destination when he left here?"

"I believe he was going down the coast to meet a friend." Moorehead's eyes narrowed. "You don't think, Mr. Pons, he may have met with foul play?"

"We shall see in good time," replied Pons. "I suggest that in any event you keep his things as they were, in case the police should want to look in."

"Perhaps you'd like to see his room, sir?"

Pons accepted the lighthouse keeper's invitation with alacrity.

Evans' room, however, was singularly bare. Pons turned up only a neat file of duplicate letters, eleven in number, which had been sent to the Right Honorable Geoffrey Crayle over a period of three months, but he did not disturb them.

"I should venture to guess," he said when at last we were on our way back to London, "that the extremely chancey method of delivering messages to Evans originated with him, and that he had some difficulty convincing his confederates of the feasibility of his plan. Hence his vigilance in the face of their temper – a vigilance which Captain Walton's trained cormorant happily foiled."

When I woke the following morning, I found myself alone.

Pons had not gone, however, without leaving cryptic word for me. Pinned to the tablecloth beside my breakfast plate was a short cutting from one of the morning papers. In sum, it set forth that the body of John T. Evans, employed at the Dungeness Lighthouse, had been found along shore in the vicinity of the long beach at Dungeness. He had been drowned, and his death was presumed to be an accident.

When I returned past midday from my round of medical calls, I found Pons just in. He was divesting himself of garb I should have thought belonged more properly on a street-hawker.

"Your message didn't escape me," I said. "No doubt you have already corrected the local verdict?"

"On the contrary," said Pons. "Mr. Evans has got his just desserts. He dealt with engaging employers, some of whom, alas! are untouchable through ordinary legal channels."

"Are diplomats forever immune?" I cried.

He nodded. "You have chronicled, I think, one or two of my little encounters with that sinister arch-criminal, the Baron Ennesfred von Kroll."

"Not he again!"

"I fear his hand in this is all too evident. Does it surprise you to learn that the house at number 17 Bourget is occupied by one Herman Albert Hauptmann, in the German government service?"

"Why, that's next door to Crayle's home."

"That is no coincidence, Parker. Moreover, Mr. Hauptmann has certain connections in Germany – he is married to a niece of Baron von Kroll. Further, he has a young son of tender years; he is nine. His name is Otto. Little Otto is an enterprising lad much given to philately. Every day he collects the discarded envelopes – 'covers,' they are called by philatelists – from the houses of all the neighbors. However unwittingly, little Otto thus serves the Vaterland. Need one be told how lovingly his father assists him at his hobby – carefully steaming off stamps, the while ungumming a flap or two?

"I was about this morning as a tradesman, and the Honorable Member's elderly housekeeper, who is evidently as kindhearted as he himself is reputed to be, turned out to be a veritable encyclopedia of information about all the neighbors. I submit that the intelligence gathered through Hauptmann's system of espionage finds its way directly to Baron von Kroll, and from him in the diplomatic pouches to Germany. There may be other Evanses in the chain, though I am inclined to doubt it, since the loss of any one link would then break and endanger the entire chain. The actual spy is somewhere in France, with access to the means of bringing his information unchallenged across the channel. Could anything be safer than a constituent's letter to his M. P.? These Germans have the guileless minds of children."

Once again in his dressing-gown, with a pipe of shag between his lips, my companion sat before the envelope and letter intended for the Right Honorable Geoffrey Crayle.

"Let us just see what we can put together," he said. "We shall send along the Member's letter, but with a little something else in place of the microfilm."

He cut out a thin strip of cellophane, and, as I watched, he pricked into it, by means of a pin, this message:

Komm schnell oder Alles ist verloren.

This he gummed to the envelope in place of the microfilm, then sealed the envelope. He put the envelope into the rack for the outgoing post and leaned back, a satisfied smile on his face.

"As soon as this reaches Herr Hauptmann, it will be safe for Captain Walton and his Adelaide to return to Kent. Meanwhile, a cautionary word to Scotland Yard, to make sure that our man is followed in his flight from London, and another to the Sureté, ought to insure a little round of trouble for Hauptmann and his French counterpart away from our own shores at the hands of a government appreciably less sensitive about the rights of espionage agents. We cannot capture Baron von Kroll, but he and I will meet again!"

Within the week, Captain Walton's dog-cart, with Adelaide perched sedately in her crate, ready for the journey back to the southeast coast, was at the kerb before Number 7. He had come back not only at Pons' invitation but also to make a token payment to Pons for his efforts on behalf of Adelaide and the cork-lined packet. On the previous day, Captain Walton and his bird had gone up country among the canals of the Thames; Adelaide had not been idle; she had caught Pons a dozen fat bream.

The morning papers had just come in, and Pons showed Captain Walton the conclusion of his adventure, chronicled therein under the heading: *Crush German Spy Ring*, which was, said Pons, somewhat "inaccurate, owing more to the enthusiasm of Scotland Yard than to the press." It set forth the dramatic shadowing of a spy from London to a meeting with a confederate in Paris, and the subsequent death of the French spy and capture of Hauptmann in a battle with the French police.

"But it says here, 'By means of close cooperation between Scotland Yard and the French Surete'...," said Captain Walton. "Not a word about you, Mr. Pons."

Pons smiled. "Ah, that, Captain Walton, is like Adelaide's discovery of the cork-lined packet – one of life's least ironies."

XI

THE ADVENTURE OF THE CAMBERWELL BEAUTY

For some time after my marriage, I had not seen my friend, Solar Pons, the consulting detective. My practise in South Norwood kept me busy, and Pons himself had been on the move in the south of France. I was not even aware that he had returned to London when, one night in May of the year 193–, I received a tantalizing message from my old friend, inviting me to take the night and perhaps the following day, to accompany him on one of those adventures of which I never tired during those happy years I had shared quarters with him at 7B Praed Street.

My wife, the most understanding of women, would hear of nothing but that I go forthwith; I had an assistant who could undertake my practise for so short a time, and I was eager to go, for, truth to tell, I had sorely missed the excitement of the game afoot. It was just past ten o'clock when I presented myself at our old quarters, where I found Pons sawing away at a tuneless melody on his violin.

"I fancy the veriest tyro at Scotland Yard would have recognized that familiar tread on the stairs, Parker. I trust you have left Mrs. Parker well. Remember to give her my regards when you return to that little island of domesticity."

To step into that cozily lit room once again was like walking into yesterday. Nothing had changed. Pons' shag was still in the toe of his bedroom slipper tacked to the right of the fireplace; letters and messages were stuck to the mantelpiece by a jack-knife; the large gasogene stood as always on the mahogany sideboard, together with a bottle of Beaune and the decanter. Pons' Inverness and deerstalker hung on a peg behind the door, where, it seemed but a few hours ago, my silk hat and overcoat had also hung.

"I must say, your violin playing has not improved, Pons."

"Quite possibly that is true. Let us see how your faculty of observation has developed during the interim." He stood his violin in a corner near his chemistry table, and came around to the mantel, from which he detached a letter which he thrust toward me. "What do you make of that, Parker?"

I read the communication with keen interest. It was written in a fine hand, in spidery script, on very thin, but expensive paper. There was no superscription save the date, which was today's, and the message itself was curiously presented: "You will honor my house if you will be so kind as to accompany my emissary when he presents himself tonight at eleven. There is a concern of some delicacy in which I beg to be served by your unique abilities." The signature was a single initial: "F."

I looked up. Pons' eyes were fixed on me in anticipation.

"It is clear you know the writer."

"Elementary. What of the writer?"

"The richness of the paper suggests he is a man of means," I ventured.

"Capital! Proceed."

"He is accustomed to giving orders and being obeyed."

Pons nodded.

"The script is that of a man advanced in years."

A little smile played about Pons' lips. "I congratulate you, Parker! Plainly, married life has sharpened your wits and increased your faculty for observation. Tell me, does not the manner strike you as strange?"

"It's different, yes."

"Oriental?"

"Now that you mention it, yes. But you know the man."

"I do." Pons sank into his arm-chair, stretched his long legs toward the coal-scuttle, and stuck his hands into the pockets of his dressing-gown.

"Who is he?"

"Let us refer to him simply as the Doctor. He is considered by some persons a financial genius, by others as the most sinister man in the complex underworld of London. He was once of singular service to me; it is not too much to say that he was instrumental in saving my life. You may recall that little matter of the Seven Sisters. I am thus in his debt."

"Is he a criminal?"

"He has never been convicted. He has never been tried. Yet he is the head of one of the most skillfully organized bands of – shall we say, secret agents? – in all London. He has, conservatively speaking, a thousand men at his disposal,"

"Yet he calls on you?" I demanded incredulously.

"Which suggests that the matter is intimately personal and not something to be entrusted to the lascars, dacoits, thugs, and assorted servants at his command."

"I don't like the sound of this, Pons."

"Ah, you are as thin-skinned as ever!" He chuckled. "Have you ever heard of the Si-Fan?"

"Indeed I have!"

"That amazing web-work of mysterious forces which, legend has it, is represented in every corner of the earth!" He chuckled again. "And the Brotherhood of the Lotus? And the much-touted Yellow Peril?" He smiled, waiting for the full effect of the images he had conjured up to strike me, and then added, "The Doctor is all of them. It is he who is the embodiment of the Yellow Peril; it is he who is the insidious mastermind of the Si-Fan and the Brotherhood of the Lotus..."

"You are leading me up the garden path, Pons!"

"Have it so, if you like."

He took out his watch and peered intently at it. "It lacks but two minutes of the hour. The Doctor's man will be prompt. Presumably, since the Doctor moves silently and unseen, he may be expected to do likewise." He cocked his head suddenly, and listened.

A cat-like step whispered along the stairs.

"He is coming," said Pons. "A light man who walks with a slight limp."

In a moment there was a discreet tap on the door.

Since I was nearer the door, I threw it open. There stood revealed not a sinister Oriental, but a slender, pale-faced young man, whose glance drove past me to fix on my companion.

"Mr. Solar Pons," he said in a pleasant, business-like voice. "I am Wayland Peters. You are expecting me."

"Come in, come in, Mr. Peters. How did you leave the Doctor?"

"In good health, if in bad spirits. You are to come with me. Is Dr. Parker accompanying us?"

"I have asked him to," said Pons. He removed his dressing-gown and slippers, and looked at our client's representative with frank interest. "An honor student at Oxford, I see. What year?"

"Two years ago, Mr. Pons."

"You are too young to have seen service in the last war. Perhaps you sustained your wound in Colonial service?"

"I had one year in India. My wound ended my service."

"Left-handed, I see."

"Yes, sir."

"The Doctor apparently disdains the typewriter even for your use. He keeps you to pen and pencil?"

"Yes, sir." A smile broke upon that pale, studious countenance, and I saw that Peters was not ill-favored in looks. Allowing him a year's military service, four years at Oxford, two years since matriculation, he would have been somewhere between twenty-five and thirty years of age.

"The Doctor told me to expect something in the way of an exercise in ratiocination, Mr. Pons," he said. "I am not disappointed. But aren't these relatively elementary deductions for you?"

"Touché!" exclaimed Pons. "You have fallen victim to the exaggeration of my poor powers of which my companion is incessantly guilty. You are right. These matters are always elementary. They consist primarily in the presentation of conclusions without the exposure of the steps between observation and conclusion, and thus seem always remarkable, though, on examination, they cannot fail but impress one with their simplicity. – But is not all such ratiocination solely the application of a little logic to the available evidence? Thus, it is easy to see that you are left-handed and given to the use of a pen; the callous is on the knuckle of the middle finger of the left hand. It is only a little less so to say that you are unmarried, you are a young man fond of his personal comfort, and one not overly burdened with scruples; though you wear a certain aspect of deference well, you are anything but obsequious; you have considerably more ambition than most young men of your age and you mean to get ahead."

Our visitor's smile had faded and vanished, but the twinkle in his pale blue eyes had not. "I'm not sure I follow you in all this, but some of it is the purest venturing," he said.

"Say rather it is what follows naturally in the circumstances of your employment. Let us be off."

Peters had come by limousine. A long, sleek Daimler stood at the kerb. It was not until Pons and I had entered it that I saw how well its occupants were protected from the gaze of passersby; the back seat was completely shut off from the street by dark curtains drawn tightly across the windows; not a glimmer of light penetrated the interior. A wave of alarm swept over me.

Pons sensed my perturbation and reassured me. "Pray do not be alarmed at the Doctor's precautions, Parker. Whatever legends have accrued to him, whatever may be whispered about the terrible and weird vengeance which has befallen his enemies, the Doctor is a man of his word. He has never broken it."

"This man could take us anywhere," I protested presently. "I know we turned east, and I thought south, but I have since lost all sense of direction."

"He'll take us directly to the Doctor, never fear. It would be as much as his life is worth to disobey."

"What manner of man is this Doctor?" I cried.

"It is hardly within my province to judge," replied Pons dryly. "I am in his debt. He has not crossed my path; I have had no occasion to cross his. I do not view with equanimity ever doing so."

We rode, I thought, interminably. The car moved smoothly, almost noiselessly along. The hour was now close to midnight. Pons sat in silence; so dark was the car's interior that I could not see him.

"Do you have any idea where we are?" I asked him presently.

"I fancy we are approaching Limehouse. The air has changed subtly; its humidity has increased, and there is that characteristic musk of the Thames. There is always a distinctive odor about the Docks. And those bells in the distance are surely those of Bow. I daresay we haven't far to go."

Within a few minutes the car slowed to a stop. The door opened under Peter's hand.

I do not know what I expected to see, but certainly it was not what I saw. We descended before a ramshackle wooden building shrouded in darkness. It shone faintly in the glow of a wan street light some distance away. It was one of a tightly-packed row of buildings, all of which appeared to need painting badly; indeed, our goal seemed never to have been painted at all. Once we were out of the car, it slid noiselessly away and vanished into the mists which were extending long fingers into the street.

Peters led the way to the door and opened it with a key. Producing a dark lantern, he pushed his way into the place, which was apparently a kind of Chinese shop. He walked directly through the shop to the far wall. There he pressed upon something; a section of the wall fell away. He unshuttered his lantern somewhat more, revealing a hallway devoid of all ornamentation. Its walls had never known paint; cobwebs hung seemingly undisturbed for years; dust lay heavily everywhere.

Peters walked the length of the corridor and disclosed another panel opening on a short flight of stairs which led down.

Since Pons followed without hesitation, I did likewise. We were soon wandering in a tortuous maze, out of which I questioned whether even Pons would have found his way.

"I suppose this secluded gentleman restores the cobwebs and dust after someone passes through," I whispered to Pons with some sarcasm.

"Nothing is beyond him, Parker. I do not doubt it."

After what seemed an endless walk through the maze of corridors and tunnels, we came into what was more substantial construction. Soon we found ourselves walking on carpets, and presently we were ushered into a fantastically luxurious room. The floor was completely covered with a thick Persian rug; the walls were hung with what struck me as priceless Oriental draperies; the spare furnishings were opulent. But the appointments of that room were completely eclipsed by its occupant.

Facing us in the pale green glow of a shaded lamp stood the tallest Chinese I had ever seen. He was thin and very old, and his tallness was such that his shoulders were slightly hunched, as if he were conscious of his height, so unusual among his countrymen. Even more remarkable was the inquiring face turned upon us. It was yellow in color, and the lustrous, hypnotic eyes which looked in our direction were green, a kind of smoky green. The head was domed, with but a few wisps of hair in an uncut tonsure, and his body was cloaked in Mandarin robes of singular richness. About his feet scampered a marmoset which, with a shrill whistling sound, ran up the Doctor's robe and came to rest on his shoulder, where it sought its master's ear and made a succession of muted sounds.

"It is good of you to come, Mr. Pons," said the Doctor. "You have brought Dr. Parker, I see. I am not surprised."

Peters stood waiting for a gesture of dismissal which did not come.

"You will stay," said the Doctor, scarcely looking at the emissary he had sent. "It will be necessary for Mr. Pons to talk with you." He turned once again to Pons and stretched forth a claw-like hand with incredibly long fingers on which gleamed and shone Oriental rings of unusual splendor, and yet in excellent taste. "Pray be seated, gentlemen."

He himself sat down. Sitting, he made as impressive a figure as he had on his feet. The light revealed him more clearly and betrayed that the old man's thin, austere face, at the moment so friendly, could be transformed in a wink of an eye into a face of sinister menace and malefic power. His eyes, I saw now, were not smoky, but filmed, and possessed a cat-like viridescence.

"You doubtless wonder that I've sent for you," he continued, speaking directly to Pons.

"I assumed the matter must be one of pressing personal concern, or it could have been dealt with in your customary manner."

A spectral smile briefly touched the Doctor's lips. Then he inclined his head a little, as if to acknowledge a compliment. He went on.

"Only a matter of such intimacy would have brought about this visit, Mr. Pons. Let me see, is it not three years since our last encounter? I believe it is. You may not have known at that time that I have had for many years a ward, who goes by the name of Karah, though her real name is Cecily Kennet. She was the daughter of Sir Cecil Kennet, who was in the consular service at Rangoon for some time, and of a woman who was very dear to me, an Eurasian with whom Sir Cecil lived. I need hardly say I have kept Karah severely apart from my way of life, save for rare visits. She has been raised in Rangoon, and came to England for her education. She was privately tutored and attended a small college, privately endowed, in Oxford, from which she was graduated with high honors two years ago. Since then she has lived a secluded life in a house in Camberwell, though her rare appearances have excited undesirable comments on the part of certain columnists who have seen her and commented on her beauty. Last night, Mr. Pons, Karah disappeared.

"The circumstances of her disappearance are these. Karah reaches me by means of a private telephone number. She informs me that she wishes to see me, and Peters is sent to bring her here. Sometimes she comes by car, sometimes by boat from London Bridge, for the principal entrance to these quarters is off the Thames. Last night she came by car. Her purpose was to take up a private matter in which I had already given my decision. The matter in question does not concern us here. She pleaded with me to alter my decision; I did not do so. She resigned herself and made ready to return home.

"Since the night was unusually fine, she expressed the wish to return by boat to London Bridge. Peters was sent to the bridge with the car, and Karah was given in charge of Ah Sen, an old faithful retainer. Peters will tell you what happened."

He nodded to Peters, who began at once to speak. "I took the car around to the bridge, got out, and went down to the landing. It was quite late, almost midnight. There was no one to be seen. That wasn't unusual. When the boat came, Ah Sen helped Karah out. Just as they were getting out of the boat, I thought I heard someone in the shadows between us and the car. I immediately asked Ah Sen to accompany us to the car.

"Just prior to reaching the car, I saw someone standing in deep shadow, evidently waiting for us to come on. I called Ah Sen's attention to him, but just as I did so, we heard a strange whistling sound, something struck Ah Sen, and he went down. Within a few seconds, it was my turn. I had seen no one except the stranger in the shadows; I had felt no one nearby. When Li King, who drove the boat, became suspicious at Ah Sen's absence, he followed and found us lying unconscious. Karah had vanished."

Peters finished, but Pons did not immediately question him.

He sat for a few moments, slouched down in his chair, in contrast to the Doctor, with his fingertips in the familiar Gothic arch before his lips.

"You spoke of a boat and driver," he said presently. "It was a motorboat?"

"A launch, similar to those used by the river police, Mr. Pons."

"You were struck by something. Can you hazard a guess as to what it was?"

"It seemed to be like a sandbag."

"It could have been thrown?"

"Some of our men are experts at such exercises," answered Peters bluntly. "If ours can do it, so can others."

"You spoke of a whistling sound. What, in your opinion, was its source?"

"Someone signalled."

"By whistle?"

"He made the sound himself. I couldn't say that it was either by lips or an instrument."

"This arrangement – your meeting the boat at the bridge – was customary?"

"Yes, sir. It has happened many times."

"So that anyone intending to abduct the lady might reasonably be expected to know of it?"

"I'm afraid so, sir."

Perceiving that Pons had finished with Peters, the Doctor tugged at a bell-rope which hung down one wall. "You will want to speak to Ah Sen, Mr. Pons."

Ah Sen came, almost upon the old man's words. He was an old-fashioned Chinese, for he still wore a pig-tail tightly coiled on his head. He walked into the room, his hands in his sleeves, and bowed to our client, who merely waved one hand languidly in Pons' direction, whereupon Ah Sen presented himself to Pons and stood waiting.

"Ah Sen speaks perfect English, Mr. Pons," said the Doctor.

"Capital!" answered Pons. "My knowledge of Oriental languages is sadly limited. We have heard Mr. Peters' story, Ah Sen. Will you tell us yours?"

Ah Sen obliged by recounting the story Peters had told us. "Did you see the man in the shadows?"

Ah Sen hesitated. "Not exactly, sir. I was just turning to look at him when I was struck. Mr. Peters was struck directly after."

"You heard the whistle described by Mr. Peters. What sort of whistle would you say it was?"

"It was a low whistle made by mouth. I believe it was a signal."

"Could the man in the shadows have made it?"

"No, sir. The whistle came from the other side, from behind Peters."

"How long were you unconscious?"

"Perhaps five minutes. We were roused by Ki Ling."

"There were mists, perhaps fog, at the bridge?" ventured Pons.

"Yes, sir. Generally so along the river."

Pons turned to the Doctor. "So you were informed at once, Doctor? And doubtless without delay all that vast machinery which you direct was set in motion."

Once again a little smile touched our client's lips. "Yes, Mr. Pons. London was literally turned inside out. I need hardly tell you there is not a nook or cranny of the city with which some of us are not familiar. And we have means of obtaining information which are not at the disposal of the Metropolitan Police or Scotland Yard. Our efforts were not entirely without results. But those results I find most troubling. They have not turned up Karah, and but very little trace of her. Yet what has been discovered is suggestive.

"You are doubtless fully aware that my enterprises are limited neither by city nor country; they are international in scope. However modest, or however widespread, they excite rivals. In this country, in certain enterprises which shall be nameless to spare you any of those qualms of conscience to which Britons are so abnormally susceptible, I have no greater rival than Baron Alfred Corvus, known in the underworld by the name of 'Old Crow'. This man, a veteran of the war, in which he lost a limb, is almost as retiring as I am; he wears a wooden peg, which is a point of some significance, and he is as unscrupulous as the members of my organization. He will, in short, stop at nothing.

"At the moment we are engaged in a desperate struggle for control of a certain aspect of the enterprise which excites our mutual interest. He lives in a secluded villa on the banks of the Thames at Teddington. Mr. Pons, our first trace of Karah was at Lambeth Bridge; she had been taken aboard a boat there. The boat was evidently waiting there under instructions, and the moment she was aboard, it sped upstream. Our second trace was along the shore of the Thames behind the gardens of Lord Corvus's villa. There were traces of three persons – two men, one of whom wore a wooden peg, one woman, whose footprints suggest those of Karah.

"I would have proceeded against Lord Corvus without delay had it not been that I must first assure myself of Karah's safety. Thus far I have received no communication from Lord Corvus; I expected none soon; he will wait until the right hour to present his demands, that hour when he believes I have no alternative but to surrender to him. Mr. Pons, I am not entirely the inhuman monster I have been depicted; I am capable of human emotions, and I love Karah as were she my own daughter. I want you to find her, to rescue her before she can come to harm. You may name any fee you like, within or beyond reason. I do not expect you to cross swords with Lord Corvus. My lascars and dacoits will deal with him. I want you to see a likeness of Karah before you begin searching for her."

The Doctor signalled to Peters, who went over to one of the wall hangings and drew it aside by means of a rope which opened the hanging like a curtain. At the same time, he pressed a wall switch, and a shaft of light came from above to shine on the portrait which the hanging had concealed. It was a portrait by the hand of one of the most eminent British artists, of a remarkably beautiful dark-haired girl with smouldering green-blue eyes, a full, sensuous mouth which yet expressed great sensitivity, and a natural charm which the artist had caught on his canvas.

The portrait was in full length, meant to be life-size. The artist had skillfully imparted a subtle sense of the mystery which tradition has it is integral in the Orient, as if to symbolize her background. Her cheekbones were high, testifying to her Eurasian origin; her skin seemed to have a lustre. She was not fair, yet she was not dark, rather somewhere between, like a girl overlong in the sun.

"Is she not beautiful?" asked our client.

"Extraordinarily so," agreed Pons.

"Please memorize her features, Mr. Pons."

"I have done so. It would be difficult to forget them."

Our client signalled again, and instantly the light went out, the portrait vanished behind the wall hanging.

"I trust you're prepared to take up the chase without delay. The launch is ready for you. Peters and Ki Ling will take you and Dr. Parker to the grounds of the villa occupied by Lord Corvus."

"I came prepared for any course," answered Pons.

"Good. When you have information for me, you will know how to reach me."

Our client took leave of us as if he had granted audience. Peters conducted us away from the Doctor's quarters. Once more we entered a maze of passageways, but now our direction was steadily downward, down pairs and trios of steps, down ramps, until at last we came out into the night on the bank of the Thames not far above the West India Docks. There a launch waited with Ki Ling, who was as Western as Ah Sen had been Oriental in appearance.

The hour was now well past midnight. The broad Thames under the ever-moving mists which shrouded it was impressive and beautiful. We swung out into the night-girt river and went up into the city, past moored ships and lesser craft, waiting out the night in spectral silence – barges, sailboats with sails furled, sea-going ships all riding the tides. The sound of our motor, though it was muffled, seemed a shattering noise.

Despite the unfamiliarity of our course, I had little difficulty finding our bearings. In but a short time, we passed under the East London Railway bridge; not far beyond came the first of the major bridges, the Tower, and thereafter, in regular succession, London Bridge, Southby, Blackfriars, Waterloo, Charing Cross, Westminster, Lambeth, and Vauxhall. It was not until we had gone beyond Putney that I turned to Pons, for by this time we were well up the river, several miles from our place of embarkation.

My companion apparently did not share my uneasiness. He sat with his angular chin cupped in one long-fingered hand; his eyes were half-closed; a ghostly smile lay on his lips. Altogether, his expression was curiously provocative. I glanced at Peters. He was watching me.

"Is it much farther?" I asked.

"Some miles," said Peters.

"You know very well where Teddington is," said Pons. "It is a little less than twenty miles. Say, an hour's journey. If you feel you must rejoin Mrs. Parker, we can let you off at Wandsworth."

"At the moment we seem to be passing Fulham Palace," I said coldly. "We passed under Wandsworth some little while ago."

Pons looked toward Peters. "I'm afraid my companion dislikes to think I may be lending my modest abilities to what would seem to be warfare between two agents engaged in a highly dubious and potentially illegal enterprise."

"I quite understand," said Peters, bestowing a nettling glance of sympathy on me.

I said no more, but gave my attention to the river. I was annoyed by Pons' amiable docility before a man like the Doctor, who was admittedly on the left side of the law, though I well knew that Pons would point out with that cold logic of his that his client's present problem was not predicated upon his status in the underworld of London.

Our goal was now soon within easy reach. The launch's taciturn driver cut speed and turned toward shore; the noise of our approach was reduced to a muffled throbbing. Close to the shore the motor was entirely cut off. The launch nosed in to the soft bank with scarcely a sound.

The area we were to examine was not far away. Once more Peters' dark lantern came into play, while Ki Ling stood guard to prevent any surprise from the house beyond the gardens, though it was plain, even in the faintly starlit night, that the villa of Lord Corvus was some distance away, shrouded by trees.

Pons took the dark lantern from our guide and examined the shore. Imprinted in the soft earth between the river's edge and the thicker lawn which thinned down toward the water was a series of footprints. At least three people had walked there. The prints were of a woman wearing high-heeled slippers, a man with a wooden peg for leg, and a third man. Pons crouched with the light flooding the footprints, his glance darting from one to another of them. No one uttered a sound.

Pons shut off the light and rose.

"Where can I reach you, Mr. Peters?"

"Perhaps it would be better to set an hour for an appointment."

"Very good. I shall expect to be back in my quarters by six o'clock tonight," said Pons. "It is now almost three in the morning. Dr. Parker and I will carry on from here without you. Pray assure the Doctor that I have every hope of some word for him by late tonight. With your permission, I'll keep your dark lantern."

Though Peters was somewhat taken aback, he acquiesced in Pons' surprising decision. The Chinese was evidently accustomed to taking orders without question; he was impassive before Pons' wish to go on alone. They returned to the launch and pushed out into the Thames to return the way we had come.

"Pons, this is madness!" I cried.

"Dear me, how readily the diagnosis comes to you," clucked Pons.

"Next thing I suppose you'll want to break into the house!" I went on, disregarding his levity.

"I need hardly ask for what reason. To rescue the fair damsel, of course!"

"What else?" I demanded in exasperation. "Pons, it is surely too great a risk to take."

"Pray be reassured, Parker. I have no intention of storming the house. The girl is not there. If Lord Corvus is everything the Doctor says he is, his villa is surely the last place he would keep Karah. No, I fancy we must look elsewhere for the Doctor's ward. But, come, you saw the footprints. They did not seem to you unusual?"

"In what way?"

"Look again."

Pons directed the light of the dark lantern to the prints. I examined them with as much care as the circumstances permitted, though I was not without some apprehension lest we be seen from the house and challenged.

"They are precisely what we were led to expect."

Pons' voice was quizzical when he answered. "I cannot determine whether that is sprung from an intelligent application of the facts, which from you is sheer genius, my dear fellow, or whether it is merely what I had expected. These footprints convey nothing to you?"

"Nothing except that a young woman wearing high-heeled slippers, a peg-legged man, and one other walked here, presumably coming off a boat of some kind," I replied.

"If you look closely, you will observe several instructive points," said Pons. "Does it not seem to you that the print of the peg is unduly uneven? As if its wearer were uncertain on his peg?"

"He might well be," I retorted, "if he were carrying the young lady."

"He could hardly have been carrying her if she were on her feet," said Pons dryly. "Moreover, if these two were carrying anything at all, their prints would go far deeper. No, Parker, whoever walked here carried nothing, far less another human being. Do not these prints seem unusually light?"

"The men who made them were not heavy."

"That is a remarkably sage deduction," said my companion with the ghost of laughter in his voice. "The size of the shoe here seems to be not more than eight and a half. That is a small foot for a man, is it not?"

"Well, it is surely below the average."

"The other would appear to be somewhat larger. Yet it is indented no further. And, save for the indentation of the heels, the prints which are presumably Karah's are uniform with the others." He brought the light closer. "Does it not seem to you that the prints have been rained upon?"

"Impossible!" I cried. "Rain has not fallen since late afternoon day before yesterday. Our client's ward was abducted last night."

"Do not these prints suggest anything more to you, Parker? Consider – they are well up from the water's edge."

"Well, that is elementary," I retorted. "The boat came in on the tide."

"Exactly," said Pons dryly. He shut off the dark lantern. "I daresay we can do no more here. Let us just make our way to the nearest street. Unfortunately, our likelihood of finding a cab at this hour is not too great. But we shall persevere, never fear."

"Pons, this is like looking for a needle in a haystack!" I cried. "The Doctor's agents have already scoured London. Where do you intend to go at this hour?"

"Where every sensible man would want to go," he answered. "To bed. Mrs. Johnson will be delighted to serve you breakfast once again. At daybreak, we can resume our search for the Doctor's ward."

All my expostulations fell on deaf ears. And to my asking to know why, if he meant only to return to 7B Praed Street, he had dismissed the launch, Pons replied only with his customary,

"You know my methods, Parker – you've known them for many years; you need only apply them."

Early morning found us once more on the Thames. Long before I had crawled somewhat tiredly from my bed to face the honest joy of the good, long-suffering lady who had for so long been my landlady as well as Pons', my companion had arranged for a launch to wait on us at Westminster Bridge. The aspect of the river was totally different by day from the eerie, almost sinister river at night, though at both times the Thames flowed along with its own majestic beauty.

I wasted no time asking Pons where he intended to go. I had learned from experience that Pons could be as uncommunicative on the scene as he could be garrulous at the conclusion of a case. Pons himself took the wheel of the launch, and it was soon evident to me that he was retracing our route of the previous night. At the breakfast table he had been poring over detailed maps of the region from Kew Gardens to Teddington; I would discover in good time whether he intended to go.

Pons' goal appeared at first to be the grounds of the Teddington villa of Lord Corvus, but in this I was mistaken, for he fell short of it, turning from the Thames at Kew into the Brent River. We soon found ourselves on the Grand Junction Canal, going through the locks at Brentford. We were now in a stretch of water which was as busy with the movement of boats as the Thames, and Pons reduced the speed of our craft. Here and there were stretches of rushes and weeds, and from time to time the canal bore the aspect of a country stream, colorful with the "monkey boats" so common to British canals.

Well past Brentford, almost within sight of the Brill's Bridge Junction and the Toll Office, Pons cut out the motor and lay in close to one bank of the canal.

"Do you not sometimes think that the canals of England are not fully appreciated?" he asked suddenly. "These are friendly waters, and I hold that the little bridges, the locks, the colored boats, as well as the inhabitants of the banks – I have reference principally to our animal friends – possess a charm which is as much the essence of the English countryside as the rolling downs and the green shires."

Doubtless Pons caught sight of the expression of bewilderment which must have reflected my feelings.

"Oh, come, Parker, brace up! I have by no means taken leave of my senses," he said.

"Forgive me," I answered. "I was under the impression that we were searching for the Doctor's ward."

"There is always time for that," said Pons, waving his hand airily. "I have a fancy this bright, sunny morning, to inform myself with the charm of the quaint boats which ply these waters. How better to acquaint one's self with the less-known aspects of England? How those lilacs hang over the water there!"

"Well, there's one of the 'monkey boats' now."

"The *Shenton*, is it not? Let us just run long shore here. I want to board her."

Thereupon Pons suited his actions to his words. There was nothing for it but that Pons must board the *Shenton*, examine her appointments, and while away time in conversation about the craft with the owner and his wife, bluff, hearty people, who were aboard. Moreover, the *Shenton* was but the beginning; thereafter as we proceeded up the canal past the West Drayton Railway station, past the lock and toll office at Cowley, toward Uxbridge Lock, it was the *Nelson*, the *Image*, the *Ivy*, the *Eve*, the *Ganpat*, the *Nottingham*, and at last, past Uxbridge, the *Lapwing*, all of which seemed as alike as peas in a pod, save for their variation in colors, each of their owners seeming to vie with one another for the brightest and sauciest of hues in which to decorate their boats, though most of the "monkey boat" people wore the traditional black and green cord of the canal folk.

Pons spent no less than five hours in this diversion. He talked with the men and women of the craft. Sometimes they were husband and wife. On occasion a boy or a girl was on board as well, and on the *Lapwing* Pons spent an unwarranted time prodding a shy, grimy-faced young fellow into conversation, provoking him with questions until the captain came along and told Pons his "nevvie" didn't know much about canal boats, having just come aboard two days before. By the time Pons had finished, it was mid-afternoon.

When we were on our way back toward the Thames, I reflected bitterly that Pons was playing a deep game. "No doubt," I said, "you've been conducting an assiduous search for the young lady, and very probably you know precisely where she is."

"I do indeed," he replied soberly. "But no more than you, for you saw her as well."

"I? Surely you are joking!" But, no, Pons would not have jested so. "The butty girl with the Ivy," I guessed.

Pons shook his head. "You are wide of the mark."

"The extra woman on the *Nottingham*."

"You're coming closer, in a sense."

"Ah!" I cried, exasperated. "Of course it was the 'nevvie' on the *Lapwing*. That was where you stopped looking."

"Elementary, my dear Parker!" said Pons, grinning.

"But why didn't you take her?"

"My assignment, I believe, was primarily to find her," said Pons. "I have done so. I was also to 'rescue' her; it did not seem to me that the young lady required that service."

At six o'clock promptly, the Doctor's emissary presented himself at our quarters. Peters came in expectantly in answer to Pons' invitation, and stood waiting near the door.

"And the Doctor – how is he?" asked Pons.

"Anticipating your report."

"I shall have to have his private telephone number, also your keys," said Pons crisply, "so that I can call on him tonight at eleven."

"I'll take you to him, Mr. Pons."

Pons' eyes twinkled. "I rather think not, Mr. Peters. By that time, unless I am very much mistaken, you will be putting considerable distance between the Doctor and yourself." Pons ignored the expression of perplexity which crossed Peters' face. "Tell me, are you prepared to leave the country? There is a flight from Croydon at nine, I believe. Unless I am in further error, you are very probably ready to leave for America at a moment's notice, together with the young lady who has been the object of your affections, despite the steadfast opposition of her guardian. We left her, by the way, all unsuspecting on the *Lapwing* at Uxbridge."

Peters' face betrayed a gamut of emotions – fear, amazement, and finally the broad smile of pure pleasure. "Mr. Pons, you are indeed a remarkable man," he said.

"On the contrary, my dear young fellow, your trail was as broad as the Thames itself – except," he added with a wry smile, "to those so confounded by the intrigues of London's underworld that the simple escapes them. I mean no disrespect to the Doctor's servants, who are superior in their own devious ways. A little more attention to matters pertinent to the tides and the weather might have made the footprints near Lord Corvus's villa more convincing. I fear, too, that a peg-leg strapped to your knee hardly permits an expert performance. But come, you will need money. Name any sum you like – I'll add it to my fee when I see the Doctor."

"Must you tell him?"

"I must. I fancy his anger will cool in good time. But until it does, I suggest you have enough respect for his methods to put the ocean between you."

Peter's response was in character. He took his departure immediately, leaving with Pons the Doctor's private telephone number – which my companion duly entered in his files for future reference – his keys, and the Doctor's car at the kerb. He did not wait to learn how Pons had hit upon his trail. My own astonishment, however, brooked no denial.

"The solution devolved upon an old tenet of mine," said Pons. "The success of circumstantial evidence depends wholly upon the correct interpretation. There were several manifest flaws in the evidence offered us. Either Lord Corvus abducted Karah in order to blackmail the Doctor, or he did not. No one seemed to consider that anyone other had done the abduction, and the 'clues' had been carefully placed for the Doctor's investigation. But even before we set out up the Thames, one question intruded insistently. If Lord Corvus had abducted Karah, surely there would have been a more opportune time to do so!

"She could have been lured from the house in some manner; her movements might have been watched pending an opportunity to take her from the Camberwell house; the abduction, taking place as it did, almost presupposed some informant in the Doctor's service, or, on the other hand, the most elaborate plans to govern every possibility, since Karah did not follow any invariable course in her way to and from Limehouse. What was most incredible, however, was the supposedly damning factor: if Lord Corvus were the author of the abduction, he himself would certainly not have appeared on or near the scene. So at the outset, it seemed to me apparent that Lord Corvus was completely innocent of complicity in Karah's abduction.

"The Doctor himself offered the key to the situation. He said, if you recall, that Karah's purpose in visiting him was 'to take up a private matter' in which he had already given his decision. She wished him to alter that decision; he did not do so. At his failure to do so, we may suppose, a plan of Peters' own was put into effect. What that 'private matter' was, I have no doubt. Karah wished to marry Peters. Indeed, Peters' presence in the Doctor's organization was predicated solely upon Karah; he wanted to be near her. They had met in Oxford. Peters told us he was graduated from Oxford two years ago; the Doctor mentioned of his ward that she had attended a smaller college in Oxford, which she had left two years ago.

"So the abduction was not an abduction at all. It was done with Karah's complicity. That alone explained all the relevant factors, and the moment it occurred to me that it was so, the elements of the puzzle fell into place with clock-work precision. The footprints were entirely the work of Peters. They had been put in at high tide a day or two before; the wavering print of the peg was made by someone quite unaccustomed to wearing such an object. The wooden-legged man's footprints, though Peters wore a larger shoe on his free foot to make them, showed the same unevenness as Peters' own prints; so did those of Karah, which Peters made with her shoes – the prints were all made by someone with a limping defect. Peters has a slightly defective leg, as you saw.

"The stage was thus set for the final act. If the Doctor failed to alter his decision, the *Lapwing* was waiting. We had evidence to show that Karah had taken to the river at Lambeth Bridge. She was probably as aware as Peters of how thoroughly the Doctor's men could comb London, of how many petty informants might be at his beck and call. If she left the boat at all, it would necessarily be for some place where she might be reasonably safe. She could have gone either up river or down; manifestly, the risk was too great to go down to the sea, even for some possible berth on a boat there, for the river-front from Wapping and Limehouse is the Doctor's especial province. It must therefore be up the Thames, and what place more unlikely offered itself than one of the 'monkey boats' common to the canals? Arrangements had unquestionably been made well in advance.

"Once the conflict between the Doctor and Lord Corvus had been joined, Karah and Peters would slip away. The attack at the bridge was simply staged. There was no 'dark shadow' standing offside; Ah Sen imagined that he saw it because Peters said it was there. Peters himself made the whistling sound and struck Ah Sen, after which Karah knocked out Peters to divert any suspicion from him. Thereafter she acted with singular dispatch and went straight to the *Lapwing* by boat. Once there, she became the nephew of the captain and his wife, who were in Peters' pay."

"I shouldn't like to be in Peters' shoes," I said, recalling the malefic menace of our mysterious client.

"Oh, I daresay the Doctor may find it easier to resign himself to Karah's marriage than to her 'abduction' and its possible consequences." Pons smiled. "I rather think our client may not have been without some apprehension of the reason for his ward's disappearance."

"Then why trouble you, Pons?"

"Our Oriental friends set great store on not 'losing face'. The Doctor has a reputation as a swift and implacable avenger. Far better that Peters and Karah should escape me, than that he should be forced to save face at their expense. He is not above either cunning or a sense of humor."

As urgently as I needed to return to my practise, I would not let Pons go alone to that incredible apartment deep in the maze of Limehouse that night. He did not telephone for an appointment until after the flight from Croydon had taken place. He made his way back to the masking storefront by car without difficulty, and he found his path among the maze of corridors with a facility that chagrined me.

Once more we sat before the sinister and impressive Chinese, who wore simultaneously the hauteur of a man of vastly superior intelligence and the humility of a supplicant at the door of Pons' power of ratiocination.

"You have found Karah, Mr. Pons?" were his first words.

"Found her – and lost her."

"Lord Corvus?"

Pons' eyes challenged his in a long, searching glance. Then he said. "I think you, too, knew that Lord Corvus himself would have had none but the author's part in the abduction of your ward."

Pons told him how he had found Karah, and where she had gone.

"So I lose both of them," said the Doctor with a weary smile. "They should be happy with each other. Peters has enterprise – the staged footprints were a little, shall we say, naive? – but on the whole, he has vision and ambition. I shall not forgive them, for they have done nothing to command forgiveness. But may they know this?" He shook his domed head gently from side to side, while his marmoset chattered at his ear. "No, never. It was not good that Karah should be so close to this world of mine. It was not meant for her. Let them go to a new world. I shall miss her grievously, Mr. Pons – but I am content to know this is what is best for her."

He paid Pons' fee without question.

Months later, when I had occasion to call at 7B, I found on the crowded mantel a set of little Chinese ivory and ebony figurines inlaid with jewels of incalculable value, in each of which the letter "F" had been engraved with consummate skill, a further expression of gratitude from the incredible occupant of that secret hideaway in Limehouse.

XII

THE ADVENTURE OF THE LITTLE HANGMAN

"My nature abhors a vacuum," said Solar Pons that evening, as he stepped into our room at the inn in Ilfracombe, "and such a holiday as this is indeed nothing less. Happily, unless I am very much mistaken, we shall soon find ourselves once again taking up one of those little problems in human behavior which never cease to enlist my deepest interest."

"Why do you say so?" I asked, for we had come to Ilfracombe at my insistence to walk some of the most charming coast paths in all England, because Pons' recent activity in the puzzles of the Lost Metternich and the Hats of M. Dulac had seemed to me to tire him unduly.

Pons chuckled. "I fear I may disappoint you, Parker. I have no great feat of deduction to offer. Only a moment ago, as I came in, I saw a constable get off his cycle just outside. Perhaps it was only vanity which suggested to me that it was more than mere coincidence that a constable in some haste should be alighting at these quarters just when we are in residence."

He cocked his head and added, "But I think not." Then, as a knock well upon the door, he called out cheerily, "Come in, Constable, come in! Pray don't stand on ceremony."

The door opened smartly. A fresh-faced young constable did indeed stand with almost military stiffness on our threshold.

"Mr. Solar Pons," he said. "Constable Ronald Borrow, Combe Martin."

Pons rubbed his hands together in pleasure, his eyes merry. "Pray come in and sit down. Constable Borrow! A delightfully suggestive name. I am fond of George Borrow; no one has ever written more effectively of wild Wales." He smiled. "But you haven't come to discuss literature."

"No, Mr. Pons. There's been a murder."

"Ah, Constable, you have no idea how sweetly your words fall upon my ear, after three days spent with the beauties of the North Devon coast. Let us hear about it."

"I telephoned to Scotland Yard, sir. Inspector Jamison told me you were here. So I came directly in the hope that you might lend us a hand. The murdered man is Kingsley Pollitt."

Pons' eyes sparkled. "The murderer of Helen Blayre! Released last month by order of the Home Secretary on a legal technicality grown from some question about the trial proceedings. 'Miscarriage of justice,' he called it. Pollitt served ten years, I believe."

"Yes, sir. But there was no miscarriage of justice, Mr. Pons. He did her in, no doubt about that. A brute of a man – hot-tempered, too. He came to Combe Martin, back to his half-brother's house. John told us at noon today that he hadn't been in last night, but no one was anxious about him. I suppose most of the people in Combe Martin just hoped he'd go away and not come back – he made them uneasy. You can understand that, sir. Well, sir, we didn't organize a search – no reason to do so. Along about sundown this evening, two boys found him. He was lying well up one of the headlands along the coast. You may know it – we call it the Little Hangman. It rises against the Great Hangman, next the sea. Mr. Pons, he was hanged!"

"Found guilty, condemned to death, reprieved, freed – and finally hanged anyway," murmured Pons. "John, I take it, is the half-brother? He had no objection to Kingsley's return to live with him?"

"I asked him that, Mr. Pons – just after Kingsley came back. He said Kingsley had no one else to go to; he couldn't close his door to him. Besides, John Pollitt is a bookish sort of man. He doesn't go out much, and I'd guess Kingsley's being there wouldn't make much difference to him as long as there was no active interference. But we ought not to take time talking here, Mr. Pons. The body's been left just as it was found. I thought you might like to look at the ground." A little self-consciously, he added. "I'm somewhat familiar with your methods, sir."

"My chronicler," said Pons, with a glance in my direction, "has done his best to glorify my little exploits, which are nothing more than the proper use of a well developed faculty of observation coupled with common sense deduction – mere exercises in logic, Constable. Very well, lead on. We'll find a conveyance somewhere in Ilfracombe, no doubt, and you can pack your cycle alongside."

I made but the semblance of a protest, reminding Pons that he had, after all, come for a holiday.

"The game's afoot, Parker," he replied, "and infinitely preferable to any holiday. Come along!"

On the way to Combe Martin, Pons prodded the constable to refresh his memory of the murder of Helen Blayre.

"I wasn't with the police then, Mr. Pons," said Constable Borrow. "But I remember it very well. Helen Blayre was an orphan, the ward of her uncle, Tom Plomer. Tom raised her brother Ned, too. She was a pretty sort of girl, not exactly what you'd call beautiful, sir, but not plain, either. Very lively, she was. Why, she was up and about the Little Hangman like a bird, and she knew the coast paths like anything. She was always to be found out there, with a book or a sheet of drawing paper or both. She was great friends with the Pollitts.

"I think, as a matter of fact, there was a distant relationship by marriage. John never went out too much, even as a younger man, but Helen was about with Kingsley here and there. It was understood they were going to be married – then there was that letter she wrote Kingsley, turning him down. He lost his head and strangled her in a fury. Hadn't meant to do it, but the brute didn't know his own strength. He was just in a rage and took it out on her – blind, you might say. But he was always a selfish man, and thought nought of anybody other."

"As I recall it, that murder took place outside, too, didn't it?"

"On the Little Hangman, yes, sir. Kingsley came on her there after she sent him the letter. They had words. He lost his temper. One thing led to another and he killed her. He ran for it, but not far. We found him drunk at the pub."

"Had she returned his ring?" asked Pons reflectively.

"Oh, it wasn't like that, Mr. Pons. These are simple people. There wasn't any ring, sir. Nothing like that. It was just something you understood. She walked out with Kingsley and she wasn't seen walking out with anybody else. She was his girl, as you might say."

"One would have thought Pollitt would have gone anywhere but Combe Martin, after Dartmoor."

"Yes, sir. But no, back here he came. Surly and moody, as always."

"The girl's uncle and brother? What of them?" asked Pons.

"Both still alive, Mr. Pons. Tom's about sixty now; Ned's close to forty." In the light from a passing car, the constable looked troubled, as if he anticipated an unpleasant task. "We'll have to talk to 'em, I have no doubt."

"All in good time, Constable."

In but a little while – for the distance was scarcely half a dozen miles – we had reached Combe Martin and were on our way along the path that led to the slope of the Little Hangman, which rose up for over seven hundred feet east of the village. A waxing moon lay low in the west, and over against the eastern sky, towering higher than our destination, loomed the Great Hangman, dark on heaven. Constable Borrow's lantern lit the path, and Pons strode along with far more vigor than he had shown during our casual holiday hikes on the coast from Ilfracombe, his Inverness spreading almost batlike in the light wind blowing from the direction of Bristol Channel.

Part way up the slope, another constable stood with a lantern on guard lest unauthorized persons pass by. A third stood virtually on the crown of the height, his lantern shining like an intimate star toward which we toiled up the gradual slope away from the last houses and fields of the combe. As we came toward our goal, the constable on duty there turned his light earthward.

There in a pool of light lay the body of Kingsley Pollitt. The dead man lay on his back, arms flung wide, his sightless eyes turned toward the stars. He was once, clearly, a thick-set, powerful man, of medium height to shortness of stature, but he had lost much of his onetime weight and his clothing fitted him poorly. He was fully dressed, except for a tie; his open shirt revealed the mark of the rope which had hanged him. At least two days' growth of beard was visible, even against the discoloration of his face, which I knew was a deep blue, though in this artificial light it looked sickeningly grey, so that Pollitt had the appearance of a mulatto.

The tableau held but a moment. Then Pons reached for Constable Borrow's lantern.

"If you please, Constable. Thank you."

He swept the light around in a wide circle, and up and down the slope.

"A singular lack," he murmured. "From what was he hanged? There is no tree within the range of the light."

"No, Mr. Pons. We observed that. We can only conjecture that he was hanged elsewhere."

"And brought here. Then there would be signs."

He began to search the ground, earnestly. He threw off his Inverness and got down upon his knees, moving around the body in steadily widening circles for a while, then crawling back down the way we had come. He went for some distance down the slope before he came to his feet and returned to where we waited.

"Something has been dragged toward this spot," he said, "and I submit it could not have been other than the body. There are barrow marks further down, some fresh, some older. Perhaps Combe Martin's reputation as a once wealthy town because of extensive silver and lead mining in the vicinity quite possibly spurs occasional native efforts toward the discovery of metal forgotten over the centuries, eh, Constable?"

"It might happen, Mr. Pons, though I'd consider it unlikely."

"So then, if Pollitt were hanged elsewhere, there is not only premeditation but also some special significance in his body's being brought to the Little Hangman."

"Mr. Pons, his crime..."

"Precisely. He murdered in the sight of heaven; so let him die there. But we have no evidence that he did die here, only that he was brought here. Have a look at him, will you, Parker?"

I examined the dead man as well as I could by the combined light of the two lanterns. Everything I saw was consistent with death by hanging. There was, however, a contusion on the back of his head, to which I called Pons' attention.

"Could it have been made in the course of transporting his body to this place?" asked Pons.

"It was made before death."

Pons smiled. "Stunned, then hanged. Most interesting. The goal was hanging, not death by any other means, for the man who stunned him could have dispatched him in any way he chose. He elected this imaginative if cumbersome method, as if to carry out the justice Pollitt escaped. Ah, what have we here?"

As he spoke, he darted forward, seized hold of what appeared to be a smooth twig projecting from beneath the body, and pulled it forth. From his fingers dangled a carved miniature gibbet.

"This little problem grows more fascinating with each moment," said Pons. "What do you make of this, Constable?"

Constable Borrow's face was lugubrious. "I'm afraid, Mr. Pons, that it puts yet another light on the matter."

"We are meant to believe, plainly, that Pollitt got what was coming to him. The motive for his death would appear to be vengeance – or simply justice, in the mind of his murderer."

"There's more than that, Mr. Pons," said the constable. "You may remember Mr. Hernshaw, the executioner?"

"That short, cherubic little man who was so disappointed at not being able to hang Pollitt!"

"Yes, Mr. Pons. He was unwise enough to say so for the newspapers, and he was retired soon afterward. You see, Mr. Pons, Mr. Hernshaw, too, is from the vicinity. He now lives in Combe Martin, where he does a little business, I am bound to say, selling wood carvings."

Pons could not repress a chuckle. "A travesty, Constable, a travesty! A hill and a man – we now have two little hangmen and a hanged man. And three named men among probably a score or more who would not be sorry to see Kingsley Pollitt dead, and might have helped him shuffle off this mortal coil!"

He turned the full light of the lantern upon the carving in his hand. It was done with broad, powerful strokes of the knife. It had a certain malignancy, a powerful suggestiveness, as no doubt it was intended to have. It was carved out of some soft wood, the identity of which was not immediately apparent.

"A professional wood carver, our Mr. Hernshaw?" murmured Pons. "But this is not the work of a professional, on the face of it."

"Unless it was meant to look unlike the work of one," I offered.

Pons agreed. "That is a point I fear we dare not overlook."

He returned to the body and fell to scrutinizing the earth anew. For awhile he crouched there in puzzled concentration. Then he rose and came back to where we stood.

"Several people have walked here," he said. "Perhaps the hanging of Kingsley Pollitt was in the nature of a community effort. One set of tracks seems to be that of a short, heavy man, walking with a rolling gait."

"That would be Hernshaw," said Constable Borrow.

Pons nodded thoughtfully. "I take it," he went on crisply, "You examined Pollitt's pockets?"

"Yes, Mr. Pons. There was nothing of significance. Some matches, four shillings, six pence, a pack of cigarettes, and a newspaper clipping on which he had marked two prospective jobs. It would seem that he had intended to find a job in Bristol, for both were offered there."

Pons stood for a moment looking thoughtfully down at the body. Then he turned away, saying, "I daresay we've finished here."

"Will you stay the night in Combe Martin, Mr. Pons?" asked Borrow.

"I think not. Let us just have a look at the items found in his pocket – and, if possible, a glance at the dossier on Helen Blayre's murder. Then we'll return to Ilfracombe and come back here in the morning."

Though the hour was midnight when we reached our quarters in Ilfracombe, Pons was far from ready for bed. He had brought with him from Combe Martin the newspaper clipping found in

Pollitt's pocket, and a photostat of the letter Helen Blayre had written Pollitt shortly before he had strangled her. He sat for some time beside the lamp, studying both of these things, his keen grey eyes veiled, his lean, hawk-like face deep in thought.

The clipping from a Bristol paper could not be construed otherwise than it was. It was barely large enough to contain the four advertisements among which Pollitt had marked two, with the numerals "1" and "2", suggesting the order in which he meant to apply for a job. The first notice which he had marked called for construction workers, and the second offered a place in an ironmonger's shop.

I protested at his long scrutiny. "It's plain to be seen that there's nothing but what meets the eye in that."

"I fancy you're right, Parker," he agreed amiably. "Yet I find a trifle of significance about it. It suggests nothing to you?"

"No, except that Pollitt meant to remove himself from Combe Martin."

"Precisely. For a month nothing happened to him in Combe Martin. Then, just as he was about to put himself quite possibly beyond his murderer's reach by going to Bristol, he was slain. I submit this suggests that his murderer had planned to kill him from the time of his first appearance in Combe Martin, and was only biding his time. Pollitt's intention to leave forced him to act." He dropped the clipping and turned to the photostat. "What do you make of this?"

The letter poor Helen Blayre had written was simplicity itself.

> "Dear Kingsley,
>
> "I know I can never marry you, and it would be dishonest to pretend otherwise. The way of life you offer me is not the same as the one we have planned. You were good to ask me, but, I am sorry, it cannot be. I wanted to write you this to spare us both next time we

> meet, so there wouldn't be any misunderstanding. We have always got along so well, I would not want this to spoil that. Let us forget that you ever spoke to me and go on as always.
>
> "In affectionate friendship – Helen."

"That is plain as a pikestaff," I said.

"I'm glad to hear you say so," replied Pons. "There are one or two little points about it that intrigue me, however. It doesn't seem to you curiously worded?"

"Oh, come, Pons," I cried, "it's nothing more than what it's meant to be. It tells us that Pollitt proposed a way of life which did not appeal to her as the ideal marriage; so she rejected him. The letter is absolutely straightforward, but I suppose it would hurt the vanity of a low type of human being like Pollitt. Obviously, they had planned something other than what he now suggested, and she couldn't agree with the change he proposed to make in their plans."

"It is always refreshing to listen to you, Parker. You have a reliable factor for reducing matters to their simplest common denominator."

"What can you find in that innocuous letter in conflict with what I've said?" I challenged him.

"I submit there are various openings. For instance, Miss Blayrc wrote: 'it would be dishonest to pretend' that she could marry Kingsley. But, if we're to believe Constable Borrow, did she not do so for some time before she wrote this letter? Secondly, what is this 'way of life' that is now so different from the 'one we have planned'? Note, please, she writes 'have', not 'had'. A minor point, true, but I cannot help calling it to your attention. Next, she proposes that both of them 'forget' that Kingsley asked him to marry her, and 'go on as always'. Now, then, how did they 'go on' before? I find that question provocative."

"Ah, Pons, you are so given to finding hidden meanings in everything that simplicity confounds you," I said.

Pons chuckled delightedly. "On the contrary, I agree wholeheartedly with you, Parker. This is a simple, straightforward missive. I am always astounded to discover how the simplest communications can be misunderstood and misinterpreted. Is that not, perhaps, symptomatic of some basic flaw in mankind? Semantic confusion abounds in this world." He put the letter down and turned out the lamp. "Let us sleep on it. We may have a clearer view in the morning."

Pons routed me out at dawn and, after a hasty breakfast, insisted upon walking to Combe Martin. Thus it was almost two hours after dawn when we reached the village. Once there, Pons went immediately to the little police station and returned the effects he had studied the previous night. Constable Borrow was at the station, and with him we set out to call on John Pollitt, for Pons had expressed a wish to look at the rooms the victim had occupied.

Combe Martin by daylight seemed somewhat drab, but it was hardly uninteresting. It lay in a long cluster of houses, many of them very old, which ran for over a mile along the combe to the beach. At one time it had been a wealthy town, as a result of the silver and lead which had been mined there, but the height of the mining was more than a century in the past, and what had once been grandeur had now faded. Though the surrounding country was beautiful enough, only a few objects of interest remained in the village to tempt the traveler, such as the eight-chimneyed Pack of Cards Inn, built on a cruciform plan, and the Standing Stone on Knap Down, northeast of the village. Its chief architectural beauty, however, was the church of St. Peter ad Vincula, which stood proudly with its hundred foot high west tower, flying buttresses, battlements, two tiers of gargoyles, and crocketed pinnacles, which Pons admired as we went by.

The Pollitt house stood on the edge of the village, near the beach. It was a very old, white-walled building with an ancient roof. Like so many Combe Martin houses, it was of three floors, and its ground floor was partly sunk into the earth. And John Pollitt, for all that he resembled a fading headmaster in a girls' school, had the undeniable appearance of belonging to the house.

He was a genteel, soft-voiced fellow, wearing a thin beard, and his rooms were crowded with books of all descriptions, occupying not only the tall shelves but scattered on chairs, tables, and even the floor. His pale blue eyes looked out apologetically from behind his spectacles, studying Pons with polite interest as Constable Borrow introduced him.

"Mr. Pons wants to ask a few questions, Mr. Pollitt," said the constable. "Just the usual enquiry."

"Of course. I understand."

Pons lost no time. "How soon after he was set free did your half-brother come here to live, Mr. Pollitt?"

"I believe he came straight on."

"You interposed no objection?"

Pollitt hesitated slightly. "He had nowhere else to go, sir," he said then. "After all, I'm his brother. I couldn't turn him out."

"You knew how people felt about him?"

"Yes, I knew. Still – " he shrugged " – there's enough of man's inhumanity to man without my adding my bit."

"He never showed any fear of his fellow townsmen?"

"None, sir. He was a strong man. Prison hadn't improved his temper."

"I should like to take a look at his quarters, if I may."

"Certainly, Mr. Pons. Come this way."

Pollitt descended to the ground floor and into one large room, beautiful with the age of its whitewashed walls and raftered ceiling.

"Nothing has been disturbed here. It's just as he left it," said Pollitt.

Pons stood for a few moments in the middle of the room, looking at the cot which had served Kingsley Pollitt as his last bed; at the table, where, presumably, he took his meals; at the two chairs, which were certainly a century old, and the product of someone's unskilled hand.

"How old is this building, Mr. Pollitt?" asked Pons.

"I believe it dates to the time of Edward I."

"It is certainly well preserved. Are those the original beams?"

"Yes, sir."

Pons pulled up a chair and mounted it to scrutinize the rafters. "Remarkable," he murmured. "How this wood endures! And the room is not at all damp."

"No, sir. The walls are at least a foot thick, Mr. Pons. We keep it dry."

"'We'?"

"Forgive me. I do not customarily live alone. I have a handyman who lives with me – George Potter – but I had to let him go because he can't – couldn't – abide Kingsley. I suppose now he'll be back."

Pons turned once again to the beams. After he had looked at several of them, he gave his attention to the remainder of the room, examining the floor with exceptional care on his hands and knees. But there was singularly little to see. The room was in good order – doubtless Kingsley Pollitt had learned how to keep his quarters in prison. One chair stood at an angle a little way from the table, as if it had been pushed back in haste and not replaced when last Kingsley had got up.

"Tell me, Mr. Pollitt, had your brother any intimation that someone still bore him a murderous grudge?" asked Pons, getting up from his knees.

"He told me one night he had had a warning to leave Combe Martin. It was unsigned. He destroyed it, but felt it had come from one of Helen's relatives."

"It came by post?"

"No, it was pushed into his hand when he walked out of one of the local pubs."

"One of Miss Blayre's relatives, eh? He did not mention which one?"

"No, Mr. Pons."

"Very well, I shall want to talk with them. Thank you, Mr. Pollitt."

Outside, Pons stood briefly looking toward the headlands. In the morning sunlight the Great and Little Hangman looked anything but sinister, the former somewhat formidable, but the latter only a pleasant upland slope rising to a rounded ridge, higher back from the coast, the peak ridge dominating the lower. The headlands stood like barriers to the sea, which added a salty tang to the morning air.

Constable Borrow waited patiently until Pons turned away. Then he set out in a rapid trot back the way we had some, out from the inland edge of Combe Martin, ourselves at his heels, until we came to a modest country house which stood before an extensive farm, separated from the road by a high hedge.

"They'll both be here," explained Borrow. "You can talk to both at once, or to each separate, as you wish."

"It makes no difference," said Pons.

As it happened, the older man, Tom Plomer, responded to Borrow's pull at the bell. He was a dour, grim-faced man, bald except for a fringe of greying hair around his head just above his ears. He was clean-shaven. Sharp black eyes darted from one to another of us before he spoke.

"Mr. Borrow," he said in a flat, and, I thought, wary, voice. Then, instead of inviting us in, he stepped outside. "Ye've come, I'll be bound, about Kingsley Pollitt."

"We have, Mr. Plomer. This is Mr. Solar Pons, who is making some inquiries for the police."

Plomer nodded curtly. "If ye expect to know where I was night before last, I'll tell ye now, I was abroad."

"Witnesses, Mr. Plomer?" asked Borrow.

"I believe they can be found," answered the older man gravely.

"Mr. Plomer," said Pons, "had you seen or spoken to Kingsley Pollitt between the time he came home and the night he met his death?"

"I saw him, yes," said Plomer grimly. "As for speaking to 'im, I'd as lief speak to the devil. Ye needn't be asking me any more questions. I'll tell ye now I won't lift a finger to harm the man who did him in. He had it coming – and more. If I'd got my hands on 'im..."

He was quiet abruptly, as a younger man came hurrying around the corner of the house, his hot brown eyes angry, his dark-skinned face flushed with irritation.

"Here, here, what's all this?" he cried. Then, catching sight of the constable, he added in a calmer tone, "Oh, it's you, Borrow."

"Don't say anything, Ted," cautioned Plomer.

"I've got nothing to hide," answered Ted Blayre.

"And where were you night before last?" asked Borrow.

"Out with a lady. And don't be asking me to name her, for I'll not drag her into this. I know what you're aiming at, Borrow, but it won't wash. I came face to face but the once with Kingsley Pollitt..."

"At a pub, Mr. Blayre?" asked Pons quietly.

"Yes, it was there – as he was coming out and I was going in. Had he not been coming out, I'd not have gone in. It wouldn't do for the likes of both of us to be together in peace under one roof. If ever a man deserved to die, it was Kingsley Pollitt. I'm hoping you never find out who did it, for the whole village is glad he's done for – the whole village. Not a soul in it but didn't love Helen – nor hate him for what he did."

"Ye talk too much," warned the older man sharply.

"I know what I'm about," answered Blayre curtly. "There's not a man in all Combe Martin who'd give testimony to say he saw anyone wheeling a body in a barrow, and if he saw it plain as day, knowing it held Kingsley Pollitt's body."

"No one has said a barrow was used, Mr. Blayre," said Pons.

"True. But it takes only a small bit of brain to see that. If it's true, as they say, he was hanged where there was no tree, then it's by barrow he'd have been wheeled up the hill. It don't take Mr. Solar Pons down from London to figure that out."

"Quite so. Elementary," agreed Pons pleasantly. "Perhaps you'll be good enough to tell us how you got that mud on your shoes. It seems unlike these surroundings, and not at all unlike that to be found on the path up the Little Hangman."

Blayre looked down quickly, a fleeting expression of alarm in his eyes. Then he glanced up again, defiantly. "There's mud of that sort all about Combe Martin," he said scornfully.

"Why don't ye go back to Lunnon?" cried Plomer angrily. "We don't need no meddling busybody coming here to pry about."

"Easy now, Mr. Plomer," said Borrow. "Mr. Pons is here at our request. We can ask you down to the station and put you through it, proper. We'll have the answer to some questions – straight now, if you please." He turned to Pons. "Go right ahead, Mr. Pons."

"There's just a trifling matter I want to inquire about," said Pons. "I'll have a look at your barrow."

Without a flicker of emotion, Ted Blayre turned and led the way across the yard and around the house to a small shed. He threw open the door. There stood the barrow, freshly washed, as clean as new.

"Commendably tidy," said Pons dryly.

"We like to keep things clean," said Blayre.

"Now, then – what else?" asked Plomer defiantly.

"Nothing else, Gentlemen," said Pons. "I bid you good-day."

As we walked away from the Plomer house, Borrow said apologetically, "Just you say the word, Mr. Pons, and we'll have them down to the station – one at a time – and we'll fair put them through it."

"No, no, Constable – I learned all I expected to learn," answered Pons enigmatically.

"Either one could have killed him," I said. "But I'll take her brother before her uncle."

"If they meant to kill him, why wait a month?" asked Pons.

"Opportunity," I added.

"A fortuitous opportunity indeed, on the eve of his departure for Bristol." He smiled. "However, let us not neglect Mr. Hernshaw. I have a fancy to speak with him."

The retired executioner likewise lived on the edge of the village, in an old two-storey stone house. We found him outside among his bees, a rotund, pink-cheeked little man. At sight of us, he came hastening eagerly forward, taking off his bee-veil, a broad smile on his face, his bird-like eyes fixed on Pons to the exclusion of Borrow and myself.

"It's a real pleasure to meet Mr. Solar Pons," he said without preamble. "I knew you, sir, the moment I caught sight of you. I used to read and hear about you while I lived in London. And there were occasions, sir, I believe, when I finished – as you might say – what you put in order." He chuckled. "I never thought I'd have the opportunity to meet you. Especially in these circumstances" – here he favored us with an elfin smile – "when it may seem impossible to find a solution to this crime – if it can be called that. Now, then, what can I do for you?"

"I understand you carve in wood, Mr. Hernshaw?" said Pons.

"I do, indeed, sir. I do. May I offer you a carving?"

"Let me purchase something of my choice. Do you have a gibbet in wood, by any chance?"

"Quite in my line, as you may say, sir. Of course."

"I'll take one then, presently. Similar to that found near Kingsley Pollitt's body."

Not an eyelash quivered at this pointed remark of Pons'. "Whatever you like, Mr. Pons," said Hernshaw, again with that smile, which was now not so much elfin as sly, as if he were laughing at us but did not dare do so openly.

"I seem to recall, Mr. Hernshaw," Pons continued, "that your unwise comment about Kingsley Pollitt cost you your position."

"It certainly contributed to it." Hernshaw nodded, still smiling engagingly. "I would dearly have loved to hang him, Mr. Pons. Not alone that he merited it, but he had a thick neck – a bull neck, I believe it is called in some quarters. He represented a challenge to a man of my skill, sir, a genuine challenge. I was very disappointed when the reprieve came through. Very disappointed. I fair cried, I did. And I spoke my piece – and that was what started the trouble for me. I found it best to resign in the face of all the todo brought about by those tender-hearted idiots who are so soft on capital punishment. Why, Mr. Pons, there was a time I'd as soon have hanged a sociologist as a murderer, I was that put out." He looked at us all archly, and laughed.

"You saw Pollitt since he came back?"

"Quite often. They'll tell you – that is, if you'll find anyone to testify," he added, with a satisfied conviction that we would not, "that I followed him about – keeping my distance, of course, for he was mortal strong – more than once. I used to speculate how I'd have done it – though his neck'd shrunk a bit in Dartmoor. All of him had."

The smile never left his face, and he looked from one to another of us as if expecting open approbation.

"It's the sort of thing that gets into your blood, Mr. Pons, and that's a fact. You take pride in a good job well done. And in all the years I served in my capacity, I never bungled an execution.

Nice, clean jobs. That's as it should be. They have a right to expect it."

"Like Kingsley Pollitt," I put in.

"Ah, was he now? I've not seen the body. But I'm happy to hear it." He gazed at me intently. "You'll be Dr. Parker, won't you? Then you must have seen the body. Tell me, was his neck broken cleanly? – Ah, I see by the expression on your face that he was more likely strangled. Not a good drop, then." He clucked in disapproval and shook his head with an expression of prim distaste.

I thought it an extraordinary conversation, and ventured a glance at Pons. I saw that his eyes positively danced with pleasure, and that he had difficulty keeping a smile from his thin lips.

"Bad as he was, Pollitt deserved a clean hanging," added Hernshaw soberly.

"Since you followed him about, perhaps you can tell us how he spent his time?" asked Pons.

"As he usually did, Mr. Pons – off by himself on solitary walks, or half drunk in the pubs. There was no work he could do. His brother sometimes found an odd job for him, but it was never for very long, nor meant to be. No one wanted him. Helen Blayre stood between him and whatever he tried to do. We're a closely-knit community, sir. We've been here for hundreds of years. We've no tolerance of murderers. It was strange he came back here – but then, he was always hardened to what others thought of him."

"Was there anyone who liked him?" asked Pons gently.

"Helen Blayre did," said Hernshaw, "And his brother. He never gave another the chance to like him. Always a surly fellow. But you don't need me to tell you that. Ask anyone – anyone at all."

"Did you see him the night he was killed, Mr. Hernshaw?"

"No, Mr. Pons, I did not. Strange, too, for I was abroad that night until quite late. You might even find my footprints on the path up the Little Hangman near to where he was found. It's a pity no one hereabouts has the knack with his hands I have – that carving you say you found would be crude compared to my work." He smiled again, that same sly, if winning smile. "But come with me – I'll show you my work."

After half an hour of looking at Hernshaw's skilled carvings, we took our leave, Pons with a beautifully done gibbet in his pocket. There was no resemblance whatsoever between this piece and that other found under Kingsley Pollitt's body, and I said so as soon as we were out of earshot.

Pons chuckled. "That means only that this one could not have been done by someone else, but that the other might have been done by Hernshaw. I fancy it was. A good carver can carve crudely, if he's a mind to, but a bad one cannot carve well, no matter how much he desires to do so," he retorted.

"A sly, devious man," I said. "Sinister, too."

"Say not so," answered Pons. "I found him delightful, with a flavor seldom encountered in our cities. Country people seem to remain individualists longer than those unhappy souls confined in closer quarters."

"I'm afraid we've not had much help," said Borrow, disappointed.

"Do not be disheartened, Constable. I did not really expect to be assisted very much. As a matter of fact, I was reasonably sure of the identity of the murderer before I went to sleep last night."

"Mr. Pons, you are having me on!" protested Constable Borrow.

"Thanks to your own assistance, Constable," continued Pons. "I daresay there is a problem to be faced when it comes to trial, for the temper of the town is such that no one will want to testify, though there must have been someone who saw the barrow with its burden being wheeled up the Little Hangman, no matter how late the hour might have been. By the way, I should lose no time impounding Plomer's barrow and subjecting it to the most careful scientific examination. I should not be surprised to learn that it had been used to transport the body – just as I am reasonably sure that it was Hernshaw who pushed that little wooden gibbet beneath the body."

"I'm gratified if I was of any assistance, Mr. Pons – but I don't understand how."

"Come along, Constable," said Pons. "We'll go to the station where we left the evidence."

Constable Borrow flashed me a mystified glance, but I could only shrug, knowing my companion's unorthodox methods.

At the small police station, Pons asked once again for the photostat of Helen Blayre's letter.

"Read it, Mr. Borrow," he directed.

Borrow did so. His eyes, when he raised them, were unenlightened.

"It suggests nothing to you?"

"Nothing, sir."

"Dear me!" exclaimed Pons. "Yet it is perfectly clear. Consider the second sentence, for example. 'The way of life you offer me is not the same as the one we have planned.' What does it mean to you?"

"Kingsley Pollitt made some change in their plans."

"I submit, Mr. Borrow, that your conclusion is as much in error as the conclusion of those who read this letter before you. Pray note, she writes 'we *have* planned' – not 'we *had* planned', which would have been proper in the circumstances you accept. You have all made a readily understandable error in concluding that the pronoun 'we' referred to Helen Blayre and Kingsley Pollitt. I suggest it did not. I submit that it referred to someone else."

"But then to whom, Mr. Pons?"

"Why, to the one man with whom she had everything in common – except her penchant for hiking. Pray reflect – she is reported repeatedly to have gone out into the hills and fields carrying books. And books are John Pollitt's life. People concluded, erroneously, that because she was seen with Kingsley Pollitt they were 'walking out' together, when, in fact, she walked with Kingsley only because his brother was sedentary. She never pretended otherwise, because it was with John, not with Kingsley Pollitt, that she had an understanding.

"Mr. Borrow, John Pollitt performed what for him was an act of justice when, anxious lest his brother escape to Bristol, he stunned and hanged him from a beam in Kingsley's own rooms. You will find the marks of the rope there still, if you hurry. I saw them plainly. I saw also slivers from the rope on the stone floor below the beam. In essence, it comes back to this – Pollitt was shunned by everyone and who else but John knew of his brother's determination to go to Bristol to work? Kingsley's body was taken to the Little Hangman not only to remove it from his lodgings, but because it was there that he had killed Helen Blayre.

"Justice failed John Pollitt, Constable – but he did not fail justice. I wish you good luck in your attempt to bring him to trial, but I am not sanguine, in the face of the temper of the people."

Pons' foresight proved correct, for the verdict against John Pollitt was "not proven," and he was set free. A fortnight after the trail, Pons received from Hernshaw a skillfully carved effigy of a hanged man, "to complete your little gibbet," as Hernshaw wrote. Its features bore a remarkable resemblance to those of the late Kingsley Pollitt.

XIII

THE ADVENTURE OF THE SWEDENBORG SIGNATURES

"I have often maintained that the science of deduction, if carried to its logical conclusion, is capable of informing the trained observer with the same certainty as any set of facts put down with concomitant proof in writing," said my friend Solar Pons from his position at the window of our quarters at 7B Praed Street.

"All of which enables me to deduce that we may quite possibly be about to entertain a client," I said.

"Capital, Parker! I am always happy to realize that these little exercises in ratiocination make somewhat of an impression on you and do indeed stimulate you to a similar observation – in degree. Come and have a look at the young lady below."

I walked to Pons' side and looked down.

Across the street, a young lady of perhaps twenty-five years pursued her way. She was dark, though not brunette. She wore a little toque on her head, and was otherwise clad in a neat grey suit with a touch of red at the lapels and cuffs. On her feet she wore sensible sandals, which had the look of the country about them. She walked up a little way, shot a glance toward our quarters, turned, and walked back.

"Now, then," said Pons, after a few moments, "what do you make of her?"

"She is obviously intending to pay us a visit," I said.

"Yes, yes. Go on."

"But there is some reason for delaying her call."

"Other than indecision?"

"She might be waiting for someone."

"I fancy not. I submit that if she were, her attention would be for the street, not for our quarters."

"She may be from the country."

"We make progress," said Pons dryly.

"Very well, then," I said, taking the plunge, "she is a lady's maid, come here at the behest of her mistress, on a mission of some delicacy."

Pons laughed heartily, his eyes twinkling. "Spoken like a Spartan!" he cried. "And, I daresay, not too wide of the mark. She is certainly in service of some kind, but I suggest a lady's companion rather than a maid. She may well be a less fortunate relative, for she dresses well, if modestly, and wears a definite, if subdued, air of independence. But she has not come at her companion's behest; she has come at her own discretion, and is nerving herself to take the final step. Moreover, she has a limited amount of time at her disposal, for she keeps glancing at her wrist-watch. Either she has another appointment, or she must catch a train. I submit it is the latter, for the hour is already late afternoon, too early for a dinner engagement, rather late for a business appointment. But she has made up her mind and is crossing the street. We shall soon hear what she has to say."

The outer bell sounded, and in a few moments Mrs. Johnson tapped on the door and ushered into our quarters the young lady we had been watching. With that intuition which seldom betrayed a client stepping into our rooms, she unerringly picked Pons as the object of her call.

"Mr. Solar Pons?"

"At your service, Miss."

"My name is Lois Graham, Mr. Pons."

"Pray be seated."

As she took the chair I propelled forward, Pons introduced me, and then went to lean against the mantel.

"Now, my dear young lady, since it is obvious that you are in haste – perhaps to catch a train – and equally so that you've been impelled to come here on a matter of some concern to you by nothing more than your own decision, I suggest we lose no time hearing your story."

A faint smile broke the tension of her face, but only momentarily. She grew grave again at once. "It's true," she began, "I don't know that I'm doing the right thing. But I wanted to come here and talk to you, because I heard from mutual friends of Octavius Grayle of the service you did them in saving Septimus from arrest for murder. I cannot let my aunt continue as she has been doing, living in fear of events. Mr. Pons, do you know the Doctrine of Signatures?"

"Ah, that doctrine which holds that all events of major significance in a life are presaged by lesser events of the same nature," said Pons. "If the major event is to be malign, than the lesser and preceding events will be malign, also; if benign, then they too will be similar. The Doctrine has been wrongfully attributed to Emanuel Swedenborg."

"Yes, that is it, Mr. Pons. My aunt is a Swedenborgian – of a sort."

"Let us just begin at the beginning, Miss Graham."

"Forgive me. I am upset. When my father died four years ago, my brother and I were left orphaned. My brother Arthur had long before gone to seek his fortune in Africa, and I had no provision for existence, since my father, though a kind and thoughtful man, was a country vicar in Dorset and not given to the accumulation of worldly goods. My brother was still somewhere in Africa, still seeking his fortune, at the time of father's death; he didn't come home and made only a brief acknowledgment of the event; indeed, I lost touch with him altogether almost three years ago. After my father's effects were sold, it was evident that I must find a position somewhere, and it was then that my Aunt Agatha Stowecroft, who lives on a country estate not far from Canterbury on the London road, offered me a position as her companion. I accepted with gratitude.

"My Aunt Agatha and her children are my only living relatives. Uncle Diomede died six years ago, and left his wife and children well provided for. His wealth was close to half a million pounds, Mr. Pons, and all of it went to his wife, who parcels it out to her children as they need it – but sparingly. There were three children. Of these, two remain at home, though both are older than I am. They are my cousins Laurel and Alexander. The third, Courtenay, who was married, lived in Dover with his wife, until two weeks ago, when both of them were killed in an accident when their automobile went out of control and plunged off the coast road.

"The household is a very strange one. Each of them has indulged himself to the utmost in his vagaries, if I may seem to speak so disrespectfully of them. My aunt, as I have said, calls herself a Swedenborgian. My cousin Laurel is a Spiritualist. My cousin Alex is an extremely erratic follower of a rather horrible man who calls himself the Great Beast."

Pons chuckled. "I fancy that will be Aleister Crowley."

"Yes, Mr. Pons, that is his name. However, I have very little to do with my cousins; my tasks lie with my aunt. I help her with her letters and such other writings as she engages in, particularly divinations. It is part of my task also to read to her, since Aunt Agatha can no longer see as well as once she could. I don't therefore see very much of my cousins, or even the servants, for the house is fully staffed, and so are the grounds, and most of the servants have been with the family for many years."

She paused and glanced swiftly at her watch, after which she went on in more rapid speech.

"About two months ago, Aunt Agatha announced that the Signatures were operating, and disaster impended. After four years in that house, no such announcement could possibly stir me. On innumerable occasions, my cousin Alex has announced that the Great Beast had had a vision and needed a thousand pounds, which my aunt refused to permit Alex to send him; or Miss Laurel has been in communication with someone in the other world and had information about the world of the future or some such thing; or my aunt has gone on about the Doctrines of Correspondences or Signatures. I paid no more attention to that announcement than to any other so common in that house.

"But then, Mr. Pons, strange things began to happen. At first they were only little things – like a broken lamp, a misplaced or lost object – but gradually they became more serious – Bannister, the butler, fell on the stairs and broke his leg; Mrs. Chenoweth, the cook, was run down in the lane approaching the London road, and seriously injured; and at last, the events which Aunt Agatha called the 'Signatures' culminated in the tragic death of my cousin Courtenay and his wife, Isobel.

"Yesterday, Mr. Pons, the 'Signatures' began again. Aunt Agatha's will disappeared. Mr. Pons, I don't believe in the Doctrine of Signatures or any other of these fantastic systems of thought or whatever they are. I have a strong Anglican faith, and that is quite enough for me. But just the same, there's something wrong in that house, and Aunt Agatha at least is convinced that the 'Signatures' predict her own death. Would it be possible for you to come to Canterbury and speak with her yourself?"

"I daresay it would. We could present ourselves tomorrow."

"Tomorrow, then, Mr. Pons," said our client, coming to her feet.

"Do not be hasty, Miss Graham. There are a few questions I would like to ask you. You spoke of Mrs. Stowecroft's will. Did you know the contents of her will?"

"Yes, Mr. Pons. I helped her and her lawyer when it was drawn up."

"In case of her death, who inherits?"

"Her children, of course. In case any one of the three predeceases her – as has now happened – the estate is to be divided among the survivors."

"And if all the children should predecease her?"

"Then to her grandchildren, if any."

"Since there are none, to whom then?"

"To myself."

"No one else is named in the document?"

"No one, Mr. Pons. My Aunt Agatha is now seventy years old, and certainly not long for this world. It is beyond the bounds of probability that all her heirs should predecease her."

"How did Mrs. Stowecroft discover that her will had disappeared?"

"She is accustomed to reading it over from time to time. Usually it is kept in a little wall-safe in the study, but sometimes it is left in a false book on the study table. It was from this book that it had vanished. I should say that my aunt frequently drew up a new will, but the only change of any importance she has ever made was the addition of my own name six months after I came to live with them."

Pons had crossed to his favorite chair, and now sat in an attitude of deep thought, his eyes closed, his feet stretched toward the coal scuttle, the fingers of one hand lightly stroking his left ear.

"You have mentioned the staff," he said presently, "as having been with the family for many years. Presumably most of them date back to a time when your late uncle still lived?"

"Yes, Mr. Pons. All but two – Bannister replaced the old butler at his death, three and a half years ago. And there's Nicholson, an assistant handyman, who was retained two years ago. But he is principally outside the house, helping Bligh, the gardener."

Pons took out his watch and glanced at it. "Canterbury is two hours from Victoria. You can be home by seven o'clock and still, perhaps, in time for dinner. We will call on you tomorrow after lunch, Miss Graham."

After our client had gone, Pons turned to me, his eyes twinkling. "Was that not an unique matter, Parker?"

"A rigmarole of superstitious nonsense!" I answered sharply.

"Miss Graham, at least, shares your views," observed Pons. "Nothing about her narrative struck you?"

"Only that the poor young woman sorely demonstrates the need for the Anglican church to take immediate steps toward increasing the living of their vicars so that young ladies left in Miss Graham's predicament need not be subjected to such environments."

"Come, come, Parker," said Pons, clucking his disapproval, "are not all things that exist of interest to the inquiring mind? I should be inclined to think so. Did not the family of the late Diomede Stowecroft impress you as decidedly different?"

"So are the occupants of any bedlam," I retorted.

"You are at your most cantankerous," said Pons, imperturbably. "I submit, nevertheless, that our client was not ill-advised to call at 7B. By Mr. and Mrs. Courtenay Stowecroft's deaths, the little circle of Mrs. Agatha Stowecroft's heirs is appreciably diminished."

"Accidents *will* increase with the tempo of living in our time."

"Spoken with appropriate sententiousness, Parker. I suggest there is more here than meets the eye."

"That is an observation which is true in any circumstances."

"Think again of the will Miss Graham mentioned. You were not aware of any significant omission?"

I threw up my hands. "My dear Pons!" I cried, "I'm convinced that the household is certifiable, lock, stock, and barrel – the inhabitants for being plainly mad, the servants for being equally touched to endure them and remain there. If there were any omission in the will, it was probably the servants, and no doubt the long list of charities which one might expect of so erratic a household – donations to the Society for Psychical Research, the furtherance of Crowleyism, and possibly a home for retired Swedenborgians."

Pons smiled. "You're in fine fettle today. Parker. I submit, however, that our client was sincere in coming here."

"Undoubtedly."

"And that she, at least, for all that she professes no belief in the Doctrine of Signatures, is convinced that the matter ought to be inquired into."

"Certainly."

"It doesn't strike you that there is one significant detail which stands out in Miss Graham's narrative?"

"It bristles with details, none significant."

"No, no, there is one detail I would call to your attention. None of the events which have gone to bear out the theory of the Signatures is incapable of manufacture."

"Ah, and the motive?"

"An interesting one begs to offer itself. We shall just see. However, in view of your scorn for the idiosyncrasies of the Stowecrofts, perhaps you would prefer to remain here tomorrow?"

"That is a wholly unwarranted assumption," I replied.

We were not destined to visit our client the following day, for in the morning a wire was delivered asking us to delay our visit. During the night, Miss Laurel Stowecroft had walked out in her sleep, had fallen into a stream which crossed the estate, and had been found drowned.

"So that is the second major event foretold by the Signatures," mused Pons, tossing the wire to the table where we were at breakfast. "We are left only with Alexander, among the children. The devotee of the Great Beast. What do you know of Crowleyism, Parker?"

"Nothing at all."

"I believe the Beast holds that his needs, physical, financial, and otherwise, are to be satisfied above all else. That is his supreme credo, and his disciples exist solely but to gratify him."

"A poor, addled lot."

"Beyond question."

"You think it is Alexander, then?"

"I have not said so," he answered, annoyingly.

Four days later, Pons and I took a train at High Holborn and were duly delivered in Canterbury. Pons chose to take lodgings near St. Dunstan's, rather than avail himself of an invitation from Miss Graham to stay at Stowecroft Hall, and then, learning that the Hall was within easy walking distance, he set out for our destination without delay, once we had taken lunch.

Stowecroft Hall was an imposing house in an estate larger than I had assumed it might be. The Hall was Georgian in architecture and rose at the far end of a double drive and a gracious lawn, broken by flower-beds and many little groves of bushes. Behind the Hall rose a yew alley, which led to some further buildings and to an adjoining wood.

Our client awaited us.

"I've explained to Aunt Agatha," she said. "She doesn't look with any confidence on your visit. I should tell you, but then, she is a strange woman, and she is not opposed to it, either. My cousin Laurel's death has shaken her badly."

"Your cousin was in the habit of walking in her sleep?"

"Yes, Mr. Pons."

"Is it not odd, Parker, that she should not have awakened at striking the water?"

"Yes, but it isn't impossible that she should not. Despite all that has been written of somnambulism, not much is known of its compulsions."

"Who discovered her?" asked Pons then.

"Bligh," answered Miss Graham.

She now turned and led the way into the Hall until she came to double doors, before which she paused and tapped gently. "Aunt Agatha?"

"Come, child."

Our client opened the doors and preceded us into the room, where she stood aside to let us pass into the presence of a tall, white-haired old lady, clad in sombre black satin. She sat in a high-backed chair at a long flat table, which appeared to be covered with divination charts and manuscript.

"Aunt Agatha, these are the gentlemen I spoke to you about," said Miss Graham.

"How do you do, Gentlemen," said the old lady. "Won't you be seated? It seems a little early for tea, but..." Her voice wandered off expectantly.

"Thank you. We have just come from lunch," said Pons.

"Ah, very well. I understand you are interested in the Doctrine of Signatures." Here she turned to Miss Graham, and said, "They have begun again, my child."

"Oh, no!"

"Yes," said the old lady, nodding gravely. "Toby has been found in the well. Dead. My cat," she added to us. "But then, if I understood my niece correctly, you gentlemen do not believe in the Signatures."

"Say rather we have open minds," replied Pons gently.

"I fear, if I read the signs properly, I am not long for this world," continued the old lady. "I have lost a son and a daughter, as well as a daughter-in-law, and still the Signatures indicate a greater tragedy that is yet to come. What could be more final than my own death? I have known the days of my years."

Pons, however, was not listening. His keen eyes darted here and there, and presently he made a sign to our client that he wished the interview to be terminated. Immediately Miss Graham rose, made excuses for us, and showed us out of the room.

"Now I should like to view the spot where Miss Laurel Stowecroft's body was found," he said.

"Certainly, Mr. Pons."

She did not question his motives, but led the way outside and around the house to where a broad brook flowed toward the highway and beyond. A pair of dogs started up from the outbuildings and followed us, looking curiously on. Miss Graham paused and showed us the place where the body had been found; much trampling of the turf and the brook's edge was still in evidence.

Pons, however, spent but a few moments at the place. He gazed back toward the house, which was in plain sight. Then he crouched and began systematically to examine the ground, moving in small half circles ever outward and back toward the house, not in the way we had come, but along a row of tall bushes paralleling our path. He darted in and out among the bushes, first on one side, then on another. Along the near side, finally, he paused and dropped to his knees.

"Someone has been carrying something heavy along here," he said. "There is depth to these prints, Parker."

"Is that not elementary, Pons?" I could not help asking. "This is the way that unfortunate woman's body was taken back to the house."

Pons favored me with a glance akin to scorn, at which I smiled, knowing his vanity had been touched.

Miss Graham, meanwhile, had watched him in perplexity. As he came to his feet, Pons suggested to her that, since he wished to speak to Bligh, she might return to the house, whither we would soon follow.

Accordingly, she took her departure.

With her going, the dogs became less friendly and followed us, barking, to the stables and out-buildings, among which stood a trim, neat greenhouse. It was to this that Pons made his way.

The first person we encountered was a short, stocky man in his early forties. He was heavily bearded, with dark, curly hair reaching well up his cheeks. His dark little eyes looked at us suspiciously.

"Bligh?" asked Pons.

"No, sir. The name is Nicholson. Bligh's inside." He touched his cap respectfully.

Pons pushed past him and confronted a tall, dour individual, who looked at us as suspiciously as his assistant had done. "Miss Graham directed us here, Bligh," said Pons disarmingly. "We understood you discovered Miss Laurel Stowecroft's body."

"Yes, sir."

"Tell me, you were on the grounds on the night of the accident?"

"I was, sir. I make my quarters in the rear of this building."

"Did you at any time during the night of Miss Laurel's death hear any sort of disturbance?"

"No, sir, I did not." He rubbed his chin reflectively. "I'm a sound enough sleeper, but I'd have heard anything that was to be heard. I'm trained for that, sir."

Pons thanked him and returned to the house where Miss Graham waited. She watched him come toward her, anxiously. "Is my aunt in any danger, Mr. Pons?" she asked as he came up.

"Let me assure you that, for the time being, Mrs. Stowecroft is in not the slightest danger," he answered.

"Thank you, Mr. Pons, I am relieved to know it."

"I shall return presently to London, but I may very probably be back in the vicinity in the near future," Pons went on. "However, before I go, there are a few further questions I should like to ask. About Mr. Alexander Stowecroft, for one. How does he occupy his time?"

"Why, he is ever about his Crowleyism," said Miss Graham disapprovingly. "He reads, writes long letters, tries to get money for the Beast."

"And fails, no doubt," said Pons, smiling. "Does he have any normal pursuits? Does he play darts, go to the pub, fish?"

"No, Mr. Pons. But he hunts. He has the hunting of the wood and the adjoining country."

"Ah. And does he have any special day for that?"

"Yes, Mr. Pons. Thursday. The hunting is perhaps the only regularity of his life. He goes out at two o'clock in the afternoon and returns at five. They say he is a good shot."

"Does he use a beater?"

"Sometimes Bligh or Nicholson or one of the men from the stables – Jepson, usually – goes along."

"If anything untoward occurs, pray do not fail to notify me, Miss Graham," said Pons then. "Though Mrs. Stowecroft is in no immediate danger, I do not doubt that someone bent on diabolical mischief is acting against the family."

On the way back to London, Pons sat in our compartment with his arms folded across his chest, and his head sunk down above, his eyes closed. His silence annoyed me, I confess, and presently I could endure it no longer.

"I've witnessed some astonishing feats of deduction on your part before this time, Pons, but I am completely at a loss to understand this latest," I said.

"I don't doubt it," he replied with some asperity. "Anyone who could look at a row of deeply-set footprints leading toward the brook and *away* from the house and loftily announce that of course they were carrying Miss Laurel Stowecroft's body to the house has, I daresay, something wanting in his ability to follow my poor powers."

"I had not noticed," I admitted. "You're one up on me."

"You are unusually flattering, Parker," he said, chuckling. "'One?' Has nothing other occurred to you about this singular business?"

"I confess I have not thought of anything. I suppose, now, that the lady was murdered."

"Her death was certainly not an accident. She was evidently carried from the house or its vicinity by her murderer, either in a somnambulistic or stunned condition, and held under the water until she was drowned. Can you doubt that the drowning of the cat, Toby, and all the other 'Signatures' were as easily arranged? I submit therefore that only someone thoroughly familiar with the household is behind this sequence of events. You will recall the action of the dogs. As soon as Miss Graham left us, they barked at us – we were strange to them. Yet Bligh could not testify to hearing any disturbance on the night of Miss Stowecroft's death. So whoever walked with her and carried her to her death was known to them. How does the picture look to you now, Parker?"

"I see clearly that Alex Stowecroft is now his mother's sole heir."

"Ah, we make progress," said Pons dryly. "And if Miss Laurel's death was arranged, certainly it is reasonable to venture that that of Courtenay and Isobel Stowecroft was also designed."

"Oh, come, Pons, any car is apt to go out of control."

"I dislike meaningful coincidences that come so opportunely," replied Pons. "I sent a wire to Dover some days ago. We should have an answer before long."

Indeed, the answer to Pons' wire awaited us at our quarters.

Pons read it, smiled, and threw the wire to the table before me, so that I too could read it. "Evidence Stowecroft

Car Tampered With Please Advise." It was signed by Police-Inspector P. H. Ramsey.

"We are about to lock horns with a determined murderer," said Pons. "Two days hence will find us once again at Stowecroft Hall. From two to five in the afternoon, Miss Graham said. We shall just see whether we can stop him three short of six."

"You talk as if you knew him," I said.

"Have I said I did not?" Pons demanded with what I thought unseemly arrogance. "Indeed, Parker, I submit that few problems have offered so patent a solution. We are handicapped only by the lack of sufficient evidence for conviction, and are therefore forced to gamble another life to win it. I dislike the course, but necessity demands it."

The following Thursday afternoon found us once again in the vicinity of Canterbury. Pons had not troubled to present himself to our client at Stowecroft Hall, but had taken us directly to the wood soon after lunch. There he had ensconced himself in a position from which he had a clear view of the Hall in his binoculars. Significantly, he was armed with both a revolver and a leaded stick, and he had insisted on my being armed as well.

At two o'clock precisely, Pons announced that Alexander Stowecroft had emerged from the house. "Now he is going to the out-buildings for a beater," he went on. "Ah, he has chosen one of them. Now he is making for the upper part of the wood. Come along, Parker."

So saying, he slid down from his eminence and moved off in a rapid trot in the direction of Alexander Stowecroft. Once in sight of him, however, he slowed.

"Keep down, Parker," he instructed me. "We must not be seen."

In this skulking fashion, we followed Stowecroft and his beater, who also served from time to time as his gun-bearer, for well over an hour. Pons' patience was the direct antithesis of my own impatience. I saw no point in this meaningless chase, and lacked only the opportunity to say so forcefully.

It was shortly after three o'clock that afternoon when Stowecroft and his man came out into a grassy glade and made for a rail fence which they obviously intended to cross. Stowecroft, who was in the lead, turned as he approached the fence, and tossed his gun to his companion. Then, as Stowecroft began to climb through between the rails, the beater ran forward, holding Stowecroft's gun at precisely the angle it might have been held if Stowecroft himself were carrying it in crossing the fence.

Pons leaped to his feet with a warning shout of "Hoi!"

But he was too late to prevent the contrived "accident" he had foreseen. The gun went off, and Alexander Stowecroft tumbled to the ground.

"Your man, Parker," said Pons.

Then, swinging his leaded stick in ever swifter circles, he loped off after the beater, who had begun to run at sight of us. Half way to the scene, Pons let fly. The heavy head of the stick caught the beater in the back of the head. He went down like a stone, not far from where Stowecroft lay groaning.

I came up to Stowecroft and dropped to my knees at his side. He was still breathing, and his wound, I saw, was not mortal, if I could manage to stanch the flow of blood. Had it been but a few inches lower! I worked hastily, and succeeded at last.

"A near thing," I said to Pons, who had been standing by. Then I glanced over toward the beater. "Whom have we here?" I saw the edge of a bearded face. "Why, it's Nicholson!"

"Mr. Arthur Graham, alias Nicholson," said Pons. "I fancy this will put an end to those mysteriously opportune 'Signatures', as well as to Mr. Graham's bloody game."

"The identity of the man whose hand was behind the events at Stowecroft Hall was never in doubt for a moment," said Pons as we sat in our compartment on our way back to London later that day. "Nicholson was the only man who had joined the staff after Miss Graham last was in touch with her brother. You will recall that our client mentioned that her benefactor had added her name to the will six months after she had come to work there. That would have been just after the new butler had come, and some months before Miss Graham last heard from her brother. Miss Graham has admitted having written her brother that she had been named in her aunt's will; soon after, she testified, she heard nothing further from him. Two years ago Nicholson turned up and took a position at Stowecroft Hall; Arthur Graham was effectively concealed behind his full beard, and his own sister never recognized him, thinking him somewhere on the dark continent.

"He spent almost two years studying his relatives, and then seized upon his aunt's superstitious beliefs to pave the way for the elimination of those people who stood between him and the fortune he sought."

"But Arthur Graham wasn't mentioned in her will," I protested.

"That was precisely the point to which I so vainly called your attention on the occasion of Miss Graham's visit to our quarters. He need not have been. If Mrs. Stowecroft died after her children, then our client inherited. If then our client herself died, Arthur was her only heir. He meant to have a fortune by one means or another. He got half way to it."

Edgar
Wallace
THE COMPLETE J. G. REEDER STORIES

E.W.
HORNUNG
THE COMPLETE RAFFLES

Edgar
Wallace
THE COMPLETE JUST MEN
VOLUME 2

Arthur
Morrison
THE COMPLETE MARTIN HEWITT COLLECTION
VOLUME 1

E. Phillips
Oppenheim
THE GREAT IMPERSONATION

Allan
Pinkerton
THE EXPRESSMAN AND THE DETECTIVE

H. Rider Haggard
MR. MEESON'S WILL

Melville Davisson Post
MASTER OF MYSTERIES
THE COMPLETE UNCLE ABNER COLLECTION

Jack London
THE ASSASSINATION BUREAU LTD.

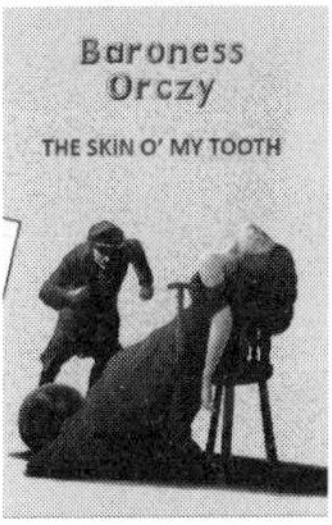
Baroness Orczy
THE SKIN O' MY TOOTH

Earl Derr Biggers
SEVEN KEYS TO BALDPATE

Horace Walpole
THE CASTLE OF OTRANTO

Sexton Blake
THE SEXTON BLAKE COLLECTION
VOLUME 1

Francis Beeding
THE HOUSE OF DR. EDWARDES

A. E. W. Mason
AT THE VILLA ROSE

Fergus Hume
THE MILLIONAIRE MYSTERY

Donald Henderson
A VOICE LIKE VELVET

Richard Hallas
YOU PLAY THE BLACK AND THE RED COMES UP